The Best American
Mystery Stories 2005

GUEST EDITORS OF
THE BEST AMERICAN MYSTERY STORIES

1997 ROBERT B. PARKER
1998 SUE GRAFTON
1999 ED McBAIN
2000 DONALD E. WESTLAKE
2001 LAWRENCE BLOCK
2002 JAMES ELLROY
2003 MICHAEL CONNELLY
2004 NELSON DeMILLE
2005 JOYCE CAROL OATES

The Best American Mystery Stories™ 2005

Edited and with an Introduction
by **Joyce Carol Oates**

Otto Penzler, *Series Editor*

HOUGHTON MIFFLIN COMPANY

BOSTON · NEW YORK   2005

Visit our Web site: www.houghtonmifflinbooks.com.

ISSN: 1094-8384
ISBN-13: 978-0-618-51744-2   ISBN-10: 0-618-51744-8
ISBN-13: 978-0-618-51745-9 (pbk.)   ISBN-10: 0-618-51745-6 (pbk.)

Printed in the United States of America

VB 10 9 8 7 6 5 4 3 2 1

These stories are works of fiction. Names, characters, places, and incidents are products of the authors' imagination or are used fictitiously. Any resemblance to actual events, locales, or persons, living or dead, is entirely coincidental.

"The Identity Club" by Richard Burgin. First published in *TriQuarterly*, Winter 2004. Copyright © 2004 by Richard Burgin. Reprinted by permission of the author.

"Disaster Stamps of Pluto" by Louise Erdrich. First published in *The New Yorker*, December 13, 2004. Copyright © 2004 by Louise Erdrich. Reprinted by permission of the Wylie Agency, Inc.

"Delmonico" by Daniel Handler. First published in *McSweeney's Enchanted Chamber of Astonishing Stories*, November 2004. Copyright © 2004 by Daniel Handler. Reprinted by permission of the author. Lyrics from "Love Me or Leave Me" by Walter Donaldson/Gus Kahn copyright 1928, copyright © renewed 1955 Donaldson Publishing Co./Gilbert Keyes Music Co. International copyright secured. All rights reserved. Used by permission. Lyrics from *Down in the Depths* by Cole Porter. Copyright © 1936 (Renewed) Chappell & Co. (ASCAP). All rights reserved. Used by permission.

"Jack Duggan's Law" by George V. Higgins. First published in *The Easiest Thing in the World*, November 2004. Copyright © 2004 by Loretta Cubberly Higgins. Reprinted by permission of Carroll & Graf Publishers, an imprint of Avalon Publishing Group, Inc.

Contents

Foreword

IT IS POSSIBLE, I suppose, that there is a smarter, harder-working, more dedicated literary figure on planet Earth than Joyce Carol Oates, but someone else will have to point out who that might be. Don't ask me to do it.

When I asked Ms. Oates to be the guest editor for this volume, I didn't quite know what I was getting into. (I could rewrite that sentence to avoid ending it with a preposition, but somehow it just sounds a bit off to say "I didn't quite know into what I was getting," so I'll just let it go.)

It is the role of the series editor for all the volumes in Houghton Mifflin's prestigious *Best American* series to select the year's fifty best stories, and then for the guest editor to select the top twenty from that group. It was a little different this year. Ms. Oates started reading before I did, and recommended stories before I even found them. She wanted batches of stories throughout the year, rather than all fifty at once, and we engaged in frequent (I might even be tempted to say relentless) correspondence, our respective fax machines humming at every hour, and eventually telephone conversations while we debated the relative merits of certain stories. This 2005 volume is certainly the most collaborative one yet. I'm not entirely certain we followed all the guidelines set by my editor at Houghton Mifflin, but I can assure you that all of the time and energy were directed at a single goal, which was to make the book the best it could be. I hope you agree that we have achieved that.

Speaking of guidelines, this is a good time to point out how great it is to work for a house like Houghton Mifflin. It is well understood

in the publishing world that if anthologies are to have any chance
of success, they must have some big names among the contributors.
Never — not once — has Houghton Mifflin suggested that these
annual volumes (this is the ninth) should have bigger names. From
the first day I started as the series editor, it was about the writing.
The best stories (or at least those I most admired) were nominated,
and the guest editors have followed that directive.

It's not about the most popular authors, and it's not about personal relationships (two close friends, both at my wedding this past
May, didn't make the cut, though both are accomplished writers,
named Grand Masters by the Mystery Writers of America, who have
been selected for this series in the past). It's about finding the best
stories, by whoever happens to have written them.

It is not uncommon for excellent writers to become famous, so
although there are a few extremely popular writers in this book
(Scott Turow, Louise Erdrich, George V. Higgins), it is doubtful
that you know very many of the others. It is equally likely, however,
that you will.

Tom Franklin's first appearance in book form was in the 1999
edition of *Best American Mystery Stories,* with a masterpiece titled
"Poachers"; he went on to publish a short story collection with William Morrow titled *Poachers and Other Stories,* followed by a novel,
Hell at the Breech. Christopher Coake had never been published in
book form until "All Through the House" was collected in *BAMS*
last year; his short story collection, *We're in Trouble,* under the prestigious imprint of Harcourt Brace, launches what should be a great
career. Scott Wolven, too, who makes his fourth consecutive appearance in *BAMS* this year, had not been published in any book
before "The Copper Kings" was selected for the 2002 volume, and
now he has a book issued by Scribner, *Controlled Burn: Stories of
Prison, Crime, and Men.* With the quality of the stories contained between these covers, it is impossible to imagine that some of the authors in *BAMS 2005* won't have more of their work published in
the satisfying permanence of books.

You know how much fun it is to read a book that you love or see a
movie that moves you and to share that with a friend who comes
back and tells you how much he loved it, too. That's one of the
things that makes editing this series such a great job. I get to recommend a lot of stories to a lot of people, almost all of whom seem to

be pretty happy about it, even though the title of the book is a little misleading for the literal-minded.

Few of these stories are detective fiction, a tale in which an official police officer, a private eye, or an amateur sleuth is confronted with a crime and pursues the culprit by making observations and deductions. It has been my practice to define a mystery story as any work of fiction in which a crime or the threat of a crime is central to the theme or plot. There is greater emphasis in these pages on why a crime was committed, or if it will be done at all, than on trying to discover the perpetrator, which has upset some readers. That simply can't be helped.

The nature of mystery fiction has changed over the years, and there are simply fewer and fewer works of pure detection than there were during the so-called golden age between World Wars I and II, when Agatha Christie, John Dickson Carr, Ellery Queen, Dorothy L. Sayers, and their peers were constructing ingenious puzzles and challenging readers to solve them before Hercule Poirot, Gideon Fell, Ellery Queen, or Lord Peter Wimsey did.

With authors focused more on the psychological aspects of crime, whether from the point of view of the detective, the victim, or the criminal, there appears to be greater strength of characterization and style than there was in the more classic form of pure detection. There are exceptions, of course, and when they occur, there is a pretty good chance that those stories will make it into these pages.

No mention of *The Best American Mystery Stories* is complete without genuflecting to Michele Slung, the fastest and smartest reader in the world, who combs every consumer magazine, every electronic zine, and as many literary journals as we can find. She scans hundreds — no, let me correct that — thousands of stories to determine which are mysteries (if you were searching for stories for this book, would you have expected "Disaster Stamps of Pluto" to qualify by virtue of its title? Or "Loyalty"? Or "Old Boys, Old Girls"?). She then culls those that have the vibe of having been scrawled with a crayon, and gives me the rest. She can read in a day what I'd need a month to do; without her dedication and intelligence, this annual volume would take three years to compile.

While I'm throwing thank-yous around, I'd like again to note the huge contributions of the guest editors, who so generously help make these wonderful books possible. It all began with Robert B. Parker in 1997, followed by Sue Grafton, Ed McBain, Donald E. Westlake, Lawrence Block, James Ellroy, Michael Connelly, Nelson DeMille, as well as Joyce Carol Oates this year, to all of whom I am forever indebted.

Although we are relentlessly aggressive in searching out mystery fiction for these pages, I live in dread that we will somehow miss a worthy story. If you are an editor, publisher, author, agent, or just care about this type of literature, please feel free to send submissions. To qualify for the 2006 collection, a story must be written by an American or Canadian and published for the first time in the 2005 calendar year in an American or Canadian publication. Unpublished stories are not eligible. If the story was published in electronic form, a hard copy must be submitted. When this series began, I did not own a computer. I do now, but I sure don't want to read from a screen, and there are just too many stories in e-zines to print them all out. Please do not ask for critical analysis of work, as I simply do not have time to do that, and please do not ask to have your material returned. If you are totally paranoid and do not believe that the postal service actually delivers mail, enclose a stamped, self-addressed postcard to confirm delivery.

Save the postage if your story was published in *Ellery Queen's Mystery Magazine* or *Alfred Hitchcock's Mystery Magazine,* as these are read cover to cover. I also see regularly *The New Yorker, Esquire, GQ, Playboy, Harper's Magazine, Atlantic, Zoetrope,* and mystery anthologies from major publishers, but it can't hurt to send your story anyway.

The earlier I see stories, the better your chance of getting a thorough reading. Any stories received after December 31, 2005, will be discarded without being read. This is not because I'm arrogant and unreasonable, or even just curmudgeonly. The book actually has a deadline, which cannot be met if I'm still reading in mid-January. If you publish in April and send me your story at Christmastime, forcing me to stay home and read while my wife and friends are out partying, you better have written a hell of a story.

Please send material to Otto Penzler, The Mysterious Bookshop, 129 West 56th Street, New York, NY 10019.

O.P.

Introduction

CRIMES CAN OCCUR without mystery. Mysteries can occur without crime. Violent and irrevocable actions can destroy lives but bring other lives together in unforeseeable, unimaginable ways.

In 1917, in the grim waterfront section called Black Rock, in Buffalo, New York, a forty-three-year-old Hungarian immigrant was murdered in a barroom fight, beaten to death with a poker. A few years later, in a rural community north of Buffalo, another recent immigrant to America, a German Jew, attacked his wife with a hammer and committed suicide with a double-barreled shotgun. Both deaths were alcohol-related. Both deaths were "senseless." The men who came to such violent ends, my mother's father and my father's grandfather, never knew each other, yet their deaths precipitated events that brought their survivors together and would continue to have an influence, haunting and obsessive, into the twenty-first century. Families disrupted by violent deaths are never quite "healed" though they struggle to regroup and redefine themselves in ways that might be called heroic.

It's an irony that I owe my life literally to those violent deaths of nearly a century ago, since they set in motion a sequence of events that resulted in my birth, but I don't think it's an irony that, as a writer, I am drawn to such material. There is no art in violence, only crude, cruel, raw, and irremediable harm, but there can be art in the strategies by which violence is endured, transcended, and transformed by survivors. Where there is no meaning, both death and life can seem pointless, but where meaning can be discovered, perhaps even violence can be redeemed, to a degree.

I grew up in a rural household in the Snowbelt of upstate New York in a household of family mysteries that were never acknowledged in my presence, and very likely never acknowledged even by the adults who safeguarded them. My father's mother, whose deranged father had blown himself away virtually in front of her, had changed her surname to a seemingly gentile name, renounced her ethnic/religious background, never acknowledged her roots even to her son, and lived among us like one without a personal, let alone a tragic, history. In this she was quintessentially "American" — self-inventing, self-defining. Her life, like the early lives of my parents, seems in retrospect to have sprung from a noir America that's the underside of the American dream, memorialized in folk ballads and blues and in the work of such disparate writers as Theodore Dreiser, Sherwood Anderson, John Steinbeck, William Faulkner, James M. Cain, Dashiell Hammett, and Raymond Chandler. It was as if, as a child, I inhabited a brightly lighted space — a family household of unusual closeness and protectiveness — surrounded by a penumbra of darkness in which malevolent shapes dwelled.

The earliest books to cast a spell on me were Lewis Carroll's *Alice in Wonderland* and *Alice Through the Looking-Glass,* nightmare adventures in the guise of a childhood classic, and Edgar Allan Poe's *Tales of the Grotesque and Arabesque.* Both Carroll and Poe create surreal worlds that seem unnervingly real, like images in a distorting mirror, and both explore mysteries without providing solutions. Why does the Red Queen scream, at the mildest provocation, "Off with his head!"? Why are hapless creatures in Wonderland and the Looking-Glass world always changing shape? Why does the narrator of "The Tell-Tale Heart" kill an old man who hasn't harmed him, and in such a bizarre manner? (Crushed and smothered beneath a heavy bed.) Why does the narrator of "The Black Cat" put out the eye of his pet cat and strangle his wife? Motiveless malignity! Individuals act out of impulse, as if to assure that irrevocable: the violent act and its consequences.

Because I grew up in an atmosphere of withheld information — a way of defining "mystery" — I can appreciate the powerful attraction of mystery as art: it's the formal, mediated, frequently ingenious and riveting simulacrum of the unexplained in our lives, the haphazard, hurtful, confusing, tragic. A crime or mystery novel is the elaboration of a riddle to which the answer is invariably less gripping than the riddle; a crime or mystery story is likely to be a single, abbreviated segment of the riddle, reduced to a few characters and a few dramatic scenes. It's a truism that mystery readers are likely to be addicts of the genre, no sooner finishing one mystery novel than taking up another, and then another, for the riddle is, while "solved," never explained. But it's perhaps less generally known that writers in the genre are likely to be addicts as well, obsessively compelled to pursue the riddle, the withheld information, the "mystery" shimmering always out of reach — in this way transforming the merely violent and chaotic into art to be shared with others in a communal enterprise.

Of contemporary mystery/crime writers, no one is more obviously haunted by a violent family past than James Ellroy (see the memoir *My Dark Places*), which accounts for the writer's compulsion to revisit, in a sense, the scene of the original crime (the unsolved murder of his mother) though it can't account, of course, for the writer's remarkable and audacious talent. In an earlier generation, Ross Macdonald is the preeminent example of the mystery/detective novelist whose carefully plotted narratives move both backward and forward, illuminating past, usually family, secrets as a way of solving a case in the present. Michael Connelly's *isolato* L.A. homicide detective Harry Bosch, as the son of a murdered woman, is temperamentally drawn to cold-case files, as are the haunted characters of Dennis Lehane's most celebrated novel *Mystic River* and the narrator of his brilliantly realized short story "Until Gwen," included in this volume. Walter Mosley's Easy Rawlins is a private "eye" in a racially turbulent, fastidiously depicted Los Angeles milieu of past decades in which the personal intersects, often violently, with the political. In this volume Louise Erdrich's beautifully composed "Disaster Stamps of Pluto" is, in its most distilled form, a "whodunit" of uncommon delicacy and art, set in a nearly extinct North Dakota town in which the past exerts a far more powerful gravitational pull than the present. Edward P. Jones's "Old Boys, Old Girls" is the life story of a man so marginalized and detached from his feelings that he seems to inhabit his life like a ghost, or a prisoner. (See Jones's remarkable story collection *Lost in the City* for further portrayals of "young lions" like Caesar Matthews.) In the unexpectedly ironic "The Last Man I Killed," David Rachel explores a Nazi past as it impinges on a banal and utterly ordinary academic career in a midwestern state university.

While mystery novels are readily available to the public in bookstores and libraries, mystery stories are relatively hidden from view. Only a very few magazines regularly publish them — *Ellery Queen's Mystery Magazine* and *Alfred Hitchcock's Mystery Magazine* come most immediately to mind; the majority of mystery stories are scattered among dozens of magazines and literary reviews with limited circulations. The inestimable value of *The Best American Mystery Stories* series is that the anthologies bring together a selection of stories in a single volume, with an appendix listing additional distinguished titles. While guest editors for the series appear for one year only, the series editor, Otto Penzler, remains a stable and galvanizing presence; any mystery volume with Penzler's name on it is likely to be very good indeed, as well as a responsible and generous representation of the current mystery scene.

Though the twenty stories in this selection are all "mysteries," the resemblances among them end just about there. Not one seems to me formulaic in the stereotypical way often charged against mystery fiction by people like the critic Edmund Wilson (see Wilson's famously peevish diatribe of 1945, "Who Cares Who Killed Roger Ackroyd?," an attack on the overplotted, psychologically superficial English-cozy whodunits by Agatha Christie, Dorothy Sayers, et al.). Not one evokes violence gratuitously, in the way of contemporary crime/action movies and video games. Not one is, in fact, driven by plot at the expense of probability and plausibility. These are all stories in which something happens, usually irrevocably, but they are not stories in which what "happens" is primarily the point. As in Kent Nelson's collectively narrated "Public Trouble," which traces the history of an adolescent boy who has committed acts of extreme violence, Oz Spies's uncomfortably intimate "The Love of a Strong Man," which tells us how it probably feels to be the publicly identified wife of a notorious serial rapist, and Tim McLoughlin's excursion into an ironic sort of nostalgia, "When All This Was Bay Ridge," it's the effect of violence upon others that is the point. As McLoughlin's stunned narrator is asked: "Who owns memory?" The expediency of ethics among professionals — in this case, police officers — that so shocks McLoughlin's protagonist is the revelation of Lou Manfredo's "Case Closed" with its street wisdom: "There is no right. There is no wrong . . . There just *is*."

It's usually claimed that short stories are distilled, sleeker, and faster-moving forms of fiction than novels, but in fact, all that one can safely say about most stories is that they are shorter than most novels. Page for page, paragraph for paragraph, sentence for sentence, some of the stories in this volume move far more deliberately, if not more poetically, than many novels: David Means's elliptical "Sault Ste. Marie" is aptly titled, for its setting is its most powerfully evoked character; Daniel Orozco's stylishly narrated "Officers Weep" is a jigsaw puzzle of a story, requiring the kind of attentive reading usually associated with poetry (or postmodernist fiction); Stuart M. Kaminsky's "The Shooting of John Roy Worth" is a fabulist tall tale that switches protagonists when we least expect it; John Sayles's teasingly oblique and cinematic "Cruisers" tempts us to read too quickly, and forces us to reread; Scott Turow's "Loyalty" is almost entirely narrated, a tour de force of suspense that uncoils with the dramatic kick of one of Turow's long, densely populated, Chicago-set novels. So far removed from its initial violent act (which occurred forty years before) is Laura Lippman's "The Shoeshine Man's Regrets" that the story is resolved as a study of character, tenderly and shrewdly reconstructed. Joseph Raiche's "One Mississippi" is similarly a reconstruction of violence after the fact, entirely absorbed in the mind of a man who has survived his wife, with no present-action drama: somewhere between story and elegy, convincing as a testament of our gun-ridden TV-tabloid culture. Daniel Handler's "Delmonico" is an artful variation on the "locked-room mystery" that pays homage to Hollywood noir. Sam Shaw's "Reconstruction" and Richard Burgin's "The Identity Club" are sui generis, feats of voice, tone, perspective, and tantalizing irresolution that argue (as Edmund Wilson could not have foreseen) for the elasticity of borders between "literary" and "mystery" stories.

Another debatable claim is that the short story is likely to be more self-consciously crafted and "shaped" than the novel. Yet at least two of the most memorable stories in this volume — Edward Jones's "Old Boys, Old Girls" and Scott Wolven's "Barracuda" — defy expectations at virtually every turn, as willfully shapeless as life. "Old Boys, Old Girls" meanders like a river over a period of many years, following a vague and haphazard chronological movement; Wolven's much shorter story cuts from scene to scene with the nervous energy of a hand-held camera. Equally memorable stories by Wolven have appeared in the last several volumes of *The Best American Mystery Stories,* each an exploration of violence among men who have become marginalized, and thus as dangerous as rogue elephants, in an economically ravaged society that places little value on traditional masculinity. For Wolven's men — loggers, tree poachers, corrupt cops — the impulse to do terrible damage to one another is as natural as watching pit bulls tear one another to pieces for sport.

George V. Higgins (1939–1999) was a unique talent. His most acclaimed novel *The Friends of Eddie Coyle* (1972) has become an American crime classic. As guest editor of this anthology I'm grateful to have the opportunity to reprint what will probably be the last of Higgins's stories to appear in this series. One might debate whether "Jack Duggan's Law" is a story or a novella, but one can't debate the verve, wit, authenticity, and wisdom of the world it memorializes: a Boston demimonde of harassed, overworked, yet quixotically zealous defense attorneys and ADAs. Higgins's ear for the rough poetry of vernacular speech has never been sharper than in this posthumously published story from a collection titled *The Easiest Thing in the World.*

As a concluding note, I should add that reading stories for this volume was a pleasure and that decisions were not easy to make. Both Otto and I read and reread. (I've read "Jack Duggan's Law" at least three times. It keeps getting better.) Each of us had the idea, I think, of wearing the other down by stubbornly clinging to favored titles. In some cases this worked, in others not. Where we couldn't finally agree, we decided to include the story in question. Our principal disagreement was over George V. Higgins: Otto preferred the even longer "The Easiest Thing in the World" to "Jack Duggan's Law." In this instance, Otto graciously deferred to me, but readers may want to decide their own preferences.

JOYCE CAROL OATES

The Best American
Mystery Stories 2005

RICHARD BURGIN

The Identity Club

FROM *TriQuarterly*

SOMETIMES YOU MEET someone who is actually achieving what you can only strive for. It's not exactly like meeting your double, it's more like seeing what you would be if you could realize your potential. Those were the feelings that Remy had about Eugene. In appearance they were similar, although Eugene was younger by a few years and taller by a few inches. But they each had fine dark hair, still untouched by any gray, and they each had refined facial features, especially their delicate noses. Eugene's body, however, was significantly more muscular than Remy's.

At the agency in New York where Remy had worked for three years writing ad copy, Eugene was making a rapid and much talked about ascent. A number of Remy's other colleagues openly speculated that Eugene was advancing because he was a masterful office politician. But when Remy began working with him on an important new campaign for a client who manufactured toothpaste, he saw that wasn't true at all. Eugene had a special kind of brilliance, not just for writing slogans or generating campaign ideas, but a deep insight into human motivations and behavior that he knew how to channel into making people buy products. Rather than being a master diplomat, Remy discovered that Eugene was aloof almost to the point of rudeness, never discussed his private life, and rarely showed any signs of a sense of humor. Yet Remy admired him enormously and wondered if Eugene, who Remy thought of as one of the wisest men he knew (certainly the wisest young man), might be a person he could confide in about the Identity Club and the important decision he had to make in the near future.

All of these thoughts were streaming through Remy's mind after work one night in his apartment when the phone rang. It was Poe calling to remind him about the Identity Club meeting that night. Remy nearly gasped as he'd inexplicably lost track of time and now had only a half hour to meet Poe and take a cab with him to the meeting.

The club itself had to be, almost by definition, a secretive organization that placed a high value on its members' trustworthiness, dependability, and punctuality. Its members assumed the identities — the appearance, activities, and personalities — (whenever they could) of various celebrated dead artists they deeply admired. At the monthly meetings, which Remy enjoyed immensely and thought of as parties, all members would be dressed in their adopted identities, drinking and eating and joking with each other. As soon as he stepped into a meeting he could feel himself transform, as if the colors of his life went from muted grays and browns to glowing reds and yellows and vibrant greens and blues. To be honest with himself, since moving to New York from New England three years ago, his life before the club had been embarrassingly devoid of both emotion and purpose. How lucky for him, he often thought, that he'd been befriended by Winston Reems — now known by club members as Salvador Dali — a junor executive at his agency who had slowly introduced him to the club.

This month's meeting was at the new Bill Evans's apartment (who had patterned himself after the famous jazz pianist) and since Remy enjoyed music he was particularly looking forward to it. He had also been told that Thomas Bernhard, named for the late, Austrian writer, would definitely be there as well. As Bernhard was renowned for being a kind of hermit it was always special when he did attend a meeting and it made sense that as a former professional musician he would go to this one.

Quickly Remy dried off from his shower and began putting on new clothes. He thought that tonight promised to be an especially interesting mix of people, which was one of the ostensible ideas of the organization, to have great artists from the different arts meet and mingle, as they never had in real life. The decision facing Remy, which he'd given a good deal of thought to without coming any closer to a conclusion, was who he was going to "become" himself. He was considered at present an "uncommitted member" and had been debating between Nathanael West and some other writers. Nabokov, whom he might have seriously considered, had already been taken. At least, since he still had a month before he had to commit, he didn't have to dress in costume — though he rather looked forward to that. Remy had been a member for four months and it was now time for him to submit to a club interview to help him decide whose identity he was best suited for. Sometimes these interviews were conducted by the entire membership, which reminded Remy of a kind of intervention, other times by the host of that evening's meeting or by some other well-established member. The new member was never informed in advance, as these "probings" were taken very seriously and the club wanted a spontaneous and true response.

One of the reasons Remy was having difficulty choosing an identity — and why he felt some anxiety about the whole process — was that he'd kept secret from the club his hidden contempt, or at least ambivalence, about the advertising business and his disappointment with the emptiness of his own life as well. No wonder he found refuge in art and in imagining the lives that famous artists led. He'd heard other members confess to those exact sentiments, but the public admission of these feelings would be difficult for Remy. He thought it was the inevitable price he had to pay to get his membership in the club, and along with his work and Eugene (whose importance to him Remy also kept secret) the club was his only interest in life, the only thing worth thinking about.

Poe was waiting for him in front of his brownstone, dressed, as Remy expected, in a black overcoat with his long recently dyed dark hair parted in the middle, the approximate match of his recently dyed mustache.

"I'm sorry I'm so late," Remy said.

Poe stared at him. "Something is preoccupying you," he said.

"You're right about that," Remy said, thinking of Eugene and wishing he could somehow be at the party.

"Do you mind if we walk?" Poe said. "There's something in the air tonight I crave, although I couldn't say exactly what it is. Some dark bell-like sound, some secret perfumed scent coming from the night that draws me forward . . . besides," he said, with a completely straight face, as he took a swallow of some kind of alcohol concealed in a brown paper bag, "it will be just as fast or just as slow as a taxi."

"Fine," Remy said; he felt he was hardly in a position to object. In the club Remy suspected that members assumed their identities with varying degrees of intensity. Clearly Poe was unusually committed to his to the point where he had renounced his former name, become a poet, short story writer, and alcoholic, and given up dating women his age. Because he worked mostly at home doing research on the Internet he was able to be in character pretty much around the clock.

"You need to focus on your choice," Poe said. "You have an important decision facing you and not much time to make it."

"I hope I'll know during the probing," Remy said. "I hope it will come to me then."

"Listen to your heart, even if it makes too much noise," Poe said, smiling ironically.

They walked in silence the rest of the way, Poe sometimes putting his hands to his ears as if Roderick Usher were reacting to too strident a sound. As they were approaching the steps to Evans's walkup, from which they could already hear a few haunting chords on the piano, Poe turned to Remy and said, "Are you aware that we're voting on the woman issue tonight?"

"Yes, I knew that."

Poe was referring to the question of whether or not the Identity Club, which was currently a de facto men's club, would begin to actively recruit women. Remy had sometimes thought of the club as practicing a form of directed reincarnation, but did that mean that in the next world the club didn't want to deal with any women? "I'm going to vote that we should recruit them. How can we fully be who we've become without women? I need them for my poetry, and to love of course. I think the organization should try to increase our chances to meet them, not isolate us from them."

"I completely agree with you," Remy said.

They rang the bell and Dali opened the door, bowing grandly and pointing toward a dark, barely furnished, yet somehow chaotic apartment.

"It's Bill Evans's home. I knew it would be a mess," Poe said quietly to Remy, drinking again from his brown paper bag.

Evans was bent over the piano, head characteristically suspended just above the keys, as he played the coda of his composition "Re: Person I Knew." He also had long dark hair but was clean-shaven.

From the small sofa — the only one in the room — Erik Satie shouted "Bravo! Encore!" Remy couldn't remember seeing any photographs of the French composer but judged his French to be authentic. As a tribute to his admirer, Evans played a version of Satie's most famous piano piece, "Gymnopedie," which Remy recalled the former Evans had recorded on his album *Nirvana*. This was the first time Remy had heard the new Bill Evans play and while he was hardly an Evans scholar he thought it sounded quite convincing. The harmony, the soft touch and plaintive melodic lines were all there (no doubt learned from a book that had printed Evans's solos and arrangements) though, of course, some mistakes were made and the new Evans's touch wasn't as elegant as the first one's. Still, Remy could see that the new Evans's immersion into his identity had been thorough. Remy had recently seen a video of the former Evans playing and could see that the new one had his body movements down pat. Could he, Remy, devote himself as thoroughly to the new identity he would soon be assuming?

"Encore, encore," said Satie again and now also Cocteau, who had joined his old friend and collaborator on the sofa. Continuing his homage to his French admirers, Evans played "You Must Believe in Spring" by the French composer Michel Legrand. When it ended Remy found himself applauding vigorously as well and becoming even more curious about the former life of the new Evans. All he knew was that he'd once been a student at Juilliard and was involved now in selling computer parts. He wished he'd paid more attention when he talked with him five months ago at the meeting but now it was too late, as members were not allowed to discuss their former identities with each other once they'd committed to a new one.

After a brief rendition of "Five," Evans took a break and Remy slowly sidled up to him, wishing again that Eugene were there. Though he was often aloof, when the situation required, Eugene always knew just what to say to people. What to say and not a word more, for Eugene had the gift of concision, just as Evans did on the piano.

"That was beautiful playing," Remy finally said.

"Thanks, man," Evans said, slowly raising his head and smiling at him. Like the first Bill Evans, his teeth weren't very good and he wore glasses.

"I know how hard it is to keep that kind of time, and to swing like that without your trio."

"I miss the guys but sometimes when I play alone I feel a oneness with the music that I just can't get any other way."

It occurred to Remy that Evans had had at least four different trios throughout his recording career and that he didn't know which trio Evans was "missing" because he didn't know what stage of Evans's life the new one was now living. Perhaps sensing this, Evans said, "When Scotty died last year I didn't even know if I could continue. I couldn't bring myself to even look for a new bassist for a long time or to record either. And when I did finally go in the studio again a little while ago, it was a solo gig."

Remy now knew that for Evans it was about 1962, since Scott LaFaro, his young former bassist, had died in a car accident in 1961.

"Do you play, man?" Evans asked.

"Just enough to tell how good you are," Remy said.

"So there's no chance you could become a musician?"

"No, no, I couldn't do it."

"I know this identity thing is difficult to handle at first."

"It is for me. It really is," Remy said, touched by the note of sympathy in Evans's voice.

"Do you do any of the arts, man?"

"Not with anything like your level of skill or Dali's or any of the other members, for that matter. I write a little at my job . . . but you could hardly call it art. There's a man, a rising star at my ad agency named Eugene who's working on a campaign with me now who has the most original ideas and comes up with the most brilliant material who really is an artist. If he were here, instead of me, he could become George Bernard Shaw or Oscar Wilde."

"Have you spoken to him about the club?"

"No, no. I don't really know him that well. I mean he barely knows I exist."

"Anyway, I've been speaking to some of the other members and there's definitely growing support to include men of letters in the club, you know, critics of a high level like Edmund Wilson or Marshall McLuhan."

"Oh no, I don't know anywhere near enough to be Edmund Wilson or McLuhan either. I figure if I become a member it will be as a novelist. I was thinking of Nathanael West, or maybe James Agee."

"Either way you'd have to go young."

Remy looked at Evans to be sure he was joking but saw that he looked quite serious. A chilling thought flitted through his mind. Did the committed members have a secret rule that they had to die at the same age their "adopted artists" did? And if so, was it merely a symbolic death of their identity or their actual physical death duplicated as closely as possible? Was the Identity Club, which he'd thought of as devoted to a form of reincarnation, then, actually devoted in the long run to a kind of delayed suicide? Of course this was probably a preposterous fantasy, still, he couldn't completely dismiss it.

"But you'll have to die young too then," Remy said, remembering that Bill Evans had died at fifty-one. He said this with a half smile so it could seem he was joking. Evans looked around himself nervously before he answered.

"I find that Zen really helps me deal with the death thing."

Remy took a step back and nodded silently. His head had begun to hurt and after he saw that Evans wanted to play again he excused himself to use the bathroom. Once there, however, he realized that he'd forgotten to bring his Tylenol. He opened the mirrored cabinet, was blinded by a variety of pharmaceuticals but found nothing he could take. He closed the cabinet and heard Evans playing the opening chorus of "Time Remembered," one of his best compositions. The music was startlingly lovely but then partially drowned out by a loud coughing in the hallway. Remy turned and saw Thomas Bernhard, face temporarily buried in a handkerchief.

"Are you looking for something?" Bernhard said in a German accent.

"I have a headache."

"How fragile we are, yet how determined. So you are looking for? . . ."

"Some Tylenol."

"Ah! You have a headache and I have some Tylenol," Bernhard said, withdrawing a small bottle from the cavernous pocket of his corduroy sports jacket.

"Since my illness I am nothing but pills, my kingdom for a pill. Here . . ." he said, handing Remy the bottle.

Remy took two and swallowed them.

"Thanks a lot," he said. Bernhard nodded, and half bowed in a gently mocking way.

"So, have you decided to become Nathanael West or not?"

"I understand that I'd have to die quite young then and quite violently," Remy said, laughing uncertainly.

Bernhard's eyes had a heightened, almost shocked expression. Then he started coughing loudly and persistently again. Remy waited a half minute, finally saying, "Why don't you drink some water?" He got out of the bathroom area, half directing Bernhard to the sink, and returned to the living room.

"Is he all right?" Poe said, meeting him in the hallway. He was drinking from a half-empty wine bottle.

"Yes, I think so," Remy said. But I'm not, he said to himself. For the first time he felt profoundly uncomfortable at a club meeting. The pressure of having to make his identity decision was oppressive and worse still were the dark fears he now had about the club's policies. The original conceit of the club had amused him in the titillating way he liked to be amused, but if he were right about his suspicions, then the club was far more literal about its directed reincarnation than he'd realized. If he were right about the death rule, to commit to an identity was to select all aspects of your fate including when you would die. And what if one changed one's mind and didn't want to cooperate after committing, what then?

The pain in Remy's head was excruciating and at the first polite opportunity he excused himself, heaping more praise on Evans for the wonderful evening before he closed the door . . . and shuddered.

He decided not to return the phone calls he got from three club members over the next two days. To say anything while he was uncertain what to do about the Identity Club could be a mistake. On the one hand he'd been profoundly upset by what he thought he might have discovered about its policies, on the other hand the club was the nucleus of what social life he had and would be very difficult to give up. Besides his job, the Identity Club was his only consistent base of human contact.

Remy began to throw himself into the new campaign with more passion than he'd ever shown at the agency. Largely due to Eugene's contributions, it was succeeding and, as expected, it was Eugene who benefited the most from it with the agency higher-ups. It was not that Eugene worked harder than Remy; it was simply that he could accomplish twice as much with less effort because he was so talented in the field. Still, Remy didn't begrudge him his success. Instead his interest in Eugene grew even stronger as he continued to watch and study him. He felt if he could become Eugene's friend and confide in him, than Eugene might know just what he should do about the Identity Club.

As Remy suspected, Eugene led a highly ritualized existence in the workplace. It wasn't difficult to arrange a "chance meeting" at the elevator banks and to quickly ask him to have a drink in a way he couldn't refuse. They went to a bar on Restaurant Row — Remy feeling happier than he had in days. But once outside the agency Eugene seemed tense and remote, and sitting across from him at the bar he avoided eye contact and spoke sparsely in a strangely clipped tone that forced Remy to become uncharacteristically aggressive.

"We're all so grateful for the work you did on the campaign. It was just amazing," Remy said. Eugene nodded and said a muted thank you. It was as if Remy had just said to him "nice shirt you're wearing."

"I'm really proud to have you as a colleague," Remy added for good measure.

Again Eugene nodded, but this time said nothing and Remy began to feel defeated and strangely desperate. He waited until their eyes locked for a moment then said, "Do you know what the Identity Club is?" The immediate reddening of Eugene's face told Remy that he did.

"What makes you think that I would know?"

"I know some of the key members in the club came from our agency."

Eugene raised his eyebrows but still said nothing.

"In fact, I'm a member myself or a potential member."

"Then what is it you think I would know about the club that you wouldn't know already?"

"Fair enough," Remy said, clearing his throat and finishing his beer.

"I'll be a little more candid. I'm a member in that I've been attending the meetings but I'm not a completely committed member. I've been trying to decide whether to commit to the club completely and since I respect you and admire your judgment so much I thought I would ask you about it."

"I tend to avoid organizations that have a strong ideology, especially ones that try to convert you to their worldview. I think they are unappetizing and often dangerous."

"Why is it dangerous?" Remy asked.

"Any organization that asks you to alter your life, or to jeopardize it and in many cases to give it up is to be avoided like the plague. *Is,* in fact, the plague . . . I'm just making this as a general statement, OK? I'm not saying anything about your club specifically," Eugene said hurriedly, looking away from Remy when he tried to make eye contact with him again.

"Thank you for your advice."

"It wasn't advice about anything specific. Remember that. It was just a general observation on the nature of organizations."

"Thank you for your observations then. I appreciate it and will keep it completely confidential."

Eugene seemed more relaxed then but five minutes later excused himself, saying he had to leave for another appointment. Remy could barely make himself stand when Eugene left, he felt so frozen with disappointment. When he did begin to move he felt strangely weightless, like a dizzy ghost passing down a dreamlike street. It was as if for the first time the universe had revealed its essential emptiness to him and he was completely baffled by it. In his life before New York there had always been some kind of support for him. First his parents, when he was a child, of course. Perhaps he left them too soon. Then his teachers when he went to school where he also met his friends who were now dispersed around the country as he was, though none of them had landed in New York. The Identity Club had filled that void, he supposed, although not completely or else Eugene wouldn't have been so important to him. But now it was clear that Eugene wanted little to do with him and it was also becoming increasingly clear (from the meeting at Evans's house to the dark advice of Eugene) that there were real problems, some of them perhaps dangerous, with the club. But how could he bear to leave it? The truth was he could hardly bring himself to focus on these problems, much less think them through in any systematic way. He could barely bring himself to get to work on time, dressed properly and able to smile, and could hardly remember that in the past he had always prided himself on being neat, on time, and amiable — the ultimate team player. After work, the next day, he went directly home as if there were some awful menace on the streets he had to flee.

In his apartment he found it difficult to sit still, and nearly impossible to sleep. He began pacing from wall to wall of his apartment, trying to move without any thought or even excess motion, like a fish in an aquarium, varying his passage as little as possible as he continued his routine.

Then, finally, a change. The phone rang in his aquarium, he picked it up for some reason, following some fish-like impulse, and heard the voice of Bill Evans saying, "I've got to talk to you, man."

"Yes, go ahead."

"Not on the phone. Are you free now?"

Remy thought of the dark streets and wasn't sure how to answer.

"It's important."

"OK," Remy said.

"You know Coliseum Books on Fifty-ninth Street?"

"Yes."

"Meet me there in half an hour. I'll be in the mystery section."

Remy hung up and continued pacing rapidly for a minute, like a fish doing double time. Then he stopped and began wondering if he should call a cab or not — would it really be any safer? And as he thought, the water around him evaporated, as did his feeling of having gills and a fish persona. He was so happy about that he decided to run the twenty blocks to the bookstore, keeping his mind as thought-free as possible although he did feel a low but persistent level of anxiety the whole way.

As promised, Evans was in the mystery section in a long black overcoat looking at or pretending to look at a book by Poe with his black-rimmed glasses. Their eyes met quickly, Evans, looking around himself, half nodding, but waiting until Remy was next to him before he spoke in a low voice barely louder than a whisper.

"We can talk here, man."

"What is it?" Remy said. He wanted to say more but couldn't, as if all those silent hours away in the aquarium made him forget how to talk.

"There are some things I think you don't know, that I want you to know."

"What things?"

"About the club and its ideas. When I was talking to you at the last meeting you looked confused when I was referring to my trio, like you didn't know how old I was."

"But then I figured it out."

"Yah, man, cause I talked about Scotty's death and the record I made a year later. You figured it out 'cause you know about my career. But let me lay it out to you in simple terms 'cause you're going to have to make an important commitment at the next meeting and when you make it it's like a complete life commitment. When you take on a new identity there are a lot of rewards, but also a lot of demands. You have to do a tremendous amount of research too and you have to have a lot of strength to leave your old self completely behind. In that sense you have to kill your old self and its old life. The only thing you can keep is your job but you have to do your job the way Nathanael West would, if you go ahead and decide to become him. That's why it takes so much courage and faith as well as work — time spent in a library, or whatever, doing as much research on him as you can. And finally, well let me ask you how old you are?"

"Twenty-nine," Remy said in a voice now barely above a whisper.

"OK, man. You'll live the life West did at twenty-nine, you'll take on his life in chronological order from twenty-nine on, so when you turn thirty West will turn thirty until . . ."

"Until when?"

"Until he dies, man. I wanted you to understand that. That's where the courage and faith part come in."

"But he died so young."

"Like I said, I'm gonna pass pretty soon too, but I'm also going to play jazz piano more beautifully than anyone's ever played it — that's the reward part — and besides, as long as the club exists I'll be reincarnated again somewhere down the line."

"But *you'll* be dead."

"No man, I'll be Bill Evans reincarnated. I might have to wait a number of years but like my song says, 'We Will Meet Again,'" Evans said with an ironic smile.

Remy looked down at the floor to get his bearings.

"Do all the members understand this when they make their commitment?"

"Don't worry about the other members. Just focus on yourself."

"But what if I lack the courage and vision to do this, to . . ."

"Have you been studying the club literature, especially the parts about reincarnation?"

"Not as much as I should have. Look, Bill, what if I decide I can't go through with this and just want to withdraw my membership?"

"I wouldn't advise that, man," Evans said with unexpected sternness. "I really think it's too late for that in your case."

Instinctively Remy took a step back — his face turning a shade of white that, in turn, made Evans's eyes grow larger and more intense.

"Do you realize the invaluable work we're doing?"

"Yes, no," Remy said.

"We're saving the most important members of the human race — allowing their beauty to continue to touch humanity."

"But you're killing them again. Why not give the, give yourself, for example, a chance to live longer to see what you could do with more time?"

Evans shook his head from side to side like a pendulum.

"You can't go against karma, man. We have to accept our limits."

Remy took another step back and Evans extended his arm and let his hand rest on his shoulder.

"This world is as beautiful as it can get. You have to accept it. You know, like the poet said, 'death is the mother of beauty.'"

"It sounds more like a suicide club than an identity club," Remy blurted.

"Sometimes when something is really important or beautiful you have to die for it, like freedom. Isn't that why all the wars are fought?"

"But most wars are stupid and preventable."

"Death isn't preventable, man. We know this. Every bar of every tune I play knows this. It's like we accept this unstated contract with the world when we're born that we understand we'll have to die but we'll live out our destiny anyway."

"But all of science and medicine is trying to extend life, to defeat death."

"They'll never succeed, man. We know that, that's why we're a club of artists. Death and reincarnation is stronger than freedom. You have to give your life to forces that are bigger than you. Isn't that the unstated contract we all understand once we realize what death is? Isn't that humility the biggest part about what being a man is, man?"

Remy bowed his head, surprised that Evans was such a forceful speaker, and spoke with such complete conviction to the point where he had almost moved himself to tears. But all Remy felt was a desire to flee, to hide under his blanket and have the Identity Club, the agency, and New York itself all turn out to be a hideous dream.

"As a matter of fact I took a risk seeing you like this and laying it all out for you."

"I appreciate that and I'll never tell anyone what we spoke about. I won't mention it to anyone at the agency, I promise. The agency is really a key player in all of this, isn't it?"

"I can't get into that, man."

Remy nodded and felt a chill spread over him.

"Again, thank you for meeting me and for everything you told me, which, of course, I'll keep completely confidential," Remy said. He thought he should shake hands with Evans then, but couldn't bring himself to do it, instead found himself backing away from him.

"Remember how important beauty is and courage," Evans said, looking him straight in the eye.

"I'll remember everything you told me."

"See you at the next meeting then."

"Yes," Remy said, "I'll see you then."

He walked out of the store dreading the streets, feeling someone from the club might be following him. It was entirely possible that Evans might have tipped off somebody and had them tail him or perhaps had already informed someone at the agency. Had he made Evans feel he would cooperate and go forward with his membership? He could only hope so.

It was cold, even for New York in December. The wind was unusually strong and seemed to blow through him as if he were hollow. It was odd how people often said that because New York had so many people you often felt anonymous or alone but to Remy that night, the abundance of people simply increased the odds that one of them was following him. And if he thought about it he could always feel that someone was, simply because it was numerically impossible to keep track of everyone walking near him.

In his apartment again, Remy went back to the aquarium and to his fish-like movements through it. He hated the aquarium, especially since he felt so feverish, but it kept him from thinking, which would be still worse. He must have stayed in it pacing for hours, sleeping only for an hour or two on his sofa in the early morning. Fortunately he had saved up all his sick days and could now call the secretary at the agency and tell her, quite honestly, that he was too ill to come in.

After making the call, Remy went to his room and lay down, too dizzy to keep moving around. But as soon as his head hit the pillow he was assailed by a steady procession of thoughts, images, and snatches of dialogue about the club. He saw the hard look in Evans's eyes as he said, "I really think it's too late for that." The worried look (the first time he'd ever seen that expression on Eugene's face) as he said, "I'm just making this as a general statement, OK? I'm not saying anything about your club specifically." He saw the horrified expression in Bernhard's eyes in the hallway and heard his coughing fit again. He should have waited till the fit ended, he thought, and gotten some kind of definitive answer from him. Then he saw an image of Poe's face as he stood in front of his apartment the night of Evans's party, heard him say again "something is preoccupying you." Was Poe in on it too? Should he try to inform him? It seemed some members knew more than others. Perhaps there really was a secret membership within the membership that had the real knowledge of what the Identity Club truly believed and what it was prepared to do to enforce its beliefs.

Remy stayed in his apartment the entire day, eating Lean Cuisines and canned soup. Intermittently he tried watching TV or listening to the radio but everything reminded him of the club, as if all the voices he heard on TV and the radio were really members of the club. He no longer was as frightened of the streets the next morning since nothing had proved to be more torturous than the last sleepless hours in his apartment. Instead he was almost happy to return to the agency and certainly eager to immerse himself in work. Somewhat to his surprise he found himself whistling a bouncy jingle in the elevator, which, in fact, was the theme song for the new toothpaste campaign he'd worked on with Eugene.

The mood in the office was decidedly different, however. The receptionist barely acknowledged him, and when he looked at her more closely, appeared to be wiping tears from her eyes. Little groups of silent, stone-like figures were whispering in the hallway as if they were in a morgue. Remy took a few steps forward toward his office, hesitated, then walked back to the receptionist's desk and stared at her until she finally looked at him.

"What happened?" Remy said.

"It's Eugene," she said tearfully. "He died last night. Here, it's in the paper," she said, handing him a *Daily News*.

"Oh my God," Remy said, immediately tucking the newspaper inside his briefcase and walking soldier straight down the rest of the hall until he reached his office, where he could close his door and lock it. On page seven he found out everything he needed to know. Eugene had fallen to his death from the balcony of his midtown Manhattan apartment. At this point, the article said, "it was yet to be determined if foul play was involved."

Remy let the paper drop on his desk, looked out his window at the maze of buildings and streets below, and shivered. Everything was suddenly starting to fall into place like the pieces of a monstrous puzzle. That so many people in the club came from the agency, that Eugene was so obviously nervous when he obliquely spoke against it, that Evans said he was "taking a risk" talking to him two days ago at Coliseum Books. Obviously, Eugene's death was no accident. He'd been punished for trying to dissuade potential members from joining, either for the warnings he gave him, Remy, or perhaps for other warnings to other people in the agency Remy didn't know about.

He nearly staggered then from the pain of losing Eugene, who'd meant so much to him and could have meant so much more not only to him but also to the world, but when he looked out the window his mood turned to terror so complete it virtually consumed his pain.

What had he done? He'd locked himself in a virtual prison near a window on the twenty-ninth floor — but surely the higher-ups in the agency had master keys that could open it and ways to open the window and arrange his fall or some other form of execution.

There was no time to do anything but leave the building, no time even to go home, for his apartment would be the most dangerous place of all, and so no time to pack anything either. The world had suddenly shrunk to the cash in his pockets, the credit card in his wallet, and the clothes on his back. His goal now was simply to get a taxi to the airport and then as far away from New York as he could. He picked up his briefcase and overcoat, then stopped just short of the door and put them down on the floor. To leave his office with briefcase in hand, much less wearing his overcoat, might well look suspicious. He had to appear as if he were merely getting a drink of water or else going to the bathroom, then take ten extra steps and reach the elevator.

He counted to seven, his lucky number, and then opened his door thinking that he could probably buy a coat in the airport. The huddle of stone-like figures was gone. He walked directly toward the elevators, eyes focused straight ahead to reduce the chance of having to talk to someone. Then he saw an elevator open and his boss, Mr. Weir, about to get out. Before their eyes could meet, Remy turned left, opened a door, and ran down a flight of stairs, then down two more flights. He thought briefly of running all the way down to the street, but if someone spotted him he'd be too easy a target. Besides, he was quite sure no one from the agency worked on the twenty-fourth floor. He stopped running, opened the new stairway door, and forced himself not to walk too fast toward the elevators. Once there he pressed the button and counted to seven again, after which an empty elevator (an almost unheard-of event) suddenly appeared.

On the ride down he thought of different cities — Boston, Philadelphia, Washington, D.C. — where he had relatives. But would it be a good idea to contact any of them? He had the feeling that the agency not only knew where his parents and other relatives lived, but who his friends were and where they lived too. It would be better to make a clean break from his past and reinvent himself — assume a new identity, as it were, and go with that for a while.

Outside the wind had picked up and it was beginning to snow slightly. Fortunately a cab came right away.

"To LaGuardia," he said to the driver, who was rough-shaven and seemed unusually old for the job. Seeing the older man, Remy thought, the old are just the reincarnation of the young. In fact, strictly speaking, each moment of time you reincarnated yourself, since you always had to attain a balance between your core, unchanging self and your constantly changing one. But when he tried to think of this further, his head started to hurt. Looking out the window to distract himself he noticed a black line of birds in the sky and thought of Eugene's falling and then thought he might cry. A man was a kind of reincarnation of a bird, a bird of a dinosaur, and so on. But it really was too difficult to think about, just as infinity itself was. That was why people wanted to shape things for themselves; it was much too difficult otherwise. And, that's why the club members wanted to act like God, because it was much too difficult to understand the real God.

Remy's eyes suddenly met the driver's and a fear went through him. He thought the driver looked like someone from the agency so as soon as the taxi slowed down at the airport, Remy handed him much more money than he needed to and left the cab without waiting for his change. Then he ran into the labyrinth of the airport trying to find a plane as fast as he could and, like those birds he'd just seen in the sky, fly away into another life.

LOUISE ERDRICH

Disaster Stamps of Pluto

FROM *The New Yorker*

THE DEAD OF PLUTO now outnumber the living, and the cemetery stretches up the low hill east of town in a jagged display of
white stone. There is no bar, no theater, no hardware store, no
creamery or car repair, just a gas pump. Even the priest comes to
the church only once a month. The grass is barely mowed in time
for his visit, and of course there are no flowers planted. But when
the priest does come, there is at least one more person for the town
café to feed.

That there is a town café is something of a surprise, and it is no
rundown questionable edifice. When the bank pulled out, the family whose drive-in was destroyed by heavy winds bought the building with their insurance money. The granite façade, arched windows, and twenty-foot ceilings make the café seem solid and even
luxurious. There is a blackboard for specials and a cigar box by the
cash register for the extra change that people might donate to the
hospital care of a local boy who was piteously hurt in a farming accident. I spend a good part of my day, as do most of the people left
here, in a booth at the café. For now that there is no point in keeping up our municipal buildings, the café serves as office space for
town-council and hobby-club members, church-society and card-
playing groups. It is an informal staging area for shopping trips to
the nearest mall — sixty-eight miles south — and a place for the
town's few young mothers to meet and talk, pushing their car-seat-
convertible strollers back and forth with one foot while hooting
and swearing as intensely as their husbands, down at the other end
of the row of booths. Those left spouseless or childless, owing to

war or distance or attrition, eat here. Also divorced or single persons like myself who, for one reason or another, have ended up with a house in Pluto, North Dakota, their only major possession.

We are still here because to sell our houses for a fraction of their original price would leave us renters for life in the world outside. Yet, however tenaciously we cling to yards and living rooms and garages, the grip of one or two of us is broken every year. We are growing fewer. Our town is dying. And I am in charge of more than I bargained for when, in 1991, in the year of my retirement from medicine, I was elected president of Pluto's historical society.

At the time, it looked as though we might survive, if not flourish, well into the next millennium. But then came the flood of 1997, followed by the cost of rebuilding. Smalls's bearing works and the farm-implement dealership moved east. We were left with flaxseed and sunflowers, but cheap transport via the interstate had pretty much knocked us out of the game already. So we have begun to steadily diminish, and, as we do, I am becoming the repository of many untold stories such as people will finally tell when they know that there is no use in keeping secrets, or when they realize that all that's left of a place will one day reside in documents, and they want those papers to reflect the truth.

My old high school friend Neve Harp, salutatorian of the class of 1942 and fellow historical-society member, is one of the last of the original founding families. She is the granddaughter of the speculator and surveyor Frank Harp, who came with members of the Dakota and Great Northern Townsite Company to establish a chain of towns along the Great Northern tracks. They hoped to profit, of course. These townsites were meticulously drawn up into maps for risktakers who would purchase lots for their businesses or homes. Farmers in every direction would buy their supplies in town and patronize the entertainment spots when they came to ship their harvests via rail.

The platting crew moved by wagon and camped where they all agreed some natural feature of the landscape or general distance from other towns made a new town desirable. When the men reached the site of what is now our town, they'd already been platting and mapping for several years and in naming their sites had used up the few words they knew of Sioux or Chippewa, presidents and foreign capitals, important minerals, great statesmen, and the names of their girlfriends and wives. The Greek and Roman gods intrigued them. To the east lay the neatly marked-out townsites of Zeus, Neptune, Apollo, and Athena. They rejected Venus as conducive, perhaps, to future debauchery. Frank Harp suggested Pluto, and it was accepted before anyone realized they'd named a town for the god of the underworld. This occurred in the boom year of 1906, twenty-four years before the planet Pluto was discovered. It is not without irony now that the planet is the coldest, the loneliest, and perhaps the least hospitable in our solar system — but that was never, of course, intended to reflect upon our little municipality.

Dramas of great note have occurred in Pluto. In 1924, five members of a family — the parents, a teenage girl, an eight- and a four-year-old boy — were murdered. A neighbor boy, apparently deranged with love over the daughter, vanished, and so remained the only suspect. Of that family, but one survived — a seven-month-old baby, who slept through the violence in a crib wedged unobtrusively behind a bed.

In 1934, the National Bank of Pluto was robbed of seventeen thousand dollars. In 1936, the president of the bank tried to flee the country with most of the town's money. He intended to travel to Brazil. His brother followed him as far as New York and persuaded him to return, and most of the money was restored. By visiting each customer personally, the brother convinced them all that their accounts were now safe, and the bank survived. The president, however, killed himself. The brother took over the job.

At the very apex of the town cemetery hill, there is a war memorial. In 1951, seventeen names were carved into a chunk of granite that was dedicated to the heroes of both world wars. One of the names was that of the boy who is generally believed to have murdered the family, the one who vanished from Pluto shortly after the bodies were discovered. He enlisted in Canada, and when notice of his death reached his aunt — who was married to a town-council member and had not wanted to move away, as the mother and father of the suspect did — the aunt insisted that his name be added to the list of the honorable dead. But unknown community members chipped it out of the stone, so that now a rough spot is all that marks his death, and on Veterans Day only sixteen flags are set into the ground around that rock.

There were droughts and freak accidents and other crimes of

passion, and there were good things that happened, too. The seven-month-old baby who survived the murders was adopted by the aunt of the killer, who raised her in pampered love and, at great expense, sent her away to an Eastern college, never expecting that she would return. When she did, nine years later, she was a doctor — the first female doctor in the region. She set up her practice in town and restored the house she had inherited, where the murders had taken place — a small, charming clapboard farmhouse that sits on the eastern edge of town. Six hundred and forty acres of farmland stretch east from the house and barn. With the lease money from those acres, she was able to maintain a clinic and a nurse, and to keep her practice going even when her patients could not always pay for her services. She never married, but for a time she had a lover, a college professor and swim coach whose job did not permit him to leave the university. She had always understood that he would move to Pluto once he retired. But instead he married a girl much younger than himself and moved to Southern California, where he could have a year-round outdoor swimming pool.

Murdo Harp was the name of the brother of the suicide banker. He was the son of the town's surveyor and the father of my friend. Neve is now an octogenarian like me; she and I take daily walks to keep our joints oiled. Neve Harp was married three times, but has returned to her maiden name and the house she inherited from her father. She is a tall woman, somewhat stooped for lack of calcium in her diet, although on my advice she now ingests plenty. Every day, no matter what the weather (up to blizzard conditions), we take our two- or three-mile walk around the perimeter of Pluto.

"We orbit like an ancient couple of moons," she said to me one day.

"If there were people in Pluto, they could set their clocks by us," I answered. "Or worship us."

We laughed to think of ourselves as moon goddesses.

Most of the yards and lots are empty. For years, there has been no money in the town coffers for the streets, and the majority have been unimproved or left to gravel. Only the main street is paved with asphalt now, but the rough surfaces are fine with us. They give more purchase. Breaking a hip is our gravest dread — once you are immobile at our age, that is the end.

Our conversations slide through time, and we dwell often on setting straight the town record. I think we've sifted through every town occurrence by now, but perhaps when it comes to our own stories there is something left to know. Neve surprised me one day.

"I've been meaning to tell you why Murdo's brother, my uncle Octave, tried to run away to Brazil," she told me, as though the scandal had just occurred. "We should write the whole thing up for the historical newsletter."

I asked Neve to wait until we had finished our walk and sat down at the café, so that I could take notes, but she was so excited by the story beating its wings inside her — for some reason so alive and insistent that morning — that she had to talk as we made our way along. Her white hair swirled in wisps from its clip. Her features seemed to have sharpened. Neve has always been angular and imposing. I've been her foil. Her best audience. The one who absorbs the overflow of her excitements and pains.

"As you remember," Neve said, "Octave drowned himself when the river was at its lowest, in only two feet of water. He basically had to throw himself upon a puddle and breathe it in. It was thought that only a woman could have caused a man to inflict such a gruesome death upon himself, but it was not love. He did not die for love." Neve jabbed a finger at me, as though I'd been the one who kept the myth of Octave's passion alive. We walked meditatively on for about a hundred yards. Then she began again. "Do you remember stamp collections? How important those were? The rage?"

I said that I did remember. People still collect stamps, I told her.

"But not like they did then, not like Octave," she said. "My uncle had a stamp collection that he kept in the bank's main vault. One of this town's best-kept secrets is exactly how much money that collection was worth. When the bank was robbed in '34, the robbers forced their way into the vault. They grabbed what cash there was and completely ignored the fifty-nine albums and twenty-two specially constructed display boxes framed in ebony. That stamp collection was worth many times what the robbers got. It was worth almost as much money as was in the entire bank, in fact."

"What happened to it?" I was intrigued, as I hadn't known any of this.

Neve gave me a sly sideways look.

"I kept it when the bank changed hands. I like looking at the

stamps, you see — they're better than television. I've decided to
sell the whole thing, and that's why I'm telling the story now. The
collection is in my front room. Stacked on a table. You've seen the
albums, but you've never commented. You've never looked inside
them. If you had, you would have been enchanted, like me, with
the delicacy, the detail, and the endless variety. You would have
wanted to know more about the stamps themselves, and the need
to know and understand their histories would have taken hold of
you, as it did my uncle and as it has me, though thankfully to a
much lesser degree. Of course, you have your own interests."

"Yes," I said. "Thank God for those."

I would be typing out and editing Neve's story for the next
month.

As we passed the church, we saw the priest there on his monthly
visit. The poor man waved at us when we called out a greeting. No
one had remembered, so he was cutting the grass. His parish was
four or six combined now.

"They treat the good ones like simple beasts," Neve said. Then
she shrugged and we pressed on. "My uncle's specialty, for all
stamp collectors begin at some point to lean in a certain direction,
was what you might call the dark side of stamp collecting."

I looked at Neve, whose excitements tend to take a shady turn,
and thought that she had inherited her uncle's twist of mind along
with his collection.

"After he had acquired the Holy Grails of philately — British
Guiana's one-cent magenta, and the one-cent Z Grill — as well as
the merely intriguing — for instance, Sweden's 1855 three-cent issue, which is orange instead of blue-green, and many stamps of the
Thurn und Taxis postal system and superb specimens of the highly
prized Mulready cover — my uncle's melancholia drew him specifically to what are called 'errors.' I think Sweden's three-cent began it all."

"Of course," I said, "even I know about the upside-down airplane
stamp."

"The twenty-four-cent carmine-rose-and-blue invert. The Jenny.
Yes!" She seemed delighted. "He began to collect errors in color,
like the Swedish stamp, very tricky, then overprints, imperforate errors, value missings, omitted vignettes, and freaks. He has one entire album devoted to the seventeen-year-old boy Frank Baptist,

who ran off stamps on an old handpress for the Confederate government."

Neve charged across a gravelly patch of road, and I hastened to stay within earshot. Stopping to catch her breath, she leaned on a tree and told me that, about six years before he absconded with the bank's money, Octave Harp had gone into disasters — that is, stamps and covers, or envelopes, that had survived the dreadful occurrences that test or destroy us. These pieces of mail, water-stained, tattered, even bloodied, marked by experience, took their value from the gravity of their condition. Such damage was part of their allure.

By then, we had arrived at the café, and I was glad to sit down and take a few notes on Neve's revelations. I borrowed some paper and a pen from the owner, and we ordered our coffee and sandwiches. I always have a Denver sandwich and Neve orders a BLT without the bacon. She is a strict vegetarian, the only one in Pluto. We sipped our coffee.

"I have a book," Neve said, "on philately, in which it says that stamp collecting offers refuge to the confused and gives new vigor to fallen spirits. I think Octave was hoping he would find something of the sort. But my father told me that the more he dwelt on the disasters the worse he felt. He would brighten whenever he obtained something valuable for his collection, though. He was in touch with people all over the globe — it was quite remarkable. I've got files and files of his correspondence with stamp dealers. He would spend years tracking down a surviving stamp or cover that had been through a particular disaster. Wars, of course, from the American Revolution to the Crimean War and the First World War. Soldiers frequently carry letters on their person, and one doesn't like to think how those letters ended up in the hands of collectors. But Octave preferred natural disasters and, to a lesser extent, man-made accidents." Neve tapped the side of her cup. "He would have been fascinated by the *Hindenburg,* and certainly there would have been a stamp or two involved, somewhere. And our modern disasters, too, of course."

I knew what she was thinking of, suddenly — those countless fluttering, strangely cheerful papers drifting through the sky in New York. . . . I went cold with dismay at the thought that many of those bits of paper were perhaps now in the hands of dealers who were selling them all over the world to people like Octave. Neve and I think very much alike, and I saw that she was about to sugar her coffee — a sign of distress. She has a bit of a blood-sugar problem.

"Don't," I said. "You'll be awake all night."

"I know." She did it anyway, then set the glass cannister back on the table. "Isn't it strange, though, how time mutes the horror of events, how they cease to affect us in the same way? But I began to tell you all of this in order to explain why Octave left for Brazil."

"With so much money. Now I'm starting to imagine he was on the trail of a stamp."

"You're exactly right," Neve said. "My father told me what Octave was looking for. As I said, he was fascinated with natural disasters, and in his collection he had a letter that had survived the explosion of Krakatoa in 1883, a Dutch postmark placed upon a letter written just before and carried off on a steamer. He had a letter from the sack of mail frozen onto the back of a New Hampshire mail carrier who died in the East Coast blizzard of 1888. An authenticated letter from the *Titanic*'s seagoing post office, too, but then there must have been quite a lot of mail recovered for some reason, as he refers to other pieces. But he was not as interested in sea disasters. No, the prize he was after was a letter from the year 79 AD."

I hadn't known there was mail service then, but Neve assured me that mail was extremely old, and that it was Herodotus whose words appeared in the motto "Neither snow, nor rain, nor gloom of night," etc., more than three hundred years before the date she'd just referred to — the year Mt. Vesuvius blew up and buried Pompeii in volcanic ash. "As you may know," she went on, "the site was looted and picked through by curiosity seekers for a century and a half after its rediscovery before anything was done about preservation. By then, quite a number of recovered objects had found their way into the hands of collectors. A letter that may have been meant for Pliny the Younger, from the Elder, apparently surfaced for a tantalizing moment in Paris, but by the time Octave could contact the dealer the prize had been stolen. The dealer tracked it, however, through a shadowy resale into the hands of a Portuguese rubber baron's wife, who was living in Brazil, a woman with obsessions similar to Octave's — though she was not a stamp collector. She was interested in all things Pompeian — had her walls painted in exact replicas of Pompeii frescoes, and so on."

"Imagine that. In Brazil."

"No stranger than a small-town North Dakota banker amassing a world-class collection of stamps. Octave was, of course, a bachelor. And he lived very modestly too. Still, he didn't have enough money to come near to purchasing the Pliny letter. He tried to leave the country with the bank's money and his stamp collection, but the stamps held him back. I think the customs officials became involved in questions regarding the collection — whether it should be allowed to leave the country, and so on. The Frank Baptist stamps were an interesting side note to American history, for instance. Murdo caught up with him a few days later, and Octave had had a breakdown and was paralyzed in some hotel room. He was terrified that his collection would be confiscated. When he returned to Pluto, he began drinking heavily, and from then on he was a wreck."

"And the Pompeii letter — what became of it?"

"There was a letter from the Brazilian lady, who still hoped to sell the piece to Octave, a wild letter full of cross-outs and stained with tears."

"A disaster letter?"

"Yes, I suppose you could say so. Her three-year-old son had somehow got hold of the Pompeii missive and reduced it to dust. So in a way it *was* a letter from a woman that broke Octave's heart."

There was nothing more to say, and we were both in a thoughtful mood by then. Our sandwiches were before us and we ate them.

Neve and I spend our evenings quietly, indoors, reading or watching television, listening to music, eating our meager suppers alone. As I have been long accustomed to my own company, I find my time from dusk to midnight wonderful. I am not lonely. I know I haven't long to enjoy the luxuries of privacy and silence, and I cherish my familiar surroundings. Neve, however, misses her two children and her grandchildren. She spends many evenings on the telephone, although they live in Fargo and she sees them often. Both Neve and I find it strange that we are old, and we are amazed at how quickly our lives passed — Neve with her marriages and I with my medical practice. We are even surprised when we catch sight of ourselves sometimes. I am fortunate in old age to have a good companion like Neve, though I have lately suspected that if she had the chance to leave Pluto she would do it.

That night, she had an episode of black moodiness, brought on by the sugar in her coffee, though I did not say so. She was still caught up in the telling of Octave's story, and she had also made an odd discovery.

Flanked by two bright reading lamps, I was quietly absorbing a rather too sweet novel sent by a book club that I belong to when the telephone rang. Speaking breathlessly, Neve told me that she had been looking through albums all evening with a magnifying glass. She had also been sifting through Octave's papers and letters. She had found something that distressed her: In a file that she had never before opened was a set of eight or nine letters, all addressed to the same person, with canceled stamps, the paper distorted as though it had got wet, the writing smudged, each stamp differing from the others by some slight degree — a minor flaw in the cancellation mark, a slight rip. She had examined them in some puzzlement and noticed that one bore a fifty-cent violet Benjamin Franklin issued two years after the cancellation mark, which was dated just before the sinking of the *Titanic*.

"I am finding it very hard to admit the obvious," she said, "because I had formed such a sympathetic opinion of my uncle. But I believe he must have been experimenting with forged disaster mail, and that what I found was no less than evidence. He was offering his fake letter to a dealer in London. There were attempts and rejections of certification letters, too." She sounded furious, as though he had tried to sell her the item himself.

I tried to talk Neve down, but when she gets into a mood like this all of her rages and sorrows come back to her and it seems she must berate the world or mourn each one. From what she could tell, all the other articles in Octave's collection were authentic, so after a while she calmed herself. She even laughed a bit, wondering if Octave's forgery would hold up if included in the context of an otherwise brilliant collection.

"It could improve the price," she said.

As soon as possible, I put the phone down, and my insipid novel as well. Neve's moods are catching. I have a notion I will soon be alone in Pluto. I try to shake off a sudden miasma of turbulent dread, but before I know it I have walked into my bedroom and am opening the chest at the foot of my bed and I am looking through my family's clothes — all else was destroyed or taken away, but the undertaker washed and kept these (kindly, I think) and he gave them to me when I moved into this house. I find the somber envelope marked "Jorghansen's Funeral Parlor" and slip from it the valentine, within its own envelope, that must have been hidden in a pocket. It may or may not be stained with blood, or rust, but it is most certainly a hideous thing, all schmaltz and paper lace. I note for the first time that the envelope bears a five-cent commemorative stamp of the Huguenot monument in Florida.

Sometimes I wonder if the sounds of fear and anguish, the thunder of the shotgun, is hidden from me somewhere in the most obscure corner of my brain. I might have died of dehydration, as I wasn't found for three days, but I don't remember that either, not at all, and have never been abnormally afraid of thirst or obsessed with food or water. No, my childhood was very happy and I had everything — a swing, a puppy, doting parents. Only good things happened to me. I was chosen Queen of the Prom. I never underwent a shock at the sudden revelation of my origins, for I was told the story early on and came to accept who I was. We even suspected that the actual killer might still be living somewhere in our area, invisible, remorseful. For we'd find small, carefully folded bills of cash hidden outdoors in places where my aunt or I would be certain to find them — beneath a flowerpot, in my tree house, in the hollow handles of my bicycle — and we'd always hold the wadded squares up and say, "He's been here again." But, truly, I am hard pressed to name more than the predictable sadnesses that pass through one's life. It is as though the freak of my survival charged my disposition with gratitude. Or as if my family absorbed all the misfortune that might have come my way. I have lived an ordinary and a satisfying life, and I have been privileged to be of service to people. There is no one I mourn to the point of madness and nothing I would really do over again.

So why, when I stroke my sister's valentine against the side of my face, and why, when I touch the folded linen of her vest, and when I reach for my brothers' overalls and the apron my mother died in that day, and bundle these things to my stomach together with my father's ancient, laundered, hay-smelling clothes, why, when I gather my family into my arms, do I catch my breath at the wild upsurge, as if a wind had lifted me, a black wing of air? And why, when that happens, do I fly toward some blurred and ineradicable set of features that seems to rush away from me as stars do? At blinding speeds, never stopping?

When Pluto is empty at last and this house is reclaimed by earth, when the war memorial is toppled and the bank/café stripped for its brass and granite, when all that remains of our town is a collection of historical newsletters bound in volumes donated to the regional collections at the University of North Dakota, what then? What shall I have said? How shall I have depicted the truth?

The valentine tells me that the boy's name should not have been scratched from the war memorial, that he was not the killer after all. For my sister loved him in return, or she would not have carried his message upon her person. And if he had had her love he probably fled out of grief and despair, not remorse or fear of prosecution. But if it was not the boy, who was it? My father? But no, he was felled from behind. There is no one to accuse. Somewhere in this town or out in the world, then, the being has existed who stalked the boys hiding in the barn and destroyed them in the hay, who saw the beauty of my sister and my mother and shot them dead. And to what profit? For nothing was taken. Nothing gained. To what end the mysterious waste?

An extremely touchy case came my way about twenty years ago, and I have submerged the knowledge of its truth. I have never wanted to think of it. But now, as with Neve, my story knocks with insistence, and I remember my patient. He was a hired man who'd lived his life on a stock farm that abutted the farthest edges of our land. Warren Wolde was a taciturn crank, who nevertheless had a way with animals. He held a number of peculiar beliefs, I am told, regarding the United States government. On these topics, his opinion was avoided. Certain things were never mentioned around him — Congress being one, and particular amendments to the Constitution. Even if one stuck to safe subjects, he looked at people in a penetrating way that they found disquieting. But Warren Wolde was in no condition to disquiet me when I came onto the farm to treat him. Two weeks before, the farm's expensive blooded bull had hooked and then trampled him, concentrating most of the damage on one leg. He'd refused to see a doctor, and now a feverish infection had set in and the wound was necrotic. He was very strong, and fought being moved to a hospital so violently that his employers had decided to call me instead to see if I could save his leg.

I could, and did, though the means were painful and awful and it meant twice-daily visits, which my schedule could ill afford. At each change of the dressing and debridement, I tried to dose Wolde with morphine, but he resisted. He did not trust me yet and feared that if he lost consciousness he'd wake without his leg. Gradually, I managed to heal the wound and also to quiet him. When I first came to treat him, he'd reacted to the sight of me with a horror unprecedented in my medical experience. It was a fear mixed with panic that had only gradually dulled to a silent wariness. As his leg healed, he opened to my visits, and by the time he was hobbling on crutches he seemed to anticipate my presence with an eager pleasure so tender and pathetic that it startled everyone around him. He'd shuck off his forbidding and strange persona just for me, they said, and sink back into an immobilizing fury once I'd left. He never healed quite enough to take on all of his old tasks, but he lasted pretty well at his job for another three years. He died naturally, in his sleep one night, of a thrown blood clot. To my surprise, I was contacted several weeks later by a lawyer.

The man said that his client Warren Wolde had left a package for me, which I asked him to send in the mail. When the package arrived, addressed in an awkward script that certainly could have been Wolde's, I opened the box immediately. Inside were hundreds upon hundreds of wadded bills of assorted denominations, and of course I recognized their folded pattern as identical to the bills that had turned up for me all through my childhood. I could perhaps believe that the money gifts and the legacy were only marks of sympathy for the tragic star of my past and, later, gratitude for what I'd done. I might be inclined to think that, were it not for the first few times I had come to treat Wolde, when he reared from me in a horror that seemed so personal. There had been something of a recalled nightmare in his face, I'd thought it even then, and I was not touched later on by the remarkable change in his character. On the contrary, it chilled me to sickness.

Those of you who have faithfully subscribed to this newsletter know that our dwindling subscription list has made it necessary to reduce the length of our articles. So I must end here. But it appears, anyway, that since only the society's treasurer, Neve Harp, and I have convened to make any decisions at all regarding the preservation and upkeep of our little collection, and as only the two of us are left to contribute more material to this record, and as we have nothing left to say, our membership is now closed. We declare our society defunct. I shall, at least, keep walking the perimeter of Pluto until my footsteps wear my orbit into the earth. My last act as the president of Pluto's historical society is this: I would like to declare a town holiday to commemorate the year I saved the life of my family's murderer. The wind will blow. The devils rise. All who celebrate it shall be ghosts. And there will be nothing but eternal dancing, dust on dust, everywhere you look.

Oh my, too apocalyptic, I think as I leave my house to walk over to Neve's to help her cope with her sleepless night. She will soon move to Fargo. She'll have the money to do it. Dust on dust! There are very few towns where old women can go out at night and enjoy the breeze, so there is that about Pluto. I take my cane to feel the way, for the air is so black I think already I am invisible.

DANIEL HANDLER

Delmonico

FROM *McSweeney's Enchanted Chamber of Astonishing Stories*

"WHAT'S A DELMONICO?"

The two gentlemen had scarcely entered the place. From where I was sitting they were only silhouettes in the shiny doorway, blaring with rude sun. It was after six but dead summer, so the sun hadn't set. I don't drink in the daytime, but if it's after six you'll probably find me at the Slow Night. It's been remarked to me that my regular spot at the bar isn't the best one, as I have to whirl around whenever somebody walks in, just to see who it is. I suppose that's true, that I could choose a better barstool if I wanted a better view of the outside world. But that's not what I like to look at when I come in.

Davis was at the cash register, her back to the door, holding two or three dollars in her palm. She was about to give them to a guy, as change for the drinks she made for him and his girlfriend. Then the guy was going to hand them back to Davis. This is how it went with Davis as long as I'd ever seen it. Davis was gorgeous, is what she was, gorgeous not in the way she looked but in the way she was. When she mixed you a drink and handed back your change you'd hand it over to her no matter what you paid and what you ordered. It wouldn't matter if you had your girl with you, waiting at one of the tables with a high-heeled foot tapping on the carpet. You'd give it back, all your puny dollars, and still you'd feel like you hadn't forked it over fast enough. "Delmonico?" Davis said, and looked back at the gentlemen. She cocked her head, but not like she was thinking, more like she was considering whether these guys deserved the real answer. They didn't move. I tried to look at them myself but the sunlight still made them nothing but shadows. All

I could notice was that one was taller than the other. Davis had probably noticed six or seven things more, and she'd just that second turned around from the register. "Delmonico," she said again. "Gin, vermouth, brandy. A clash of bitters."

The shorter gentleman gave his friend a little tap with his hand. "I told you she was smart," he said, and then the two of them stepped inside and let the door shut behind them. Davis put her hands on her hips like this offhand compliment wasn't nearly enough. The guy slid his money back to Davis and took his seat.

Time and time I want to tell Davis that I love her, but she's so smart there's no way she hasn't figured it out already.

The Slow Night is on a fairly main drag, more or less half a block away from two other bars and just about across the street from another. These bars are called Mary's, and O'Malley's, and The something. I've never been inside them and never intend to. One of them — Mary's, I think — has those little flags all over the ceiling, fluttering like a used-car lot. You can see it from the street because they prop the door open. All of them have the neon in the window and even on a quick walk-by you can hear the roar of music and laughing and the little earthquakes of bottle caps falling to the floor. The bars are full in the evenings, because I guess there are lots of people in the world who like to have a pitcher of something, and sit underneath a TV yelling at each other. In the daytime they're dead like anyplace, with just a few puttering around. One of them has a pool table and people gather for that, with the chattering of the balls like teeth on a chilly day. I don't wish any of these people any harm and am grateful that these other bars take them away. The Slow Night looks closed from the outside, with heavy draperies on the windows and no real sign, just the name fading away over the entrance. The doors are closed except when someone is walking through them. From the doorway are two steps down into the bar — mostly for show, I think, because it's not a basement place. Inside, all the furniture's real — real barstools, real tables and chairs, and a real jukebox giving the world the music of the lonely, with Julie London and Hank Williams, and some quieter jazz things I never can determine. They don't serve food although sometimes a bowl of nuts might appear from someplace, and the only thing one might call entertainment is a few sections of the day's paper stacked up at the very end of the bar, in case one needs to check on something outside. Nowhere is any advertisement of any sort, except the clock which says Quill, right in the middle of the face. Davis doesn't know what that is. It came with the place.

The bar has something of a reputation, in guidebooks fools buy and read. "Don't let the exterior fool you," is the sort of thing that passes as praise, "the Slow Night is the real deal — the sort of place in which your parents might have met, with real leather booths and a lady behind the counter who will mix you any poison you can dream up." But these lazy lies — no booths, you don't dream up cocktails — aren't really the thing. Below the surface of the city, murmured between I don't know who, is the story that Davis is very smart. Not smart like a bartender who knows his World Series, but *smart*, like if you have a problem you can bring it up after you've ordered a drink and she will likely solve it for you. I've seen this in action — actually seen it happen. Divorce lawyers. Grad students. Geological survey men. She fixes their puzzles, although they're no less puzzled, really, when they leave. The gentlemen must have known this, too, although the tall one had to ask his quizmaster question before he believed it. They took off their hats and sat down.

"Holy —" the guy said from the table, but his girlfriend shushed him. The tall gentleman gave the guy a real angry look, and the guy lowered his eyes and took a long, long sip from his drink. Martinis, both of them, the guy and the girl both. That's the kind of couple that stays together.

"My friend here," said the short gentleman, "was hoping not to be recognized."

"You wander around hoping not to be recognized," Davis said, "then you ought not to let everybody know."

"Do you know who I am?" the tall gentleman asked.

"A customer, I'm guessing," Davis said. "I recognize everyone who comes in that way. I ask them what they want to drink and they tell me and we go from there. So far it's worked OK. Do you gentlemen really want Delmonicos? It's no drink for beginners."

"Scotch," said the shorter one, "for both of us, please," at the same time as his friend said, "I'm not sure I like your attitude."

Davis just kept her hands on her hips. I looked down at the rest of my bourbon. Davis has offered to make me something nicer, time and time again, but just a little bourbon on ice is what I get, and what she gives me. The shorter one coughed a little into his hand, and looked at his friend. "You'll have to excuse him," he said to Davis. "He's going through a lot."

Davis wasn't sure this was enough, but she nodded. "What kind of Scotch?"

"What kind is there?" the tall one said.

"There's cheap," she said, "there's good, and there's pretentious."

"I usually drink Banquo Gold," he said. "Eight-year-old, if you have it."

"Pretentious it is," she said, and his friend smiled. "Ice? Lemon?"

"I don't have to take this," growled the taller one. "It's a stupid idea, anyway. Bruno, let's get out of here. I should get out of here. I should have my *head* examined. I have a lawyer taking my money fast enough. I don't have to chase after some legendary bar skirt."

Bruno, a short name if there ever was one, tried to grab his friend again. "Relax, OK?" he said. "So she jokes around, so what?"

"I've had enough of women *joking around*," the taller one said. "Let's go."

"Look, why don't we have a drink?" Bruno said. "You want one anyway, right?"

"We can go across the street," the taller one said.

"You think they won't know you across the street?" Bruno said.

"Sure," Davis said. "Everybody across the street'll want to buy a drink for the guy who killed his wife."

The girlfriend gasped at her table. The two gentlemen flicked her a look of annoyance. "So you do know me," the taller one said. "You recognize me, what, from the papers?"

"Papers, TV," Davis said, shrugging. "You think that hat makes you invisible? Callahan Jeffers. That's who you are."

"I didn't kill my wife," the man snarled. "But I suppose you won't believe that unless it's in the papers, too."

"Don't you want it in the papers?" Davis asked. "I believe that's known as clearing your name."

"Let's go," Callahan Jeffers said to Bruno. "She's not going to help me if she thinks I did it."

"I don't think you did it," Davis said. "But I still don't help people who get rude in my bar."

"What have I done that's rude?" Jeffers asked. "You've been mocking me since I sat down."

"You haven't sat down," Davis said.

"You know what I mean."

"What I mean," Davis said, "is why don't you sit down, drink some good Scotch, and ask me what you want to ask me?"

Callahan Jeffers looked at her for a second or two, and put his hat down on the bar. "Ice," he said, "and lemon."

"For two," Bruno said.

Davis poured, and the gentlemen took their drinks — the way you might take a hike if a very dangerous person suggested it. Bruno laid a bill on the table I couldn't see, but from her bored glance it must have been enormous. She turned around and rang out change, placing her hard-earned cash on the bar before she even picked up the bill. The men let it stand. They were going to tip her later. I hated those guys. They weren't gentlemen after all.

Jeffers took a seat and took a sip and nodded. "So," he said, "there's no invisibility potion in a Delmonico, right? Or the gin, brandy, and whatever don't turn into an invisibility potion?"

"When your mother told you that there was no such thing as a stupid question," Davis said, "you didn't believe her, did you?"

"He's not used to women like you is all," Bruno said. "Since I've known him he goes for a different type."

"I don't want to hear about the type," Davis said. "I want to hear about the girl."

"She's no girl," Jeffers said. "She's my wife. Or was. Or *is*. She's gone."

"So you say," Davis said. "Do me a favor and don't tell me things I know already. You're Callahan Jeffers. You're very rich. You've never worked a day in your life, and neither did your father. You were sent to Europe for what rich people call 'schooling' and what everybody else calls 'school.' When you returned you made a big splash as an eligible bachelor. You invested in things for what we might call a living. You beat up a room-service waiter during a seventy-two-hour birthday party in an enormous suite, and you gave him a lot of money and two years later the mayor had you on some special citizens' commission on crime."

"I was drunk," Jeffers said. "That night in the hotel. I was very drunk and it was wrong. I've said it a thousand times. I had a drinking problem, and I worked it out."

"There are many people who come into my bar and order Scotch," Davis said. "None of them are reformed alcoholics."

"I just said I worked it out," Jeffers said. "That's what I believe. What you say about paying off the waiter was true. He was a fag and I bought him what fags want, which is a condo on the beach and a handsome face. I don't think that's a crime. People who resent me for money would do the same thing if they had it."

"And yet," Davis said, "with these statements, the police nevertheless suspect you of some sort of crime."

Callahan Jeffers stood up, although not without first taking another gulp of his drink. If you spend time in a bar you hear a number of men snarl. I don't know if they snarl more in bars or if that's just where I hear them snarl, but they snarl, like some animal you find messing around in the trash, or out in the angry woods where stupid people camp. *"I didn't kill my wife!"* he said. "I don't know how she did it, but she set me up. She's a bitch, a bitch someplace laughing at me. And she'll keep laughing until I'm all locked up."

"They're not going to lock you up," Bruno said.

"Says you." Callahan didn't sit down but he finished his drink. It made him look weak, the grab for the glass but still standing like he might leave.

"Says everyone, including the lawyer," Bruno said. "There's no body, so there's no crime. You haven't even been arrested."

"Arrested," Jeffers said. "Everything's gone now even if the police never touch me. I killed her is what everyone thinks. Mayor's special commission. I was going to be *mayor.*"

"He was weighing the odds of running, yes," Bruno said. "Those odds have changed."

"My whole odds have changed with this," Jeffers said. He looked around like he was going to spit on the floor and then looked at Davis again. What would have happened if this guy had spat on the floor? I think of that sometimes on sleepless nights, when the sugar from the bourbon wakes me up and makes me look at life. "I'm not the mayor now. I'm just a man who killed his wife. I'm gone and she's laughing. She's not dead any more than I'm Santa Claus. She fucked me somehow. I don't get it. No one gets it. Bruno said maybe you might."

"No," Davis said. "I certainly don't get why anyone would fuck you. You want another Scotch?"

"Take mine," Bruno said quickly, and handed over his drink. Where do they get guys like him? All the way back in his family tree maybe there were whipping boys.

"Tell me the thing," Davis said, "while I get everybody another round. Mr. Jones, you OK back there?"

I stay quiet when the bar's got customers, so I just nodded into my bourbon. It was half-gone. Maybe six months before it was a man with stolen eels. He was a marine something — you know, not like he'd actually ever been in the Marines. The eels were valuable and shipped across the ocean from a faraway sea, or maybe it was the other way around. When the man opened the tanks there was nothing but grime and seaweed. The eels were valuable but only if they were alive, and it was hard enough keeping them alive if you were a specialist with a government grant, let alone some black-market eel thug. Davis found them. She drew a little map on a cock-tail napkin with the words "Slow Night" written on it, the address below, because the man was from out of town and didn't know where the warehouse district was. You'd think a man who spent too much time with eels would have lost some social skills, but he was gorgeously grateful.

"I'll tell you the thing," Bruno said. "Mr. Jeffers met Nathalie at a club."

"The circus was in town," Jeffers said.

"It's true," Bruno said. "This girl was trash, I told him. Her parents were from different countries and ate fire for a living. She spun around on one of those things they dangle from the top of the tent."

"Trapeze," Davis said. "I remember the wedding pictures."

"I told him she'd never clean up," Bruno said. "Girls like that, from a circus? No. He made me go to her last show. She leaped through a hoop; I don't know what else she did. She takes a bow with the clowns and the Chinamen and he wants to marry her?"

"She was a beautiful woman," Davis said. "I remember the pictures."

Callahan Jeffers looked at her and almost smiled. "She was," he said. "She hit me like a ton of bricks."

Davis put two fresh Scotches down on the counter. Behind her the guy and his girlfriend were listening, their martinis forgotten. "And what'd you hit her like?" Davis said.

"It was just some fights," Jeffers said. "She had a temperament, you know? I guess it was wrecked from the start. I bought us a beautiful house, furnished it up, but she just couldn't sit still."

"A Wesson, wasn't it?" Davis asked. "One of the last untouched Wessons in this town."

"You know architecture?" Bruno asked.

"Why is it," Davis asked, "that people think a girl sitting around a deserted bar all day is *less* likely to be well-read?"

"It's completely restored," Jeffers said, with what would have passed for pride among the very dim. "The staircases, the banisters, the window dressings, the whole bit. I paid a flouncy faggot to track down as much of the pricey crap as he could dig up. Two benches in the front hall. The dining table and twelve chairs. You know, black and square — all that German minimal stuff he did. Nathalie was crazy about it. She said it calmed her down — *no*. What was the word? Whittled her down. The whole place was whittled down. The living room had one couch and a mirror balanced in the corner. The bedroom had just two huge black bureaus with square drawers. My study had one of Wesson's only rugs, a big black thing with one gray stripe, and a chandelier from his personal collection, all spidery on the ceiling. And a desk that looked like a fucking altar. It was enormous. It cost everything. But I bought it to show her I cared."

"The study," Davis said, "where you last saw her?"

"We were fighting," Callahan Jeffers said.

"What else is new?" Bruno said.

"She got home late," Jeffers said. "I don't know how it started. Bruno and I went to the fights. She'd never do that with me. We got home around ten but she still wasn't home. An hour later she walks in with Timothy Speed."

"The designer," Davis said.

"The *fag*," Callahan Jeffers said. He put one fist down, very gently, on the bar, like a man showing his gun. "The fag I paid a fortune to spend my fortune on furniture to whittle down my wife. I threw him out."

"Mr. Jeffers'd had a drink or two," Bruno said with a very small shrug.

"She yelled at me, I yelled at her, she pushed me around a little . . ." Callahan stopped talking. "I know what you're going to say. I shouldn't hit women."

"You shouldn't hit women," Davis said.

"I know that," Jeffers said. "But it was fighting. It was a fight. We were always getting worse. She thought I was catting around, which I was a little. But she drove me there! As soon as I married her she went a little crazy."

"She couldn't take it, with the swells," Bruno said. "A circus performer, Mr. Jeffers. She was climbing the walls because she climbed walls for a living. You can't dress that up."

"She dressed up fine," Jeffers said, "but nothing made her happy. I couldn't take it forever, you know? You want to make someone happy, but if the first fucking fifteen thousand tries don't do it, you get tired of an unhappy person and her yelling."

"So she locked herself in the study," Bruno said. "It locks from the inside. She wouldn't come out."

"What did you do?" Davis asked.

Callahan Jeffers looked at her like a horse I saw once. Some kids were making fun of it. The horse's eyes said, *Some day I will not be pulling this flatbed hayride. I will come to your room when you are sleeping and I will stomp on you, you damn kids.* The rich man lifted both fists and pounded in slow, heavy beats. Everybody's drinks bounced. "Come out!" he yelled. "Come out! Come out! *Come out! Come out!*"

He stopped and sat down. The jukebox finished a song — "And here I am, facing tomorrow, alone in my sorrow, down in the depths of the ninetieth floor" — and stopped, out of money, like much of this town. The guy and his girl shared one quick glance and skedaddled. When the door swung open and shut, it was much darker outside. For a moment I couldn't remember anything I'd done before Callahan Jeffers entered the Slow Night and started yelling. The rich man, once an eligible bachelor and probably one again, drew a handkerchief out of his pocket and wiped his face. I took a sip, mostly melted ice.

"It's true," Bruno muttered. "That's what he did."

"She didn't come out," Jeffers said. "We waited all night, Bruno and I."

"Bruno and you," Davis said. "Where did you wait?"

"Outside," Jeffers said. "Just outside that locked door. There's a little space with two chairs that hurt to sit in. We sat in them."

"Could you hear anything?"

"She made a crying phone call," Jeffers said. "It was Timothy Speed. He told me. I practically had to beat it out of him. He said she called and went through the whole blow by blow, and cried. She said I was going to kill her. That's what he told the police. He said she said. Why they would believe that of me —"

"You, a known drunk who beats people up," Davis said.

I didn't kill her! Jeffers said. "She cried to the fag and she hung up. She hung up and ordered a drink."

"What?" Davis asked.

"She said she wanted a drink," Jeffers said. "A Delmonico. She always liked the fancy things. When I met her she was asking for a Singapore Sling."

"Gin again," Davis said. "Gin, cherry brandy, bitters, lime, ginger beer. There are some who say you can't trust a gin woman. How did you make her a Delmonico if you didn't know what it was?"

"I don't make the drinks in my home," Jeffers said. "I have a man."

"He woke up Gregor," Bruno said. "It was late."

"Gregor loved it," Jeffers said. "Gregor loves Nathalie and he loves . . . I don't know. *Drama.* The trick with the mixing and the right glass for a lady who asks. He made one and brought it on a tray with a shaker and everything. He knocked on the door and she made him swear we were at least fifteen feet away."

"Which we were," Bruno said.

"He handed her the tray and she slammed the door again and locked it. We heard the cocktail shaker pour and then we heard nothing."

"Nothing?" Davis said.

"For two hours," Jeffers said. "It was morning, almost morning. Gregor went back to bed. Bruno fell asleep in the ugly chair. I paced outside and pounded some more. Bruno woke up."

"I did," Bruno said. "I woke up and made the point that perhaps you should go to bed rather than pounding on a door that incidentally cost a fortune. You were making marks."

"And then we heard a shattering of glass," Jeffers said. "Give me another Scotch."

"I'll think about it," Davis said. "You're making enough noise without another round. You scared two customers away before the martinis were over."

"Not my problem," Jeffers said.

"No," Davis agreed, and walked out of the bar to collect the glasses the kids had left behind. "Mine. If the study is the rounded room on the ground floor, then there are three enormous windows —"

"Painted shut," Jeffers said. "We were going to redo them. They hadn't been touched."

"And a small one in the far corner," Davis finished.

"That's the one that broke," Bruno said. "But the window doesn't go anywhere. It's a what's-it. A *lightwell*. Even if she could have fit through that window, which she couldn't —"

"She might," Jeffers said. "She was wasting away. I know she looked fine in the picture but she was starving herself. She wasn't doing well. She was making herself skinny to make me angry."

"That's not usually how it goes," Davis said.

"She was depressed, she said." Jeffers shook his head. "What's that thing where girls make themselves skinny for attention?"

"Marriage," Davis said.

Jeffers gave her one curt laugh. "I heard the window, I didn't know what to think. One day we were fighting and she found a nail on the ground. A nail! And scratched herself across the arm. With broken glass, I didn't want her to —"

"We used one of the chairs to break the door down," Bruno said. "Gregor heard us and came upstairs. The chair was broken too."

"Now what else is really in this room?" Davis said. "Rug and desk, you said. Curtains?"

"Heavy dark things," Jeffers said. "Like in here. Just like in this place. Timothy Speed made her get them. That's the first place we looked. We thought she'd thrown herself out one of the big windows, although she was so light they might not have broken. Who knows. But she wasn't there. And don't think behind the door because I looked there and kicked the goddamn wall. I'm telling you she wasn't hiding. She must have gone out the other one."

"It's a *lightwell*," Bruno said. "It goes up to a skylight made of marble you can shine light through. The light is yellowy. I don't like it. But that's where it goes."

"Up to a skylight," Davis said, "and down to where?"

"To another window, in the basement," Bruno said. "Painted shut. Not messed with. The police used what I have read was a fine-tooth comb."

"She was gone," Jeffers said. "When we saw the window we ran downstairs to the basement. There were four cases of wine stacked up against that window. They were dusty. She wasn't there. We ran all the way up to the roof. The sun was coming up over the park, I'm telling you, the goddamn birds were singing but my wife was not on the roof and there's no way she was ever on the roof."

Davis stopped wiping the table. "Afraid of heights?"

"No," Jeffers said. "You can't open that marble thing. It's old. Wesson didn't build it to be opened."

"Who went up on the roof?" Davis said. "All of you? Gregor too?"

"Gregor's old," Jeffers said. "He dozed in the other chair."

"The police have been with him a million times," Bruno said. "That's why they haven't arrested Mr. Jeffers, I think. They believe that I'd help him murder somebody and hide a body, but not Gregor. They thought maybe they couldn't shake me, but two hours with the cops and Gregor would cry like a baby."

"He lost his mom young," Jeffers said. "That's why he's such a fucking baby."

"I really don't like you," Davis said. She walked back to the bar and ran a thoughtful hand down the wood, close to where I was sitting. I couldn't help watching her even though it must have looked schoolboy. "A girl," she said, "goes into a room with nothing in it but antique furniture and closed windows. Someone brings her a drink. Glass breaks. A tiny window that goes nowhere is broken. The other ones aren't, and you're sure, right? Because they're tall. You might have missed a small break at the top."

"When we got back from the roof I ripped those drapes down myself," Jeffers said.

"Which hasn't helped your case," Bruno said. "He trashed that whole room and then had to tell the cops that nothing had been broken but the window. We got an Italian guy doing the wiring and an old man with a shop in his garage. He's the only man who can fix a Wesson chair, so he says."

"Yes," Jeffers said. "I threw the chair."

"The chair that broke the door?" Davis asked.

"No," Jeffers said. "Another chair. The chair by the desk. It was like a throne but I lifted it and I snapped it over the desk."

"So there was another chair in the room," Davis said. "What else?"

"Papers in the desk," Jeffers said. "I don't know. Nothing. A letter opener, maybe? When I tipped it over I didn't notice anything missing."

"The drink," Bruno said.

"What?" Davis asked.

"The Delmonico," Bruno said. "The tray was there and the little shaker full of melting ice. But the glass and the drink were gone. Gin, vermouth, brandy, dash of bitters."

"An invisibility potion," Jeffers said. "Like I said. Gone like her."

"Mr. Jones," Davis said, "put something on the jukebox."

She handed me two of Callahan's unearned dollars. He glared at me. I walked to the jukebox and chose Chet Baker, which is what I do often.

"What was she wearing?" Davis asked.

"A necklace," Jeffers said. "A lot of money around her neck. Diamonds and I think sapphires, I don't know. A vintage thing somebody found for me. A present after a fight. And a silk dress I ripped. And her shoes, but her shoes were sitting on the desk, right next to the phone which I ripped out of the wall. Just tell me where the fuck she is or stop with the stupid questions. I'm so tired of this. The cops ask all the same things, what was she wearing, like I would have forgot to mention jet-pack."

"I'm going to pour you one more Scotch," Davis said. "And you'll drink it and I'll tell you something and you'll leave. And you'll pay for another bourbon for Mr. Jones."

"Who the hell is Mr. Jones?" Jeffers asked.

"A customer who doesn't give me any trouble," Davis said, her back to the bottles. She poured, and then she reached up and coaxed two martini glasses from a rack above her head. I always forget about that. The gentlemen sipped and I sipped and she filled the two glasses with ice and left them on the bar, while she busied herself with a shaker. Gin. Brandy. You know where this is going. She trembled the bitters bottle over the shaker, stirred, and shut the lid. The ice shifted in the glass. The jukebox played.

There's something about this I'm not telling right. How nasty Jeffers was, maybe, or the sheer implausible mess of a circus wife, a thuggish friend, a tale of an old butler and a locked-up room. The gorgeous shadow of the Slow Night while outside the sun sank, and the quiet of an early drink you didn't deserve. You do not meet people very often like Davis, with a smile from nowhere and a wavering frown, thinking things over so beautifully just to watch her was beauty enough, like the lilt in a good jazz singer, the curve of a good lyric like a secret closing in on itself. *This suspense is killing me. I can't stand uncertainty. Tell me now. I've got to know whether you want me to stay or go. Love me, or leave me and let me be lonely. You won't believe me. I love you only. I'd rather be lonely than happy with somebody else. You might find the nighttime the right time for kissing, but nighttime is my time for just reminiscing, regretting instead of forgetting with somebody else. There'll be no one unless that someone is you. I intend to be independently blue. I want your love, but I don't want to borrow — to have it today, to give back tomorrow. For my love is your love. There's no love for nobody else.*

When the song ended Jeffers lifted his glass to drain it. It finished, and the sliver of lemon hit his grimacing mouth. "Well?" he said, and pointed to the icy glasses. "What're those?"

"Delmonicos," Davis said. "Like the one that vanished. But it didn't vanish. She threw the glass at the window. Both broke. You couldn't tell one from the other."

Jeffers turned his glass over. This wasn't polite. The Scotch was on the rocks, and the bar got wet with the slop of his ice. The puddle stopped before the two glasses, the ice ghosting into water, that Davis had ready for I couldn't imagine who. "And my wife?"

"That I can't tell you," Davis admitted. She opened her palm and brushed the pile of money, very slowly, into the puddle of Callahan's drink. "Time to go, fellas."

"She's not smart," Jeffers said to Bruno, pointing at him and sneering. "She doesn't know."

"I'm smart enough," Davis said. "If you don't stand up and leave I will walk out of this bar myself. Across the street is a roomful of drunk cops. I'll tell them that Callahan Jeffers, a man finished in this town, is harassing me."

It was true. Funny thing: Davis lets cops drink for free, but hardly anybody ever takes her up. Across the way, O'Malley's lets them drink for half price, and by closing there's a whole platoon staggering outside. Bruno grabbed Callahan's shoulder. Callahan put on his hat. When the door swung open the light was almost gone, and when it swung shut Davis poured the ice out of the glasses and drained the cocktails from the shaker. "Join me," she said. "I haven't had one of these in years."

I put my bourbon aside. "It's not a drink for beginners," I said.

"You're not a beginner," she said. She'd overmeasured, or maybe some of the ice had melted — the glasses were brimming full. Carefully, carefully, she walked them both over, nearly teetering. "All those fishbowls I had to carry in Miss Brimley's class," she said. "Finally coming in handy. To us, Mr. Jones. To our good health."

I didn't drink. "Where is she?" I said.

Davis shrugged, which was a sight to see, each shoulder rising and falling like a sheet in the wind. "I don't know. Probably in some summer cottage of Timothy Speed's. Dyeing her hair or however that goes. Everybody wants to join the circus when they run away from home, but that might be too easy. He'd look for her there, maybe. But a dead girl'll need money."

"Speed could help her sell the necklace," I said.

"That'd be a start," she said, and sighed. "When did you figure it?"

"When you reached for those glasses," I said. "Nobody ever remembers to look up. The drink broke the window and made them look the wrong way. Just the time she needed. They took a trip to the basement, they took a trip to the room, and by the time they got back from the roof she was out the front door like a person. Speed left a car maybe."

"And Gregor? Really dozing, you think?"

"Really dozing, I think," I said. "Without shoes she could tiptoe past him. Or maybe he could lie to the cops after all. Maybe he watched her swing down from that chandelier, as skinny as she was, and let her go after all the fights he saw. She must have been very scared."

"Scared?" Davis said. "She hatched a plan to ruin her husband. It's like he said. They'll never charge him but he'll never be mayor, either. He'll just be a rich guy who got away with murder."

"That's what he is anyway," I said. "That's why she was scared. Scared to fall. If she fell it'd be the end of her — maybe from hitting the floor, or maybe from her husband hitting her. It was a risk. Even an acrobat. Even someone who'd whittled herself away to almost nothing."

"Then she had almost nothing to lose," Davis said. She took a sip and pursed her lips. It's a bitter drink, or maybe bitter's not what I mean. It's sharp and sour. It's complicated. It's difficult to get down

unless that's the sort of thing you like. "I feel that way myself sometimes," she said. "Almost nothing, or maybe that's just Chet Baker
nudging me to say that. You think I was wrong not to tell him."

"You told him where the drink went," I said. "That's enough for
someone like that. Without a body they won't charge him. He'll
never know for sure. Maybe Timothy Speed will even blackmail
him."

"Or just keep overcharging him for furniture," Davis said. "Wesson never made any rugs. The whole point of a Wesson is the sheer
lines of the place. The floors are bare so you can see the wood."

"Callahan Jeffers," I said, "would never see the wood."

"Not for the trees," Davis agreed. She put her drink down and
walked to the jukebox with one of Jeffers's damp bills. She
punched a number in and her hair just slayed me in the red lights
shining inside the machine that sits in the Slow Night waiting for
people to ask it to sing. I tried the drink myself but didn't like it,
but I liked watching the tilt of the surface of the drink as I moved
the glass, like water too cold to swim in. When we're alone like this
the room sinks in a bit, like we're locked away from all the people.
There are some who can't stand to stay in a room like that but this
is my regular spot, right here at the bar where I can see her. Time
and time I want to tell Davis that I love her, but of course she's so
smart — of course she is — there's no way she hasn't figured it out
already.

GEORGE V. HIGGINS

Jack Duggan's Law

FROM *The Easiest Thing in the World*

LATE IN THE MORNING, the Coupe de Ville — slate gray, black vinyl roof, five years old — emerged from the road in the woods and moved too quickly down the curving highway. There was a building at the bottom of the hill. It was low, one-story, painted white, and peeling. It was surrounded by an eight-foot board fence which had been barn red at one time but had not been painted for years. The fence enclosed a trapezoidal area. The enclosure was filled with old tires piled two and three feet higher than the fence. The fence sagged and bulged around the tires. There was a marsh-land which surrounded the fence. It was crowded with cat-o'-nine-tails and scrub brush.

The Cadillac swung around to the front of the building and stopped with some hastiness. There was an old Texaco gas pump in front, the mechanism exposed from the midsection to the top, the top crowned by a white disk emblazoned with the fire chief hat symbol. There was a sign on the front of the building, above two sagging barn doors. One of the doors was ajar. The sign read: TEX-ACO. GIFFORD'S. BRAKES. SERVICE. LUBRICATION. The let-ters had started out black, but had faded to gray. There were old tires scattered around the outside of the fence, and a row of old au-tomobile batteries against it.

The driver of the Cadillac backed it up slightly and ran over the signal bell hose again. The bell rang in the stillness. The driver opened the door of the car and got out. He was in his middle for-ties. He had dark hair and he was getting thick in the middle. He wore a white shirt with french cuffs and onyx links that were too large. He wore a red tie that was too shiny. He had left his suit coat in the car; the pants were dark blue and well-cut. They did not look appropriate with his brown jodhpur boots. He wore wraparound mirror sunglasses and a Texas Instruments calculator watch. He ran his right hand through his hair, making it stand up. He put his fists on his hips and stared at the garage. He slammed the door of the car and started toward the garage doors.

When the driver was about eight feet from the doors, a very large chow-chow emerged with immense dignity. The dog had a mane and a black tongue. It stood half-in, half-out of the space between the doors and slavered. It looked at the driver with interest, as though it had not had a square meal in some time.

"Nice boy," the driver said politely. He continued to approach the doors. The dog continued to stare at him. The driver reached a point about six feet from the doors. The dog roared and lunged at him, rearing up on its hind legs. It was snubbed up by a chain with half-inch links. The dog sat down. The driver backed up. "Nice boy," the driver said. The dog hung its black tongue out and slavered, measuring the driver.

"Halloo," the driver said to the building. The dog panted. "Halloo," the driver said to the building.

The dog lurched backward, jerked off its front feet, and vanished into the building.

"Is it OK to come in?" the driver said. There was no reply. The driver advanced tentatively toward the doors. He peered around the edge of the one that was ajar. He went inside. The interior was dim and it took him a moment to regain his vision. Dead ahead there was an old man in a khaki cardigan and a dark blue wool ski hat. He was sitting in an old maroon armchair. There was an old floor lamp to the right of the armchair. There was a kerosene heater next to the armchair. It was stiflingly hot in the garage. To the left there was a double rack of new tires. To the left there was a double rack of new batteries. Behind the man in the armchair there was a wooden case, fronted and topped with glass, filled with candies. The dog sat beside the man in the armchair. The dog was still slavering.

"Careful," the old man said. "Grease pit, front of you."

The driver looked down. There was a lubrication pit in front of him.

"Help you?" the old man said. He was reading something, or had been. The magazine was open in his lap. It was open to a double-page spread of a naked woman.

"Yeah," the driver said, "I need some directions."

"Ain't seen you before," the old man said.

"Ain't been here before," the driver said. "What I need's directions."

"No gas," the old man said.

"Nope," the driver said, "no gas."

"Just as well," the old man said. "Ain't got any. Quit pumpin' that stuff six year ago. Damned nuisance."

"Directions," the driver said.

"Directions," the old man said. "Montreal's north. Go to the border. Turn left. You want Quebec, turn right. Simple." He cackled.

The driver did not laugh. When the old man had finished, the driver said: "Ellis house."

"Ellis house," the old man said.

"Yeah," the driver said.

"You from Boston?" the old man said.

"Yeah," the driver said.

"Thought so," the old man said.

"The Ellis house," the driver said.

"Never heard of 'em," the old man said, complacently.

"Bullshit," the driver said.

"Seen my dog?" the old man said.

"Yeah," the driver said.

"Big dog," the old man said.

"Seen my car?" the driver said.

"Nope," the old man said.

"Out front," the driver said. "Big car. Bigger'n your dog."

"No foolin'," the old man said.

"Yup," the driver said. "I bet I could fire that sucker up and run right over your big dog in about twenny seconds, and peel right outta here and scrape him off the wheels onna first turn."

"Ellis house," the old man said.

"Ellis house," the driver said.

"Third white house on the left," the old man said. "There's a farm pond just before it. It's on the hill."

"Thanks," the driver said.

"I'm Gifford," the old man said. "Dog's Magician."

"I believe in magic," the driver said.

"Who're you?" the old man said.

"Duggan," the driver said. "Jack Duggan."

Mrs. Ellis was elderly and she wore an apron and she peered at Duggan through thick spectacles so that she resembled the Easter Bunny, but she was not stupid. She sat him down in the kitchen and put the black kettle on the black iron stove to boil, and she gave him a homemade blueberry muffin. The tablecloth was a gingham pattern, but it was done on oilcloth. There was a vase of flowers in the middle of the table, but they were plastic flowers.

"I haven't seen him," she said. "I have not seen Frederick."

"Mrs. Ellis," Duggan said, "of course you haven't seen Frederick. Frederick is in the slammer down in Boston town. It is not an overtime parking ticket. Frederick is in the cooler because the police are under the impression that he went and killed a guy, and they think that they can prove it. If it is not too much trouble, while we are waiting for the blasted water to boil, I'd like a few facts here and there."

"I haven't seen him," she repeated.

"I have," Duggan said. "I didn't want to. I was appointed by the court to represent Frederick Ellis on a murder charge because he doesn't have enough money to get his own lawyer. Now I see that his mummy has a whole lot of prime land and a pond to go with it, not to mention some cattle."

"Jerseys," she said.

"Frederick," he said. "He can get his own T-shirts. Tell me all about Frederick, or I will go back into that court down in Boston and recite to that judge that Frederick Ellis may be a thing you might see floating in the gutter, but his family has some money. And then prepare to mortgage the cows."

"Jerseys," she said.

"Cows is cows," Duggan said.

Duggan in the First Session, Criminal, Suffolk Superior Court, waived the reading of the indictment. He stood next to Maurice Morse, a young black man, while the clerk, Don Sherman, informed Morse that he was charged with the forcible rape of Rose Walters.

"What say you?" Sherman said. "Are you guilty or not guilty?"

"Not guilty," Morse said.

"Counsel?" Judge Shanahan said.

"May I have thirty days to file special pleas, Your Honor?" Duggan said. "As you know, I have the Ellis case to prepare as well."

"Ten," Judge Shanahan said. Sherman wrote on the docket file.

"Your Honor," Duggan said, "I haven't had a chance for a real conference with my client as yet. As the court is aware, I am presently on trial in a capital case. May I press my request for thirty days in which to *file* special pleas?"

"You are not presently on trial, Counselor," Shanahan said, "you are about to be presently on trial. Presently you will file any motions that you may have in Commonwealth versus Morse, *presently* meaning: within ten days. During that time you can press your requests or your pants, just as you choose. You'd look better if you chose your pants.

"The Commonwealth," Judge Shanahan said, "will furnish all statements of the defendant, all material which may be exculpatory in nature, all transcripts of wiretaps, a list of all laboratory tests or other scientific tests which the Commonwealth has conducted and intends to introduce at trial, a list of all witnesses whom the Commonwealth may call at trial, all photographs and other physical evidence, to be inspected at the convenience of defense counsel. So ordered."

"Your Honor," Edie said, getting up, "I scarcely know what the case is about myself. And I also have the Ellis case. I don't know whether there's any of the evidence that you describe. I haven't even seen the file. As the court is aware, I too am currently on trial."

"Work nights," Shanahan said, "same as him. Bail?"

"May I be heard, Your Honor?" Edie said.

"Most likely," Shanahan said.

"This is one of several cases of rape in the same neighborhood," she said.

"Right," Shanahan said. "This is one case. This man is charged with one rape. Go ahead."

"The women in the neighborhood are extremely fearful for their safety," she said.

"Can't help that," Shanahan said. "This man hasn't been convicted of harming a single one of them."

"This is a serious charge," she said.

"Certainly is," Shanahan said. "I'd imagine the defendant would wholeheartedly agree with you on that point. The Constitution of the United States is a serious document. It says the purpose of bail is to ensure that the defendant shall appear for trial. Doesn't say anything at all about making nervous ladies feel better, no matter where they live. What are you asking for bail?"

"One hundred thousand dollars, with surety," she said.

"Ten grand for the bondsman," Shanahan said. "Counselor Duggan, what have you got to say about this?"

"Your Honor," Duggan said, "the defendant has a steady job. He has roots in the community. He's never been charged with anything before. There's no reason whatsoever to believe that he will not show up as ordered by this court."

"Lemme see that file, Don," Shanahan said to Sherman. He put on pince-nez glasses and leafed through it. He looked up over the glasses. "Morse," he said, "Mr. Morse, are you really broke, like you told the clerk?"

"Yessah," Morse said.

"Never mind that plantation talk," Shanahan said. "You broke or not?"

"I can't afford a lawyer, Your Honor," Morse said.

"Mr. Morse," Shanahan said, removing the glasses, "nobody can afford a lawyer. The question is whether you're broke. If you're not broke, Mr. Duggan doesn't have to represent you at huge expense to the taxpayers. If you are broke, he does. You broke or not?"

"I only make a small amount of money, Your Honor," Morse said. "I make two hundred and ten dollars a week, take-home. My rent's sixty a week. I pay maybe forty a week for food and stuff. I haven't got any money or anything."

"You own any real estate?" Shanahan said.

"No, sir," Morse said.

"You got a car?" Shanahan said.

"Yes, sir," Morse said.

"What is it?" Shanahan said.

"It's just a car," Morse said.

"One of those rectangular things with a wheel on each corner, right?" Shanahan said. This drew a laugh from the regular spectators. "Is there a brand name on it?"

"Yes, sir," Morse said.

"What does the brand name say?" Shanahan said.

"Pontiac," Morse said.

"Good," Shanahan said. "Now we are making progress. You own a Pontiac. What model is it?"

"It's a two-door," Morse said.

"That isn't what I asked you," Shanahan said. "Let me try again. What model is it?"

"It's a Firebird," Morse said.

"See?" Shanahan said. "We're making progress left and right here. Let me see if I can speed things up a little more. Is it by any chance a Firebird Trans Am?"

"Yes, sir," Morse said.

"Time passes so quickly when you're having fun," Shanahan said. "What is the year of its manufacture? When was it made, in other words?"

"Last year, Your Honor," Morse said.

"Did you buy it new?" Shanahan said.

"Yes, Your Honor," Morse said.

"How much did you pay for it?" Shanahan said.

Morse sighed: "Eleven thousand, three hundred and change."

"Where did you get the money?" Shanahan said.

"From the bank," Morse said.

"Did you borrow it?" Shanahan said.

"No, sir," Morse said, "I took it out of my account, I saved up for that car."

"You don't owe anything on it, then," Shanahan said.

"No, sir," Morse said.

"How much is it worth, do you figure?" Shanahan said.

"I dunno," Morse said.

"Eight thousand?" Shanahan said.

"I doubt it," Morse said.

"How about seven thousand?" Shanahan said.

"Maybe," Morse said.

"And that's the only thing you own," Shanahan said.

"Well," Morse said, "I got my furniture and stuff."

"What does the stuff consist of?" Shanahan said.

"My bike and stuff," Morse said.

"Let's deal with the bike," Shanahan said. "We'll get to the stuff as need be. It is a ten-speed bike?"

"Ten-speed?" Morse said.

"Yeah," Shanahan said. "What kind of bike is it?"

"It's a Kawasaki," Morse said.

"Oh," Shanahan said, "when you say *bike*, you mean it's a *motorcycle*."

"Yeah," Morse said.

"Yeah," Shanahan said. "When'd you get that and how much did it cost you?"

"Last year," Morse said. "Thirty-eight hundred dollars."

"Borrow the money?" Shanahan said.

"No, Your Honor," Morse said.

"Get it out of that bank account?" Shanahan said.

"Yeah," Morse said.

"What?" Shanahan said.

"Yeah," Morse said, louder.

"I can't hear you, Mr. Defendant," Shanahan said. "You get that money out of your savings account?"

"Say 'Yes, Your Honor,'" Duggan whispered to Morse.

"Yes, Your Honor," Morse said.

"That makes over fifteen thousand dollars you took out of that bank account to buy wheels last year," Shanahan said. "That's a pretty nice bank account. I wish I had one like it. Where is it?"

"I got the book home in my apartment," Morse said.

"Which bank?" Shanahan said.

"Oh," Morse said. "River Trust."

"How much you got in that account now?" Shanahan said.

"Your Honor," Morse said, "I worked hard for that money and I saved it up."

Shanahan held up his right hand. "Spare me, Mr. Morse," he said. "I'm sure you denied yourself many of life's pleasures in order to prepare for your future. You are asking me to confirm Mr. Duggan's worst fears that he will be forced to represent you for small change paid late by the Commonwealth. This will require Mr. Duggan to deny himself many of life's pleasures in order to represent you. How much money is left in that bank account?"

"I'm not sure," Morse said.

"Take a guess," Shanahan said.

"About nine thousand dollars," Morse said.

"OK," Shanahan said, "that saves us from going into the value of the furniture and stuff. Mr. Sherman: The court finds that the defendant, Maurice Morse, is not without resources with which to retain counsel, that he is not indigent. The case is continued for one week so that Mr. Morse may secure counsel. Bail is set at twenty-five thousand dollars, with surety. Case on trial."

"Your Honor," Morse said, as the court officer started toward him.

"Mr. Morse," Shanahan said, "you are remanded to the custody of the sheriff of Suffolk County. Your case is continued for one week so that you may secure counsel."

"I want Duggan here," Morse said.

"I'm sure Mr. Duggan will be happy to confer with you at the Charles Street Jail," Shanahan said. "You will want to discuss a fee with him, no doubt. Mr. Duggan is currently on trial. If you want to see him, make an appointment that will suit his convenience. For the time being, you have lots of convenience, at least until you make bail. Case on trial. Afternoon recess."

Morse was led away.

The judge stood up and marched off the bench. The spectators moved toward the doors. Edie approached Duggan. "Nice, huh?" she said.

"In my next life," Duggan said, "I am going to make my living doing something easy. Brain surgery, I think."

"Yeah," she said. "But in this one?"

"In this one," Duggan said, "I am going back to my office to see Fred Ellis, because thanks to your incompetence, he got out."

In the early evening, Duggan parked the Cadillac in front of the bait shop at Neponset Circle in Dorchester. The bait shop, which advertised its appointment by the Commonwealth as an official fish-weighing center, occupied the ground floor of a three-story wooden building. The building was covered with tarpaper that was supposed to resemble brick. The window frames and doors were painted cream. There were apartments for single old people on the third floor. Duggan, a bill collector named Mullins who called himself the Commonwealth Adjustment Agency, and the law firm of Kunkel and Concannon had offices on the second floor. Kunkel was over eighty. Concannon was Kunkel's daughter. They specialized in divorce law.

Duggan used his key to open the door in the center of the building. He shut it and locked it firmly behind him. The floor in the hall was linoleum. It had buckled badly and he was careful of his footing. It was lighted by one 60-watt bulb. He reached the stairway, which had a curved banister with knurled supports on the right and a dowel banister on the left, and climbed it. The steel treads were loose and creaked under him. At the top of the stairs he turned right, into the corridor leading to the offices. The corridor was lighted badly. The door to his office was half-frosted glass. There was scroll painting on it: JOHN F. DUGGAN. ATTORNEY AND COUNSELOR AT LAW. He opened the door and went in.

There were two people in the reception area. Cynthia, Duggan's secretary, was at her desk, which was synthetic blond mahogany. Cynthia had an extremely good figure and an extremely slow brain. She chewed gum. Her husband made a halfway-decent living as the manager of a hamburger stand on Morrissey Boulevard, about seven hundred yards west of the bait shop. Cynthia was incapable of conceiving a child. She was twenty-six years old and she was restless. Cynthia's husband was agreeable to allowing her to do poor work for very little money, so long as it was close by and he thought her boss was harmless. This arrangement was agreeable to Duggan, especially the part about the small salary.

The second person in the reception area was Frederick Ellis. He was sitting on a sofa-bed slipcovered in beige. The sofa looked as though Duggan had slept on it. He had. Ellis had a two-day growth of beard and he did not look good in it. He had dark hair that stuck up and looked greasy, and he wore a denim jacket and jeans which also could have been improved by washing. He looked disdainful. There were two cops seated next to him.

Duggan spoke to Ellis first. "You're sitting down already, and you haven't said anything yet. Therefore, keep up the good work." Then he said to the cops: "Whadda you guys want."

The two cops were in full uniform in Duggan's reception area, along with Frederick Ellis. One of the cops was Panther Ahearn, a stern man in his middle forties with heavy jowls and a permanent expression of exasperation. The other was Roderick Franklin, a man in his late thirties, who sat with his hands clasped in his lap and looked at the floor. Franklin's holster was empty, and the strap which secured the revolver which belonged in it hung loose. Roderick Franklin was black.

"Ahearn," Duggan said, "I needed you like a sore tooth this day.

Tell me what is on your mind and make it fast. I've got a living to make."

"Done and done," Ahearn said. He gestured with his head. "Franklin here has got a little problem." He nudged Franklin with his elbow. "This is correct, is it not, Roderick?"

Franklin nodded, miserably.

"Roderick," Ahearn said, standing up and hitching his pants higher, "Roderick shot a fellow last night."

"Shot a fellow," Duggan said.

"Exactly," Ahearn said.

"Where, precisely, did he shoot the fellow?" Duggan said.

"In the chest," Ahearn said. "Just like we are trained. Right below the heart. Three in a circle you could cover with a quarter. Roderick is a damned good shot." Ahearn looked at Franklin. Franklin did not look up.

"I presume there was some reason for all of this commotion," Duggan said.

"There was that," Ahearn said. "There was a silent alarm going off at the all-night grocery, and me and Roderick were dispatched thereto to see if perhaps there might be something going on. When we got there in the blue-and-white, there was sure-God something going on. So we drew our service revolvers and we exited the official vehicle and we entered the establishment and there was quite a lot going on. There were two young gentlemen in there, who had entered posing as customers. One of them had a rather large knife. The other one had a revolver.

"The young gentleman with the knife," Ahearn said, "is a reasonable fellow, and that is why he is still breathing air. As soon as he saw my revolver, he saw the wisdom of obedience to my command to drop the stinking knife. The other gentleman, the one with the revolver, was not as agreeable. He brought it up and pointed it at me. Thereupon, Patrolman Franklin plugged him. Three times. I was very glad of it. Roderick blew him back to last Wednesday."

"Ahh," Duggan said. "I see that Patrolman Franklin does not have any revolver on his person."

"They took it away from me," Franklin said. He did not look up.

"He's up on charges," Ahearn said.

"Charges," Duggan said.

"Departmental hearing," Ahearn said.

"Indictment to follow," Duggan said.

"If the department says he shouldn't've plugged the kid," Ahearn said.

"And?" Duggan said.

"You are going to make damned sure that hearing comes out the right way," Ahearn said.

"Ahearn," Duggan said, "you must be losing your memory. You hate my guts, remember? You told me so. If there was one miserable piece of stuff floating in at low tide tomorrow, it'd be better'n I am. Remember that?"

"That was different," Ahearn said. "That was when you got a little snotbag off on a case that he should've gone to jail."

"That's what I do," Duggan said.

"Right," Ahearn said, "and that is what you're gonna do for Roderick, here." He put his hand on Franklin's shoulder. "You got that, Counselor? You are gonna work your magic in behalf of Roderick, who saved my everlasting life. And you are gonna get his gun back for him. And you are gonna see that Roderick does not get indicted. That is what you are gonna do."

Franklin spoke. He did not look up, but he spoke. He said: "I don't want any favors from this honkey."

Ahearn lifted his hand and slapped it down hard on Franklin's shoulder. "You just shut your mouth, cotton-chopper. I got a wife and I got kids, and they go through groceries like they were lawn mowers. I'm on the earth this morning, not in it, and that is thanks to you. You did me one, I'll do you one."

"You're gonna pay me, I assume," Duggan said to Ahearn.

"Right," Ahearn said. "Cup of coffee? I'll go for a doughnut, even."

"Nifty," Duggan said.

Franklin looked up. There was misery all over his face. "He don't want this case, Terry," Franklin said. "I can't pay him. You told me already, long before this, what a rat he is."

Ahearn did not look at Franklin. He stared at Duggan instead. He spoke slowly and softly. "He is a rat, Roderick," Ahearn said. "He walked a guy on me the last time I brought in a guy that should've burned, and then he laughed in my face afterwards. You did that, Duggan."

"I did that, Ahearn," Duggan said.

"Roderick," Ahearn said, "this Duggan is the biggest rat in the

Western world. He bites and he's probably got rabies too. You need a rat, my friend. You need something that will bite and get the other guys infected. Duggan is your rat."

Franklin looked up again. "I can't afford to pay you anything, Mr. Duggan," he said.

Duggan started to speak. Ahearn silenced both of them. "Nothin' to worry about, Roderick," he said. "Mr. Duggan isn't charging for this one."

"You're not charging?" Franklin said.

"He's not charging," Ahearn said.

"I didn't ask you," Franklin said.

"I'm not charging," Duggan said. "And the rest of what he said is also true."

Duggan then spoke to Cynthia. "What bad things have happened today that I do not wish to know about but people called me about?"

Cynthia snapped her gum. Duggan said: "Don't do that."

She paid no attention to him. She riffled through a stack of telephone messages. "Well," she said, "they're mostly all from people in the court, and I'm not sure.

Duggan interrupted her. "It's after six, for the luvva Mike, I'm at least three hours late, trying to get back to somebody in the courts."

"There was one," Cynthia said, reflectively, snapping the gum. "Said she'd wait for your call."

"There's a happy note," Duggan said. "Who the hell was it?"

"Said her name," Cynthia said, frowning, "said her name was Edie and you'd know her."

"Edie," Duggan said.

"Edie," Cynthia said. "From the DA's office."

"Uh-huh," Duggan said. "OK, I'll call Edie from the DA's office."

He turned to look at Ellis. "For your information, Mr. Ellis, Edie from the DA's office is Assistant District Attorney Edith Washburn, and she has got a strong inclination to fit your very large tail into a very small crack. If it is all right with you, I will excuse myself for a moment and call her."

Ellis stared at him. Ellis did not look happy. "You already kept me waiting a long time," he said.

"Put it on my bill," Duggan said.

*

The district attorney was Harold Gould. He was a large and powerful man in a large and powerful office. He was in his early sixties,
and he knew what his values were. He also knew that some other
people did not share his values, and he resented it. His office in the
New Courthouse at Pemberton Square was spare. There was one
glass-fronted bookcase which contained a selection of lawbooks
that he had not opened in years. His diplomas from Boston College and the Harvard Law School were on the walls, along with his
membership certificates in nine organizations. There were two pictures of Harold Gould shaking hands with John F. Kennedy. Harold
Gould wore a PT-109 tie clasp. There were two pictures of Harold
Gould with Richard Cardinal Cushing. There was one picture of
Harold Gould with Francis Cardinal Spellman. There was a certificate attesting to the elevation of Harold Gould to the rank of
Knight of Malta. There was a large oak desk that was covered with
file folders. Harold Gould sat in an oak chair that creaked. His visitors sat in oak chairs that did not creak. Harold Gould, in the early
evening, was not happy.

Edith Washburn was uneasy. She was in her early thirties and she
had a lawyer's job in a town full of lawyers; she wished to keep it.
She disliked Harold Gould, who had appointed her to the job she
wished to keep. Once married and divorced, with custody of a son
who had not yet seen his sixth birthday and an ex-husband who
had managed to elude his child-support payments — there had
never been any alimony payments, because she was too proud to
accept those or even ask for them — she needed the job that Harold Gould could take away from her if she became too saucy.

"You booted it," Gould said. He had a voice with an edge like a
pitted razor blade. "I told you I didn't want that Ellis punk on the
street."

Edie controlled herself. "Boss," she said, "I did not boot it. I am
not Judge Wilcox. I did not release him on personal recognizance.
I asked a hundred thou bail, and Judge Wilcox let him loose. Judge
Wilcox is black. He thinks all defendants're the unfortunate victims of society. That's not my fault, either."

"That punk," Gould said, "is a murderer."

She sighed. "So I'm told," she said.

"He should be in jail," Gould said.

"So I'm told," she said.

"He isn't," Gould said.

"He hasn't been convicted yet," she said.

"Who's got the case for trial," Gould said.

"Judge Shanahan," she said.

Gould nodded. "Good," he said, "good. Shanahan's a standup guy. No continuances. Get that little scumbag in here and convict him and put him in the damned can. Right?"

Edie sighed again. "Boss," she said, "Duggan just got the case. He's gonna want time to get ready. He's gonna ask for it and Shanahan or any other judge's gonna give it to him. The guy's appointed, for God's sake. He's not making any money off this. He's got to eat. He'll be out on the street."

"Who'd Duggan kill?" Gould said.

"Far as I know," she said, "nobody."

"Right," Gould said. "So therefore I don't care if Duggan's onna street. I don't like him, but he ain't dangerous. Ellis is dangerous."

Duggan tilted back in his desk chair and looked at Frederick Ellis with extreme distaste. The chair was a tufted Naugahyde Eames model. The desk was a large construction of blond mahogany. Ellis slouched in an armchair upholstered in nubby cerulean blue fabric, and smoked a thin cigar. The walls of Duggan's office were absolutely bare, painted white, and somewhat dirty.

"You, my friend," Duggan said, "you are more trouble'n you're worth. That lady is really mad at you, and I think you are going to go away for a while if she has anything to say about it. Which she does."

Ellis tipped the ash from the cigar onto the brown tweed rug. "I can do time," he said.

"So can Big Ben," Duggan said. "Any jerk can do time, just like any clock. Clocks're made of metal. Some of them've got glass onna front. They're *made* to do time."

Ellis shrugged. "Maybe I was, too" he said.

"Maybe you were," Duggan said. He allowed his shoulders to slump. "And in the meantime, I've got to do time for you, because that lady wants to see me. *Tonight.*"

In the remnants of the twilight, Frederick Ellis emerged from the door next to the bait shop, turned right, and walked rapidly along

Gallivan Boulevard until he came to the International House of Pancakes. He stopped at the entrance to the parking lot and looked around. There was a maroon Cougar XR7 in one of the spaces, pointing toward the street. Ellis approached it, glanced around, opened the passenger door, and got inside.

There was another man inside, sitting in the driver's seat. He was smoking a cigar, and the car was filled with the smoke of it. Ellis did not look at him directly, but it would not have mattered if he had.

"I am in the gravy," Ellis said. "I am in the gravy up to my belt-buckle. They are heating up the gravy. I think they are planning to cook me. I am getting nervous."

"Not good," the driver said. "Not good to get nervous. Makes the Man nervous when people get nervous. That is very seldom good for the nervous people."

"Look," Ellis said, "all right?" He turned his body in the passenger's bucket seat so that he could look at the cloud of smoke around the driver. He gestured with his hands. "I got some problems, all right? This guy Duggan that I win, you know what he did? He drove up to see my mother, for God's sake. I haven't seen my mother since the Chicago Cubs won the World Series, for God's sake. I can't stand my mother and she can't stand me and he goes to see her and eat one of her damned muffins and now I got that to think about. This guy Duggan takes things *serious,* Franco. He wants to win this case and he tells me he does not think that I am telling him everything I know."

"Umm," the driver said through the smoke.

"It gets worse," Ellis said, slumping back against the seat and facing the windshield. "This broad they got prosecuting me? Duggan makes me think she is another one of those eager types that always plans to win. Between the two of them, I am going to end up at the wrong end of the chain saw."

"You got problems," the driver said.

Ellis became angry. "Problems?" he said. "I had problems before. I bite my fingernails sometimes and I have been constipated. I borrowed some money off a guy and I didn't have the dough to pay him back. Those, I thought that those were problems when I had them. Now I am looking at all day in the Massachusetts Correctional Institution at Walpole because I borrowed some money off a guy, and you are telling me I got problems? Compared to me, the president has got it easy."

The driver leaned forward and started the car. "I think," he said, "I think we'd better go and see the Man."

Duggan escaped from the darkness of Tremont Street into Dini's restaurant. The light inside was tinted rose colored, and there were pictures of fish and aquariums in strategic locations. There was a truculent woman in a tight pink jersey dress at the door, with a sheaf of menus. She challenged him. "Yesss?" she said.

"Look," Duggan said, "I had a hard day. I'm supposed to meet a lady here. Her name is Washburn."

The woman clearly did not believe this. "What is your name, please?"

"For God's sake," Duggan said, "have I got to get references to meet somebody for dinner in a place of public refreshment? What difference does it make, who I am? I told you who she is. Is she here? I'm not trying to cash a bum check or anything."

The woman's face grew stern. "I'm merely trying to help you, sir," she said. "There are several ladies sitting alone tonight. I don't know any of their names. If you would give me your name, I could inquire whether any of them is waiting for you."

Duggan sighed. "I got a better idea," he said. "Lemme look around." He brushed past the woman and turned to his right, walking up a slight incline into another rosily lighted room. It was lined with small booths on the right and larger booths on the left. There was one person in the room. That was Edith Washburn. She was seated at one of the small booths. She was drinking a glass of white wine. Duggan caught her eye as he walked down the narrow corridor between the small booths and the large booths. She smiled, wanly. He gestured with his head toward the large booth across from her. She looked quizzical. He grinned. When he reached her, he said: "I don't like these tables. When they put me in one of them, I feel like I'm a dog getting into one of those pet carriers the airlines use. Move."

Edith Washburn got up swiftly and crossed the aisle. They sat down simultaneously at one of the large booths. She grinned at him.

"Hard day?" he said.

"An absolute bitch of a day," she said. "Yours?"

"I could use a drink," he said. "Do they have any waitresses left tonight that aren't candidates for autopsies?"

"I saw one a while ago that seemed to be breathing," she said. "I can't be sure, though. Didn't take her pulse."

"OK?" Duggan said. He put his fingers in his mouth and whistled piercingly.

"Good heavens," Edie said. She started to laugh. "You mustn't have any trouble getting cabs."

"Or birds, neither," Duggan said. "Called in a penguin once, from Antarctica. Walked all the way, poor little critter. Took him to the zoo."

An alarmed and elderly woman appeared at the door leading into the room. Duggan waved her toward them, using the traffic cop's signal.

"How did he like the zoo?" Edie said.

"Wonderful," Duggan said. "We had such a good time, next day I took him to the ball game. Sox lost."

The waitress reached their table. "Just two of you for dinner?" she said.

"That's a quorum, ma'am," Duggan said. "But first I would like about a pail of vodka martinis. Put some ice in it."

"Vodka martini on the rocks," the waitress said. She wrote it down. "But if you're not expecting anyone else, I'll have to ask you to take one of the smaller tables."

"Go to it," Duggan said. "Ask away, we're not going to move. There's room enough in this joint tonight for the Second Armored Division. When they show up and the place gets crowded, we will meekly move. Until that happens, I would like my drink and enough space to sit comfortably."

"We do have rules, sir," the waitress said.

"I do have a nasty disposition, begging your pardon and all, ma'am," Duggan said. "I am not moving. My drink, please, and the menus."

The waitress hobbled away. Duggan leaned toward Edie. "Tell you what," he said, "you show me yours, I'll show you mine."

She began to laugh again. "You were mean to that woman."

"OK," Duggan said, "I show mine first. My guy will not plead out. I think he should. If I had a reasonable client, we could belt this thing out on a second-degree in a minute. He is not reasonable."

"He confessed," she said.

"He made a statement," Duggan said. "I have read that statement, which you so kindly provided to me."

"He had his rights read to him," she said.

"Yup," Duggan said. "Signed a document to prove it. Said he'd been to the tidal creek. Said he knew Thomas Monaghan. Said he knew Monaghan was dead. Said he believed Monaghan'd gotten shot by somebody."

"Oh, come on, Jack," she said. "He led the cops to the scene."

"Right," Duggan said. "Now you are going to tell me that the cops didn't know there was a tidal creek there until he told them about it."

"No," she said.

"No," Duggan said. "And probably the cops didn't know about Monaghan being dead until they pulled him out of the water, all green and swollen, and he wasn't breathing very much. You are going to tell me that."

"No," she said.

"Edie," Duggan said, "it was in all the papers. Frederick Ellis, my esteemed client, is dumber'n some rocks that I have met. But he can *read*. He can listen to the wireless and he can watch the television. Everybody who ever laid eyes on Monaghan knew he wasn't getting around much anymore. This is not proof beyond a reasonable doubt that Frederick Ellis did him in."

"Jack," she said, "I have some more bad news to improve your day."

"Go ahead," he said. "Everybody else has."

"Gould won't take a plea," she said. "He wants murder one."

The waitress limped down the aisle with Duggan's drink. "Oh good," he said as she arrived. "That is extremely good. That was just what I needed. I've got an unreasonable client and you've got an unreasonable boss." The waitress set the drink down on the table. Duggan picked it up immediately and swigged from it. "Another one of these little buggers," he said, "and some fried clams, french fries, slaw." To Edie he said: "Order."

"Same thing," she said.

"Martini also?" the waitress said.

"White wine," Edie said. "White wine."

The Man was short and thin and wizened. He was in his late sixties. He had a shock of white hair that he combed straight back. He wore a white broadcloth shirt with a medium spread collar and a tie made of dark blue silk. He wore a well-cut Ivy-League suit, dark blue, just slightly nipped in at the waist. He wore black wing-tipped shoes. He sat behind an ornate antique desk, made of oak and carved with elaborate scrolling. He sipped at a pony of anisette and then from a cup of coffee. He did not show any expression on his face.

The cigar-smoking driver was in his middle forties, rather flush of face and somewhat overweight. He wore a blue blazer and tan slacks. He sat in an armchair, padded and then covered with tufted leather. Ellis had a straight chair opposite the driver.

"He is worried, Mr. Caruso," the driver said. "Frederick here tells me that he is worried."

Caruso shifted his gaze to Ellis. He spoke mildly. "Worry is bad for a man, Freddie. Worried people tend to die before their time."

Ellis's tone betrayed considerable anxiety. He spread his hands and leaned forward in the chair. He spoke earnestly. "Mr. Caruso," he said, "it is not just me who should be worried. Walsh should be worried and Charlie Carnival should be worried."

"Walsh and Carnival are not around," Caruso said. "They are vacationing and cannot be reached."

"They should still be worried," Ellis said.

"And Francesco," Caruso said, nodding toward the driver, "should he be worried?"

"Probably," Ellis said.

"And I, perhaps," Caruso said, "should I perhaps be worried?"

"Considering what's happening," Ellis said, "you should think about it at least."

Caruso glanced at Francesco. He looked back at Ellis. He leaned forward and steepled his fingers. "You have succeeded, Freddie," he said. "Now I also am worried, and I am an old man who must think also of his health. How can we end all of this worry?"

"The cops haven't got a hard case against me," Ellis said. "They got all excited when they got the tip and they left a lot of things out."

"Then there is no worry," Caruso said.

"It's the lawyers," Ellis said. "This guy Duggan that I got is some kind of a crazy man, I think, and he is beating all over me that I am not telling him the truth. The DA is this broad that is beating all over Duggan because I will not plead out. One or the other of those damned lawyers is going to get all haired up and that will finish me off. The DA wants murder one. I do not."

"What could you do, Freddie?" Caruso said it very softly.

"I could run," Ellis said.

"Any man can run," Caruso said. "The question is: how far?"

"I could go on vacation, like Walshie and Carnival," Ellis said anxiously.

"I think that many people would miss you," Caruso said.

Duggan was in the 99 Restaurant on Pearl Street in Boston. His red tie was loosened from his collar and his speech was somewhat slurred. He was drinking vodka martinis and he was talking to a small blond woman in her early twenties who had bleached her hair and gained a little weight since she had purchased her flowered blouse and tan skirt. She had undone the top three buttons of her blouse to avoid getting overheated. "You're married," she said.

"Yup," Duggan said.

"My God," she said, "I never thought I'd see the day when one of you guys admitted it. You still living with her, or what?"

"Yes," he said.

"Yes what?" she said. "When you go home at night, do you go home at night or do you go somewhere else?"

"Yes," he said. "Depends on the night. I do one or I do the other."

"Hot damn," she said. "Which you like better?"

"The other," he said. "Much better."

She linked her left arm through his right arm. "I think we could be friends," she said.

"Until morning," he said, thickly.

"With an option year," she said, "like the other guys who play ball."

Edie Washburn in the morning met Lieutenant Walter Nolan outside the District One Police Headquarters on New Chardon Street in the Government Center complex in Boston. "Lieutenant," she said, "we have got to talk."

Nolan was in his early thirties. He wore a plain tan raincoat and a somewhat mischievous expression. "This is so sudden, Edie," he said. He smiled at her and stuck his hands in his pockets.

"Time passes so quickly when you're having fun," she said. She grabbed him by the left elbow.

"Whoa," he said, pulling loose. "Not here in the middle of a public thoroughfare."

"I've got to talk to you," she said.

"Can we have some coffee, maybe?" Nolan said.

"Coffee," she said, taking him by the arm again. "Now, walk, and let's see if we can do that at the same time we're talking."

They headed up the hill on New Chardon toward Center Plaza. "Look, Walter," she said.

"I have been," he said.

"You're married," she said, "and I like Annie. This's business. I think we have got a little problem with this Ellis guy."

"He should faw down, go boom," Walter said.

"He ain't gonna," she said grimly. "There're two reasons why he won't. There is Harold Gould. The second one is Jack Duggan."

"He drew Duggan?" Walter said. "Son of a gun, I thought Duggan spent most of his time moaning and groaning about his life. He still alive?"

"Very much so," she said. "Not only alive, but very well, thank you."

"He hasn't had a murder case in two, three years," Walter said. "The heaviest thing he's had, I heard about, was a couple smalltime hoods robbed a gas station, and that was about six months ago."

"How'd it come out?" she said.

"Not guilty," Walter said.

"You're a detective," she said. "That a clue to something, maybe?"

"Hell, Edie," Walter said, "it wasn't an ironclad case."

"Is Ellis ironclad?" she said, pulling Nolan to a halt.

"No, Edie, for cryin' out loud," Walter said. "No case's ironclad. You've been at this long enough to know that."

"Right," she said. "And so's Duggan. And now let me tell you another thing: Gould won't take a plea."

"Oh, oh," Walter said.

"I am going to have to try this case," she said.

"Sounds like it," he said.

"I have read the file again," she said. "I do not feel cheerful."

Mrs. Ellis was waiting in Duggan's office when he arrived in the morning. She was wearing a nubby pale violet coat and a black pillbox hat and black sensible shoes. She had curled her hair. She sat clutching her black vinyl purse on her lap. As Duggan entered the office, she was glancing surreptitiously and disapprovingly at Cynthia.

Cynthia was drinking coffee from a paper cup. She slurped it. She was chewing gum at the same time and reading the paper.

Duggan looked dreadful. He had not shaved. He was wearing the same clothes he had been wearing the night before. He had not gotten much sleep and his eyes showed it. So did his expression. He closed the door. He stared blearily at Mrs. Ellis. "Mrs. Ellis," he said.

She pursed her lips. She looked him up and down. Cynthia paid no attention to either of them. Mrs. Ellis said, "I came to see you."

"So I see," Duggan said. "I don't recall inviting you, but I see you're here."

"I'm surprised you can," she said sternly.

"Oh, Mrs. Ellis," Duggan said, "there are many things I cannot see this morning. One, for example, is the money to defend Frederick on a murder charge. You will recall, we had some discussion about that. You weren't interested. Another thing I cannot see is your appointment at this ungodly hour."

"You didn't have an appointment to see me," she said. "You came anyway, at your convenience."

"You are not defending my son on a murder charge," Duggan said. "And losing your shirt on it."

Mrs. Ellis surveyed him again. "Your son might do better if I did," she said.

"Would you like to talk about sons, Mrs. Ellis?" Duggan said. "Do you really want to do that? I'm willing if you are. I ain't perfect, but until one of my kids gets hauled up on a murder charge, I'm way ahead of you. And if one of my kids does, I'll pay for his defense. No welfare for Duggan, no sir."

She paused and looked down at her handbag. Then she looked up at Duggan. "I want to talk to you," she said.

"So I gathered," Duggan said. He looked at his watch. "It is nine-oh-five, Mrs. Ellis. I am due in court at eleven. I can get there in twenty minutes if I'm lucky. That gives us almost two hours. You must've left home early. Go get something to eat and come back at ten."

"I don't know this area," she said with a whine in her voice.

"Walk around and get acquainted with it," Duggan said. "You won't like it. No cows. Now beat it."

Her lower lip trembled.

"I mean it," Duggan said.

She stood up and straightened her coat. She headed for the open door.

"Cynthia," Duggan said. Cynthia looked up. "Did I wake you?" Duggan said. She gazed at him as though she had just noticed that he was in the office. "Of course I did," Duggan said. "Go and get me a fried egg sandwich with two strips of bacon inside, and two large coffees."

"You want toast?" she said, chewing the gum.

"I would like the sandwich on toast," Duggan said. "I do not want the sandwich and the toast on the side."

"I haven't got any money," she said.

He reached into his pocket and pulled out a crumpled five, which he threw on her desk. He stalked to his office.

"What about the phones, Mr. Duggan," Cynthia said.

"They'll be here when you get back, Cynthia," he said.

He was taking off his jacket, loosening his tie and pulling it down, and unbuttoning his shirt as he walked.

Duggan entered the Fifth Criminal Session of the Suffolk Superior Court through the swinging oak doors. The benches were empty and the high windows spilled sunlight into the courtroom. There was one court officer on duty, a heavyset man about fifty. The officer was smoking a Salem.

"Not supposed to smoke in court, Bailey," Duggan said. He was clean-shaven. He wore a clean yellow shirt. He wore a gray hopsack suit and a blue-and-gold tie.

Bailey looked at Duggan. "My, my," he said, "and what a fine figure of a fellow we're cutting this morning."

"Clean living," Duggan said, "that's what does it."

"Got a shower in your office, huh?" Bailey said.

"Nope," Duggan said. "Complete wardrobe, though, and a men's room with running water, sometimes hot."

Bailey shook his head. "I wished I was a lawyer," he said. "Way it is, I got to work for a living."

"Lemme know when you start," Duggan said. "Judge in?"

"Judge Shanahan?" Bailey said. "Oh, Judge Shanahan is in all right. He's been in since eleven, when you were supposed to be here. So's Edie." He got up from his chair and started toward the judge's chambers. Over his shoulder he said: "Hope your shaving lotion's nice."

Judge Shanahan had a rosy, pudgy face, a roly-poly body, sparse graying hair and an unfiltered Lucky Strike. He was short and he had an executioner's sense of humor. He was seated behind the scarred desk in chambers and regaling Edie and defense counsel Sam Waldstein when Duggan entered. He gave Duggan a perfunctory greeting and continued.

"So," Shanahan said, "this jerk Cangelosi gets up on his hind legs and asks the cop when he first wrote down someplace that the defendant was suspected of being a drug dealer. Now there is a beauty. You can see the cop cocking his bat already. He looks like Ted Williams, up against a slow pitcher. And the cop says he wrote it down a long time ago.

"Now," Shanahan said, "even I know this. I read the damned reports. They are full of the most scandalous gossip you can imagine. There is stuff in those reports that would be enough to hang the pope if you could prove it. The trouble is that Gould can't prove any of it. And if Edie, for example, offered all that hearsay, I would take her head off. But the DA isn't offering all that hearsay, and for some reason or other, the DA is not objecting to Cangelosi bringing it in. I think I know what the reason is, but that is beside the point. I leave him do it.

"Well," Shanahan said, leaning back in the chair and blowing smoke rings, "Cangelosi asks the cop when he wrote it down. And the cop says he wrote it down in the same damned report that Cangelosi's waving around like a damned flag. Which, of course, he did. And Cangelosi demands to have the cop show him where it is written down. And he throws the report at the cop and invites him to read from it.

"So," Shanahan said, "the cop does. He does it slowly. He considers every word like it was cole slaw and he had to chew it, so as to get all the flavor.

"It was in the report, all right," Shanahan said. He was grinning. "*Everything* was in the report. The report said the cop knew the defendant was a dirty, rotten, no-good, lousy, miserable dope pusher. It said the cops had good reason to believe he was a pimp who beat up on his ladies. It said there was no question that he carried a gun and used it to pistol-whip the people that he didn't find it necessary to shoot. It went on and on. The jury was eating it up. It was really good stuff.

"In the middle of this recital," Shanahan said, leaning forward, "Cangelosi *objects*. Now, that was a new one to me. I never had an objection before from a lawyer who was asking the question. 'You're objecting to your own question Mr. Cangelosi,' I said. He tells me he is not objecting to his own question. He is objecting to the cop's answer to the question. I can see why he might. It is blowing his boat right out of the water. The trouble is, when you ask the question, you don't get to object to the answer."

"'He is putting in hearsay and undocumented evidence,' Cangelosi says. 'He certainly is,' I smartly reply. 'He is able to do that because you invited him to do it.' Well, there was a great tussle, and in the meantime the prosecutor is sitting there with a grin that the Cheshire Cat would've envied."

Shanahan rocked back in his chair and clasped his hands behind his head. "And that, ladies and gentlemen," he said, "is today's lesson in trial practice. Sam, you are excused."

As Waldstein arose, Shanahan stubbed out his Lucky and lit another one. He surveyed Duggan critically. "You look reasonably good today, Jackie boy," he said. "What did you do, go through the car wash on foot?"

"No," Duggan said, "I went to your embalmer and told him I wanted the same discount special you bought."

Shanahan began to laugh. "No respect for the court as usual, I see." Waldstein pursed his lips and gazed disapprovingly at Duggan.

"Hiya, Sam," Duggan said. "Didn't notice you before. Course, you're easy to overlook."

Shanahan guffawed.

"I don't think . . ." Waldstein said.

"I know it," Duggan said. "You should try it some time. Whyncha beat it now, so I can talk to the judge. OK?"

Waldstein glanced toward Shanahan, who only smiled. Waldstein left chambers. Duggan took his chair.

"Tell me about this twerp Ellis," Shanahan said. "We gonna belt this out or what?"

"Or what," Edie said. "Gould wants a murder one."

"Wonderful," Shanahan said. "Duggan?"

"Ellis says he's innocent," Duggan said.

"Trial, then," Shanahan said. "Confound it. Blasted nuisance." He pulled his calendar over and studied it. "This's a pain in the neck, you know."

"Life's full of hardships, Your Honor," Duggan said.

Duggan was at his desk. He was speaking urgently into the phone and the door to his office was closed. He said: "Look, honey, I'll be there by five-thirty. I will really be there. You can count on it. I am not going to let you down."

Frederick Ellis emerged in the darkness from the Sheraton Boston Hotel. He was wearing a leather car-coat and an anxious expression. He stood in the doorway and gazed at the street. The maroon Cougar came into view. It pulled up at the entrance. Ellis opened the passenger door and climbed in. "Francesco," he said.

"Frederick," the driver said. He was smoking a cigar. The car was filled with the smoke.

"Francesco," Ellis said, "where the hell're we going?"

"Frederick," the driver said, "the Man is concerned. He is worried. Just like you wanted. He is just as worried as you are."

"Now I am even more worried," Ellis said.

"You must stop worrying," Francesco said, putting the car in gear. "In the position you're in, when you get worried, everybody else gets worried."

The Cadillac slowed to a halt in the driveway of the yellow colonial garrison house in a western suburb of Boston. The side door, leading to the breezeway, immediately opened. A girl about nine years old came out. She was prancing. She wore a blue melton coat with red embroidery around the buttonholes and sleeves. She wore white knee socks and black Mary Janes. She had long blond hair and she wore barrettes. She began to run toward the car, but she had breath enough to scream. She screamed: "Daddy."

Behind the girl there was a boy, about three years older. He came out more slowly, ushered by a woman who remained inside the jalousied breezeway, and shut the door behind him. He put his hands in his pockets and studied the sky for a while. He wore a tweed overcoat and L.L. Bean boots.

The girl embraced Duggan exuberantly. He was only halfway out of the car and he was off-balance, but he recovered himself and picked her off the ground. He hugged her and swung her. He carefully concealed from her the tears that came up in his eyes. He made his voice gruff and said: "Mark."

The girl said: "I'm so glad to see you, Daddy."

Duggan said: "Right. Get Mark." He turned away from her. The boy came down the walk very slowly. The girl ran up to him and took him by the left hand. She skipped. He lagged. She brought him up to the car.

Duggan said: "Hi, Mark. Hungry?"

Mark stared at him for what seemed like several minutes. Then he said: "Can I have steak?"

"Sure," Duggan said. He was forcing heartiness. "Gino'll make braciole for you, we ask. Politely."

The boy pondered that. He nodded. "I would like that," he said.

Gino Ferraro was holding court at his restaurant, close by the Boston Garden. He wore a blue blazer and tan slacks and a red-striped tie. He needed glasses and he had had them made in gold-filled aviator frames. When Duggan and his kids came in, Gino was effusive. He said: "Annie. Mark. So good to see you." They shook his hand. Gino said to Duggan: "Table for three, Jack?"

"Please," Duggan said.

Gino clapped him on the back. "It's good to see you, my friend," he said. "When're we goin' the track?"

"Tomorrow is out," Duggan said. "Police hearing. You hear about that guy Franklin?"

"Poor guy," Gino said. He shook his head.

"I got him," Duggan said.

"Poor guy, you," Gino said. "He got any money?"

"If he has," Duggan said, "he's hangin' onto it."

"Ahh," Gino said. He ushered them into the dining area.

He spoke to Mark. "And you, young man, are you goin' the game?"

"Steak," Mark said, as he sat down.

"Ahh," Gino said, "braciolettine. And for you, Mr. Duggan?"

"Gimme a beer, Gino," Duggan said.

"It's a pleasure, Jack, see you with the kids in here," Gino said.

Duggan slumped. "Out on dates," he said. "Out on dates with my own damned kids."

Gino patted him again. "It'll get better, Jack. It'll get better."

Harold Gould had been to morning Mass and had a cup of coffee. He was dressed in a gray cheviot suit and he was madder than a hornet. He slammed his fist on the desk when he sat down in the creaking oak chair. He shouted at Edie Washburn. His face was inflamed and his veins stood out.

"I dunno," she said.

"He isn't here," Gould said.

"He isn't here," she said.

"Can't fool you, can they?" Gould said.

"Nope," she said.

"Find him," Gould said.

"OK," she said.

"Find him before noon," Gould said.

"This may be hard to do," she said.

"Struggle," Gould said. "Life is very hard."

In the early morning, Walter Nolan stood with his shoulders hunched under the tan raincoat on the macadam launching ramp at the marina. There was some cold gray sunshine. There was an object floating in the water. It was Ellis. Edie Washburn stood next to him. She wore a tan raincoat.

"This," Walter said, "does not look like a plea bargain to me, under any circumstances."

"The defendant appears to be dead," she said.

"Terminally dead," Nolan said.

Duggan showed up at his office fairly early in the morning. He did not look good. Cynthia snapped her gum and snapped at him. "Hard night, Counselor?"

"Very," he said.

"You should go home at night," she said.

"I did," he said.

"Frederick Ellis is dead," she said.

Duggan sat down fast in the reception area. "Dead," he said.

"Dead," she said. She snapped her gum again.

"Cause of death?" he said.

"Gunshot," Cynthia said. "He's on the slab. Southern Mortuary."

Duggan did not say anything for a while. "I appreciate the address. I don't think I care to see him."

"He didn't pay ya, did he?" Cynthia said.

"Nope," Duggan said, getting up.

"Then the hell with him," Cynthia said. She went back to her coffee and her newspaper.

"Exactly," Duggan said. "Exactly."

The hearing room was windowless. The walls were walnut paneling, halfway up. Above waist level, the walls were white. They needed paint. The commissioner and two uniformed officers sat behind a long oak table. The commissioner wore a gray flannel suit and a stern expression. He said: "Mr. Duggan. Have you any more questions?"

Duggan turned and glanced at Franklin. Franklin shook his head once. Duggan turned back to the commissioner. "I have nothing further," he said.

"Would you care to be heard?" the commissioner said.

"Actually," Duggan said, "I think I've been heard enough at this proceeding. I can talk some more if you like, but I don't think I'm going to add much to the supply of human wisdom."

The commissioner did not cover his grin quickly enough. "That will be fine, Counselor," he said. He rapped the gavel. "The hearing will be in recess while we deliberate." The spectators began to shift in their chairs, collecting coats. "We will deliberate right here," the commissioner said. "No need to leave unless you wish to."

The commissioner leaned to the officer on his right and spoke behind his hand. He nodded and turned to the officer on his left. He spoke behind his hand again. He nodded again. He rapped the gavel. "The board is agreed," he said. "We find the charges against Patrolman Franklin to be without merit, and that he acted with prudence and discretion in protecting the life and safety of a fellow officer. Anything further?"

"Nothing further," Duggan said.

The commissioner banged the gavel again. "Hearing is adjourned." Franklin stood up very slowly. Ahearn came out of the spectators' section and shook his hand. Each of them had tears in his eyes. Ahearn took Duggan by the hand. "Thanks," he said.

"Yeah," Franklin said. "Thanks."

"Nothing to it," Duggan said. "Lead pipe cinch."

"See?" Ahearn said. "I told you he was a rotten louse."

EDWARD P. JONES

Old Boys, Old Girls

FROM *The New Yorker*

THEY CAUGHT HIM after he had killed the second man. The law would never connect him to the first murder. So the victim — a stocky fellow Caesar Matthews shot in a Northeast alley only two blocks from the home of the guy's parents, a man who died over a woman who was actually in love with a third man — was destined to lie in his grave without anyone officially paying for what had happened to him. It was almost as if, at least on the books the law kept, Caesar had got away with a free killing.

Seven months after he stabbed the second man — a twenty-two-year-old with prematurely gray hair who had ventured out of Southeast for only the sixth time in his life — Caesar was tried for murder in the second degree. During much of the trial, he remembered the name only of the first dead man — Percy, or "Golden Boy," Weymouth — and not the second, Antwoine Stoddard, to whom everyone kept referring during the proceedings. The world had done things to Caesar since he'd left his father's house for good at sixteen, nearly fourteen years ago, but he had done far more to himself.

So at trial, with the weight of all the harm done to him and because he had hidden for months in one shit hole after another, he was not always himself and thought many times that he was actually there for killing Golden Boy, the first dead man. He was not insane, but he was three doors from it, which was how an old girlfriend, Yvonne Miller, would now and again playfully refer to his behavior. Who the fuck is this Antwoine bitch? Caesar sometimes thought during the trial. And where is Percy? It was only when the judge sentenced him to seven years in Lorton, D.C.'s prison in Virginia, that matters became somewhat clear again, and in those last moments before they took him away he saw Antwoine spread out on the ground outside the Prime Property night club, blood spurting out of his chest like oil from a bountiful well. Caesar remembered it all: sitting on the sidewalk, the liquor spinning his brain, his friends begging him to run, the club's music flooding out of the open door and going *thumpety-thump-thump* against his head. He sat a few feet from Antwoine, and would have killed again for a cigarette. "That's you, baby, so very near insanity it can touch you," said Yvonne, who believed in unhappiness and who thought happiness was the greatest trick God had invented. Yvonne Miller would be waiting for Caesar at the end of the line.

He came to Lorton with a ready-made reputation, since Multrey Wilson and Tony Cathedral — first-degree murderers both, and destined to die there — knew him from his Northwest and Northeast days. They were about as big as you could get in Lorton at that time (the guards called Lorton the House of Multrey and Cathedral), and they let everyone know that Caesar was good people, "a protected body," with no danger of having his biscuits or his butt taken.

A little less than a week after Caesar arrived, Cathedral asked him how he liked his cellmate. Caesar had never been to prison but had spent five days in the D.C. jail, not counting the time there before and during the trial. They were side by side at dinner, and neither man looked at the other. Multrey sat across from them. Cathedral was done eating in three minutes, but Caesar always took a long time to eat. His mother had raised him to chew his food thoroughly. "You wanna be a old man livin on oatmeal?" "I love oatmeal, Mama." "Tell me that when you have to eat it every day till you die."

"He all right, I guess," Caesar said of his cellmate, with whom he had shared fewer than a thousand words. Caesar's mother had died before she saw what her son became.

"You got the bunk you want, the right bed?" Multrey said. He was sitting beside one of his two "women," the one he had turned out most recently. "She" was picking at her food, something Multrey had already warned her about. The woman had a family — a wife and three children — but they would not visit. Caesar would never have visitors, either.

"It's all right." Caesar had taken the top bunk, as the cellmate had already made the bottom his home. A miniature plastic panda from his youngest child dangled on a string hung from one of the metal bedposts. "Bottom, top, it's all the same ship."

Cathedral leaned into him, picking chicken out of his teeth with an inch-long fingernail sharpened to a point. "Listen, man, even if you like the top bunk, you fuck him up for the bottom just cause you gotta let him know who rules. You let him know that you will stab him through his motherfuckin heart and then turn around and eat your supper, cludin the dessert." Cathedral straightened up. "Caes, you gon be here a few days, so you can't let nobody fuck with your humanity."

He went back to the cell and told Pancho Morrison that he wanted the bottom bunk, couldn't sleep well at the top.

"Too bad," Pancho said. He was lying down, reading a book published by the Jehovah's Witnesses. He wasn't a Witness, but he was curious.

Caesar grabbed the book and flung it at the bars, and the bulk of it slid through an inch or so and dropped to the floor. He kicked Pancho in the side, and before he could pull his leg back for a second kick Pancho took the foot in both hands, twisted it, and threw him against the wall. Then Pancho was up, and they fought for nearly an hour before two guards, who had been watching the whole time, came in and beat them about the head. "Show's over! Show's over!" one kept saying.

They attended to themselves in silence in the cell, and with the same silence they flung themselves at each other the next day after dinner. They were virtually the same size, and though Caesar came to battle with more muscle, Pancho had more heart. Cathedral had told Caesar that morning that Pancho had lived on practically nothing but heroin for the three years before Lorton, so whatever fighting dog was in him could be pounded out in little or no time. It took three days. Pancho was the father of five children, and each time he swung he did so with the memory of all five and what he had done to them over those three addicted years. He wanted to return to them and try to make amends, and he realized on the morning of the third day that he would not be able to do that if

Caesar killed him. So fourteen minutes into the fight he sank to the floor after Caesar hammered him in the gut. And though he could have got up he stayed there, silent and still. The two guards laughed. The daughter who had given Pancho the panda was nine years old and had been raised by her mother as a Catholic.

That night, before the place went dark, Caesar lay on the bottom bunk and looked over at pictures of Pancho's children, which Pancho had taped on the opposite wall. He knew he would have to decide if he wanted Pancho just to move the photographs or to put them away altogether. All the children had toothy smiles. The two youngest stood, in separate pictures, outdoors in their First Communion clothes. Caesar himself had been a father for two years. A girl he had met at an F Street club in Northwest had told him he was the father of her son, and for a time he had believed her. Then the boy started growing big ears that Caesar thought didn't belong to anyone in his family, and so after he had slapped the girl a few times a week before the child's second birthday she confessed that the child belonged to "my first love." "Your first love is always with you," she said, sounding forever like a television addict who had never read a book. As Caesar prepared to leave, she asked him, "You want back all the toys and things you gave him?" The child, as if used to their fighting, had slept through this last encounter on the couch, part of a living-room suite that they were paying for on time. Caesar said nothing more and didn't think about his 18k.-gold cigarette lighter until he was eight blocks away. The girl pawned the thing and got enough to pay off the furniture bill.

Caesar and Pancho worked in the laundry, and Caesar could look across the noisy room with all the lint swirling about and see Pancho sorting dirty pieces into bins. Then he would push uniform bins to the left and everything else to the right. Pancho had been doing that for three years. The job he got after he left Lorton was as a gofer at construction sites. No laundry in the outside world wanted him. Over the next two weeks, as Caesar watched Pancho at his job, his back always to him, he considered what he should do next. He wasn't into fucking men, so that was out. He still had not decided what he wanted done about the photographs on the cell wall. One day at the end of those two weeks, Caesar saw the light above Pancho's head flickering and Pancho raised his head and looked for a long time at it, as if thinking that the answer to all his problems lay in fixing that one light. Caesar decided then to let the pictures remain on the wall.

Three years later, they let Pancho go. The two men had mostly stayed at a distance from each other, but toward the end they had been talking, sharing plans about a life beyond Lorton. The relationship had reached the point where Caesar was saddened to see the children's photographs come off the wall. Pancho pulled off the last taped picture and the wall was suddenly empty in a most forlorn way. Caesar knew the names of all the children. Pancho gave him a rabbit's foot that one of his children had given him. It was the way among all those men that when a good-luck piece had run out of juice it was given away with the hope that new ownership would renew its strength. The rabbit's foot had lost its electricity months before Pancho's release. Caesar's only good-fortune piece was a key chain made in Peru; it had been sweet for a bank robber in the next cell for nearly two years until that man's daughter, walking home from third grade, was abducted and killed.

One day after Pancho left, they brought in a thief and three-time rapist of elderly women. He nodded to Caesar and told him that he was Watson Rainey and went about making a home for himself in the cell, finally plugging in a tiny lamp with a green shade which he placed on the metal shelf jutting from the wall. Then he climbed onto the top bunk he had made up and lay down. His name was all the wordplay he had given Caesar, who had been smoking on the bottom bunk throughout Rainey's efforts to make a nest. Caesar waited ten minutes and then stood and pulled the lamp's cord out of the wall socket and grabbed Rainey with one hand and threw him to the floor. He crushed the lamp into Rainey's face. He choked him with the cord. "You come into my house and show me no respect!" Caesar shouted. The only sound Rainey could manage was a gurgling that bubbled up from his mangled mouth. There were no witnesses except for an old man across the way, who would occasionally glance over at the two when he wasn't reading his Bible. It was over and done with in four minutes. When Rainey came to, he found everything he owned piled in the corner, soggy with piss. And Caesar was again on the top bunk.

They would live in that cell together until Caesar was released, four years later. Rainey tried never to be in the house during waking hours; if he was there when Caesar came in, he would leave.

Rainey's name spoken by him that first day were all the words that would ever pass between the two men.

A week or so after Rainey got there, Caesar bought from Multrey a calendar that was three years old. It was large and had no markings of any sort, as pristine as the day it was made. "You know this one ain't the year we in right now," Multrey said as one of his women took a quarter from Caesar and dropped it in her purse. Caesar said, "It'll do." Multrey prized the calendar for one thing: its top half had a photograph of a naked woman of indeterminate race sitting on a stool, her legs wide open, her pussy aimed dead at whoever was standing right in front of her. It had been Multrey's good-luck piece, but the luck was dead. Multrey remembered what the calendar had done for him and he told his woman to give Caesar his money back, lest any new good-fortune piece turn sour on him.

The calendar's bottom half had the days of the year. That day, the first Monday in June, Caesar drew in the box that was January 1 a line that went from the upper left-hand corner down to the bottom right-hand corner. The next day, a June Tuesday, he made a line in the January 2 box that also ran in the same direction. And so it went. When the calendar had all such lines in all the boxes, it was the next June. Then Caesar, in that January 1 box, made a line that formed an X with the first line. And so it was for another year. The third year saw horizontal marks that sliced the boxes in half. The fourth year had vertical lines down the centers of the boxes.

This was the only calendar Caesar had in Lorton. That very first Monday, he taped the calendar over the area where the pictures of Pancho's children had been. There was still a good deal of empty space left, but he didn't do anything about it, and Rainey knew he couldn't do anything, either.

The calendar did right by Caesar until near the end of his fifth year in Lorton, when he began to feel that its juice was drying up. But he kept it there to mark off the days and, too, the naked woman never closed her legs to him.

In that fifth year, someone murdered Multrey as he showered. The killers — it had to be more than one for a man like Multrey — were never found. The Multrey woman who picked at her food had felt herself caring for a recent arrival who was five years younger

than her, a part-time deacon who had killed a Southwest bartender
for calling the deacon's wife "a woman without one fuckin brain
cell." The story of that killing — the bartender was dropped head-
first from the roof of a ten-story building — became legend, and
in Lorton men referred to the dead bartender as "the Flat-Head
Insulter" and the killer became known as "the Righteous Desulter."
The Desulter, wanting Multrey's lady, had hired people to butcher
him. It had always been the duty of the lady who hated food to
watch out for Multrey as he showered, but she had stepped away
that day, just as she had been instructed to by the Desulter.

In another time, Cathedral and Caesar would have had enough
of everything — from muscle to influence — to demand that
someone give up the killers, but the prison was filling up with
younger men who did not care what those two had been once upon
a time. Also, Cathedral had already had two visits from the man he
had killed in Northwest. Each time, the man had first stood before
the bars of Cathedral's cell. Then he held one of the bars and
opened the door inward, like some wooden door on a person's
house. The dead man standing there would have been sufficient to
unwrap anyone, but matters were compounded when Cathedral
saw a door that for years had slid sideways now open in an impossible fashion. The man stood silent before Cathedral, and when he
left he shut the door gently, as if there were sleeping children in
the cell. So Cathedral didn't have a full mind, and Multrey was
never avenged.

There was an armed-robbery man in the place, a tattooer with
homemade inks and needles. He made a good living painting on
both muscled and frail bodies the names of children; the Devil
in full regalia with a pitchfork dripping with blood; the words
"Mother" or "Mother Forever" surrounded by red roses and angels
who looked sad, because when it came to drawing happy angels the
tattoo man had no skills. One pickpocket had had a picture of his
father tattooed in the middle of his chest; above the father's head,
in medieval lettering, were the words "Rotting in Hell," with the letter "H" done in fiery yellow and red. The tattoo guy had told
Caesar that he had skin worthy of "a painter's best canvas," that he
could give Caesar a tattoo "God would envy." Caesar had always
told him no, but then he awoke one snowy night in March of his

sixth year and realized that it was his mother's birthday. He did not know what day of the week it was, but the voice that talked to him had the authority of a million loving mothers. He had long ago forgotten his own birthday, had not even bothered to ask someone in prison records to look it up.

There had never been anyone or anything he wanted commemorated on his body. Maybe it would have been Carol, his first girlfriend twenty years ago, before the retarded girl entered their lives. He had played with the notion of having the name of the boy he thought was his put over his heart, but the lie had come to light before that could happen. And before the boy there had been Yvonne, with whom he had lived for an extraordinary time in Northeast. He would have put Yvonne's name over his heart, but she went off to work one day and never came back. He looked for her for three months, and then just assumed that she had been killed somewhere and dumped in a place only animals knew about. Yvonne was indeed dead, and she would be waiting for him at the end of the line, though she did not know that was what she was doing. "You can always trust unhappiness," Yvonne had once said, sitting in the dark on the couch, her cigarette burned down to the filter. "His face never changes. But happiness is slick, can't be trusted. It has a thousand faces, Caes, all of them just ready to reform into unhappiness once it has you in its clutches."

So Caesar had the words "Mother Forever" tattooed on his left bicep. Knowing that more letters meant a higher payment of cigarettes or money or candy, the tattoo fellow had dissuaded him from having just plain "Mother." "How many hours you think she spent in labor?" he asked Caesar. "Just to give you life." The job took five hours over two days, during a snowstorm. Caesar said no to angels, knowing the man's ability with happy ones, and had the words done in blue letters encased in red roses. The man worked from the words printed on a piece of paper that Caesar had given him, because he was also a bad speller.

The snow stopped on the third day and, strangely, it took only another three days for the two feet of mess to melt, for with the end of the storm came a heat wave. The tattoo man, a good friend of the Righteous Desulter, would tell Caesar in late April that what happened to him was his own fault, that he had not taken care of himself as he had been instructed to do. "And the heat ain't helped

you neither." On the night of March 31, five days after the tattoo
had been put on, Caesar woke in the night with a pounding in his
left arm. He couldn't return to sleep so he sat on the edge of his
bunk until morning, when he saw that the "e"s in "Mother Forever"
had blistered, as if someone had taken a match to them.

He went to the tattoo man, who first told him not to worry, then
patted the "e"s with peroxide that he warmed in a spoon with a
match. Within two days, the "e"s seemed to just melt away, each dissolving into an ugly pile at the base of the tattoo. After a week,
the diseased "e"s began spreading their work to the other letters
and Caesar couldn't move his arm without pain. He went to the
infirmary. They gave him aspirin and Band-Aided the tattoo. He
was back the next day, the day the doctor was there.

He spent four days in D.C. General Hospital, his first trip back to
Washington since a court appearance more than three years before. His entire body was paralyzed for two days, and one nurse
confided to him the day he left that he had been near death. In the
end, after the infection had done its work, there was not much left
of the tattoo except an "o" and an "r," which were so deformed they
could never pass for English, and a few roses that looked more like
red mud. When he returned to prison, the tattoo man offered to
give back the cigarettes and the money, but Caesar never gave him
an answer, leading the man to think that he should watch his back.
What happened to Caesar's tattoo and to Caesar was bad advertising, and soon the fellow had no customers at all.

Something had died in the arm and the shoulder, and Caesar
was never again able to raise the arm more than thirty-five degrees.
He had no enemies, but still he told no one about his debilitation.
For the next few months he tried to stay out of everyone's way,
knowing that he was far more vulnerable than he had been before
the tattoo. Alone in the cell, with no one watching across the way,
he exercised the arm, but by November he knew at last he would
not be the same again. He tried to bully Rainey Watson as much as
he could to continue the façade that he was still who he had been.
And he tried to spend more time with Cathedral.

But the man Cathedral had killed had become a far more constant visitor. The dead man, a young bachelor who had been Cathedral's next-door neighbor, never spoke. He just opened Cathedral's cell door inward and went about doing things as if the cell

were a family home — straightening wall pictures that only Cathedral could see, turning down the gas on the stove, testing the shower water to make sure that it was not too hot, tucking children into bed. Cathedral watched silently.

Caesar went to Cathedral's cell one day in mid-December, six months before they freed him. He found his friend sitting on the bottom bunk, his hands clamped over his knees. He was still outside the cell when Cathedral said, "Caes, you tell me why God would be so stupid to create mosquitoes. I mean, what good are the damn things? What's their function?" Caesar laughed, thinking it was a joke, and he had started to offer something when Cathedral looked over at him with a devastatingly serious gaze and said, "What we need is a new God. Somebody who knows what the fuck he's doing." Cathedral was not smiling. He returned to staring at the wall across from him. "What's with creatin bats? I mean, yes, they eat insects, but why create those insects to begin with? You see what I mean? Creatin a problem and then havin to create somethin to take care of the problem. And then comin up with somethin for that second problem. Man oh man!" Caesar slowly began moving away from Cathedral's cell. He had seen this many times before. It could not be cured even by great love. It sometimes pulled down a loved one. "And roaches. Every human bein in the world would have the sense not to create roaches. What's their function, Caes? I tell you, we need a new God, and I'm ready to cast my vote right now. Roaches and rats and chinches. God was out of his fuckin mind that week. Six wasted days, cept for the human part and some of the animals. And then partyin on the seventh day like he done us a big favor. The nerve of that motherfucker. And all your pigeons and squirrels. Don't forget them. I mean really."

In late January, they took Cathedral somewhere and then brought him back after a week. He returned to his campaign for a new God in February. A ritual began that would continue until Caesar left: determine that Cathedral was a menace to himself, take him away, bring him back, then take him away when he started campaigning again for another God.

There was now nothing for Caesar to do except try to coast to the end on a reputation that was far less than it had been in his first years at Lorton. He could only hope that he had built up enough good will among men who had better reputations and arms that worked a hundred percent.

In early April, he received a large manila envelope from his attorney. The lawyer's letter was brief. "I did not tell them where you are," he wrote. "They may have learned from someone that I was your attorney. Take care." There were two separate letters in sealed envelopes from his brother and sister, each addressed to "My Brother Caesar." Dead people come back alive, Caesar thought many times before he finally read the letters, after almost a week. He expected an announcement about the death of his father, but he was hardly mentioned. Caesar's younger brother went on for five pages with a history of what had happened to the family since Caesar had left their lives. He ended by saying, "Maybe I should have been a better brother." There were three pictures as well, one of his brother and his bride on their wedding day, and one showing Caesar's sister, her husband, and their two children, a girl of four or so and a boy of about two. The third picture had the girl sitting on a couch beside the boy, who was in Caesar's father's lap, looking with interest off to the left, as if whatever was there were more important than having his picture taken. Caesar looked at the image of his father — a man on the verge of becoming old. His sister's letter had even less in it than the lawyer's: "Write to me, or call me collect, whatever is best for you, dear one. Call even if you are on the other side of the world. For every step you take to get to me, I will walk a mile toward you."

He had an enormous yearning at first, but after two weeks he tore everything up and threw it all away. He would be glad he had done this as he stumbled, hurt and confused, out of his sister's car less than half a year later. The girl and the boy would be in the back seat, the girl wearing a red dress and black shoes, and the boy in blue pants and a T-shirt with a cartoon figure on the front. The boy would have fallen asleep, but the girl would say, "Nighty-night, Uncle," which she had been calling him all that evening.

An ex-offenders' group, the Light at the End of the Tunnel, helped him to get a room and a job washing dishes and busing tables at a restaurant on F Street. The room was in a three-story building in the middle of the 900 block of N Street, Northwest, a building that, in the days when white people lived there, had had two apartments of eight rooms or so on each floor. Now the first-floor apartments were uninhabitable and had been padlocked for years. On the two other floors, each large apartment had been divided into five rented rooms, which went for twenty to thirty dollars a week, depending on the size and the view. Caesar's was small, twenty dollars, and had half the space of his cell at Lorton. The word that came to him for the butchered, once luxurious apartments was "warren." The roomers in each of the cut-up apartments shared two bathrooms and one nice-sized kitchen, which was a pathetic place because of its dinginess and its 50-watt bulb, and because many of the appliances were old or undependable or both. Caesar's narrow room was at the front, facing N Street. On his side of the hall were two other rooms, the one next to his housing a mother and her two children. He would not know until his third week there that along the other hall was Yvonne Miller.

There was one main entry door for each of the complexes. In the big room to the left of the door into Caesar's complex lived a man of sixty or so, a pajama-clad man who was never out of bed in all the time Caesar lived there. He *could* walk, but Caesar never saw him do it. A woman, who told Caesar one day that she was "a home health-care aide," was always in the man's room, cooking, cleaning, or watching television with him. His was the only room with its own kitchen setup in a small alcove — a stove, icebox, and sink. His door was always open, and he never seemed to sleep. A green safe, three feet high, squatted beside the bed. "I am a moneylender," the man said the second day Caesar was there. He had come in and walked past the room, and the man had told the aide to have "that young lion" come back. "I am Simon and I lend money," the man said as Caesar stood in the doorway. "I will be your best friend, but not for free. Tell your friends."

He worked as many hours as they would allow him at the restaurant, Chowing Down. The remainder of the time, he went to movies until the shows closed and then sat in Franklin Park, at Fourteenth and K, in good weather and bad. He was there until sleep beckoned, sometimes as late as two in the morning. No one bothered him. He had killed two men, and the world, especially the bad part of it, sensed that and left him alone. He knew no one, and he wanted no one to know him. The friends he had had before Lorton seemed to have been swept off the face of the earth. On the penultimate day of his time at Lorton, he had awoken terrified and thought that if they gave him a choice he might well stay. He might find a life and a career at Lorton.

He had sex only with his right hand, and that was not very often. He began to believe, in his first days out of prison, that men and women were now speaking a new language, and that he would never learn it. His lack of confidence extended even to whores, and this was a man who had been with more women than he had fingers and toes. He began to think that a whore had the power to crush a man's soul. "What kinda language you speakin, honey? Talk English if you want some." He was thirty-seven when he got free.

He came in from the park at two-forty-five one morning and went quickly by Simon's door, but the moneylender called him back. Caesar stood in the doorway. He had been in the warren for less than two months. The aide was cooking, standing with her back to Caesar in a crisp green uniform and sensible black shoes. She was stirring first one pot on the stove and then another. People on the color television were laughing.

"Been out on the town, I see," Simon began. "Hope you got enough poontang to last you till next time." "I gotta be goin," Caesar said. He had begun to think that he might be able to kill the man and find a way to get into the safe. The question was whether he should kill the aide as well. "Don't blow off your friends that way," Simon said. Then, for some reason, he started telling Caesar about their neighbors in that complex. That was how Caesar first learned about an "Yvonny," whom he had yet to see. He would not know that she was the Yvonne he had known long ago until the second time he passed her in the hall. "Now, our sweet Yvonny, she ain't nothin but an old girl." Old girls were whores, young or old, who had been battered so much by the world that they had only the faintest wisp of life left; not many of them had hearts of gold. "But you could probably have her for free," Simon said, and he pointed to Caesar's right, where Yvonne's room was. There was always a small lump under the covers beside Simon in the bed, and Caesar suspected that it was a gun. That was a problem, but he might be able to leap to the bed and kill the man with one blow of a club before he could pull it out. What would the aide do? "I've had her myself," Simon said, "so I can only recommend it in a pinch." "Later, man," Caesar said, and he stepped away. The usual way to his room was to the right as soon as he entered the main door, but that morning he walked straight ahead and within a few feet was passing Yvonne's door. It was slightly ajar, and he heard music from a radio. The aide might even be willing to help him rob the moneylender if he could talk to her alone beforehand. He might not know the language men and women were speaking now, but the language of money had not changed.

It was a cousin who told his brother where to find him. That cousin, Nora Maywell, was the manager of a nearby bank, at Twelfth and F Streets, and she first saw Caesar as he bused tables at Chowing Down, where she had gone with colleagues for lunch. She came in day after day to make certain that he was indeed Caesar, for she had not seen him in more than twenty years. But there was no mistaking the man, who looked like her uncle. Caesar was five years older than Nora. She had gone through much of her childhood hoping that she would grow up to marry him. Had he paid much attention to her in all those years before he disappeared, he still would not have recognized her — she was older, to be sure, but life had been extraordinarily kind to Nora and she was now a queen compared with the dirt-poor peasant she had once been.

Caesar's brother came in three weeks after Nora first saw him. The brother, Alonzo, ate alone, paid his bill, then went over to Caesar and smiled. "It's good to see you," he said. Caesar simply nodded and walked away with the tub of dirty dishes. The brother stood shaking for a few moments, then turned and made his unsteady way out the door. He was a corporate attorney, making nine times what his father, at fifty-seven, was making, and he came back for many days. On the eighth day, he went to Caesar, who was busing in a far corner of the restaurant. It was now early September and Caesar had been out of prison for three months and five days. "I will keep coming until you speak to me," the brother said. Caesar looked at him for a long time. The lunch hours were ending, so the manager would have no reason to shout at him. Only two days before, he had seen Yvonne in the hall for the second time. It had been afternoon and the dead light bulb in the hall had been replaced since the first time he had passed her. He recognized her, but everything in her eyes and body told him that she did not know him. That would never change. And, because he knew who she was, he nodded to his brother and within minutes they were out the door and around the corner to the alley. Caesar lit a cigarette right away. The brother's gray suit had cost $1,865.98. Caesar's apron was filthy. It was his seventh cigarette of the afternoon. When it wasn't in his mouth, the cigarette was at his side, and as he raised it up and down to his mouth, inhaled, and flicked ashes, his hand never shook.

"Do you know how much I want to put my arms around you?" Alonzo said.

"I think we should put an end to all this shit right now so we can get on with our lives," Caesar said. "I don't wanna see you or anyone else in your family from now until the day I die. You should understand that, mister, so you can do somethin else with your time. You a customer, so I won't do what I would do to somebody who ain't a customer."

The brother said, "I'll admit to whatever I may have done to you. I will, Caesar. I will." In fact, his brother had never done anything to him, and neither had his sister. The war had always been between Caesar and their father, but Caesar, over time, had come to see his siblings as the father's allies. "But come to see me and Joanie, one time only, and if you don't want to see us again then we'll accept that. I'll never come into your restaurant again."

There was still more of the cigarette, but Caesar looked at it and then dropped it to the ground and stepped on it. He looked at his cheap watch. Men in prison would have killed for what was left of that smoke. "I gotta be goin, mister."

"We are family, Caesar. If you don't want to see Joanie and me for your sake, for our sakes, then do it for Mama."

"My mama's dead, and she been dead for a lotta years." He walked toward the street.

"I know she's dead! I know she's dead! I just put flowers on her grave on Sunday. And on three Sundays before that. And five weeks before that. I know my mother's dead."

Caesar stopped. It was one thing for him to throw out a quick statement about a dead mother, as he had done many times over the years. A man could say the words so often that they became just another meaningless part of his makeup. The pain was no longer there as it had been those first times he had spoken them, when his mother was still new to her grave. The words were one thing, but a grave was a different matter, a different fact. The grave was out there, to be seen and touched, and a man, a son, could go to that spot of earth and remember all over again how much she had loved him, how she had stood in her apron in the doorway of a clean and beautiful home and welcomed him back from school. He could go to the grave and read her name and die a bit, because it would feel as if she had left him only last week.

Caesar turned around. "You and your people must leave me alone, mister."

"Then we will," the brother said. "We will leave you alone. Come to one dinner. A Sunday dinner. Fried chicken. The works. Then we'll never bother you again. No one but Joanie and our families. No one else." Those last words were to assure Caesar that he would not have to see their father.

Caesar wanted another cigarette, but the meeting had already gone on long enough.

Yvonne had not said anything that second time, when he said "Hello." She had simply nodded and walked around him in the hall. The third time they were also passing in the hall, and he spoke again, and she stepped to the side to pass and then turned and asked if he had any smokes she could borrow.

He said he had some in his room, and she told him to go get them and pointed to her room.

Her room was a third larger than his. It had an icebox, a bed, a dresser with a mirror over it, a small table next to the bed, a chair just beside the door, and not much else. The bed made a T with the one window, which faced the windowless wall of the apartment building next door. The beautiful blue-and-yellow curtains at the window should have been somewhere else, in a place that could appreciate them.

He had no expectations. He wanted nothing. It was just good to see a person from a special time in his life, and it was even better that he had loved her once and she had loved him. He stood in the doorway with the cigarettes.

Dressed in a faded purple robe, she was looking in the icebox when he returned. She closed the icebox door and looked at him.

He walked over, and she took the unopened pack of cigarettes from his outstretched hand. He stood there.

"Well, sit the fuck down before you make the place look poor." He sat in the chair by the door, and she sat on the bed and lit the first cigarette. She was sideways to him. It was only after the fifth drag on the cigarette that she spoke. "If you think you gonna get some pussy, you are sorely mistaken. I ain't givin out shit. Free can kill you."

"I don't want nothin."

"'I don't want nothin. I don't want nothin.'" She dropped ashes into an empty tomato-soup can on the table by the bed. "Mister, we all want somethin, and the sooner people like you stand up and stop the bullshit, then the world can start bein a better place. It's the bullshitters who keep the world from bein a better place." Together, they had rented a little house in Northeast and had been planning to have a child once they had been there two years. The night he came home and found her sitting in the dark and talking about never trusting happiness, they had been there a year and a half. Two months later, she was gone. For the next three months, as he looked for her, he stayed there and continued to make it the kind of place that a woman would want to come home to. "My own mother was the first bullshitter I knew," she continued. "That's how I know it don't work. People should stand up and say, 'I wish you were dead,' or 'I want your pussy,' or 'I want all the money in your pocket.' When we stop lyin, the world will start bein heaven." He had been a thief and a robber and a drug pusher before he met her, and he went back to all that after the three months, not because he was heartbroken, though he was, but because it was such an easy thing to do. He was smart enough to know that he could not blame Yvonne, and he never did. The murders of Percy "Golden Boy" Weymouth and Antwoine Stoddard were still years away.

He stayed that day for more than an hour, until she told him that she had now paid for the cigarettes. Over the next two weeks, as he got closer to the dinner with his brother and sister, he would take her cigarettes and food and tell her from the start that they were free. He was never to know how she paid the rent. By the fourth day of bringing her things, she began to believe that he wanted nothing. He always sat in the chair by the door. Her words never changed, and it never mattered to him. The only thanks he got was the advice that the world should stop being a bullshitter.

On the day of the dinner, he found that the days of sitting with Yvonne had given him a strength he had not had when he had said yes to his brother. He had Alonzo pick him up in front of Chowing Down, because he felt that if they knew where he lived they would find a way to stay in his life.

At his sister's house, just off Sixteenth Street, Northwest, in an area of well-to-do black people some called the Gold Coast, they welcomed him, Joanie keeping her arms around him for more than a minute, crying. Then they offered him a glass of wine. He had not touched alcohol since before prison. They sat him on a dark-green couch in the living room, which was the size of ten prison cells. Before he had taken three sips of the wine, he felt good enough not to care that the girl and the boy, his sister's children, wanted to be in his lap. They were the first children he had been around in more than ten years. The girl had been calling him Uncle since he entered the house.

Throughout dinner, which was served by his sister's maid, and during the rest of the evening, he said as little as possible to the adults — his sister and brother and their spouses — but concentrated on the kids, because he thought he knew their hearts. The grownups did not pepper him with questions and were just grateful that he was there. Toward the end of the meal, he had a fourth glass of wine, and that was when he told his niece that she looked like his mother and the girl blushed, because she knew how beautiful her grandmother had been.

At the end, as Caesar stood in the doorway preparing to leave, his brother said that he had made this a wonderful year. His brother's eyes teared up and he wanted to hug Caesar, but Caesar, without smiling, simply extended his hand. The last thing his brother said to him was "Even if you go away not wanting to see us again, know that Daddy loves you. It is the one giant truth in the world. He's a different man, Caesar. I think he loves you more than us because he never knew what happened to you. That may be why he never remarried." The issue of what Caesar had been doing for twenty-one years never came up.

*

His sister, with her children in the back seat, drove him home. In front of his building, he and Joanie said goodbye and she kissed his cheek and, as an afterthought, he, a new uncle and with the wine saying, *Now, that wasn't so bad,* reached back to give a playful tug on the children's feet, but the sleeping boy was too far away and the girl, laughing, wiggled out of his reach. He said to his niece, "Good night, young lady," and she said no, that she was not a lady but a little girl. Again, he reached unsuccessfully for her feet. When he turned back, his sister had a look of such horror and disgust that he felt he had been stabbed. He knew right away what she was thinking, that he was out to cop a feel on a child. He managed a goodbye and got out of the car. "Call me," she said before he closed the car door, but the words lacked the feeling of all the previous ones of the evening. He said nothing. Had he spoken the wrong language, as well as done the wrong thing? Did child molesters call little girls "ladies"? He knew he would never call his sister. Yes, he had been right to tear up the pictures and letters when he was in Lorton.

He shut his eyes until the car was no more. He felt a pained rumbling throughout his system and, without thinking, he staggered away from his building toward Tenth Street. He could hear music coming from an apartment on his side of N Street. He had taught his sister how to ride a bike, how to get over her fear of falling and hurting herself. Now, in her eyes, he was no more than an animal capable of hurting a child. They killed men in prison for being that kind of monster. Whatever avuncular love for the children had begun growing in just those few hours now seeped away. He leaned over into the grass at the side of the apartment building and vomited. He wiped his mouth with the back of his hand. "I'll fall, Caesar," his sister had said in her first weeks of learning how to ride a bicycle. "Why would I let that happen?"

He ignored the aide when she told him that the moneylender wanted to talk to him. He went straight ahead, toward Yvonne's room, though he had no intention of seeing her. Her door was open enough for him to see a good part of the room, but he simply turned toward his own room. His shadow, cast by her light behind him, was thin and went along the floor and up the wall, and it was seeing the shadow that made him turn around. After noting that the bathroom next to her room was empty, he called softly to her from the doorway and then called three times more before he gave the door a gentle push with his finger. The door had not opened all the way when he saw her half on the bed and half off. Drunk, he thought. He went to her, intending to put her full on the bed. But death can twist the body in a way life never does, and that was what it had done to hers. He knew death. Her face was pressed into the bed, at a crooked angle that would have been uncomfortable for any living person. One leg was bunched under her, and the other was extended behind her, but both seemed not part of her body, awkwardly on their own, as if someone could just pick them up and walk away.

He whispered her name. He sat down beside her, ignoring the vomit that spilled out of her mouth and over the side of the bed. He moved her head so that it rested on one side. He thought at first that someone had done this to her, but he saw money on the dresser and felt the quiet throughout the room that signaled the end of it all, and he knew that the victim and the perpetrator were one and the same. He screwed the top on the empty whiskey bottle near her extended leg.

He placed her body on the bed and covered her with a sheet and a blanket. Someone would find her in the morning. He stood at the door, preparing to turn out the light and leave, thinking this was how the world would find her. He had once known her as a clean woman who would not steal so much as a needle. A woman with a well-kept house. She had been loved. But that was not what they would see in the morning.

He set about putting a few things back in place, hanging up clothes that were lying over the chair and on the bed, straightening the lampshade, picking up newspapers and everything else on the floor. But, when he was done, it did not seem enough.

He went to his room and tore up two shirts to make dust rags. He started in a corner at the foot of her bed, at a table where she kept her brush and comb and makeup and other lady things. When he had dusted the table and everything on it, he put an order to what was there, just as if she would be using them in the morning.

Then he began dusting and cleaning clockwise around the room, and by midnight he was not even half done and the shirts were dirty with all the work, and he went back to his room for two more. By three, he was cutting up his pants for rags. After he had cleaned and dusted the room, he put an order to it all, as he had done with the things on the table — the dishes and food in mouseproof cannisters on the table beside the icebox, the two framed posters of mountains on the wall that were tilting to the left, the five photographs of unknown children on the bureau. When that work was done, he took a pail and a mop from her closet. Mice had made a bed in the mop, and he had to brush them off and away. He filled the pail with water from the bathroom and soap powder from under the table beside the icebox. After the floor had been mopped, he stood in the doorway as it dried and listened to the mice in the walls, listened to them scurrying in the closet.

At about four, the room was done and Yvonne lay covered in her unmade bed. He went to the door, ready to leave, and was once more unable to move. The whole world was silent except the mice in the walls.

He knelt at the bed and touched Yvonne's shoulder. On a Tuesday morning, a school day, he had come upon his father kneeling at his bed, Caesar's mother growing cold in that bed. His father was crying, and when Caesar went to him his father crushed Caesar to him and took the boy's breath away. It was Caesar's brother who had said they should call someone, but their father said, "No, no, just one minute more, just one more minute," as if in that next minute God would reconsider and send his wife back. And Caesar had said, "Yes, just one minute more." *The one giant truth . . .* , his brother had said.

Caesar changed the bed clothing and undressed Yvonne. He got one of her large pots and filled it with warm water from the bathroom and poured into the water cologne of his own that he never used and bath-oil beads he found in a battered container in a corner beside her dresser. The beads refused to dissolve, and he had to crush them in his hands. He bathed her, cleaned out her mouth. He got a green dress from the closet, and underwear and stockings from the dresser, put them on her, and pinned a rusty cameo on the dress over her heart. He combed and brushed her hair, put barrettes in it after he sweetened it with the rest of the cologne, and laid her head in the center of the pillow now covered with one of his clean cases. He gave her no shoes and he did not cover her up, just left her on top of the made-up bed. The room with the dead woman was as clean and as beautiful as Caesar could manage at that time in his life. It was after six in the morning, and the world was lighting up and the birds had begun to chirp. Caesar shut off the ceiling light and turned out the lamp, held on to the chain switch as he listened to the beginnings of a new day.

He opened the window that he had cleaned hours before, and right away a breeze came through. He put a hand to the wind, enjoying the coolness, and one thing came to him: he was not a young man anymore.

He sat on his bed smoking one cigarette after another. Before finding Yvonne dead, he had thought he would go and live in Baltimore and hook up with a vicious crew he had known a long time ago. Wasn't that what child molesters did? Now, the only thing he knew about the rest of his life was that he did not want to wash dishes and bus tables anymore. At about nine-thirty, he put just about all he owned and the two bags of trash from Yvonne's room in the bin in the kitchen. He knocked at the door of the woman in the room next to his. Her son opened the door, and Caesar asked for his mother. He gave her the hundred and forty-seven dollars he had found in Yvonne's room, along with his radio and tiny black-and-white television. He told her to look in on Yvonne before long and then said he would see her later, which was perhaps the softest lie of his adult life.

On his way out of the warren of rooms, Simon called to him. "You comin back soon, young lion?" he asked. Caesar nodded. "Well, why don't you bring me back a bottle of rum? Woke up with a taste for it this mornin." Caesar nodded. "Was that you in there with Yvonny last night?" Simon said as he got the money from atop the safe beside his bed. "Quite a party, huh?" Caesar said nothing. Simon gave the money to the aide, and she handed Caesar ten dollars and a quarter. "Right down to the penny," Simon said. "Give you a tip when you get back." "I won't be long," Caesar said. Simon must have realized that was a lie, because before Caesar went out the door he said, in as sweet a voice as he was capable of, "I'll be waitin."

He came out into the day. He did not know what he was going to do, aside from finding some legit way to pay for Yvonne's funeral. The D.C. government people would take her away, but he knew where he could find and claim her before they put her in potter's field. He put the bills in his pocket and looked down at the quarter in the palm of his hand. It was a rather old one, 1967, but shiny enough. Life had been kind to it. He went carefully down the steps in front of the building and stood on the sidewalk. The world was going about its business, and it came to him, as it might to a man who had been momentarily knocked senseless after a punch to the face, that he was of that world. To the left was Ninth Street and all the rest of N Street, Immaculate Conception Catholic Church at Eighth, the bank at the corner of Seventh. He flipped the coin. To his right was Tenth Street, and down Tenth were stores and the house where Abraham Lincoln had died and all the white people's precious monuments. Up Tenth and a block to Eleventh and Q Streets was once a High's store where, when Caesar was a boy, a pint of cherry-vanilla ice cream cost twenty-five cents, and farther down Tenth was French Street, with a two-story house with his mother's doilies and a foot-long porcelain black puppy just inside the front door. A puppy his mother had bought for his father in the third year of their marriage. A puppy that for thirty-five years had been patiently waiting each working day for Caesar's father to return from work. *The one giant truth . . . Just one minute more.* He caught the quarter and slapped it on the back of his hand. He had already decided that George Washington's profile would mean going toward Tenth Street, and that was what he did once he uncovered the coin.

At the corner of Tenth and N, he stopped and considered the quarter again. Down Tenth was Lincoln's death house. Up Tenth was the house where he had been a boy, and where the puppy was waiting for his father. A girl at the corner was messing with her bicycle, putting playing cards in the spokes, checking the tires. She watched Caesar as he flipped the quarter. He missed it and the coin fell to the ground, and he decided that that one would not count. The girl had once seen her aunt juggle six coins, first warming up with the flip of a single one and advancing to the juggling of three before finishing with six. It had been quite a show. The aunt had shown the six pieces to the girl — they had all been old and heavy one-dollar silver coins, huge monster things, which nobody made anymore. The girl thought she might now see a reprise of that event. Caesar flipped the quarter. The girl's heart paused. The man's heart paused. The coin reached its apex and then it fell.

STUART M. KAMINSKY

The Shooting of John Roy Worth

FROM *Ellery Queen's Mystery Magazine*

And a hard-drinking woman or a slow-thinking man will be the
death of me yet.
— *"Hard-Drinking Woman" by John Roy Worth*

WALLY CZERBIAK WAS SANE. At least he was as sane as Monty
Vitalle, who stood behind the second of three chairs at The Clean
Cut barbershop, five dollars for a haircut, three barbers, no wait-
ing. But sometimes there were only two barbers. Sometimes only
one. Actually, there was usually only one, Monty. It didn't matter.
There was never much of a wait, if any, at The Clean Cut.

Wally listened to Monty talk as Monty cut his hair. Monty was a
throwback. He had seen barbers in movies, old movies where the
barber just talks and talks. That was a major reason Monty had become a barber. He liked to talk about anything. Baseball, the market, the latest gossip about drug abuse by some million-million-dol-
lar basketball player, Rhoda Brian's stomach stapling.

Wally just sat and listened. Songs ran through his head, background music that fit the scene. For Wally, the major factor in his
becoming a sign painter was that his father was a sign painter till arthritis crippled him and he turned over his brushes and paints to
Wally. Wally had a natural talent, and it was easier to just paint signs
than do what was necessary to become a doctor or something. The
fact was that Wally couldn't think fast on his feet. School had always
been a puzzle he couldn't solve, a game whose rules he could never
learn.

Besides, Wally was proud of some of his work, the real chal-
lenges, like the sign he did a few months ago, black letters on yel-

low, Old English: PIECE OF CAKE, with a picture Wally drew of a
cake with white icing in a flowing, delicate pattern.

The cake was vanilla with cherries inside. You couldn't tell that
by looking at the sign, but Wally knew it. It was important to him to
know things like that so he could make the cake look real. Without
knowing what was inside, it was just a hollow shell.

Sometimes Wally felt like a hollow shell. When that happened,
he quickly filled the shell with food. He was thinking of a Big Mac
while Monty kept talking. He was thinking of a Big Mac and how he
would kill John Roy Worth.

"You understand?" Monty said.

Monty looked like a twig, a bald twig with wide brown suspenders. Monty had blue eyes and peppermint breath. He popped Certs
like Wally's cousin Kenneth had popped uppers back in the 1980s,
when they were kids.

"Yes," said Wally, looking at himself in the mirror, watching the
hair fall in ringlets as Monty cut and talked, narrow knobby shoulders huddled, holding today's suspenders. The Clean Cut was old,
ceiling a patterned tin, floor white tile with cracks that ran like me-
andering rivers, walls covered in paper with repeating pictures of
ancient airplanes. Monty was alone today. The other barber chairs
sat empty, and only Mr. Rosenberg, who lived in the Garden Gables
Assisted Living facility, sat waiting. Mr. Rosenberg had been driven
by the bus from the Garden Gables. It would be back for him in an
hour. Mr. Rosenberg didn't care if it was five hours. He liked the
smell of the barbershop. He liked fingering the curled edges of the
magazines that flopped on the small table next to him. He liked listening to Monty and throwing in an observation when he could.

"So, it's a miracle," Monty said. "All this."

He paused to wave his comb and point it around the shop. Wally
could see him in the mirror.

"You gotta think about it, Wally," he went on. "People were on
the earth with nothing, nothing at all, no thing at all. Just people
and the earth and the animals and whatever was growing. And they
made from it houses and cars and computers and cake mixers."

"And streets and telephones and airplanes," said Mr. Rosenberg.

"I'm going to shoot someone today," said Wally softly, looking at
the elegant letters painted on the window more than forty years
ago by his father, saying this, indeed, was The Clean Cut Barbershop.

"That a fact?" said Monty. "Something eating you?"

"No, nothing special. It's just the day I'm going to shoot someone," said Wally again, very softly, calmly, looking in the mirror to be sure Monty was cutting his hair just the way he liked it, not too short. Too short and his face looked like a balloon, like John Candy.

"You got to kill somebody, kill Dwight Spenser," said Mr. Rosenberg. "No loss there. You gotta kill somebody, kill Spenser, get it out of your system, rid the world of an anti-Semite."

"I don't know Spenser," said Wally.

"Room next to mine," said Rosenberg. "Must be a hundred years old. God's keeping him alive to punish those around him who've screwed up their lives. I'm eighty-six. He'll outlive me. The bad die ancient. You know what I'm saying?"

"I know what you're saying," said Wally. "But I've got to kill someone important."

"Like who?" asked Rosenberg. "Who's important in Bardo?"

"John Roy Worth," said Wally.

"And that's who?" asked Rosenberg.

"Country singer," said Monty dreamily, still thinking about the miracle of the world, the wonders of a comb, the marvel of the scissors in his hand. "Born and grew up right here in Bardo. Mother and father still here. Won the Grammy last year for singing something about dirty women. He in town?"

"'Hard-Drinking Woman,'" Wally said. "Youngest country-and-western singer to win a Grammy. Yes, he's in town."

"Done," said Monty, sweeping the sheet out from under Wally's chin so that the hairs on it floated neatly to the floor like snowfall in a glass bulb. Monty twirled the sheet like a toreador and laid it neatly in one movement on the empty barber chair next to him. It was Monty's trademark. That little move.

Wally got out of the chair. He always gave Monty a dollar tip. Monty always said, "Thank you kindly, Mr. Czerbiak, sir."

He did this time too. Rosenberg had put down the magazine and was walking slowly, stoop-shouldered, toward the chair. He looked like a gnome with a secret. Rosenberg had perfected the knowing look to hide his basic lack of intelligence.

Such, thought Wally, is the way of the world.

"You got a gun?" asked Monty, wrapping the cloth around Rosenberg's wrinkled neck.

"Yeah," said Wally as he went out the door and onto Fourth Street. The gun in his pocket belonged to his father. Kept it loaded in a drawer in the shop.

And this is what John Roy Worth was doing in Bardo, Texas. He was visiting his father and mother. He came back when he was in the area. He brought them something they didn't need or want whenever he made his brief visits. John Roy's mother and father always acted pleased to get the modern-looking lamp or new television to replace their new television. John Roy never stayed long, an hour or two at the most. He was always in a hurry, had someplace to go. John Roy's mother had come to expect this.

"Go, Johnny," she would say. "I know you're busy. We're proud of you."

"Very proud," John Roy's father, Lee, would say with a smile he didn't mean, happy that his son, who had dyed his hair and wore an earring and a cowboy hat, would be out of his life. Lee was a cop, retired. Sheriff's office. He couldn't carry a tune. Neither could his wife, and Lee didn't think their son John Roy did an awful god-damn good job of it, either. Besides, Lee could tell from his breath that John Roy had been smoking. The smell was also on his son's clothes. He was glad when John Roy, named for his mother's father, was gone, back on the television and the radio and the tapes, where he could be turned off.

It was toward the apartment of Mr. and Mrs. Lee Worth that Wally, clean-shaven, freshly cut hair, determined look on his face, headed. He walked. He could have taken his car. He had a 1997 Geo Prizm. It was blue. He kept it in good condition, but didn't have much of anywhere to drive it.

He didn't need his car. Not today. He was going to shoot John Roy Worth with the gun in his pocket and then wait for the police. There might be someone with John Roy. He would shoot him or her or them too. He might have to shoot John Roy three or four or more times. There were enough bullets in the gun. He wanted to be sure. He didn't want to be the man who tried to kill the sort-of-famous John Roy Worth. He wanted to be the man who killed the celebrity.

He walked. Nice sunny day. Slight breeze. Crows cawing some-where but he couldn't see them. The streets were almost empty. He was just turning into the driveway of the Fair Breeze Condos on

Second Street. A lady came out of the doorway, putting on white gloves as she walked toward him with a smile. She was a friend of Wally's mother. Her name was Stella Armstrong.

"Wally," she said.

"Mrs. Armstrong."

"You visiting someone?"

"No," he said. "I'm here to shoot John Roy Worth."

Mrs. Armstrong thought Wally meant he was going to take the singer's photograph. He wasn't carrying a camera, but they were so small nowadays that you could carry one in your pocket. Wally was a painter, not a photographer, but maybe, Mrs. Armstrong thought, he took photographs and then went back and painted pictures from them — not that she recalled any paintings of real people Wally had ever done.

"Got to get to an appointment with my doctor," she said apologetically. "I've got a thing on my back. Down here, you see? My best to your mother."

Wally nodded and smiled at her as she passed him. She smelled like lilacs.

Now, if someone were to ask Wally why he wanted to kill John Roy Worth, he would have had an answer. He would have had a different answer for whoever asked the question. He had a list of answers in his head depending on the questioner and when they asked him. He wondered what, if anything, he would tell the police. He was curious about how the system would work once he was under arrest. He looked forward to being questioned, talking to a lawyer, getting a uniform, lying on a cell cot, going to trial. He would definitely plead "not guilty." No plea-bargaining. What was the point in plea-bargaining when part of the point was seeing himself on trial?

He tried to hum "Hard-Drinking Woman" as he nodded at Richie Stawn, who manned the desk, wore a uniform, and was responsible for security. Richie liked his uniform, his job. Gave him plenty of time to write poetry. He had given a lot of it to John Roy Worth when the famous singer came to see his parents in Apartment 4G. John Roy had always taken the ring binder filled with what Richie was certain, or at least hoped, were lyrics for a big hit.

"Who you going to see, Wally?" Richie asked.

"Going to shoot John Roy Worth."

"Little camera?"

"Yes," said Wally, thinking only now that he should have brought a camera or something. He had not considered the possibility that people would think what he meant by shooting was something quite different.

Richie had been three years ahead of Wally at Lyndon Johnson High. They hadn't been friends. They hadn't been enemies. All they shared was the fact that neither participated in anything at school. Not football, baseball, basketball, wrestling, the photo club, the collectors club, the herpetology club, the Young Republicans, nothing. Wally had painted all the signs for school dances, elections, meetings, none of which he attended. Everything he had created had been thrown away or washed away by wind, rain, and time. All these years since he barely graduated, Wally had continued to do the signs for homecomings, graduation, the town's annual Founder's Day, the Prairie Flower Festival.

Reasons, Wally thought as he waited for the elevator, reasons he could have given had he been asked about what he planned to do in a few minutes:

John Roy Worth had been against the war with Iraq. He was unpatriotic.

John Roy Worth had done nothing for the very town in which he was born.

John Roy Worth took the Lord's name in vain in his songs.

John Roy Worth fornicated.

John Roy Worth was planning something big and evil. Wally wasn't sure what it was, but it was clearly spelled out in his songs.

John Roy Worth had one of those smug I'm-a-star faces that let you know he thought you were a dust mite and he knew something funny and embarrassing about you.

John Roy Worth's death would make Wally famous for a little while. He'd be interviewed by Diane Sawyer just before the weather on *Good Morning America*.

John Roy Worth's death would put Wally in prison forever and he'd never have to make another decision again about much of anything. Maybe they'd let him paint signs till the arthritis got him the way it had gotten his father. Did they need someone to paint signs in prison?

These were all reasons he might give. One or two of them might even be right, or maybe not.

"Worths expecting you, Wally?" asked Richie.

"No."

"Gotta call them up, then," he said with a deep sigh, as if the sigh were a major task.

The elevator doors opened while Richie was dialing. Out stepped John Roy Worth. He was wearing a cowboy hat, nice tan one with a black band and a tiny feather. His face was shaved clean, a concession to his parents, because when he did his videos or TV appearances John Roy always looked like he needed a shave.

He was also wearing clean, new-looking jeans and a Dallas Cowboys shirt, not the T kind but a white one with a collar and just a little Dallas Cowboys insignia on the pocket.

He was smoking, looked deep in thought, didn't see Richie or Wally. He walked past them toward the door.

"Mr. Worth," Richie called.

John Roy paused and turned, his mind still somewhere, maybe upstairs with his parents, maybe in some studio in Nashville or in bed with some girl. He looked at Richie.

"Wally wants to shoot you," Richie said. "That all right?"

John Roy Worth looked at Wally, head to foot, maybe recognizing something.

"Shoot me?"

"Picture, photograph, you know," Richie explained.

Wally's hand was in his pocket. The gun felt surprisingly warm. He imagined, tasted gunmetal in his mouth, on his tongue.

"Wally Czerbiak?" asked John Roy, taking a step toward Wally.

Wally nodded.

"You painted the horse on the sidewalk in front of Lyndon Johnson High for the homecoming when I graduated."

"Yeah," said Wally.

John Roy smiled. "Great horse. Forgot about that till just now. Funny how you forget things and they just come back."

"I've got a poem about a horse," Richie lied. "I can get it to you at the hotel before you leave."

John Roy wasn't listening.

"You still painting?" John Roy asked, taking a deep drag on his cigarette.

"Signs," said Wally.

"That horse," John Roy said, looking up at the ceiling, maybe trying to see the horse. "All white and wide-eyed. It had wings or a horn on its head or something."

"Both," said Wally. "A flying unicorn."

"Flying unicorn," John Roy repeated almost to himself.

"Well, I'll be damned," Richie lied again. "My poem is about a white flying unicorn."

"It'd make a good album cover," John Roy said, looking at Wally. "I could write a song about homecoming, that horse, Connie Appleton, but I wouldn't use her name. You know."

Richie sighed. He wasn't getting through. He knew it. He was doomed to his uniform.

"You got a card?" John Roy asked.

"No," said Wally.

"Well, you can write your name and number down for me and I'll have someone call you."

"You'd forget," said Wally. "You'd shove it in your pocket and forget and five months from now you'd forget why you wrote my name and number and throw it away."

John Roy adjusted his cowboy hat and grinned.

"You may be right, but don't count on it. You want to take my picture?"

"No," said Wally, taking the gun out of his pocket and aiming it at the singer.

"Wally," Richie cried out from behind the desk.

John Roy Worth looked at the gun and lost his grin.

"Hold it, Wally. I've got about five hundred dollars in my wallet. I'll just pull it out and hand it over. Put the gun away and we'll call it a loan, no, a first payment for the flying-horse album cover."

"Not about money," said Wally. "I've got eleven thousand, four hundred and six dollars in savings at First Farmers."

"I do something to you?" asked John Roy. "I mean, you got a grudge, something? I knock up your sister or cousin or something, insult you or your family? Hell, I was a kid."

"You're everybody," Wally said as John Roy started to raise his arms, though no one had asked him to.

John Roy glanced at Richie for help. Richie had none.

The idea had just come to Wally. Right out of the blue nowhere.

John Roy Worth was everybody. John Roy Worth wasn't just a country singer who used to live in Bardo, Texas. John Roy was Texas, was the United States, was the world. The world had no meaning. That's what had started Wally down this gun-weighted road. It was all made up. All a story people told each other to make them forget they were going to die and the world was going to blow up or blow away or freeze or burn someday.

Maybe Monty had said something like this once and the idea had just slept all curled up inside him and woke up just now wondering what was going on.

Wally was going to be a shooting star. He was going to be a bright light for a few seconds. He was going to shoot a star. He was going to be a star. It was that or just keep painting signs till his fingers got too much arthritis like his father's had and then he'd live alone in the house and watch television with his mother and father and eat cereal with freeze-dried fruit in it that got soggy when you added milk.

Richie said, "Wally, no."

Wally pulled the trigger. He was no more than a dozen feet from John Roy Worth, but he had never fired a gun before and missed, shattering the window behind the man who had written and sung "Hard-Drinking Woman."

Then, in that little snip of an instant that hardly covered any real time and seemed like a dream, Wally saw the young cowboy drop to the floor and pull something out of his pocket.

Wally was going to fire again. Maybe he did. He didn't remember. The thump on his chest like someone jabbing him to make a point pushed him back a step. Then something stuck in his throat the way a big vitamin pill did sometimes. He dropped to his knees and felt like coughing and sneezing at the same time. And then Wally fell forward on his face into shattered glass from the window.

The gun was no longer in his hand. Nothing was in his hand. His head was to his left side. He could see shards and bits of glass forming some kind of figure. He imagined chance or God or his own imagination was starting to make a stained-glass window. A flying white horse?

Someone turned him over. He looked up at John Roy Worth, who held a little gun in his hand. John Roy was shouting, "Call the police!"

Wally wanted to talk but words wouldn't come.

"You crazy son of a bitch," John Roy said.

Somewhere far away, maybe as far as Houston, Richie was talking to someone on the phone.

"Hero," Wally gasped, and choked.

John Roy brushed some shards of glass from Wally's face.

"You're no hero," said John Roy. "Just be quiet. Police are coming."

"No," said Wally. "You. You're the hero. Shot it out with a crazy sign painter. Beat him to the draw. All over the news. That gun registered?"

John Roy nodded and tilted his cowboy hat back like Roy Rogers or James Garner.

Wally wanted to say something else. He wasn't sure what it was, but it didn't matter because he could no longer speak. He closed his eyes. John Roy lifted Wally's head and Wally suddenly, vividly saw the flying white unicorn and John Roy Worth astride it, cowboy hat in one hand, horse bucking in the clouds.

Someone was breathing into his mouth. John Roy was trying to keep him alive. Hero.

It was then that Wally Czerbiak decided not to die. And he didn't.

DENNIS LEHANE

Until Gwen

FROM *The Atlantic Monthly*

YOUR FATHER picks you up from prison in a stolen Dodge Neon, with an 8-ball of coke in the glove compartment and a hooker named Mandy in the back seat. Two minutes into the ride, the prison still hanging tilted in the rearview, Mandy tells you that she only hooks part-time. The rest of the time she does light secretarial for an independent video chain and tends bar, two Sundays a month, at the local VFW. But she feels her calling — her true calling in life — is to write.

You go, "Books?"

"Books." She snorts, half out of amusement, half to shoot a line off your fist and up her left nostril. "Screenplays!" She shouts it at the dome light for some reason. "You know — movies."

"Tell him the one about the psycho saint guy." Your father winks at you in the rearview, like he's driving the two of you to the prom. "Go ahead. Tell him."

"OK, OK." She turns on the seat to face you, and your knees touch, and you think of Gwen, a look she gave you once, nothing special, just looking back at you as she stood at the front door, asking if you'd seen her keys. A forgettable moment if ever there was one, but you spent four years in prison remembering it.

". . . so at his canonization," Mandy is saying, "something, like, happens? And his spirit comes *back* and goes into the body of this priest. But, like, the priest? He has a brain tumor. He doesn't know it or nothing, but *he* does, and it's fucking up his, um —"

"Brain?" you try.

"Thoughts," Mandy says. "So he gets this saint in him and that *does it,* because, like, even though the guy was a saint, his spirit has become evil, because his soul is gone. So this priest? He spends the rest of the movie trying to kill the Pope."

"Why?"

"Just listen," your father says. "It gets good."

You look out the window. A car sits empty along the shoulder. It's beige, and someone has painted gold wings on the sides, fanning out from the front bumper and across the doors. A sign is affixed to the roof with some words on it, but you've passed it by the time you think to wonder what it says.

"See, there's this secret group that works for the Vatican? They're like a, like a . . ."

"A hit squad," your father says.

"Exactly," Mandy says, and presses her finger to your nose. "And the lead guy, the, like, head agent? He's the hero. He lost his wife and daughter in a terrorist attack on the Vatican a few years back, so he's a little fucked up, but —"

You say, "Terrorists attacked the Vatican?"

"Huh?"

You look at her, waiting. She has a small face, eyes too close to her nose.

"In the *movie,*" Mandy says. "Not in real life."

"Oh. I just — you know, four years inside, you assume you missed a couple of headlines, but . . ."

"Right." Her face is dark and squally now. "Can I finish?"

"I'm just saying," you say and snort another line off your fist, "even the guys on death row would have heard about that one."

"Just go with it," your father says. "It's not, like, real life."

You look out the window, see a guy in a chicken suit carrying a can of gas in the breakdown lane, think how real life isn't like real life. Probably more like this poor dumb bastard running out of gas in a car with wings painted on it. Wondering how the hell he ever got here. Wondering who he'd pissed off in that previous real life.

Your father has rented two rooms at an Econo Lodge so that you and Mandy can have some privacy, but you send Mandy home after she twice interrupts the sex to pontificate on the merits of Michael Bay films.

You sit in the blue-wash flicker of ESPN and eat peanuts from a plastic bag you got out of a vending machine and drink plastic cupfuls of Jim Beam from a bottle your father presented when you reached the motel parking lot. You think of the time you've lost, and how nice it is to sit alone on a double bed and watch TV, and you think of Gwen, can taste her tongue for just a moment, and you think about the road that's led you here to this motel room on this night after forty-seven months in prison, and how a lot of people would say it was a twisted road, a weird one, filled with curves, but you just think of it as a road like any other. You drive down it on faith, or because you have no other choice, and you find out what it's like by the driving of it, find out what the end looks like only by reaching it.

Late the next morning your father wakes you, tells you he drove Mandy home and you've got things to do, people to see.

Here's what you know about your father above all else: people have a way of vanishing in his company.

He's a professional thief, a consummate con man, an expert in his field — and yet something far beyond professionalism is at his core, something unreasonably arbitrary. Something he keeps within himself like a story he heard once, laughed at maybe, yet swore never to repeat.

"She was with you last night?" you say.

"You didn't want her. Somebody had to prop her ego back up. Poor girl like that."

"But you drove her home," you say.

"I'm speaking Czech?"

You hold his eyes for a bit. They're big and bland, with the heartless innocence of a newborn's. Nothing moves in them, nothing breathes, and after a while you say, "Let me take a shower."

"Fuck the shower," he says. "Throw on a baseball cap and let's get."

You take the shower anyway, just to feel it, another of those things you would have realized you'd miss if you'd given it any thought ahead of time — standing under the spray, no one near you, all the hot water you want for as long as you want it, shampoo that doesn't smell like factory smoke.

Drying your hair and brushing your teeth, you can hear the old man flicking through channels, never pausing on one for more than thirty seconds: Home Shopping Network — zap. Springer — zap. Oprah — zap. Soap-opera voices, soap-opera music — zap. Monster-truck show — pause. Commercial — zap, zap, zap.

You come back into the room, steam trailing you, pick your jeans up off the bed, and put them on.

The old man says, "Afraid you'd drowned. Worried I'd have to take a plunger to the drain, suck you back up."

You say, "Where we going?"

"Take a drive." Your father shrugs, flicking past a cartoon.

"Last time you said that, I got shot twice."

Your father looks back over his shoulder at you, eyes big and soft. "Wasn't the car that shot you, was it?"

You go out to Gwen's place, but she isn't there anymore. A couple of black kids are playing in the front yard, black mother coming out on the porch to look at the strange car idling in front of her house.

"You didn't leave it here?" your father says.

"Not that I recall."

"Think."

"I'm thinking."

"So you didn't?"

"I told you — not that I recall."

"So you're sure."

"Pretty much."

"You had a bullet in your head."

"Two."

"I thought one glanced off."

You say, "Two bullets hit your fucking head, old man, you don't get hung up on the particulars."

"That how it works?" Your father pulls away from the curb as the woman comes down the steps.

The first shot came through the back window, and Gentleman Pete flinched. He jammed the wheel to the right and drove the car straight into the highway exit barrier, air bags exploding, water barrels exploding, something in the back of your head exploding, glass pebbles filling your shirt, Gwen going, "What happened? Jesus. What happened?"

You pulled her with you out the back door — Gwen, your Gwen — and you crossed the exit ramp and ran into the woods and the second shot hit you there but you kept going, not sure how, not sure why, the blood pouring down your face, your head on fire, burning so bright and so hard that not even the rain could cool it off.

"And you don't remember nothing else?" your father says. You've driven all over town, every street, every dirt road, every hollow you can stumble across in Sumner, West Virginia.

"Not till she dropped me off at the hospital."

"Dumb goddamn move if ever there was one."

"I seem to remember I was puking blood by that point, talking all funny."

"Oh, you remember that. Sure."

"You're telling me in all this time you never talked to Gwen?"

"Like I told you three years back, that girl got gone."

You know Gwen. You love Gwen. This part of it is hard to take. You remember Gwen in your car and Gwen in the cornstalks and Gwen in her mother's bed in the hour just before noon, naked and soft. You watched a drop of sweat appear from her hairline and slide down the side of her neck as she snored against your shoulder blade, and the arch of her foot was pressed over the top of yours, and you watched her sleep, and you were so awake.

"So it's with her," you say.

"No," the old man says, a bit of anger creeping into his puppy-fur voice. "You called me. That night."

"I did?"

"Shit, boy. You called me from the pay phone outside the hospital."

"What'd I say?"

"You said, 'I hid it. It's safe. No one knows where but me.'"

"Wow," you say. "I said all that? Then what'd I say?"

The old man shakes his head. "Cops were pulling up by then, calling you 'motherfucker,' telling you to drop the phone. You hung up."

The old man pulls up outside a low red-brick building behind a tire dealership on Oak Street. He kills the engine and gets out of the car, and you follow. The building is two stories. Facing the street are the office of a bail bondsman, a hardware store, a Chinese takeout place with greasy walls the color of an old dog's teeth, and a hair salon called Girlfriend Hooked Me Up that's filled with black women. Around the back, past the whitewashed windows of what was once a dry cleaner, is a small black door with the words TRUE-LINE EFFICIENCY EXPERTS CORP. stenciled on the frosted glass.

The old man unlocks the door and leads you into a ten-by-ten room that smells of roast chicken and varnish. He pulls the string of a bare light bulb, and you look around at a floor strewn with envelopes and paper, the only piece of furniture a broken-down desk probably left behind by the previous tenant.

Your father crab-walks across the floor, picking up envelopes that have come through the mail slot, kicking his way through the paper. You pick up one of the pieces of paper and read it.

Dear Sirs,

Please find enclosed my check for $50. I look forward to receiving the information packet we discussed as well as the sample test. I have enclosed a SASE to help facilitate this process. I hope to see you someday at the airport!

Sincerely,
Jackson A. Willis

You let it drop to the floor and pick up another one.

To Whom It May Concern:

Two months ago, I sent a money order in the amount of fifty dollars to your company in order that I may receive an information packet and sample test so that I could take the US government test and become a security handler and fulfill my patriotic duty against the al Qadas. I have not received my information packet as yet and no one answers when I call your phone. Please send me that information packet so I can get that job.

Yours truly,
Edwin Voeguarde
12 Hinckley Street
Youngstown, OH 44502

You drop this one to the floor too, and watch your father sit on the corner of the desk and open his fresh pile of envelopes with a penknife. He reads some, pauses only long enough with others to shake the checks free and drop the rest to the floor.

You let yourself out, go to the Chinese place and buy a cup of Coke, go into the hardware store and buy a knife and a couple of tubes of Krazy Glue, stop at the car for a minute, and then go back into your father's office.

"What're you selling this time?" you say.

"Airport security jobs," he says, still opening envelopes. "It's a booming market. Everyone wants in. Stop them bad guys before they get on the plane, make the papers, serve your country, and maybe be lucky enough to get posted near one of them Starbucks kiosks. Hell."

"How much you made?"

Your father shrugs, though you're certain he knows the figure right down to the last penny.

"I've done all right. Hell else am I going to do, back in this shit town for three months, waiting on you? 'Bout time to shut this down, though." He holds up a stack of about sixty checks. "Deposit these and cash out the account. First two months, though? I was getting a thousand, fifteen hundred checks a week. Thank the good Lord for being selective with the brain tissue, you know?"

"Why?" you say.

"Why what?"

"Why you been hanging around for three months?"

Your father looks up from the stack of checks, squints. "To prepare a proper welcome for you."

"A bottle of whiskey and a hooker who gives lousy head? That took you three months?"

Your father squints a little more, and you see a shaft of gray between the two of you, not quite what you'd call light, just a shaft of air or atmosphere or something, swimming with motes, your father on the other side of it looking at you like he can't quite believe you're related.

After a minute or so your father says, "Yeah."

Your father told you once you'd been born in New Jersey. Another time he said New Mexico. Then Idaho. Drunk as a skunk a few months before you got shot, he said, "No, no. I'll tell you the truth. You were born in Las Vegas. That's in Nevada."

You went on the Internet to look yourself up but never did find anything.

*

Your mother died when you were seven. You've sat up at night occasionally and tried to picture her face. Some nights you can't see her at all. Some nights you'll get a quick glimpse of her eyes or her jawline, see her standing by the foot of her bed, rolling her stockings on, and suddenly she'll appear whole cloth, whole human, and you can smell her.

Most times, though, it's somewhere in between. You see a smile she gave you, and then she'll vanish. See a spatula she held turning pancakes, her eyes burning for some reason, her mouth an O, and then her face is gone and all you can see is the wallpaper. And the spatula.

You asked your father once why he had no pictures of her. Why hadn't he taken a picture of her? Just one lousy picture?

He said, "You think it'd bring her back? No, I mean, do you? Wow," he said, and rubbed his chin. "Wouldn't that be cool."

You said, "Forget it."

"Maybe if we had a whole album of pictures?" your father said. "She'd, like, pop out from time to time, make us breakfast."

Now that you've been in prison, you've been documented, but even they'd had to make it up, take your name as much on faith as you. You have no Social Security number or birth certificate, no passport. You've never held a job.

Gwen said to you once, "You don't have anyone to tell you who you are, so you don't *need* anyone to tell you. You just are who you are. You're beautiful."

And with Gwen that was usually enough. You didn't need to be defined — by your father, your mother, a place of birth, a name on a credit card or a driver's license or the upper left corner of a check. As long as her definition of you was something she could live with, then you could, too.

You find yourself standing in a Nebraska wheat field. You're seventeen years old. You learned to drive five years earlier. You were in school once, for two months when you were eight, but you read well and you can multiply three-digit numbers in your head faster than a calculator, and you've seen the country with the old man. You've learned people aren't that smart. You've learned how to pull lottery-ticket scams and asphalt-paving scams and get free meals with a slight upturn of your brown eyes. You've learned that if you hold ten dollars in front of a stranger, he'll pay twenty to get his hands on it if you play him right. You've learned that every good lie is threaded with truth and every accepted truth leaks lies.

You're seventeen years old in that wheat field. The night breeze smells of wood smoke and feels like dry fingers as it lifts your bangs off your forehead. You remember everything about that night because it is the night you met Gwen. You are two years away from prison, and you feel like someone has finally given you permission to live.

This is what few people know about Sumner, West Virginia: every now and then someone finds a diamond. Some dealers were in a plane that went down in a storm in '51, already blown well off course, flying a crate of Israeli stones down the eastern seaboard toward Miami. Plane went down near an open mineshaft, took some swing-shift miners with it. The government showed up, along with members of an international gem consortium, got the bodies out of there, and went to work looking for the diamonds. Found most of them, or so they claimed, but for decades afterward rumors persisted, occasionally given credence by the sight of a miner, still grimed brown by the shafts, tooling around town in an Audi.

You'd been in Sumner peddling hurricane insurance in trailer parks when word got around that someone had found a diamond as big as a casino chip. Miner by the name of George Brunda, suddenly buying drinks, talking to his travel agent. You and Gwen shot pool with him one night, and you could see his dread in the bulges under his eyes, the way his laughter exploded too high and too fast.

He didn't have much time, old George, and he knew it, but he had a mother in a rest home, and he was making the arrangements to get her transferred. George was a fleshy guy, triple-chinned, and dreams he'd probably forgotten he'd ever had were rediscovered and weighted in his face, jangling and pulling the flesh.

"Probably hasn't been laid in twenty years," Gwen said when George went to the bathroom. "It's sad. Poor sad George. Never knew love."

Her pool stick pressed against your chest as she kissed you, and you could taste the tequila, the salt, and the lime on her tongue.

"Never knew love," she whispered in your ear, an ache in the whisper.

*

"What about the fairground?" your father says as you leave the office of True-Line Efficiency Experts Corp. "Maybe you hid it there. You always had a fondness for that place."

You feel a small hitch. In your leg, let's say. Just a tiny clutching sensation in the back of your right calf. But you walk through it, and it goes away.

You say to your father as you reach the car, "You really drive her home this morning?"

"Who?"

"Mandy?"

"Who's . . .?" Your father opens his door, looks at you over it. "Oh, the whore?"

"Yeah."

"Did I drive her home?"

"Yeah."

Your father pats the top of the door, the cuff of his denim jacket flapping around his wrist, his eyes on you. You feel, as you always have, reflected in them, even when you aren't, couldn't be, wouldn't be.

"Did I drive her home?" A smile bounces in the rubber of your father's face.

"Did you drive her home?" you say.

That smile's all over the place now — the eyebrows, too. "Define home."

You say, "I wouldn't know, would I?"

"You're still pissed at me because I killed Fat Boy."

"George."

"What?"

"His name was George."

"He would have ratted."

"To who? It wasn't like he could file a claim. Wasn't a fucking lottery ticket."

Your father shrugs, looks off down the street.

"I just want to know if you drove her home."

"I drove her home," your father says.

"Yeah?"

"Oh, sure."

"Where'd she live?"

"Home," he says, and gets behind the wheel, starts the ignition.

*

You never figured George Brunda for smart, and only after a full day in his house, going through everything down to the point of removing the drywall and putting it back, resealing it, touching up the paint, did Gwen say, "Where's the mother stay again?"

That took uniforms, Gwen as a nurse, you as an orderly, Gentleman Pete out in the car while your father kept watch on George's mine entrance and monitored police activity over a scanner.

The old lady said, "You're new here, and quite pretty," as Gwen shot her up with phenobarbital and Valium and you went to work on the room.

This was the glitch: You'd watched George drive to work, watched him enter the mine. No one saw him come back out again, because no one was looking on the other side of the hill, at the exit of a completely different shaft. So while your father watched the front, George took off out the back, drove over to check on his investment, walked into the room just as you pulled the rock from the back of the mother's radio, George looking politely surprised, as if he'd stepped into the wrong room.

He smiled at you and Gwen, held up a hand in apology, and backed out of the room.

Gwen looked at the door, looked at you.

You looked at Gwen, looked at the window, looked at the rock filling the center of your palm, the entire center of your palm. Looked at the door.

Gwen said, "Maybe we —"

And George came through the door again, nothing polite in his face, a gun in his hand. And not any regular gun — a motherfucking six-shooter, like they carried in Westerns, long, thin barrel, a family heirloom maybe, passed down from a great-great-great-grandfather, not even a trigger guard, just the trigger, and crazy fat George the lonely unloved pulling back on it and squeezing off two rounds, the first of which went out the window, the second of which hit metal somewhere in the room and then bounced off that. The old lady went *"Ooof,"* even though she was doped up and passed out, and it sounded to you like she'd eaten something that didn't agree with her. You could picture her sitting in a restaurant, halfway through coffee, placing a hand to her belly, saying it: *"Ooof."* And George would come around to her chair and say, "Is everything OK, Mama?"

But he wasn't doing that now, because the old lady went ass-end-up out of the bed and hit the floor, and George dropped the gun and stared at her and said, "You shot my mother."

And you said, "*You* shot your mother," your entire body jetting sweat through the pores all at once.

"No, you did. No, you did."

You said, "Who was holding the fucking gun?"

But George didn't hear you. George jogged three steps and dropped to his knees. The old lady was on her side, and you could see blood staining the back of her white johnny.

George cradled her face, looked into it, and said, "Mother. Oh, Mother, oh, Mother, oh, Mother."

And you and Gwen ran right the fuck out of that room.

In the car Gwen said, "You saw it, right? He shot his own mother."

"He did?"

"He did," she said. "Baby, she's not going to die from that."

"Maybe. She's old."

"She's old, yeah. The fall from the bed was worse."

"We shot an old lady."

"We didn't shoot her."

"In the ass."

"We didn't shoot anyone. He had the gun."

"That's how it'll play, though. You know that. An old lady. Christ."

Gwen's eyes were the size of that diamond as she looked at you, and then she said, *"Ooof."*

"Don't start," you said.

"I can't help it, Bobby. Jesus."

She said your name. That's your name — Bobby. You loved hearing her say it.

Sirens were coming up the road behind you now, and you were looking at her and thinking, This isn't funny, it isn't, it's fucking sad, that poor old lady, and thinking, OK, it's sad, but God, Gwen, I will never, ever live without you. I just can't imagine it anymore. I want to . . . What?

Wind was pouring into the car, and the sirens were growing louder, an army of them, and Gwen's face was an inch from yours, her hair falling from behind her ear and whipping across her mouth, and she was looking at you, she was seeing you — really *see-*

ing you. Nobody'd ever done that, nobody. She was tuned to you like a radio tower out on the edge of the unbroken fields of wheat, blinking red under a dark-blue sky, and that night breeze lifting your bangs was her, for Christ's sake, her, and she was laughing, her hair in her teeth, laughing because the old lady had fallen out of the bed and it wasn't funny, it wasn't, and you said the first part in your head, the "I want to" part, but you said the second part aloud: "Dissolve into you."

And Gentleman Pete, up there at the wheel, on this dark country road, said, "What?"

But Gwen said, "I know, baby. I know." And her voice broke around the words, broke in the middle of her laughter and her fear and her guilt, and she took your face in her hands as Pete drove up on the interstate, and you saw all those siren lights washing across the back window like Fourth of July ice cream. Then the window came down like yanked netting and chucked glass pebbles into your shirt, and you felt something in your head go all shifty and loose and hot as a cigarette coal.

The fairground is empty, and you and your father walk around for a bit. The tarps over some of the booths have come undone at the corners, and they rustle and flap, caught between the wind and the wood, and your father watches you, waiting for you to remember, and you say, "It's coming back to me. A little."

Your father says, "Yeah?"

You hold up your hand, tip it from side to side.

Out behind the cages where, in summer, they set up the dunking machine and the bearded lady's chair and the fast-pitch machines, you see a fresh square of dirt, recently tilled, and you stand over it until your old man stops beside you, and you say, "Mandy?"

The old man chuckles softly, scuffs at the dirt with his shoe, looks off at the horizon.

"I held it in my hand, you know," you say.

"I'd figure," the old man says.

It's quiet, the land flat and metal-blue and empty for miles in every direction, and you can hear the rustle of the tarps and nothing else, and you know that the old man has brought you here to kill you. Picked you up from prison to kill you. Brought you into the world, probably, so eventually he could kill you.

"Covered the center of my palm."

"Big, huh?"

"Big enough."

"Running out of patience, boy," your father says.

You nod. "I'd guess you would be."

"Never my strong suit."

"No."

"This has been nice," your father says, and sniffs the air. "Like old times, reconnecting and all that."

"I told her that night to just go, just put as much country as she could between you and her until I got out. I told her to trust no one. I told her you'd stay hot on her trail even when all logic said you'd quit. I told her even if I told you I had it, you'd have to cover your bets — you'd have to come looking for her."

Your father looks at his watch, looks off at the sky again.

"I told her if you ever caught up to her, to take you to the fair-ground."

"Who's this we're talking about?"

"Gwen." Saying her name to the air, to the flapping tarps, to the cold.

"You don't say." Your father's gun comes out now. He taps it against his outer knee.

"Told her to tell you that's all she knew. I'd hid it here. Some-where here."

"Lotta ground."

You nod.

Your father turns so you are facing, his hands crossed over his groin, the gun there, waiting.

"The kinda money that stone'll bring," your father says, "a man could retire."

"To what?" you say.

"Mexico."

"To what, though?" you say. "Mean old man like you? What else you got, you ain't stealing something, killing somebody, making sure no one alive has a good fucking day?"

The old man shrugs, and you watch his brain go to work, some-thing bugging him finally, something he hasn't considered until now.

"It just come to me," he says.

"What's that?"

"You've known for, what, three years now that Gwen is no more?"

"Dead."

"If you like," your father says. "Dead."

"Yeah."

"Three years," your father says. "Lotta time to think."

You nod.

"Plan."

You give him another nod.

Your father looks down at the gun in his hand. "This going to fire?"

You shake your head.

Your father says, "It's loaded. I can feel the mag weight."

"Jack the slide," you say.

He gives it a few seconds and then tries. He yanks back hard, bending over a bit, but the slide is stone.

"Krazy Glue," you say. "Filled the barrel too."

You pull your hand from your pocket, open up the knife. You're very talented with a knife. Your father knows this. He's seen you win money this way, throwing knives at targets, dancing blades between your fingers in a blur.

You say, "Wherever you buried her, you're digging her out."

The old man nods. "I got a shovel in the trunk."

You shake your head. "With your hands."

Dawn is coming up, the sky bronzed with it along the lower reaches, when you let the old man use the shovel. His nails are gone, blood crusted black all over the older cuts, red seeping out of the newer ones. The old man broke down crying once. Another time he got mean, told you you weren't his anyway, some whore's kid he found in a barrel, decided might come in useful on a missing-baby scam they were running back then.

You say, "Was this in Las Vegas? Or Idaho?"

When the shovel hits bone, you say, "Toss it back up here," and step back as the old man throws the shovel out of the grave.

The sun is up now, and you watch the old man claw away the dirt for a while, and then there she is, all black and rotted, bones exposed in some places, her rib cage reminding you of the scales of a large fish you saw dead on a beach once in Oregon.

The old man says, "Now what?" and tears flee his eyes and drip off his chin.

"What'd you do with her clothes?"

"Burned 'em."

"I mean, why'd you take 'em off in the first place?"

The old man looks back at the bones, says nothing.

"Look closer," you say. "Where her stomach used to be."

The old man squats, peering, and you pick up the shovel.

Until Gwen, you had no idea who you were. None. During Gwen, you knew. After Gwen, you're back to wondering.

You wait. The old man keeps cocking and recocking his head to get a better angle, and finally, finally, he sees it.

"Well," he says, "I'll be damned."

You hit him in the head with the shovel, and the old man says, "Now, hold on," and you hit him again, seeing her face, the mole on her left breast, her laughing once with a mouth full of popcorn. The third swing makes the old man's head tilt funny on his neck, and you swing once more to be sure and then sit down, feet dangling into the grave.

You look at the blackened, shriveled thing lying below your father, and you see her face with the wind coming through the car and her hair in her teeth and her eyes seeing you and taking you into her like food, like blood, like what she needed to breathe, and you say, "I wish . . ." and sit there for a long time with the sun beginning to warm the ground and warm your back and the breeze returning to make those tarps flutter again, desperate and soft.

"I wish I'd taken your picture," you say finally. "Just once."

And you sit there until it's almost noon and weep for not protecting her and weep for not being able to know her ever again, and weep for not knowing what your real name is, because whatever it is or could have been is buried with her, beneath your father, beneath the dirt you begin throwing back in.

LAURA LIPPMAN

The Shoeshine Man's Regrets

FROM *Murder . . . and All That Jazz*

"BRUNO MAGLI?"

"Uh-uh. Bally."

"How can you be so sure?"

"Some kids get flashcards of farm animals when they're little. I think my mom showed me pictures of footwear cut from magazines. After all, she couldn't have her only daughter bringing home someone who wore white patent loafers, even in the official season between Memorial Day and Labor Day. Speaking of which — there's a full Towson."

"Wow — white shoes *and* white belt and white tie, and ten miles south of his natural habitat, the Baltimore County courthouse. I thought the full Towson was on the endangered clothing list."

"Bad taste never dies. It just keeps evolving."

Tess Monaghan and Whitney Talbot were standing outside the Brass Elephant on a soft June evening, studying the people ahead of them in the valet parking line. A laundry truck had blocked the driveway to the restaurant's lot, disrupting the usually smooth operation, so the restaurant's patrons were milling about, many agitated. There was muttered talk of symphony tickets and the Orioles game and the Herzog retrospective at the Charles Theatre.

But Tess and Whitney, mellowed by martinis, eggplant appetizers, and the perfect weather, had no particular place to go and no great urgency about getting there. They had started cataloging the clothes and accessories of those around them only because Tess had confided to Whitney that she was trying to sharpen her powers of observation. It was a reasonable exercise in self-improvement for a private detective — and a great sport for someone as congenitally catty as Whitney.

The two friends were inventorying another man's loafers — Florsheim, Tess thought, but Whitney said good old-fashioned Weejuns — when they noticed a glop of white on one toe. And then, as if by magic, a shoeshine man materialized at the elbow of the Weejun wearer's elbow.

"You got something there, mister. Want me to give you a quick shine?"

Tess, still caught up in her game of cataloging, saw that the shoeshine man was old, but then, all shoeshine men seemed old these days. She often wondered where the next generation of shoeshine men would came from, if they were also on the verge of extinction, like the Towson types who sported white belts with white shoes. This man was thin, with a slight stoop to his shoulders and a tremble in his limbs, his salt-and-pepper hair cropped close. He must be on his way home from the train station or the Belvedere Hotel, Tess concluded, heading toward a bus stop on one of the major east-west streets farther south, near the city's center.

"What the — ?" Mr. Weejun was short and compact, with a yellow polo shirt tucked into lime green trousers. A golfer, Tess decided, noticing his florid face and sunburned bald spot. She was not happy to see him waiting for a car, given how many drinks he had tossed back in the Brass Elephant's Tusk Lounge. He was one of the people who kept braying about his Orioles tickets.

Now he extended his left foot, pointing his toe in a way that reminded Tess of the dancing hippos in *Fantasia,* and stared at the white smear on his shoe in anger and dismay.

"You *bastard,*" he said to the shoeshine man. "How did you get that shit on my shoe?"

"I didn't do anything, sir. I was just passing by, and I saw that your shoe was dirty. Maybe you tracked in something in the restaurant."

"It's some sort of scam, isn't it?" The man appealed to the restless crowd, which was glad for any distraction at this point. "Anyone see how this guy got this crap on my shoe?"

"He didn't," Whitney said, her voice cutting the air with her usual conviction. "It was on your shoe when you came out of the restaurant."

It wasn't what Mr. Weejun wanted to hear, so he ignored her.

"Yeah, you can clean my shoe," he told the old man. "Just don't expect a tip."

The shoeshine man sat down his box and went to work quickly. "Mayonnaise," he said, sponging the mass from the shoe with a cloth. "Or salad dressing. Something like that."

"I guess you'd know," Weejun said. "Since you put it there."

"No, sir. I wouldn't do a thing like that."

The shoeshine man was putting the finishing touches on the man's second shoe when the valet pulled up in a Humvee. Taxicab yellow, Tess observed, still playing the game. Save the Bay license plates and a sticker that announced the man as a member of an exclusive downtown health club.

"Five dollars," the shoeshine man said, and Weejun pulled out a five with great ostentation — then handed it to the valet. "No rewards for scammers," he said with great satisfaction. But when he glanced around, apparently expecting some sort of affirmation for his boorishness, all he saw were shocked and disapproving faces.

With the curious logic of the disgraced, Weejun upped the ante, kicking the man's shoeshine kit so its contents spilled across the sidewalk. He then hopped into his Humvee, gunning the motor, although the effect of a quick getaway was somewhat spoiled by the fact that his emergency brake was on. The Humvee bucked, then shot forward with a squeal.

As the shoeshine man's hands reached for the spilled contents of his box, Tess saw him pick up a discarded soda can and throw it at the fender of the Humvee. It bounced off with a hollow, harmless sound, but the car stopped with a great squealing of brakes and Weejun emerged, spoiling for a fight. He threw himself on the shoeshine man.

But the older man was no patsy. He grabbed his empty box, landing it in his attacker's stomach with a solid, satisfying smack. Tess waited for someone, anyone, to do something, but no one moved. Reluctantly she waded in, tossing her cell phone to Whitney. Longtime friends who had once synched their movements in a women's four on the rowing team at Washington College, the two could still think in synch when necessary. Whitney called 911 while Tess grabbed Weejun by the collar and uttered a piercing scream as close to his ear as possible. "Stop it, asshole. The cops are coming."

The man nodded, seemed to compose himself — then charged

the shoeshine man again. Tess tried to hold him back by the belt, and he turned back, swinging out wildly, hitting her in the chin. Sad to say, this physical contact galvanized the crowd in a way that his attack on an elderly black man had not. By the time the blue-and-whites rolled up, the valet parkers were holding Weejun and Whitney was examining the fast-developing bruise on Tess's jaw with great satisfaction.

"You are so going to file charges against this asshole," she said.

"Well, I'm going to file charges against him, then," Weejun brayed, unrepentant. "He started the whole thing."

The patrol cop was in his midthirties, a seasoned officer who had broken up his share of fights, although probably not in this neighborhood. "If anyone's adamant about filing a report, it can be done, but it will involve about four hours down at the district."

That dimmed everyone's enthusiasm, even Whitney's.

"Good," the cop said. "I'll just take the bare details and let everyone go."

The laundry truck moved, the valet parking attendants regained their usual efficiency, and the crowd moved on, more anxious about their destinations than this bit of street theater. The shoeshine man started to walk away, but the cop motioned for him to stay, taking names and calling them in, along with DOBs. "Just routine," he told Tess, but his expression soon changed in a way that indicated the matter was anything but routine. He walked away from them, out of earshot, clicking the two-way on his shoulder on and off.

"You can go," he said to Whitney and Tess upon returning. "But I gotta take him in. There's a warrant."

"Him?" Whitney asked hopefully, jerking her chin at Weejun.

"No, him." The cop looked genuinely regretful. "Could be a mix-up, could be someone else using his name and DOB, but I still have to take him downtown."

"What's the warrant for?" Tess asked.

"Murder, if you really want to know."

Weejun looked at once gleeful and frightened, as if he were wondering just whom he had taken on in this fight. It would make quite a brag around the country club, Tess thought. He'd probably be telling his buddies he had taken on a homicidal maniac and won.

Yet the shoeshine man was utterly composed. He did not protest his innocence or insist that it was all a mistake, things that even a guilty man might have said under the circumstances. He simply sighed, cast his eyes toward the sky, as if asking a quick favor from his deity of choice, then said: "I'd like to gather up my things, if I could."

"It's the damnedest thing, Tess. He couldn't confess fast enough. Didn't want a lawyer, didn't ask any questions, just sat down and began talking as fast as he could."

Homicide detective Martin Tull, Tess's only real friend in the Baltimore Police Department, had caught the shoeshine man's case simply by answering the phone when the patrol cop called him about the warrant. He should be thrilled — it was an easy stat, about as easy as they come. No matter how old the case, it counted toward the current year's total of solved homicides.

"It's a little too easy," Tull said, sitting with Tess on a bench near one of their favorite coffeehouses, watching the water taxis zip back and forth across the Inner Harbor.

"Everyone gets lucky, even you," Tess said. "It's all too incredible that the warrant was lost all these years. What I don't get is how it was found."

"Department got some grant for computer work. Isn't that great? There's not enough money to make sure DNA samples are stored safely, but some think tank gave us money so college students can spend all summer keystroking data. The guy moved about two weeks after the murder, before he was named in the warrant. Moved all of five miles, from West Baltimore to the county, but he wasn't the kind of guy who left a forwarding address. Or the cop on the case was a bonehead. At any rate, he's gone forty years wanted for murder, and if he hadn't been in that fight night before last, he might've gone another forty."

"Did he even know there was a warrant on him?"

"Oh, yeah. He knew exactly why he was there. Story came out of him as if he had been rehearsing it for years. Kept saying, 'Yep, I did it, no doubt about it. You do what you have to do, Officer.' So we charged him, the judge put a hundred-grand bail on him, a bail bondsman put up ten thousand, and he went home."

"I guess someone who's lived at the same address for thirty-nine years isn't considered a flight risk."

"Flight risk? I think if I had left this guy in the room with all our opened files, he would have confessed to every homicide in Baltimore. I have never seen someone so eager to confess to a crime. I almost think he wants to go to jail."

"Maybe he's convinced that a city jury won't lock him up, or that he can get a plea. How did the victim die?"

"Blunt-force trauma in a burglary. There's no physical evidence, and the warrant was sworn out on the basis of an eyewitness who's been dead for ten years."

"So you probably couldn't get a conviction at all if it went to trial."

"Nope. That's what makes it so odd. Even if she were alive, she'd be almost ninety by now, pretty easy to break down on the stand."

"What's the file say?"

"Neighbor lady said she saw William Harrison leave the premises, acting strangely. She knew the guy because he did odd jobs in the neighborhood, even worked for her on occasion, but there was no reason for him to be at the victim's house so late at night."

"Good luck recovering the evidence from Evidence Control."

"Would you believe they still had the weapon? The guy's head was bashed in with an iron. But that's all I got. If the guy hadn't confessed, if he had stonewalled me or gotten with a lawyer, I wouldn't have anything."

"So what do you want me to tell you? I never met this man before we became impromptu tag-team wrestlers. He seemed pretty meek to me, but who knows what he was like forty years ago? Maybe he's just a guy with a conscience, who's been waiting all these years to see if someone's going to catch up with him."

Tull shook his head. "One thing. He didn't know what the murder weapon was. Said he forgot."

"Well, forty years. It's possible."

"Maybe." Tull, who had already finished his coffee, reached for Tess's absent-mindedly, grimacing when he realized it was a latte. Caffeine was his fuel, his vice of choice, and he didn't like it diluted in any way.

"Take the easy stat, Martin. Guy's named in a warrant, and he said he did it. He does have a temper, I saw that much. Last night it was a soda can. Forty years ago, it very well could have been an iron."

"I've got a conscience, too, you know." Tull looked offended.

Tess realized that it wasn't something she knew that had prompted Tull to call her up, but something he wanted her to do. Yet Tull would not ask her directly, because then he would be in her debt. He was a man, after all. But if she volunteered to do what he seemed to want, he would honor *her* next favor, and Tess was frequently in need of favors.

"I'll talk to him. See if he'll open up to his tag-team partner."

Tull didn't even so much as nod to acknowledge the offer. It was as if Tess's acquiescence were a belch, or something else that wouldn't be commented on in polite company.

The shoeshine man — William Harrison, Tess reminded herself, she had a name for him now — lived in a neat bungalow just over the line in what was known as the Woodlawn section of Baltimore County. Forty years ago, Mr. Harrison would have been one of its first black residents, and he would have been denied entrance to the amusement park only a few blocks from his house. Now the neighborhood was more black than white, but still middle class.

A tiny woman answered the door to Mr. Harrison's bungalow, her eyes bright and curious.

"Mrs. Harrison?"

"*Miss.*" There was a note of reprimand for Tess's assumption.

"My name is Tess Monaghan. I met your brother two nights ago in the, um, fracas."

"Oh, he felt so bad about that. He said it was shameful, how the only person who wanted to help him was a girl. He found it *appalling.*"

She drew out the syllables of the last word, as if it gave her some special pleasure.

"It was so unfair what happened to him. And then this mix-up with the warrant . . ."

The bright catlike eyes narrowed a bit. "What do you mean by mix-up?"

"Mr. Harrison just doesn't seem to me to be the kind of man who could kill someone."

"Well, he says he was." Spoken matter-of-factly, as if the topic were the weather or something else of little consequence. "I knew nothing about it, of course. The warrant or the murder."

"Of course," Tess agreed. This woman did not look like someone who had been burdened with a loved one's secret for four decades. Where her brother was stooped and grave, she had the regal posture of a short woman intent on using every inch given her, but there was something blithe, almost gleeful, beneath her dignity. Did she not like her brother?

"It was silly of William" — she stretched the name out, giving it a grand, growling pronunciation, Will-yum — "to tell his story and sign the statement, without even talking to a lawyer. I told him to wait, to see what they said, but he wouldn't."

"But if you knew nothing about it . . ."

"Nothing about it until two nights ago," Miss Harrison clarified. That was the word that popped into Tess's head, *clarified*, and she wondered at it. Clarifications were what people made when things weren't quite right.

"And were you shocked?"

"Oh, he had a temper when he was young. Anything was possible."

"Is your brother at home?"

"He's at work. We still have to eat, you know." Now she sounded almost angry. "He didn't think of that, did he, when he decided to be so noble. I told him this house may be paid off, but we still have to eat and buy gas for my car. Did you know they cut your Social Security off when you go to prison?"

Tess did not. She had relatives who were far from pure, but they had managed to avoid doing time. So far.

"Well," Miss Harrison said, "they do. But Will-yum didn't think of that, did he? Men are funny that way. They're so determined to be *gallant*"— again, the word was spoken with great pleasure, with the tone of a child trying to be grand — "that they don't think things through. He may feel better, but what about me?"

"Do you have no income, then?"

"I worked as a laundress. You don't get a pension for being a laundress. My brother, however, was a custodian for Social Security, right here in Woodlawn."

"I thought he shined shoes."

"Yes, *now*." Miss Harrison was growing annoyed with Tess. "But not always: William was enterprising, even as a young man. He worked as a custodian at Social Security, which is why he has Social Security. But he took on odd jobs, shined shoes. He hates to be idle. He won't like prison, no matter what he thinks."

"He did odd jobs for the man he killed, right?"

"Some. Not many. Really, hardly any at all. They barely knew each other."

Miss Harrison seemed to think this mitigated the crime somehow, that the superficiality of the relationship excused her brother's deed.

"Police always thought it was a burglary?" Tess hoped her tone would invite a confidence, or at least another clarification.

"Yes," she said. "Yes. That, too. Things were taken. Everyone knew that."

"So you were familiar with the case, but not your brother's connection to it?"

"Well, I knew the man. Maurice Dickman. We lived in the neighborhood, after all. And people talked, of course. It was a big deal, murder, forty years ago. Not the *happenstance* that it's become. But he was a showy man. He thought awfully well of himself, because he had money and a business. Perhaps he shouldn't have made such a spectacle of himself, and then no one would have tried to steal from him. You know what the Bible says, about the rich man and the camel and the eye of the needle? It's true, you know. Not always, but often enough."

"Why did your brother burglarize his home? Was that something else he did to supplement his paycheck? Is that something he still does?"

"My brother," Miss Harrison said, drawing herself up so she gained yet another inch, "is not a thief."

"But —"

"I don't like talking to you," she said abruptly. "I thought you were on our side, but I see now I was foolish. I know what happened. You called the police. You talked about pressing charges. If it weren't for you, none of this would have happened. You're a terrible person. Forty years, and trouble never came for us, and then you undid everything. You have brought us nothing but grief, which we can ill afford."

She stamped her feet, an impressive gesture, small though they were. Stamped her feet and went back inside the house, taking a moment to latch the screen behind her, as if Tess's manners were so suspect that she might try to follow where she clearly wasn't wanted.

*

The shoeshine man did work at Penn Station, after all, stationed in front of the old-fashioned wooden seats that always made Tess cringe a bit. There was something about one man perched above another that didn't sit quite right with her, especially when the other man was bent over the enthroned one's shoes.

Then again, pedicures probably looked pretty demeaning, too, depending on one's perspective.

"I'm really sorry, Mr. Harrison, about the mess I've gotten you into." She had refused to sit in his chair, choosing to lean against the wall instead.

"Got myself into, truth be told. If I hadn't thrown that soda can, none of this would have happened. I could have gone another forty years without anyone bothering me."

"But you could go to prison."

"Looks that way." He was almost cheerful about it.

"You should get a lawyer, get that confession thrown out. Without it, they've got nothing."

"They've got a closed case, that's what they've got. A closed case. And maybe I'll get probation."

"It's not a bad bet, but the stakes are awfully high. Even with a five-year sentence, you might die in prison."

"Might not," he said.

"Still, your sister seems pretty upset."

"Oh, Mattie's always getting upset about something. Our mother thought she was doing right by her, teaching her those Queen of Sheba manners, but all she did was make her perpetually disappointed. Now, if Mattie had been born just a decade later, she might have had a different life. But she wasn't, and I wasn't, and that's that."

"She did seem . . . refined," Tess said, thinking of the woman's impeccable appearance and the way she loved to stress big words.

"She was raised to be a lady. Unfortunately, she didn't have a lady's job. No shame in washing clothes, but no honor in it either, not for someone like Mattie. She should have stayed in school, become a teacher. But Mattie thought it would be easy to marry a man on the rise. She just didn't figure that a man on the rise would want a woman on the rise, too, that the manners and the looks wouldn't be enough. A man on the rise doesn't want a woman to get out of his bed and then wash his sheets, not unless she's already his wife. Mattie should never have dropped out of school. It was a shame, what she gave up."

"Being a teacher, you mean."

"Yeah," he said, his tone vague and faraway. "Yeah. She could have gone back, even after she dropped out, but she just stomped her feet and threw back that pretty head of hers. Threw back her pretty head and cried."

"Threw back her pretty head and cried — why does that sound familiar?"

"I couldn't tell you."

"Threw back her pretty head . . . I know that, but I can't place it."

"Couldn't help you." He began whistling a tune, "Begin the Beguine."

"Mr. Harrison — you didn't kill that man, did you?"

"Well, now, I say I did, and why would anyone want to argue with me? And I was seen coming from his house that night, sure as anything. That neighbor, Edna Buford, she didn't miss a trick on that block."

"What did you hit him with?"

"An iron," he said triumphantly. "An iron!"

"You didn't know that two days ago."

"I was nervous."

"You were anything but, from what I hear."

"I'm an old man. I don't always remember what I should."

"So it was an iron?"

"Definitely, one of those old-fashioned ones, cast iron. The kind you had to heat."

"The kind," Tess said, "that a man's laundress might use."

"Mebbe. Does it really matter? Does any of this really matter? If it did, would they have taken forty years to find me? I'll tell you this much — if Maurice Dickman had been a white man, I bet I wouldn't have been walking around all this time. He wasn't a nice man, Mr. Dickman, but the police didn't know that. For all they knew, he was a good citizen. A man was killed, and nobody cared. Except Edna Buford, peeking through her curtains. They should have found me long ago. Know something else?"

"What?" Tess leaned forward, assuming a confession was about to be made.

"I *did* put the mayonnaise on that man's shoe. It had been a light day here, and I wanted to pick up a few extra dollars on my way home. I'm usually better about picking my marks, though. I won't make that mistake again."

A lawyer of Tess's acquaintance, Tyner Gray, asked that the court throw out the charges against William Harrison on the grounds that his confession was coerced. A plea bargain was offered instead — five years probation. "I told you so," Mr. Harrison chortled to Tess, gloating a little at his prescience.

"Lifted up her lovely head and cried," Tess said.

"What?"

"That's the line I thought you were quoting. You said 'threw,' but the line was lifted. I had to feed it through Google a few different ways to nail it, but I did. 'Miss Otis Regrets.' It's about a woman who kills her lover, and is then hanged on the gallows."

"Computers are interesting," Mr. Harrison said.

"What did you really want? Were you still trying to protect your sister, as you've protected her all these years? Or were you just trying to get away from her for a while?"

"I have no idea what you're talking about. Mattie did no wrong in our mother's eyes. My mother loved that girl, and I loved for my mother to be happy."

So Martin Tull got his stat and a more-or-less clean conscience. Miss Harrison got her protective older brother back, along with his Social Security checks.

And Tess got an offer of free shoeshines for life, whenever she was passing through Penn Station. She politely declined Mr. Harrison's gesture. After all, he had already spent forty years at the feet of a woman who didn't know how to show gratitude.

TIM McLOUGHLIN

When All This Was Bay Ridge

FROM *Brooklyn Noir*

STANDING IN CHURCH at my father's funeral, I thought about being arrested on the night of my seventeenth birthday. It had occurred in the train yard at Avenue X, in Coney Island. Me and Pancho and a kid named Freddie were working a three-car piece, the most ambitious I'd tried to that point, and more time-consuming than was judicious to spend trespassing on city property. Two Transit cops with German shepherds caught us in the middle of the second car. I dropped my aerosol can and took off, and was perhaps two hundred feet along the beginning of the trench that becomes the IRT line to the Bronx, when I saw the hand. It was human, adult, and severed neatly, seemingly surgically, at the wrist. My first thought was that it looked bare without a watch. Then I made a whooping sound, trying to take in air, and turned and ran back toward the cops and their dogs.

At the 60th Precinct, we three were ushered into a small cell. We sat for several hours, then the door opened and I was led out. My father was waiting in the main room, in front of the counter.

The desk sergeant, middle-aged, black, and noticeably bored, looked up briefly. "Him?"

"Him," my father echoed, sounding defeated.

"Goodnight," the sergeant said.

My father took my arm and led me out of the precinct. As we cleared the door and stepped into the humid night he turned to me and said, "This was it. Your one free ride. It doesn't happen again."

"What did it cost?" I asked. My father had retired from the police department years earlier, and I knew this had been expensive.

He shook his head. "This once, that's all."

I followed him to his car. "I have two friends in there."

"Fuck 'em. Spics. That's half your problem."

"What's the other half?"

"You have no common sense," he said, his voice rising in scale as it did in volume. By the time he reached a scream he sounded like a boy going through puberty. "What do you think you're doing out here? Crawling 'round in the dark with the niggers and the spics. Writing on trains like a hoodlum. Is this all you'll do?"

"It's not writing. It's drawing. Pictures."

"Same shit, defacing property, behaving like a punk. Where do you suppose it will lead?"

"I don't know. I haven't thought about it. You had your aimless time, when you got out of the service. You told me so. You bummed around for two years."

"I always worked."

"Part-time. Beer money. You were a roofer."

"Beer money was all I needed."

"Maybe it's all I need."

He shook his head slowly, and squinted, as though peering through the dirty windshield for an answer. "It was different. That was a long time ago. Back when all this was Bay Ridge. You could live like that then."

When all this was Bay Ridge. He was masterful, my father. He didn't say *when it was white,* or *when it was Irish,* or even the relatively tame *when it was safer.* No. When all this was Bay Ridge. As though it were an issue of geography. As though, somehow, the tectonic plate beneath Sunset Park had shifted, moving it physically to some other place.

I told him about seeing the hand.

"Did you tell the officers?"

"No."

"The people you were with?"

"No."

"Then don't worry about it. There's body parts all over this town. Saw enough in my day to put together a baseball team." He drove in silence for a few minutes, then nodded his head a couple of times, as though agreeing with a point made by some voice I could not hear. "You're going to college, you know," he said.

*

That was what I remembered at the funeral. Returning from the altar rail after receiving Communion, Pancho walked past me. He'd lost a great deal of weight since I'd last seen him, and I couldn't tell if he was sick or if it was just the drugs. His black suit hung on him in a way that emphasized his gaunt frame. He winked at me as he came around the casket in front of my pew, and flashed the mischievous smile that — when we were sixteen — got all the girls in his bed and all the guys agreeing to the stupidest and most dangerous stunts.

In my shirt pocket was a photograph of my father with a woman who was not my mother. The date on the back was five years ago. Their arms were around each other's waists and they smiled for the photographer. When we arrived at the cemetery I took the picture out of my pocket, and looked at it for perhaps the fiftieth time since I'd first discovered it. There were no clues. The woman was young to be with my father, but not a girl. Forty, give or take a few years. I looked for any evidence in his expression that I was misreading their embrace, but even I couldn't summon the required naiveté. My father's countenance was not what would commonly be regarded as a poker face. He wasn't holding her as a friend, a friend's girl, or the prize at some retirement or bachelor party; he held her like a possession. Like he held his tools. Like he held my mother. The photo had been taken before my mother's death. I put it back.

I'd always found his plodding predictability and meticulous planning of insignificant events maddening. For the first time that I could recall, I was experiencing curiosity about some part of my father's life.

I walked from Greenwood Cemetery directly to Olsen's bar, my father's watering hole, feeling that I needed to talk to the men that nearly lived there, but not looking forward to it. Aside from my father's wake the previous night, I hadn't seen them in years. They were all Irish. The Irish among them were perhaps the most Irish, but the Norwegians and the Danes were Irish, too, as were the older Puerto Ricans. They had developed, over time, the stereotypical hooded gaze, the squared jaws set in grim defiance of whatever waited in the sobering daylight. To a man they had that odd trait of the Gaelic heavy-hitter, that — as they attained middle age — their faces increasingly began to resemble a woman's nipple.

The door to the bar was propped open, and the cool damp odor of stale beer washed over me before I entered. That smell has always reminded me of the Boy Scouts. Meetings were Thursday nights in the basement of Bethany Lutheran Church. When they were over, I would have to pass Olsen's on my way home, and I usually stopped in to see my father. He would buy me a couple of glasses of beer — about all I could handle at thirteen — and leave with me after about an hour so we could walk home together.

From the inside looking out: Picture an embassy in a foreign country. A truly foreign country. Not a Western European ally, but a fundamentalist state perennially on the precipice of war. A fill-the-sandbags-and-wait-for-the-airstrike enclave. That was Olsen's, home to the last of the donkeys, the white dinosaurs of Sunset Park. A jukebox filled with Kirsty MacColl and the Clancy Brothers, and fliers tacked to the flaking walls advertising step-dancing classes, Gaelic lessons, and the memorial run to raise money for a scholarship in the name of a recently slain cop. Within three blocks of the front door you could attend a cockfight, buy crack, or pick up a streetwalker, but in Olsen's, it was always 1965.

Upon entering the bar for the first time in several years, I found its pinched dimensions and dim lighting more oppressive, and less mysterious, than I had remembered. The row of ascetic faces, and the way all conversation trailed off at my entrance, put me in mind of the legendary blue wall of silence in the police department. It is no coincidence that the force has historically been predominantly Irish. The men in Olsen's would be pained to reveal their zip code to a stranger, and I wasn't sure if even they knew why.

The bar surface itself was more warped than I'd recalled. The mirrors had oxidized and the white tile floor had been torn up in spots and replaced with odd-shaped pieces of green linoleum. It was a neighborhood bar in a neighborhood where such establishments are not yet celebrated. If it had been located in my part of the East Village, it would have long since achieved cultural-landmark status. I'd been living in Manhattan for five years and still had not adjusted to the large number of people who moved here from other parts of the country, and overlooked the spectacle of the city only to revere the mundane. One of my coworkers, herself a transplant, remarked that the coffee shop on my corner was *authentic*. In that they served coffee, I suppose she was correct.

I sat on an empty stool in the middle of the wavy bar and ordered a beer. I felt strangely nervous there without my father, like a child about to be caught doing something bad. Everyone knew me. Marty, the round-shouldered bartender, approached first, breaking the ice. He spoke around an enormous, soggy stub of a cigar, as he always did. And, as always, he seemed constantly annoyed by its presence in his mouth; as though he'd never smoked one before, and was surprised to discover himself chewing on it.

"Daniel. It's good to see you. I'm sorry for your loss."

He extended one hand, and when I did the same, he grasped mine in both of his and held it for a moment. It had to have been some sort of signal, because the rest of the relics in the place lurched toward me then, like some nursing-home theater guild performing *Night of the Living Dead*. They shook hands, engaged in awkward stiff hugs, and offered unintelligible condolences. Frank Sanchez, one of my father's closest friends, squeezed the back of my neck absently until I winced. I thanked them as best I could, and accepted the offers of free drinks.

Someone — I don't know who — thought it would be a good idea for me to have Jameson's Irish whiskey, that having been my father's drink. I'd never considered myself much of a drinker. I liked a couple of beers on a Friday night, and perhaps twice a year I would get drunk. I almost never drank hard liquor, but this crew was insistent, they were matching me shot for shot, and they were paying. It was the sort of thing my father would have been adamant about.

I began to reach for the photograph in my pocket several times and stopped. Finally I fished it out and showed it to the bartender. "Who is she, Marty?" I asked. "Any idea?"

The manner in which he pretended to scrutinize it told me that he recognized the woman immediately. He looked at the picture with a studied perplexity, as though he would have had trouble identifying my father.

"Wherever did you get such a thing?" he asked.

"I found it in the basement, by my father's shop."

"Ah. Just come across it by accident then."

The contempt in his voice seared through my whiskey glow, and left me as sober as when I'd entered. He knew, and if he knew they all knew. And a decision had been reached to tell me nothing.

"Not by accident," I lied. "My father told me where it was and asked me to get it."

Our eyes met for a moment. "And did he say anything about it?" Marty asked. "Were there no instructions or suggestions?"

"He asked me to take care of it," I said evenly. "To make everything all right."

He nodded. "Makes good sense," he said. "That would be best served by letting the dead sleep, don't you think? Forget it, son, let it lie." He poured me another drink, sloppily, like the others, and resumed moving his towel over the bar, as though he could obliterate the mildewed stench of a thousand spilled drinks with a few swipes of the rag.

I drank the shot down quickly and my buzz returned in a rush. I hadn't been keeping track, but I realized that I'd had much more than what I was used to, and I was starting to feel dizzy. The rest of the men in the room looked the same as when I walked in, the same as when I was twelve. In the smoke-stained bar mirror I saw Frank Sanchez staring at me from a few stools away. He caught me looking and gestured for me to come down.

"Sit, Danny," he said when I got there. He was drinking boilermakers. Without asking, he ordered each of us another round. "What were you talking to Marty about?"

I handed Frank the picture. "I was asking who the woman is."

He looked at it and placed it on the bar. "Yeah? What'd he say?"

"He said to let it lie."

Frank snorted. "Typical donkey," he said. "Won't answer a straight question, but has all kinds of advice on what you should do."

From a distance in the dark bar I would have said that Frank Sanchez hadn't changed much over the years, but I was close to him now, and I'd seen him only last night in the unforgiving fluorescent lighting of the funeral home. He'd been thin and handsome when I was a kid, with blue-black hair combed straight back, and the features and complexion of a Hollywood Indian in a John Wayne picture. He'd thickened in the middle over the years, though he still wasn't fat. His reddish brown cheeks were illuminated by the roadmap of broken capillaries that seemed an entrance requirement for "regular" status at Olsen's. His hair was still shockingly dark, but now with a fake Jerry Lewis sheen and plenty of scalp showing through in the back. He was a retired homicide detective. His had been one of the first Hispanic families in this neighborhood. I knew he'd moved to Fort Lee, New Jersey, long ago, though my father said that he was still in Olsen's every day.

Frank picked up the picture and looked at it again, then looked over it at the two sloppy rows of bottles along the back bar. The gaps for the speed rack looked like missing teeth.

"We're the same," he said. "Me and you."

"The same, how?"

"We're on the outside, and we're always looking to be let in."

"I never gave a damn about being on the inside here, Frank."

He handed me the photo. "You do now."

He stood then, and walked stiffly back to the men's room. A couple of minutes later Marty appeared at my elbow, topped off my shot, and replaced Frank's.

"It's a funny thing about Francis," Marty said. "He's a spic who's always hated the spics. So he moves from a spic neighborhood to an all-white one, then has to watch as it turns spic. So now he's got to get in his car every day and drive back to his old all-spic neighborhood, just so he can drink with white men. It's made the man bitter. And," he nodded toward the glasses, "he's in his cups tonight. Don't take the man too seriously."

Marty stopped talking and moved down the bar when Frank returned.

"What'd Darby O'Gill say to you?" he asked.

"He told me you were drunk," I said, "and that you didn't like spics."

Frank widened his eyes. "Coming out with revelations like that, is he? Hey, Martin," he yelled, "next time I piss tell him JFK's been shot!" He drained his whiskey, took a sip of beer, and turned his attention back to me. "Listen. Early on, when I first started on the job — years back, I'm talking — there was almost no spades in the department; even less spics. I was the only spic in my precinct, only one I knew of in Brooklyn. I worked in the seven-one, Crown Heights. Did five years there, but this must've been my first year or so.

"I was sitting upstairs in the squad room typing attendance reports. Manual typewriters back then. I was good too, fifty or sixty words a minute — don't forget, English ain't my first language.

See, I learned the forms. The key is knowin' the forms, where to plug in the fucking numbers. You could type two hundred words a minute, but you don't know the forms, all them goddamn boxes, you're sitting there all day.

"So I'm typing these reports — only uniform in a room full of bulls, only spic in a room full of harps — when they bring in the drunk."

Frank paused to order another shot, and Marty brought one for me too. I was hungry and really needed to step outside for some air, but I wanted to hear Frank's story. I did want to know how he thought we were similar, and I hoped he would talk about the photo. He turned his face to the ceiling and opened his mouth like a child catching rain, and he poured the booze smoothly down his throat.

"You gotta remember," he continued, "Crown Heights was still mostly white back then, white civilians, white skells. The drunk is just another mick with a skinful. But what an obnoxious cock-sucker. And loud.

"Man who brought him in is another uniform, almost new as me. He throws him in the cage and takes the desk next to mine to type his report. Only this guy can't type, you can see he's gonna be there all day. Takes him ten minutes to get the paper straight in the damn machine. And all this time the goddamn drunk is yelling at the top of his lungs down the length of the squad room. You can see the bulls are gettin' annoyed. Everybody tells him to shut up, but he keeps on, mostly just abusing the poor fuck that brought him in, who's still struggling with the report, his fingers all smudged with ink from the ribbons.

"On and on he goes: 'Your mother blows sailors . . . Your wife fucks dogs . . . You're all queers, every one of you.' Like that. But I mean, really, it don't end, it's like he never gets tired.

"So the guy who locked him up gets him outa the cage and walks him across the room. Over in the corner they got one of these steam pipes, just a vertical pipe, no radiator or nothing. Hot as a motherfucker. So he cuffs the drunk's hands around the pipe, so now the drunk's gotta stand like this" — Frank formed a huge circle with his arms, as if he were hugging an invisible fat woman — "or else he gets burned. And just bein' that close to the heat, I mean, it's fuckin' awful. So the uniform walks away, figuring that'll shut the scumbag up, but it gets worse.

"Now, the bulls are all pissed at the uniform for not beatin' the drunk senseless before he brought him in, like any guy with a year on the street would know to do. The poor fuck is still typing the paperwork at about a word an hour, and the asshole is still at it, 'Your daughter fucks niggers. When I get out I'll look your wife up — again.' Then he looks straight at the uniform, and the uniform looks up. Their eyes lock for a minute. And the drunk says this: 'What's it feel like to know that every man in this room thinks you're an asshole?' Then the drunk is quiet and he smiles."

Marty returned then, and though I felt I was barely hanging on, I didn't dare speak to refuse the drink. Frank sat silently while Marty poured, and when he was done Frank stared at him until he walked away.

"After that," he continued in a low voice, "it was like slow motion. Like everything was happening underwater. The uniform stands up, takes his gun out, and points it at the drunk. The drunk never stops smiling. And then the uniform pulls the trigger, shoots him right in the face. The drunk's head like explodes, and he spins around the steam pipe — all the way — once, before he drops.

"For a second everything stops. It's just the echo and the smoke and blood on the wall and back window. Then, time speeds up again. The sergeant of detectives, a little leprechaun from the other side — must've bribed his way past the height requirement — jumps over his desk and grabs up a billy club. He lands next to the uniform, who's still holding the gun straight out, and he clubs him five or six times on the forearm, hard and fast, *whap-whap-whap*. The gun drops with the first hit but the leprechaun don't stop till the bone breaks. We all hear it snap.

"The uniform pulls his arm in and howls, and the sergeant throws the billy club down and screams at him: 'The next time . . . the next time, it'll be your head that he breaks before you were able to shoot him. Now get him off the pipe before there's burns on his body.' And he storms out of the room."

Frank drank the shot in front of him and finished his beer. I didn't move. He looked at me and smiled. "The whole squad room," he said, "jumped into action. Some guys uncuffed the drunk; I helped the uniform out. Got him to a hospital. Coupla guys got rags and a pail and started cleaning up.

"Now, think about that," Frank said, leaning in toward me and lowering his voice yet again. "I'm the only spic there. The only

other uniform. There had to be ten bulls. But the sergeant, he
didn't have to tell anybody what the plan was, or to keep their
mouth shut, or any fucking thing. And there was no moment where
anybody worried about me seeing it, being a spic. We all knew that
coulda been any one of us. That's the most on-the-inside I ever felt.
Department now, it's a fucking joke. Affirmative action, cultural-di-
versity training. And what've you got? Nobody trusts anybody. Guys
afraid to trust their own partners." He was whispering, and starting
to slur his words.

I began to feel nauseated. It's a joke, I thought. A cop's made-up
war story. "Frank, did the guy die?"

"Who?"

"The drunk. The man that got shot."

Frank looked confused, and a bit annoyed. "Of course he died."

"Did he die right away?"

"How the fuck should I know? They dragged him outa the room
in like a minute."

"To a hospital?"

"Was a better world's all I'm saying. A better world. And you
always gotta stay on the inside, don't drift, Danny. If you drift,
nobody'll stick up for you."

Jesus, did he have a brogue? He certainly had picked up that lilt
to his voice that my father's generation possessed. That half-accent
that the children of immigrants acquire in a ghetto. I had to get out
of there. A few more minutes and I feared I'd start sounding like
one of these tura-lura-lura motherfuckers myself.

I stood, probably too quickly, and took hold of the bar to steady
myself. "What about the picture, Frank?"

He handed it to me. "Martin is right," he said slowly, "let it lie.
Why do you care who she was?"

"Who she *was*? I asked who she *is*. Is she dead, Frank? Is that what
Marty meant by letting the dead rest?"

"Martin . . . Marty meant . . ."

"I'm right here, Francis," Marty said, "and I can speak for myself." He turned to me. "Francis has overindulged in a few jars," he
said. "He'll nap in the back booth for a while and be right as rain
for the ride home."

"Is that the way it happened, Frank? Exactly that way?"

Frank was smiling at his drink, looking dreamily at his better
world. "Who owns memory?" he said.

"Goodnight, Daniel," Marty said. "It was good of you to stop in."

I didn't respond, just turned and slowly walked out. One or two guys gestured at me as I left, the rest seemed not to notice or care.

I removed the picture from my pocket again when I was outside, an action that had taken on a ritualistic feel, like making the sign of the cross. I did not look at it this time, but began tearing it in strips, lengthwise. Then I walked, and bent down at street corners, depositing each strip in a separate sewer along Fourth Avenue.

He'd told me that he'd broken his arm in a car accident, pursuing two black kids who had robbed a jewelry store.

As I released the strips of paper through the sewer gratings, I thought of the hand in the subway tunnel, and my father's assertion that there were many body parts undoubtedly littering the less frequently traveled parts of the city. Arms, legs, heads, torsos; and perhaps all these bits of photo would find their way into disembodied hands. A dozen or more hands, each gripping a strip of photograph down in the wet slime under the street. Regaining a history, a past, that they lost when they were dismembered, making a connection that I never would.

LOU MANFREDO

Case Closed

FROM *Brooklyn Noir*

The fear enveloped her, and yet despite it, or perhaps because of it, she found herself oddly detached, being from body, as she ran frantically from the stifling grip of the subway station out into the rainy, darkened street.

Her physiology now took full control, independent of her conscious thought, and her pupils dilated and gathered in the dim light to scan the streets, the storefronts, the randomly parked automobiles. Like a laser, her vision locked onto him, undiscernible in the distance. Her brain computed: one hundred yards away. Her legs received the computation and turned her body toward him, propelling her faster. How odd, she thought through the terror, as she watched herself from above. It was almost the flight of an inanimate object. So unlike that of a terrified young woman.

When her scream came at last, it struck her deeply and primordially, and she ran even faster with the sound of it. A microsecond later the scream reached his ears and she saw his head snap around toward her. The silver object at the crest of his hat glistened in the misty streetlight, and she felt her heart leap wildly in her chest.

Oh my God, she thought, a police officer. Thank you, dear God, a police officer!

As he stepped from the curb and started toward her, she swooned, and her being suddenly came slamming back into her body from above. Her knees weakened and she faltered, stumbled, and as consciousness left her, she fell heavily down and slid into the grit and slime of the wet, cracked asphalt.

Mike McQueen sat behind the wheel of the dark gray Chevrolet Impala and listened to the hum of the motor idling. The intermittent *slap-slap* of the wipers and the soft sound of the rain falling on the sheet-metal body were the only other sounds. The Motorola two-way on the seat beside him was silent. The smell of stale cigarettes permeated the car's interior. It was a slow September night, and he shivered against the dampness.

The green digital on the dash told him it was almost 1:00 AM. He glanced across the seat and through the passenger window. He saw his partner, Joe Rizzo, pocketing his change and about to leave the all-night grocer. He held a brown bag in his left hand. McQueen was a six-year veteran of the New York City Police Department, but on this night he felt like a first-day rookie. Six years as a uniformed officer first assigned to Manhattan's Greenwich Village, then, most recently, its Upper East Side. Sitting in the car, in the heart of the Italian-American ghetto that was Brooklyn's Bensonhurst neighborhood, he felt like an out-of-towner in a very alien environment.

He had been a detective, third grade, for all of three days, and this night was to be his first field exposure, a midnight-to-eight tour with a fourteen-year detective first grade, the coffee-buying Rizzo.

Six long years of a fine, solid career, active in felony arrests, not even one civilian complaint, medals, commendations, and a file full of glowing letters from grateful citizens, and it had gotten for him only a choice assignment to the East Side Precinct. And then one night, he swings his radio car to the curb to pee in an all-night diner, hears a commotion, takes a look down an alleyway, and just like that, third grade detective, the gold shield handed to him personally by the mayor himself just three weeks later.

If you've got to fall ass-backwards into an arrest, fall into the one where the lovely young college roommate of the lovely young daughter of the mayor of New York City is about to get raped by a nocturnal predator. Careerwise, it doesn't get any better than that.

McQueen was smiling at the memory when Rizzo dropped heavily into the passenger seat and slammed the door.

"Damn it," Rizzo said, shifting his large body in the seat. "Can they put some fucking springs in these seats, already?"

He fished a container of coffee from the bag and passed it to McQueen. They sat in silence as the B train roared by on the overhead elevated tracks running above this length of Eighty-sixth Street. McQueen watched the sparks fly from the third rail contacts and then sparkle and twirl in the rainy night air before flickering and dying away. Through the parallel slots of the overhead tracks, he watched the twin red taillights of the last car vanish into the distance. The noise of the steel-on-steel wheels and a thousand rattling steel parts and I-beams reverberated in the train's wake. It made the deserted, rain-washed streets seem even more dismal. McQueen found himself missing Manhattan.

The grocery had been the scene of a robbery the week before, and Rizzo wanted to ask the night man a few questions. McQueen wasn't quite sure if it was the coffee or the questions that had come as an afterthought. Although he had only known Rizzo for two days, he suspected the older man to be a somewhat less than enthusiastic investigator.

"Let's head on back to the house," Rizzo said, referring to the 62nd Precinct station house, as he sipped his coffee and fished in his outer coat pocket for the Chesterfields he seemed to live on. "I'll write up this here interview I just did and show you where to file it."

McQueen eased the car out from the curb. Rizzo had insisted he drive, to get the lay of the neighborhood, and McQueen knew it made sense. But he felt disoriented and foolish: He wasn't even sure which way the precinct was.

Rizzo seemed to sense McQueen's discomfort. "Make a U-turn," he said, lighting the Chesterfield. "Head back up Eighty-sixth and make a left on Seventeenth Avenue." He drew on the cigarette and looked sideways at McQueen. He smiled before he spoke again. "What's the matter, kid? Missing the bright lights across the river already?"

McQueen shrugged. "I guess. I just need time, that's all."

He drove slowly through the light rain. Once off Eighty-sixth Street's commercial strip, they entered a residential area comprised of detached and semidetached older, brick homes. Mostly two stories, the occasional three-story. Some had small, neat gardens or lawns in front. Many had ornate, well-kept statues, some illuminated by flood lamps, of the Virgin Mary or Saint Anthony or Joseph. McQueen scanned the home fronts as he drove. The occasional window shone dimly with night lights glowing from within. They looked peaceful and warm, and he imagined the families inside, tucked into their beds, alarm clocks set and ready for the coming workday. Everyone safe, everything secure, everyone happy and well.

And that's how it always seemed. But six years had taught him what was more likely going on in some of those houses. The drunken husbands coming home and beating their wives; the junkie sons and daughters, the sickly, lonely old, the forsaken parent found dead in an apartment after the stench of decomposition had reached a neighbor and someone had dialed 911.

The memories of an ex–patrol officer. As the radio crackled to life on the seat beside him and he listened with half an ear, he wondered what the memories of an ex-detective would someday be.

He heard Rizzo sigh. "All right, Mike. That call is ours. Straight up this way, turn left on Bay Eighth Street. Straight down to the Belt Parkway. Take the parkway east a few exits and get off at Ocean Parkway. Coney Island Hospital is a block up from the Belt. Looks like it might be a long night."

When they entered the hospital, it took them some minutes to sort through the half-dozen patrol officers milling around the emergency room. McQueen found the right cop, a tall, skinny kid of about twenty-three. He glanced down at the man's nametag. "How you doing, Marino? I'm McQueen, Mike McQueen. Me and Rizzo are catching tonight. What d'ya got?"

The man pulled a thick leather note binder from his rear pocket. He flipped through it and found his entry, turned it to face McQueen, and held out a Bic pen.

"Can you scratch it for me, detective? No sergeant here yet."

McQueen took the book and pen and scribbled the date, time, and CIHOSP E/R across the bottom of the page, then put his initials and shield number. He handed the book back to Marino.

"What d'ya got?" he asked again.

Marino cleared his throat. "I'm not the guy from the scene. That was Willis. He was off at midnight, so he turned it to us and went home. I just got some notes here. Female Caucasian, Amy Taylor, twenty-six, single, lives at 1860 Sixty-first Street. Coming off the subway at Sixty-second Street about eleven o'clock, twenty-three hundred, the station's got no clerk on duty after nine. She goes into one of them — what d'ya call it? — one-way exit-door turnstile things, the ones that'll only let you out, not in. Some guy jumps out of nowhere and grabs her."

At that point, Rizzo walked up. "Hey, Mike, you OK with this for a while? My niece is a nurse here, I'm gonna go say hello, OK?"

Mike glanced at his partner. "Yeah, sure, OK, Joe, go ahead."

McQueen turned back to Marino. "Go on."

Marino dropped his eyes back to his notes. "So this guy pins her in the revolving door and shoves a knife in her face. Tells her he's gonna cut her bad if she don't help him."

"Help him with what?"

Marino shrugged. "Who the fuck knows? Guy's got the knife in one hand and his johnson in the other. He's trying to whack off on her. Never says another word to her, just presses the knife against her throat. Anyway, somehow he drops the weapon and she gets loose, starts to run away. The guy goes after her. She comes out of the station screaming, Willis is on a foot post doing a four-to-midnight, sees her running and screaming, and goes over her way. She takes a fall, faints or something, bangs up her head and swells up her knee and breaks two fingers. They got her upstairs in a room, for observation on account of the head wound."

McQueen thought for a moment. "Did Willis see the guy?"

"No, never saw him."

"Any description from the girl?"

"I don't know, I never even seen her. When I got here she was upstairs."

"OK, stick around till your sergeant shows up and cuts you loose."

"Can't you, Detective?"

"Can't I what?"

"Cut me loose?"

McQueen frowned and pushed a hand through his hair. "I don't know. I think I can. Do me a favor, though, wait for the sarge, OK?"

Marino shook his head and turned his lips downward. "Yeah, sure, a favor. I'll go sniff some ether or something." He walked away, his head still shaking.

McQueen looked around the brightly lit emergency room. He saw Rizzo down a hall, leaning against a wall, talking to a bleached-blond nurse who looked to be about Rizzo's age: fifty. McQueen walked over.

"Hey, Joe, you going to introduce me to your niece?"

Joe turned and looked at McQueen with a puzzled look, then smiled.

"Oh, no, no, turns out she's not working tonight. I'm just making a new friend here, is all."

"Well, we need to go talk to the victim, this Amy Taylor."

Rizzo frowned. "She a ditsoon?"

"A what?" McQueen asked.

Rizzo shook his head. "Is she black?"

"No, cop told me Caucasian. Why?"

"Kid, I know you're new here to Bensonhurst, so I'm gonna be patient. Anybody in this neighborhood named Amy Taylor is either a ditsoon or a yuppie pain-in-the-ass moved here from Boston to be an artist or a dancer or a Broadway star, and she can't afford to live in Park Slope or Brooklyn Heights or across the river. This here neighborhood is all Italian, kid, everybody — cops, crooks, butchers, bakers, and candlestick makers. Except for you, of course. You're the exception. By the way, did I introduce you two? This here is the morning-shift head nurse, Rosalie Mazzarino. Rosalie, say hello to my boy wonder partner, Mike Mick-fucking-Queen."

The woman smiled and held out a hand. "Nice to meet you, Mike. And don't believe a thing this guy tells you. Making new friends! I've known him since he was your age and chasing every nurse in the place." She squinted at McQueen then and slipped a pair of glasses out of her hair and over her eyes. "How old are you — twelve?"

Mike laughed. "I'm twenty-eight."

She twisted her mouth up and nodded her head in an approving manner. "And a third-grade detective already? I'm impressed."

Rizzo laughed. "Yeah, so was the mayor. This boy's a genuine hero with the alma mater gals."

"Okay, Joe, very good. Now, can we go see the victim?"

"You know, kid, I got a problem with that. I can tell you her whole story from right here. She's from Boston, wants to be a star, and as soon as you lock up the guy raped her, she's gonna bring a complaint against you 'cause you showed no respect for the poor shit, a victim of society and all. Why don't you talk to her, I'll go see the doctor and get the rape kit and the panties, and we'll get out of here."

McQueen shook his head. "Wrong crime, partner. No rape, some kind of sexual assault or abuse or whatever."

"Go ahead, kid, talk to her. It'll be good experience for you. Me and Rosalie'll be in one of these linen closets when you get back. I did tell you she was the *head* nurse, right?"

McQueen walked away with her laughter in his ear. It was going to be a long night. Just like Joe had figured.

He checked the room number twice before entering. It was a small room with barely enough space for the two hospital beds it held. They were separated by a seriously despondent-looking curtain. The one nearest the door was empty, the mattress exposed. In the dim lighting, McQueen could see the foot of the second bed. The outline of someone's feet showed through the bedding. A faint and sterile yet vaguely unpleasant odor touched his nostrils. He waited a moment longer for his eyes to adjust to the low light, so soft after the harsh fluorescent glare of the hall. He glanced around for something to knock on to announce his presence. He settled on the footboard of the near bed and rapped gently on the cold metal.

"Hello?" he said softly. "Hello, Ms. Taylor?"

The covered feet stirred. He heard the low rustle of linens. He raised his voice a bit when he spoke again.

"Ms. Taylor? I'm Detective McQueen, police. May I see you for a moment?"

A light switched on, hidden by the curtain but near the head of the bed. McQueen stood and waited.

"Ms. Taylor? Hello?"

The voice was sleepy, possibly sedated. It was a gentle and clear voice, yet it held a tension, an edginess. McQueen imagined he had awoken her and now the memories were flooding through her, the reality of it: yes, it had actually happened, no, it hadn't been a dream. He had seen it a thousand times: the burglarized, the beaten, the raped, robbed, shot, stabbed, pissed on whole lot of them. He had seen it.

"Detective? Did you say 'detective'? Hello? I can't see you."

He stepped further into the room, slowly venturing past the curtain. Slow and steady, don't move fast and remember to speak softly. Get her to relax, don't freak her out.

Her beauty struck him immediately. She was sitting, propped on two pillows, the sheet raised and folded over her breasts. Her arms lay beside her on the bed, palms down, straight out. She appeared to be clinging to the bed, steadying herself against some unseen, not possible force. Her skin was almost translucent, a soft glow emanating from it. Her wide-set eyes were like liquid sapphire, and they met and held his own. Her lips were full and rounded and sat perfectly under her straight, narrow nose, her face framed with shoulder-length black hair. She wore no makeup, and an ugly purple-yellow bruise marked her left temple and part of her cheekbone. Yet she was the most beautiful woman McQueen had ever seen.

After almost three years working the richest, most sophisticated square mile in the world, here, now, in this godforsaken corner of Brooklyn, he sees this woman. For a moment, he forgot why he had come.

"Yes? Can I help you?" she asked as he stood in her sight.

He blinked himself back and cleared his throat. He glanced down to the blank page of the notepad in his hand, just to steal an instant more before he had to speak.

"Yes, yes, Ms. Taylor. I'm Detective McQueen, six-two detective squad. I need to see you for a few minutes. If you don't mind."

She frowned, and he saw pain in her eyes. For an instant he thought his heart would break. He shook his head slightly. What the hell? What the hell was this?

"I've already spoken to two or three police officers. I've already told them what happened." Her eyes closed. "I'm very tired. My head hurts." She opened her eyes and they were welled with tears. McQueen used all his willpower not to move to her, to cradle her head, to tell her it was OK, it was all over, he was here now.

"Yeah, yeah, I know that," he said instead. "But my partner and I caught the case. We'll be handling it. I need some information. Just a few minutes. The sooner we get started, the better chance we have of catching this guy."

She seemed to think it over as she held his gaze. When she tried to blink the tears away, they spilled down onto her cheeks. She made no effort to brush them away. "All right," was all she said.

McQueen felt his body relax, and he realized he had been holding himself so tightly that his back and shoulders ached. "May I sit down?" he asked softly.

"Yes, of course."

He slid the too-large-for-the-room chair to the far side of the bed and sat with his back to the windows. He heard rain rattle against the panes and the sound chilled him and made him shiver. He found himself hoping she hadn't noticed.

"I already know pretty much what happened. There's no need to go over it all, really. I just have a few questions. Most of them are formalities, please don't read anything into it. I just need to know certain things. For the reports. And to help us find this guy. OK?"

She squeezed her eyes closed again and more tears escaped. She nodded yes to him and reopened her eyes. He couldn't look away from them.

"This happened about eleven, eleven-ten?"

"Yes, about."

"You had gotten off the train at the Sixty-second Street subway station?"

"Yes."

"Alone?"

"Yes."

"What train is that?"

"The N."

"Where were you going?"

"Home."

"Where were you coming from?"

"My art class in Manhattan."

McQueen looked up from his notes. Art class? Rizzo's inane preamble resounded in his mind. He squinted at her and said, "You're not originally from Boston, are you?"

For the first time she smiled slightly, and McQueen found it disproportionately endearing. "No, Connecticut. Do you think I sound like a Bostonian?"

He laughed. "No, no, not at all. Just something somebody said to me. Long story, pay no attention."

She smiled again, and he could see it in her eyes that the facial movement had caused her some pain. "A lot of you Brooklyn-ites think anyone from out of town sounds like they come from Boston."

McQueen sat back in his chair and raised his eyebrows in mock indignation. "'Brooklynite?' You think I sound like a Brooklynite?"

"Sure do."

"Well, Ms. Taylor, just so you know, I live in the city. Not Brooklyn." He kept his voice light, singsong.

"Isn't Brooklyn in the city?"

"Well, yeah, geographically. But the city is Manhattan. I was born on Long Island but I've lived in the city for fifteen years."

"All right, then," she said, with a pitched nod of her head.

McQueen tapped his pen on his notepad and looked at the ugly bruise on her temple. He dropped his gaze to the splinted, bandaged broken fingers of her right hand.

"How are you doing? I know you took a bad fall and had a real bad scare. But how are you doing?"

She seemed to tremble briefly, and he regretted having asked. But she met his gaze with her answer.

"I'll be fine. Everything is superficial, except for the fingers, and they'll heal. I'll be fine."

He nodded to show he believed her and that yes, of course, she was right, she would be fine. He wondered, though, if she really would be.

"Can you describe the man to me?"

"It happened very fast. I mean, it seemed to last for hours, but . . . but . . ."

McQueen leaned forward and spoke more softly so she would have to focus on the sound of his voice in order to hear, focus on hearing the words and not the memory at hand.

"Was he taller than you?"

"Yes."

"How tall are you?"

"Five-eight."

"And him?"

She thought for a moment. "Five-nine or -ten."

"His hair?"

"Black. Long. Very dirty." She looked down at the sheet and nervously picked at a loose thread. "It . . . It . . ."

McQueen leaned in closer, his knees against the side of the bed. He imagined what it would be like to touch her. "It what?" he asked gently.

"It smelled." She looked up sharply with the near panic of a frightened deer in her eyes. She whispered, "His hair was so dirty, I could smell it."

She started to sob. McQueen sat back in his chair.

He needed to find this man. Badly.

*

"I want to keep this one."

McQueen started the engine and glanced down at his wristwatch as he spoke to Rizzo. It was two in the morning, and his eyes stung with the grit of someone who had been too long awake.

Rizzo shifted in the seat and adjusted his jacket. He settled in and turned to the younger detective.

"You what?" he asked absently.

"I want this one. I want to keep it. We can handle this case, Joe, and I want it."

Rizzo shook his head and frowned. "Doesn't work that way, kid. The morning shift catches and pokes around a little, does a rah-rah for the victim, and then turns the case to the day tour. You know that, that's the way it is. Let's get us back to the house and do the reports and grab a few Z's. We'll pick up enough of our own work next day-tour we pull. We don't need to grab something ain't our problem. OK?"

McQueen stared out of the window into the falling rain on the dark street. He didn't turn his head when he spoke.

"Joe, I'm telling you, I want this case. If you're in, fine. If not, I go to the squad boss tomorrow and ask for the case and a partner to go with it." Now he turned to face the older man and met his eyes. "Up to you, Joe. You tell me."

Rizzo turned away and spoke into the windshield before him. He let his eyes watch McQueen's watery reflection. "Pretty rough for a fuckin' guy with three days under his belt." He sighed and turned slowly before he spoke again.

"One of the cops in the ER told me this broad was a looker. So now I get extra work 'cause you got a hard-on?"

McQueen shook his head. "Joe, it's not like that."

Rizzo smiled. "Mike, you're how old? Twenty-seven, twenty-eight? It's like that, all right, it's always like that."

"Not this time. And not me. It's wrong for you to say that, Joe."

At that, Rizzo laughed aloud. "Mike," he said through a lingering chuckle, "there ain't no wrong. And there ain't no right. There just *is,* that's all."

Now it was McQueen who laughed. "Who told you that, a guru?"

Rizzo fumbled through his jacket pockets and produced a battered and bent Chesterfield. "Sort of," he said as he lit it. "My grandfather told me that. Do you know where I was born?"

McQueen, puzzled by the question, shook his head. "How would I know? Brooklyn?"

"Omaha-fuckin'-Nebraska, that's where. My old man was a lifer in the Air Force stationed out there. Well, when I was nine years old he dropped dead. Me and my mother and big sister came back to Brooklyn to live with my grandparents. My grandfather was a first-grade detective working Chinatown back then. The first night we was home, I broke down, crying to him about how wrong it was, my old man dying and all, how it wasn't right and all like that. He got down on his knees and leaned right into my face. I still remember the smell of beer and garlic sauce on his breath. He leaned right in and said, 'Kid, nothing is wrong. And nothing is right. It just is.' I never forgot that. He was dead-on correct about that, I'll tell you."

McQueen drummed his fingers lightly on the wheel and scanned the mirrors. The street was empty. He pulled the Impala away from the curb and drove back toward the Belt Parkway. After they had entered the westbound lanes, Rizzo spoke again.

"Besides, Mike, this case won't even stay with the squad. Rapes go to sex crimes and they get handled by the broads and the guys with the master's degrees in fundamental and advanced bullshit. Can you imagine the bitch that Betty Friedan and Bella Abzug would pitch if they knew an insensitive prick like me was handling a rape?"

"Joe, Bella Abzug died about twenty years ago."

Rizzo nodded. "Whatever. You get my point."

"And I told you already, this isn't a rape. A guy grabbed her, threatened her with a blade, and was yanking on his own chain while he held her there. No rape. Abuse and assault, tops."

For the first time since they had worked together, McQueen heard a shadow of interest in Rizzo's voice when the older man next spoke.

"Blade? Whackin' off? Did the guy come?"

McQueen glanced over at his partner. "What?" he asked.

"Did the guy bust a nut, or not?"

McQueen squinted through the windshield: Had he thought to ask her that? No. No, he hadn't. It simply hadn't occurred to him.

"Is that real important to this, Joe, or are you just making a case for your insensitive-prick status?"

Rizzo laughed out loud and expelled a gray cloud of cigarette smoke in the process. McQueen reached for the power button and cracked his window.

"No, no, kid, really, official request. Did this asshole come?"

"I don't know. I didn't ask her. Why?"

Rizzo laughed again. "Didn't want to embarrass her on the first date, eh, Mike? Understandable, but totally unacceptable detective work."

"Is this going somewhere, Joe?"

Rizzo nodded and smiled. "Yeah, it's going toward granting your rude request that we keep this one. If I can catch a case I can clear up quick, I'll always keep it. See, about four, five years ago we had some schmuck running around the precinct grabbing girls and forcing them into doorways and alleyways. Used a knife. He'd hold them there and beat off till the thing started to look like a stick of chop meat. One victim said she stared at a bank clock across the street the whole time to sort of distract herself from the intimacy of the situation, and she said the guy was hammering himself for twenty-five minutes. But he could never get the job done. Psychological, probably. Sort of a major failure at his crime of choice. Never hurt no one, physically, but one of his victims was only thirteen. She must be popping Prozac by the handful now somewheres. We caught the guy. Not me, but some guys from the squad. Turned out to be a strung-out junkie shitbag we all knew. Thing is, junkies don't usually cross over into the sex stuff. No cash or H in it. I bet this is the same guy. He'd be long out by now. And except for the subway, it's his footprint. We can clear this one, Mike. You and me. I'm gonna make you look like a star, first case. The mayor will be so proud of himself for grabbing that gold shield for you, he'll probably make you the fuckin' commissioner!"

Two days later, McQueen sat at his desk in the cramped detective squad room, gazing once again into the eyes of Amy Taylor. He cleared his voice before he spoke, and noticed the bruise at her temple had subsided a bit and that no attempt to cover it with makeup had been made.

"What I'd like to do is show you some photographs. I'd like you to take a look at some suspects and tell me if one of them is the perpetrator."

Her eyes smiled at him as she spoke. "I've talked to about five police officers in the last few days, and you're the first one to say 'perpetrator.'"

He felt himself flush a little. "Well," he said with a forced laugh,
"it's a fairly appropriate word for what we're doing here."

"Yes, it is. It's just unsettling to hear it actually said. Does that
make sense?"

He nodded. "I think I know what you mean."

"Good," she said with the pitched nod of her head that he
suddenly realized he had been looking forward to seeing again.
"I didn't mean it as an insult or anything. Do I look at the mug
books now?"

This time McQueen's laugh was genuine. "No, no, that's your
words now. We call it a photo array. I'll show you eight photos of
men roughly matching the description you gave me. You tell me if
one of them is the right one."

"All right, then." She straightened herself in her chair and
folded her hands in her lap. She cradled the broken right fingers
in the long slender ones of her left hand. The gentleness made
McQueen's head swim with — what? — grief? — pity? He didn't
know.

When he came around to her side of the desk and spread out the
color photos before her, he knew immediately. She looked up at
him — and the sapphires swam in tears yet again. She turned back
to the photos and lightly touched one.

"Him," was all she said.

"You know," Rizzo said, chewing on a hamburger as he spoke, "you
can never overestimate the stupidity of these assholes."

It was just after nine on a Thursday night, and the two detectives
sat in the Chevrolet and ate their meals. The car stood backed into
a slot at the rear of the Burger King's parking lot, nestled in the
darkness between circles of glare from two lampposts. Three weeks
had passed since the assault on Amy Taylor.

McQueen turned to his partner. "Which assholes we talking
about here, Joe?" In the short time he had been working with
Rizzo, McQueen had developed a grudging respect for the older
man. What Rizzo appeared to lack in enthusiasm, he more than
made up for in experience and with an ironic, grizzled sort of

street smarts. McQueen had learned much from him and knew he was about to learn more.

"Criminals," Rizzo continued. "Skells in general. This burglary call we just took reminded me of something. Old case I handled seven, eight years ago. Jewelry store got robbed, over on Thirteenth Avenue. Me and my partner, guy named Giacalone, go over there and see the victim. Old Sicilian lived in the neighborhood forever, salt-of-the-earth type. So me and Giacalone, we go all out for this guy. We even called for the fingerprint team, we were right on it. So we look around, talk to the guy, get the description of the perp and the gun used, and we tell the old guy to sit tight and wait for the fingerprint team to show up and we'll be in touch in a couple of days. Well, the old man is so grateful, he walks us out to the car. Just as we're about to pull away, the guy says, 'You know, the guy that robbed me cased the joint first.' Imagine that? — 'cased the joint' — Musta watched a lot of TV, this old guy. So I say to him, 'What d'ya mean, cased the joint?' And he says, 'Yeah, two days ago the same guy came in to get his watch fixed. Left it with me and everything. Even filled out a receipt card with his name and address and phone number. Must have been just casing the place. Well, he sure fooled me.'"

Rizzo chuckled and bit into his burger. "So," he continued through a full mouth, "old Giacalone puts the car back into park and he leans across me and says, 'You still got that receipt slip?' The old guy goes, 'Yeah, but it must be all phony. He was just trying to get a look around.' Well, me and Giacalone go back in and we get the slip. We cancel the print guys and drive out to Canarsie. Guess what? The asshole is home. We grab him and go get a warrant for the apartment. Gun, jewelry, and cash, bing-bang-boom. The guy cops to rob-three and does four-to-seven."

Rizzo smiled broadly at McQueen. "His girlfriend lived in the precinct, and while he was visiting her, he figured he'd get his watch fixed. Then when he sees what a mark the old guy is, he has an inspiration! See? Assholes."

"Yeah, well, it's a good thing," McQueen said. "I haven't run across too many geniuses working this job."

Rizzo laughed and crumpled up the wrappings spread across his lap. "Amen," he said.

They sat in silence, Rizzo smoking, McQueen watching the people and cars moving around the parking lot.

"Hey, Joe," McQueen said after a while. "Your theory about this neighborhood is a little bit off base. For a place supposed to be all Italian, I notice a lot of Asians around. Not to mention the Russians."

Rizzo waved a hand through his cigarette smoke. "Yeah, somebody's got to wait the tables in the Chinese restaurants and drive car service. You still can't throw a rock without hitting a fucking guinea."

The Motorola crackled to life at McQueen's side. It was dispatch directing them to call the precinct via telephone. McQueen took his cell from his jacket pocket as Rizzo keyed the radio and gave a curt "Ten-four."

McQueen placed the call and the desk put him through to the squad. A detective named Borrelli came on the line. McQueen listened. His eyes narrowed and, taking a pen from his shirt, he scribbled on the back of a newspaper. He hung up the phone and turned to Rizzo.

"We've got him," he said softly.

Rizzo belched loudly. "Got who?"

McQueen leaned forward and started the engine. He switched on the headlights and pulled away. After three weeks in Bensonhurst, he no longer needed directions. He knew where he was going.

"Flain," he said. "Peter Flain."

Rizzo reached back, pulled on his shoulder belt, and buckled up. "Imagine that," he said with a faint grin. "And here we was, just a minute ago, talking about assholes. Imagine that."

McQueen drove hard and quickly toward Eighteenth Avenue. Traffic was light, and he carefully jumped a red signal at Bay Parkway and turned left onto Seventy-fifth Street. He accelerated to Eighteenth Avenue and turned right.

As he drove, he reflected on the investigation that was now about to unfold.

It had been Rizzo who had gotten it started when he recalled the prior crimes with the same pattern. He had asked around the precinct and someone remembered the name of the perp. Flain. Peter Flain.

The precinct computer had spit out his last known address in the Bronx and the parole officer assigned to the junkie ex-con. A call to the officer told them that Flain had been living in the Bronx for some years, serving out his parole without incident. He had been placed in a methadone program and was clean. Then, about three months ago, he disappeared. His parole officer checked around in the Bronx, but Flain had simply vanished. The officer put a violation on Flain's parole and notified the state police, the New York Supreme Court, and NYPD headquarters. And that's where it had ended, as far as he was concerned.

McQueen had printed a color print from the computer and assembled the photo array. Amy Taylor picked Flain's face from it. Flain had returned to the Six-two Precinct.

Then Rizzo had really gone to work. He spent the better part of a four-to-midnight hitting every known junkie haunt in the precinct. He had made it known he wanted Flain. He had made it known that he would not be happy with any bar, poolroom, candy store, or after-hours joint that would harbor Flain and fail to give him up with a phone call to the squad.

And tonight, that call had been made.

McQueen swung the Chevy into the curb, killing the lights as the car rolled to a slow stop. Three storefronts down, just off the corner of Sixty-ninth Street, the faded fluorescent of the Keyboard Bar shone in the night. He twisted the key to shut off the engine. As he reached for the door handle and was about to pull it open, he felt the firm, tight grasp of Rizzo's large hand on his right shoulder. He turned to face him.

Rizzo's face held no sign of emotion. When he spoke, it was in a low, conversational tone. McQueen had never heard the older man enunciate more clearly. "Kid," Rizzo began, "I know you like this girl. And I know you took her out to dinner last week. Now, we both know you shouldn't even be working this collar since you been seeing the victim socially. I been working with you for three weeks now, and you're a good cop. But this here is the first bit of real shit we had to do. Let me handle it. Don't be stupid. We pinch him and read him the rights and off he goes." Rizzo paused and let his dark brown eyes run over McQueen's face. When they returned to the cold blue of McQueen's own eyes, they bored in.

"Right?" Rizzo asked.

McQueen nodded. "Just one thing, Joe."

Rizzo let his hand slide gently off McQueen's shoulder.

"What?" he asked.

"I'll process it. I'll walk him through central booking. I'll do the paperwork. Just do me one favor."

"What?" Rizzo repeated.

"I don't know any Brooklyn ADAs. I need you to talk to the ADA writing tonight. I want this to go hard. Two top counts, D felonies. Assault two and sexual abuse one. I don't want this prick copping to an A misdemeanor assault or some bullshit E felony. OK?"

Rizzo smiled, and McQueen became aware of the tension that had been hidden in the older man's face only as he saw it melt away. "Sure, kid," he nodded. "I'll go down there myself and cash in a favor. No problem." He pushed his face in the direction of the bar and said, "Now, let's go get him."

Rizzo walked in first and went directly to the bar. McQueen hung back near the door, his back angled to the bare barroom wall. His eyes adjusted to the dimness of the large room and he scanned the half-dozen drinkers scattered along its length. He noticed two empty barstools with drinks and money and cigarettes spread before them on the worn Formica surface. At least two people were in the place somewhere, but not visible. He glanced over at Joe Rizzo.

Rizzo stood silently, his forearms resting on the bar. The bartender, a man of about sixty, was slowly walking toward him.

"Hello, Andrew," McQueen heard Rizzo say. "How the hell you been?" McQueen watched as the two men, out of earshot of the others, whispered briefly to one another. McQueen noticed the start of nervous stirrings as the drinkers came to realize that something was suddenly different here. He saw a small envelope drop to the floor at the feet of one man.

Rizzo stepped away from the bar and came back to McQueen.

He smiled. "This joint is so crooked, old Andrew over there would give up Jesus Christ Himself to keep me away from here." With a flick of his index finger, Rizzo indicated the men's room at the very rear in the left corner.

"Our boy's in there. Ain't feeling too chipper this evening, according to Andrew. Flain's back on the junk, hard. He's been sucking down Cokes all night. Andrew says he's been in there for twenty minutes."

McQueen looked at the distant door. "Must have nodded off."

Rizzo twisted his lips. "Or he read Andrew like a book and climbed out the fucking window. Lets us go see."

Rizzo started toward the men's room, unbuttoning his coat with his left hand as he walked. McQueen suddenly became aware of the weight of the 9mm Glock automatic belted to his own right hip. His groin broke into a sudden sweat as he realized he couldn't remember having chambered a round before leaving his apartment for work. He unbuttoned his coat and followed his partner.

The men's room was small. A urinal hung on the wall to their left, brimming with dark urine and blackened cigarette butts. A cracked mirror hung above a blue-green stained sink. The metallic rattle of a worn, useless ventilation fan clamored. The stench of disinfectant surrendered to — what? — vomit? Yes, vomit.

The single stall stood against the wall before them. The door was closed. Feet showed beneath it.

McQueen reached for his Glock and watched as Rizzo slipped an ancient-looking Colt revolver from under his coat.

Then Rizzo leaned his weight back, his shoulder brushing against McQueen's chest, and heaved a heavy foot at the stress point of the stall door. He threw his weight behind it, and as the door flew inward, he stepped deftly aside, at the same time gently shoving McQueen the other way. The door crashed against the stall occupant and Rizzo rushed forward, holding the bouncing door back with one hand, pointing the Colt with the other.

Peter Flain sat motionless on the toilet. His pants and underwear lay crumpled around his ankles. His legs were spread wide, pale and varicosed, and capped by bony knees. His head hung forward onto his chest, still. McQueen's eyes fell on the man's greasy black hair. Flain's dirty gray shirt was covered with a brown, foamy, blood-streaked vomit. More blood, dark and thick, ran from his nostrils and pooled in the crook of his chin. His fists were clenched.

Rizzo leaned forward and, carefully avoiding the fluids, lay two fingers across the jugular.

He stood erect and holstered his gun. He turned to McQueen.

"Morte," he said. "The prick died on us!"

McQueen looked away from Rizzo and back to Flain. He tried to feel what he felt, but couldn't. "Well," he said, just to hear his own voice.

Rizzo let the door swing closed on the sight of Flain. He turned to McQueen with sudden anger on his face. "You know what this means?" he said.

McQueen watched as the door swung slowly back open. He looked at Flain, but spoke to Rizzo.

"It means he's dead. It's over."

Rizzo shook his head angrily. "No, no, that's not what it fucking means. It means no conviction. No guilty plea. It means, 'Investigation abated by death'! That's what it means."

McQueen shook his head. "So?" he asked. "So what?"

Rizzo frowned and leaned back against the tiled wall. Some of the anger left him. "So what?" he said, now more sad than angry. "I'll tell you 'so what.' Without a conviction or a plea, we don't clear this case. We don't clear this case, we don't get credit for it. We don't clear this case, we did all this shit for nothing. Fucker would have died tonight anyway, with or without us bustin' our asses to find him."

They stood in silence for a moment. Then, suddenly, Rizzo brightened. He turned to McQueen with a sly grin, and when he spoke, he did so in a softer tone.

"Unless," he said, "unless we start to get smart."

In six years on the job, McQueen had been present in other places, at other times, with other cops, when one of them had said, "Unless . . ." with just such a grin. He felt his facial muscles begin to tighten.

"What, Joe? Unless what?"

"Un-less when we got here, came in the john, this guy was still alive. In acute respiratory distress. Pukin' on himself. Scared, real scared 'cause he knew this was the final overdose. And we, well, we tried to help, but we ain't doctors, right? So he knows he's gonna die and he says to us, 'I'm sorry.' And we say, 'What, Pete, sorry about what?' And he says, 'I'm sorry about that girl, that last pretty girl, in the subway. I shouldn'ta done that.' And I say to him, 'Done what, Pete, what'd you do?' And he says, 'I did like I did before, with the others, with the knife.' And then, just like that, he drops dead!"

McQueen wrinkled his forehead. "I'm not following this, Joe. How does that change anything?"

Rizzo leaned closer to McQueen. "It changes everything," he whispered, holding his thumb to his fingers and shaking his hand, palm up, at McQueen's face. "Don't you get it? It's a deathbed confession, rock-solid evidence, even admissible in court. Bang — case closed! And we're the ones who closed it. Don't you see? It's fucking beautiful."

McQueen looked back at the grotesque body of the dead junkie. He felt bile rising in his throat, and he swallowed it down.   ·

He shook his head slowly, his eyes still on the corpse.

"Jesus, Joe," he said, the bile searing at his throat. "Jesus Christ, Joe, that's not right. We can't do that. That's just fucking wrong!"

Rizzo reddened, the anger suddenly coming back to him.

"Kid," he said, "don't make me say you owe me. Don't make me say it. I took this case on for you, remember?"

But it was not the way McQueen remembered it. He looked into the older man's eyes.

"Jesus, Joe," he said.

Rizzo shook his head, "Jesus got nothin' to do with it."

"It's wrong, Joe," McQueen said, even as his ears flushed red with the realization of what they were about to do. "It's just wrong."

Rizzo leaned in close, speaking more softly, directly into McQueen's ear. The sound of people approaching the men's room forced an urgency into his voice. McQueen felt the warmth of Rizzo's breath touching him.

"I tole you this, kid. I already tole you this. There is no right. There is no wrong." He turned and looked down at the hideous corpse. "There just *is*."

DAVID MEANS

Sault Ste. Marie

FROM *Harper's Magazine*

ERNIE DUG IN with the tip of his penknife, scratching a line into the plastic top of the display case, following the miniature lock system as it stepped down between Lake Superior and Lake Huron. At the window, Marsha ignored us both and stood blowing clouds of smoke at the vista . . . a supertanker rising slowly in the lock, hefted by water . . . as if it mattered that the system was fully functioning and freight was moving up and down the great seaway. As if it mattered that ore was being transported from the hinterlands of Duluth (a nullifyingly boring place) to the eastern seaboard and points beyond. As if it mattered that the visitor's center stood bathed in sunlight, while behind the gift counter an old lady sat reading a paperback and doing her best to ignore the dry scratch of Ernie's knife, raising her rheumy eyes on occasion, reaching up to adjust her magnificent hair with the flat of her hand. — I'm gonna go see that guy I know, Tull, about the boat I was telling you about, Ernie announced, handing me the knife. He tossed his long black hair to the side, reached into his pants, yanked out his ridiculously long-barreled .44 Remington Magnum, pointed it at the lady, and said — But first I'm going to rob this old bag. — Stick 'em up, he said, moving toward the lady, who stared over the top of her paperback. Her face was ancient; the skin drooped from her jaw, and on her chin bits of hair collected faintly into something that looked like a Vandyke. A barmaid beauty remained in her face, along with a stony resilience. Her saving feature was a great big poof of silvery hair that rose like a nest and stood secured by an arrangement of bobby pins and a very fine hairnet. — Take whatever you want, she said in a husky voice, lifting her hands out in a gesture of offering. — As a matter of fact, shoot me if you feel inclined. It's not going to matter to me. I'm pushing eighty. I've lived the life I'm going to live and I've seen plenty of things and had my heart broken and I've got rheumatoid arthritis in these knuckles so bad I can hardly hold a pencil to paper. (She lifted her hand and turned it over so we could see the claw formation of her fingers.) — And putting numbers into the cash register is painful. — Jesus Christ, Ernie said, shooting you would just be doing the world a favor, and too much fun, and he tucked the gun back in his pants, adjusted the hem of his shirt, and went to find this guy with the boat. Marsha maintained her place at the window, lit another cigarette, and stared at the boat while I took Ernie's knife from the top of the display case and began scratching where he left off. Finished with the matter, the old lady behind the gift counter raised the paperback up to her face and began reading. Outside, the superfreighter rose with leisure; it was one of those long ore boats, a football field in length, with guys on bicycles making the journey from bow to stern. There was probably great beauty in its immensity, in the way it emerged from the lower parts of the seaway, lifted by the water. But I didn't see it. At that time in my life, it was just one more industrial relic in my face.

A few minutes later, when Ernie shot the guy named Tull in the parking lot, the gun produced a tight little report that bounced off the side of the freighter that was sitting up in the lock, waiting for the go-ahead. The weight line along the ship's hull was far above the visitor's station; below the white stripe, the skin of the hull was shoddy with flakes of rust and barnacle scars. The ship looked ashamed of itself exposed for the whole world to see, like a lady with her skirt blown up. The name on the bow, in bright white letters, was Henry Jackman. Looking down at us, a crew member raised his hand against the glare. What he saw was a sad scene: a ring of blue gun smoke lingering around the guy Ernie shot, who was muttering the word fuck and bowing down while blood pooled around his crotch. By the time we scrambled to the truck and got out of there, he was trembling softly on the pavement, as if he were trying to limbo-dance under an impossibly low bar. I can assure you now, the guy didn't die that morning. A year later we came face-to-face at an amusement park near Bay City, and he looked perfectly fine, strapped into a contraption that would — a few seconds after our eyes met — roll him into a triple corkscrew at eighty miles an hour. I like to imagine that the roller-coaster ride shook his vision of me into an aberration that stuck in his mind for the rest of his earthly life.

For what it's worth, the back streets of Sault Ste. Marie, Michigan, were made of concrete with nubs of stone mixed in, crisscrossed with crevices, passing grand old homes fallen into disrepair — homes breathing the smell of mildew and dry rot from their broken windows. Ernie drove with his hand up at the noon position while the police sirens wove through the afternoon heat behind us. The sound was frail, distant, and meaningless. We'd heard the same thing at least a dozen times in the past three weeks, from town to town, always respectfully distant, unraveling, twisting around like a smoke in a breeze until it disappeared. Ernie had a knack for guiding us out of bad situations. We stuck up a convenience store, taking off with fifty bucks and five green-and-white cartons of menthol cigarettes. Then a few days later we hogtied a liquor-store clerk and made off with a box of Cutty Sark and five rolls of Michigan scratch-off Lotto tickets. Under Ernie's leadership, we tied up our victims with bravado, in front of the fish-eyed video monitors, our heads in balaclavas. We put up the V sign and shouted: Liberation for all! For good measure, we turned to the camera and yelled: Patty Hearst lives! The next morning the *Detroit Free Press* Sunday edition carried a photo, dramatically smudgy, of the three of us bent and rounded off by the lens, with our guns in the air. The accompanying article speculated on our significance. According to the article, we were a highly disciplined group with strong connections to California, our gusto and verve reflecting a nationwide resurgence of Weathermen-type radicals. — A place to launch the boat will provide itself, Ernie said, sealing his lips around his dangling cigarette and pulling in smoke. Marsha rooted in the glove box and found a flaying knife, serrated and brutal-looking, with a smear of dried blood on the oak handle. She handed it to me, dug around some more, and found a baggie with pills, little blue numbers; a couple of bright reds, all mystery and portent. She spun it around a few times and then gave out a long yodel that left our ears tingling. Marsha was a champion yodeler. Of course we popped the pills and swallowed them dry while Ernie raged through the center of town, running two red lights, yanking the boat behind us like an afterthought. Marsha had her feet on the dash, and her hair tangled beautifully around her eyes and against her lips. It was the best feeling in the world to be running from the law with a boat in tow, fishtailing around corners, tossing our back wheels into the remnants of the turn, rattling wildly over the potholes, roaring through a shithole town that was desperately trying to stay afloat in the modern world and finding itself sinking deeper into squalor beneath a sky that unfurled blue and deep. All this along with drugs that were, thank Christ, swiftly going about their perplexing work, turning the whole show inside out and making us acutely aware of the fact that above all we were nothing much more than a collection of raw sensations. Marsha's legs emerging beautiful from her fringed cutoff shorts — the shorts are another story — and her bare toes, with her nails painted cherry red, wiggling in the breeze from the window. The seaway at the bottom of the street, spread out in front of a few lonely houses, driftwood gray, rickety and grand, baking in the summer heat. They crackled with dryness. They looked ready to explode into flames. They looked bereft of all hope. In front of a Victorian, a single dog, held taut by a long length of rope, barked and tried to break free, turning and twisting and looping the full circumference of his plight. We parked across the street, got out of the truck, and looked at him while he, in turn, looked back. He was barking SOS. Over and over again. Bark bark bark. Bark bark bark. Bark bark bark. Bark bark bark. Bark bark bark. Until finally Ernie yanked his gun from his belt, pointed quickly, with both hands extended out for stability, and released a shot that materialized as a burst of blooming dust near the dog; then another shot that went over his head and splintered a porch rail. The dog stopped barking and the startled air glimmered, got brighter, shiny around the edges, and then fell back into the kind of dull haze you find only in small towns in summer, with no one around but a dog who has finally lost the desire to bark. The dog sat staring at us. He was perfectly fine but stone-still. Out in the water a container ship stood with solemnity, as if dumbfounded by its own passage, covered in bright green tarps. — We're gonna drop her right here, Ernie said, unleashing the boat, throwing back restraining straps, trying to look like he knew what he was doing. The water was a five-foot fall from the corrugated steel and poured cement buttress of the wall. The Army Corps of Engineers had constructed a breakwall of ridiculous proportions. We lifted the hitch, removed it from the ball, and wiggled the trailer over so that the bow of the boat hung over the edge. Then without consultation — working off the mutual energies of our highs — we lifted the trailer and spilled the boat over the edge. It landed in the water with a plop, worked hard to right itself, coming to terms with its new place in the world, settling back as Ernie manipulated the rope and urged it along to some ladder rungs. To claim this was anything but a love story would be to put Sault Ste. Marie in a poor light. The depleted look in the sky and the sensation of the pills working in our bloodstream, enlivening the water, the slap and pop of the metal hull over the waves. The superfreighter (the one with green tarps) looming at our approach. To go into those details too much would be to bypass the essential fact of the matter. I was deeply in love with Marsha. Nothing else in the universe mattered. I would have killed for her, I would have swallowed the earth like an egg-eating snake. I would have turned inside out in my own skin. I was certain that I might have stepped from the boat and walked on the water, making little shuffling movements, conserving my energy, doing what Jesus did but only better. Jesus walked on water to prove a point. I would have done it for the hell of it. Just for fun. To prove my love. Up at the bow Ernie stood with his heel on the gunwale, one elbow resting on a knee, looking like the figurehead on a Viking ship. I sat in the back with Marsha, watching as she held the rubber grip and guided the motor with her suspiciously well-groomed fingers. I could see in the jitteriness of her fingers that she was about to swing the boat violently to the side. Maybe not as some deeply mean-spirited act but just as a joke on Ernie, who was staring straight ahead, making little hoots, patting his gun, and saying, — We're coming to get you. We're gonna highjack us a motherfucking superfreighter, boys. I put my hand over Marsha's and held it there. Her legs, caught in the fringed grip of her tight cutoff jeans, were gleaming with spray. (She'd amputated the pants back in a hotel in Manistee, laying them over her naked thighs while we watched, tweaking the loose threads out to make them just right.) Tiny beads of water clung to the downy hairs along the top of her thighs, fringed with her cutoff jeans, nipping and tucking up into her crotch. Who knows? Maybe she was looking at my legs, too, stretched against her own, the white half-moon of my knees poking through the holes in my jeans. When I put my hand over hers I felt our forces conjoin into a desire to toss Ernie overboard.

Two nights later we were alone in an old motel, far up in the nether regions of the Upper Peninsula, near the town of Houghton, where her friend Charlene had OD'ed a few years back. Same hotel, exactly. Same room too. She'd persuaded me that she had to go and hold a wake for her dead friend. (— I gotta go to the same hotel, she said. — The same room.) The hotel was frequented mainly by sailors, merchant-marine types, a defiled place with soggy rank carpet padding and dirty towels. In bed we finished off a few of Tull's pills. Marsha was naked, resting on her side as she talked to me in a solemn voice about Charlene and how much they had meant to each other one summer, and how, when her own father was on a rage, they would go hide out near the airport, along the fence out there, hanging out and watching the occasional plane arrive, spinning its propellers wildly and making tipping wing gestures as if in a struggle to conjure the elements of flight. Smoking joints and talking softly, they poured out secrets the way only stoner girls can — topping each other's admissions, one after the other, matter-of-factly saying yeah, I did this guy who lived in Detroit and was a dealer and he, like, he like was married and we took his car out to the beach and spent two days doing it. Listening to her talk, it was easy to imagine the two of them sitting out there in the hackweed and elderberry on cooler summer nights, watching the silent airstrips, cracked and neglected, waiting for the flight from Chicago. I'd spent my own time out in that spot. It was where Marsha and I figured out that we were bound by coincidence: our fathers had both worked to their deaths in the paint booth at Fisher Body, making sure the enamel was spread evenly, suffering from the gaps in their masks, from inhaled solvents, and from producing quality automobiles.

I was naked on the bed with Marsha, slightly buzzed, but not stoned out of my sense of awareness. I ran my hand along her hip and down into the concave smoothness of her waist while she, in turn, reached around and pawed and cupped my ass, pulling me forward against her as she cried softly in my ear, just wisps of breath, about nothing in particular except that we were about to have sex. I was going to roll her over softly, expose her ass, find myself against her, and then press my lips to her shoulder blades as I sank in. When I got to that point, I became aware of the ashen cinder-block smell of the hotel room, the rubber of the damp carpet padding, the walls smeared with mildew, and the large russet stains that marked the dripping zone inside the tub and along the upper rim of the toilet. Outside, the hotel — peeling pink stucco, with a pale blue slide curling into an empty pool — stood along an old road, a logging route, still littered with the relics of a long-past tourist boom. The woods across from the place were thick with undergrowth, and the gaps between trees seemed filled with the dark matter of interstellar space. When we checked in it was just past sunset, but the light was already drawn away by the forest. It went on for miles and miles. Just looking at it too long would be to get lost, to wander in circles. You could feel the fact that we were far up along the top edge of the United States; the north pole began its pull around there, and the aurora borealis spread across the sky. I like to think that we both came out of our skin, together, in one of those orgasmic unifications. I like to think that two extremely lonely souls — both fearing that they had just killed another human being — united themselves carnally for some wider, greater sense of the universe; I like to think that maybe for one moment in my life, I reached up and ran my hand through God's hair. But who knows? Who really knows? The truth remains lodged back in that moment, and that moment is gone, and all I can honestly attest to is that we did feel a deep affection for our lost comrade Ernie at the very moment we were both engaged in fornication. (That's the word Ernie used: I'd like to fornicate with that one over there, or I'm going to find me some fornication.) We lay on the bed and let the breeze come through the hotel window — cool and full of yellow pine dust — across our damp bellies. The air of northern Michigan never quite matches the freshness of Canada. There's usually a dull iron-ore residue in it, or the smell of dead flies accumulating between the stones onshore. Staring up at the ceiling, Marsha felt compelled to talk about her dead friend. She lit a smoke and took a deep inhalation and let it sift from between her teeth. (I was endlessly attracted to the big unfixed gap-tooth space between her two front ones.) Here's the story she told me in as much detail as I can muster:

Charlene was a hard-core drifter, born in Sarnia, Ontario, across the lake from Port Huron. Her grandmother on her mother's side raised her, except for a few summers — the ones in our town — with her deranged auto-worker father. She was passed on to her grandfather on her father's side for some reason, up in Nova Scotia. Her grandfather was an edgy, hard drinker who abused her viciously. Along her ass were little four-leaf-clover scar formations. She ran away from her grandfather, back to her grandmother in Sarnia, and then ran away from her and crossed the International Bridge to Detroit, where she hooked up with a guy named Stan, a maintenance worker at a nursing home, who fixed air conditioners and cleared dementia-plugged toilets. Stan was into cooking crank in his spare time. They set up a lab in a house near Dearborn, in a pretty nice neighborhood, actually. Then one day there was an explosion and Stan got a face full of battery acid. She left him behind and hooked up with another cooker, named King, who had a large operation in a house near Saginaw. She worked with him and helped out, but she never touched the stuff and was angelic and pious about it. Even King saw a kind of beauty in Charlene's abstinence, Marsha said. For all the abuse she had suffered she had a spiritual kind of calm. Her eyes were, like, this amazingly deep blue color. Aside from her scars and all, she still had the whitest, purest skin, Snow White skin, the kind that you just want to touch, like a cool smooth stone. She just got more and more beautiful until eventually the guy named King couldn't stand the gentleness in her eyes and, maybe to try to change things around, he started to beat her face like a punching bag. One afternoon, under the influence of his own product, he had a couple of friends hold her down while he struck her face with a meat pounder, just hammered it, until she was close to death — maybe actually dead. Maybe she left her body and floated above herself and looked down and saw a guy with long shaggy hair and a silver meat hammer bashing her face in and decided it just wasn't worth dying in that kind of situation and so went back into her body. (Marsha was pretty firm in her belief about this part.) Charlene's cheekbones were broken, her teeth shattered. It took about twenty operations on her jaw and teeth just to chew again. Even then, chewing never felt right; her fake teeth

slipped from the roof of her mouth, she talked funny, and a ringing
sounded in her ears when she tried to smile. When she laughed too
hard, her mouth would clamp up and she'd hear a chiming sound,
high in pitch, like bells, and then the sound of windswept rain, or
wind in a shell, or wind through guy wires, or a dry, dusty windswept street, or the rustling of tissue paper, or a sizzling like a single
slice of bacon in a pan, or a dial tone endlessly unwinding in her
eardrum. Forever she was up over herself looking down, watching
King go at her, the two guys holding onto her shoulders, her legs
scissor-kicking, the flash of the hammer until it was impossible to
know what was going on beneath the blood. When Marsha met her
again — a year or so later, in the break room at Wal-Mart, she had
this weirdly deranged face; the out-of-place features demanded
some thought to put straight. I mean it was a mess, Marsha said.
Her nose was folded over. The Detroit team of plastic and oral sur-
geons just couldn't put poor Charlene back together again. A total
Humpty Dumpty. No one was going to spend large amounts of
money on a face of a drifter, anyway. Marsha forced herself to look.
Then Charlene told her the story of King, the reasons for the damage, and the whole time Marsha didn't remove her eyes from the
nose, the warped cheeks, the fishlike mouth. She tried as hard as
she could to see where the beauty had gone and what Charlene
must've been like before King mashed her face, the angelic part,
because she kind of doubted her on that part of the story. As far as
she could remember, from their nights together getting stoned
outside the airport fence, Charlene had been, well, just a normal-
looking kid. But listening to her talk, she put the pieces together
and saw that, yeah, yeah, yeah, maybe this mishmash of features
had once been beautiful. Her eyes were certainly bright blue, and
wide, and she had pale milky skin. That night after work they decided to go out together, not to a bar where she'd get hassled but
just to buy some beer and go to Charlene's apartment and drink.
She had some little pills she called goners, good God goners, something like that. So they went to her apartment, took the pills, drank
some beer, and decided to watch *Blue Velvet*. Whatever transpired
next, according to Marsha, was amazing and incredibly sensual;
they were stoned together, watching the movie, and suddenly between them there grew a hugely powerful sense of closeness; when
Marsha looked down at her on the couch, Charlene appeared to
her too gorgeous not to kiss (that's how she put it, exactly). Her

mouth was funny because her teeth were out, so it was just softness and nothing else, and then, somehow, they undressed — I mean it wasn't like a first for either of us, Marsha said — and she fell down between Charlene's knees, and made her come, and then they spent the night together. A few days later, Charlene quit her job and split for Canada, back over the bridge, and then the next thing Marsha heard she was up north at this hotel with some guys and then she OD'ed.

The story — and the way she told it to me, early in the morning, just before dawn — as both of us slid down from our highs, our bodies tingling and half asleep, turned me on in a grotesque way. To get a hard-on based on a story of abuse seemed wrong, but it happened, and we made love to each other again, for the second time, and we both came wildly and lay there for a while until she made her confession. — I made that up, completely. I never knew a drifter named Charlene from Canada, and I certainly wouldn't sleep with a fuckface reject like that. No way. I just felt like telling a story. I felt like making one up for you. I thought it would be interesting and maybe shed some light on the world. The idea — the angelic girl, the perfect girl, the one with perfect beauty getting all mashed up like that. That's something I think about a lot. She sat up, smoking a cigarette, stretching her legs out. Dawn was breaking outside. I imagined the light plunging through the trees, and the log trucks roaring past. For a minute I felt like knocking her on the head. I imagined pinning her down and giving her face a go with a meat hammer. But I found it easy to forgive her because the story she made up had sparked wild and fanciful sex. I kissed her and looked into her eyes and noticed that they were sad and didn't move away from mine (but that's not what I noticed). What did I notice? I can't put words to it except to say she had an elegiac sadness there, and an unearned calm, and that something had been stolen from her pupils. — You weren't making that up, I said. — You couldn't make that shit up, she responded, holding her voice flat and cold. — So it was all true. — I didn't say that. I just said you couldn't make that shit up.

*

We're gonna get nailed for what we did, she said, later, as we ate breakfast. Around us truckers in their long-billed caps leaned into plates of food, clinking the heavy silverware, devouring eggs in communal silence. A waitress was dropping dirty dishes into the slop sink, lifting each of them up and letting them fall, as if to test the durability of high-grade, restaurant-quality plates. — We're gonna get nailed, I agreed. I wasn't up for an argument about it. The fact was, our stream of luck would go on flowing for a while longer. Then I'd lose Marsha and start searching for a Charlene. For his part, the world could devour plenty of Ernies; each day they vaporized into the country's huge horizon. — He's probably dead. He knew how to swim, but he didn't look too confident in his stroke. — Yeah, I agreed. Ernie had bobbed up to the surface shouting profanities and striking out in our direction with a weird sidestroke. His lashing hands sustained just his upper body. The rest was sunken out of sight and opened us up to speculation as to whether his boots were on or off. After he was tossed from the boat, he stayed under a long, long time. When he bobbed up, his face had a wrinkled, babyish look of betrayal. He blew water at us, cleared his lips, and in a firm voice said, — You're dead, man, both of you. Then he cursed my mother and father and the day they were born, Marsha's cunt and her ass and her mother and father and God and the elements and the ice-cold water of the seaway and the ship, which was about four hundred yards away (— come on, motherfuckers, save my ass). He kept shouting like this until a mouthful of water gagged him. We were swinging around, opening it up full-throttle, looping around, sending a wake in his direction and heading in. When we got to the breakwall we turned and saw that he was still out there, splashing, barely visible. The ship loomed stupidly in the background, oblivious to his situation. A single gull spiraled overhead, providing us with an omen to talk about later. (Gulls are God's death searchers, Marsha told me. Don't be fooled by their white feathers or any of that shit. Gulls are best at finding the dead.) Then we got back in Tull's truck and headed through town and out, just following roads north toward Houghton, leaving Ernie to whatever destiny he had as one more aberration adrift in the St. Lawrence Seaway system. For a long time we didn't say a word. We just drove. The radio was playing an old Neil Young song. We turned it up, and then up some more, and left it loud like that, until it was just so much rattling noise.

KENT NELSON

Public Trouble

FROM *The Antioch Review*

WE SHOULD HAVE BEEN more alert, all of us, more aware. Those closer to the circumstances, like Ivo Darius and his wife, Frieda, might have figured out something was wrong, but they were busy feeding cattle and had used the downtime in winter to build an aluminum storage shed. The dental hygienist, Sara Warren, who also lived out there, could have said more, but why would she? Of course Emily Jefferson's silence was understandable, but she didn't enter the picture until later, when it was too late to change the course of events. We have all pointed at social services, but they can't be involved until someone comes forward, unless there's public trouble — malnourishment, truancy from school, a suspicious bruise. And there wasn't. But even with full knowledge in advance, could we have done anything? Even if all of us together had been vigilant for the signs, even if someone had spoken up, could we have prevented it from happening?

Everyone knew the Olshanskys. The father, Del, worked part-time at the loading dock at Wal-Mart, and we often saw him in town at the Silver Nugget on Main Street or on the town's embarrassing highway strip at the bowling alley, or Taco Bell, or the Branding Iron. He was a handsome man — dark eyes, a strong nose, chin and jaw unshaved, the way movie stars appear these days. If he'd cared at all for appearances, he might have been called dashing. He looked like the sort who'd lose his temper and get into bar fights, but no, he was calm, offhand, halfway pleasant, no matter what he'd had to drink. His appearance was rough — his jeans had holes in the knees, and his shirts were torn — and he didn't have much ambition. That isn't a crime. The sheriff, all of us in town, had seen a lot of men worse than Del, lots of couples worse than Del and Billie Jean.

The Olshanskys lived out past the landfill in the piñon-juniper foothills where there wasn't much water. They had dug a well and watered a patch of grass bordered by rocks worn smooth by the river. There was an Elcar-fenced pen for a dog, too, though when we were there — in the winter, when this all happened — there wasn't a dog. The house was really a trailer they'd added on to. In front they'd built a porch with a green plastic snowshed roof slanting to one side, and a façade of cinder blocks to hide the cheap vinyl siding. In back, they'd cobbled on two bedrooms with views of the Sangre de Cristos. Billie Jean was a nurse's assistant at the hospital, just a hundred beds, but apparently she had time for a garden because there was a raised bed inside railroad ties and hauled-in topsoil. We don't know what she grew because the plants were black and draped in snow.

Most of us don't blame Del and Billie Jean. We think it started at that school, though who knows whether a beginning to such a thing can be deciphered. Even if it didn't start at the school, the place was a catalyst. It had to be. Before that, for the first several years they were around, the Olshansky kids had gone to the public school. They lived in town most of that time, and even for two years after they moved to the trailer, the kids took the school bus in. Danielle, the oldest, was Billie Jean's daughter from a former marriage. She was a smart kid, and one of the English teachers, Mary Padua, thought Danielle had a photographic memory, because she recited "The Rime of the Ancient Mariner" and often wrote answers on exams in the exact same words that were in the texts. If she'd wanted to, she could have gone to college, but college wasn't an ambition for most high school students here, and after graduation she moved upriver to Nathrop and worked as a scheduler for raft trips.

Six years younger was Marya, Del's first. She was the athlete. A lot of us had kids in school, and all through junior high and high school we saw Marya play basketball. She was not just good, she was great. She leaped higher than any other girl we'd seen, and her jump shot floated to the basket. She was pretty, too, tall and lithe, and ambitious. Often when we delivered our children to school in the mornings, Marya had ridden her bike six miles in from the trailer and was at the playground shooting baskets.

The youngest was Carlos, two grades behind Marya. No one understood naming a child Carlos when he wasn't Hispanic, but, as someone said, it's no different from naming a child Danielle or Kurt. The thing about Carlos was — how do you say it about a boy? — he was easy to look at. He had long blond hair, high cheekbones, a perfect nose. His eyes were deep set, shadowed, and such a pale shade of blue that when you saw them in a certain light, they reminded you of sky. Many of us, when we first laid eyes on him, said, "There is the most beautiful boy in the world."

During the school year we heard about Carlos every day. Our children came home saying Carlos this, Carlos that, how good he was at sports, how pretty he was. When he walked by in the hall, apparently everyone, all grades, boys and girls both, stopped whatever they were doing and watched him pass.

He wasn't a big kid, but he played halfback and ran track, and he was a good student, all A's. The girls loved him, and the boys admired him, too, though they were all a little afraid of him. Because of his beauty, he wasn't one of them.

"He doesn't choose one girl." That's what all our kids said. That's what the parents heard. "He likes everybody," they said. Or, "He barely talks. We can't tell what girl he likes."

"What would you like him to say?" we asked.

The kids didn't know what Carlos should say. Silence was power. It made them uneasy he was so quiet. He went days without saying anything. He wouldn't even answer questions in class.

The Olshanskys came from up north, Wyoming or Montana, no one knew for sure. Del was pretty vague on the subject. When we first knew them, they lived on River Street, right downtown, six blocks from the water, in a rented house barely big enough for a couple, let alone a family. At that time, Del did home repair, mowed lawns, worked freelance as an auto mechanic. We all gave him work. When Fred Larsen put a garage on his split-level, he hired Del for the crew, and when Jerry Matuzcek's Blazer broke down, he paid Del to fix it. Del was quiet but personable, and talked if he was spoken to. They lived in that house on River Street for several years, and there was never any trouble. Nedda Saenz owned the house, and she said they were late every month with the rent, but eventually they got the money to her. "I don't know why it wasn't on the first," Nedda said, "but at least they paid."

They weren't first-of-the-month people. They had a way about them that made people unsure. They *looked* unreliable. Billie Jean, for instance, never looked right at you when she spoke, and she was frequently late to work at the hospital. Once there was a dispute about some missing money. Everyone thought she'd taken it — she never denied it — but it was later proved to be a clerical error. Why wouldn't she have said she was not guilty? And though Del never had enough money for new clothes, he had enough to buy beer. They never saved for another car, or a newer used one, but Del managed to keep their '81 Dodge truck running, even if it wasn't the most efficient vehicle. They weren't shiftless, exactly, but no one would have been surprised if one day the whole family was up and gone. We thought of them as about to disappear.

At first we admired them, reluctantly perhaps, for buying the trailer and settling in. At the same time, it was foolish because the land was glacial moraine, and they had to put in a deep well. They had payments to make every month on the land, and in general it cost more to live out of town. Telephone and trash pickup was more expensive; appliance repairmen and plumbers charged mileage; Billie Jean had to drive farther to work. And you're isolated — that's a hidden cost. There weren't many neighbors if you needed help.

For a few years there, we in town were less attentive to them. Ivo and Frieda Darius and Luther and Sara Warren lived farther west up the gravel road where the creek came out of the mountains, and they saw the Olshanskys more often than anyone else. Sara worked in a dentist's office, and she drove by every morning. She frequently saw the Olshansky kids at the bus stop — the three of them standing alone on the highway. In warmer weather, coming home late in the day, she sometimes saw Del working on the façade of the trailer or Billie Jean digging in the garden. Ivo Darius was older, a rancher, and was frequently laid up with real or imaginary illnesses. He said he had heard gunshots a few times — target practice, he assumed — out in the arroyo. There was nothing unusual about that. Ivo owned two rifles himself and sometimes shot marauding skunks or coyotes.

The only occasion anyone had close contact with one of the Olshanskys was on a spring morning when Sara Warren saw Carlos running to the bus stop. Carlos was twelve or thirteen then, and the Olshanskys had lived in the trailer more than a year. At the bottom of the hill, the bus was pulling away, and Carlos accepted a lift to school. Sara asked the predictable general questions — how was school? How do you like living out here? What are you doing this summer? But Carlos made no reply beyond a few guttural sounds. Carlos stared straight out the windshield as if he were fixated or drugged, or so focused inward he hadn't heard the questions. Sara said later she wasn't sure Carlos could speak. Sara remembered that particular morning because an eagle had dived down right next to the gravel road into the piñons and killed a fawn, and Carlos never looked.

The Christian school started three years ago. We knew there were splinter sects in our town, groups besides the Episcopalians and the Lutherans and the Catholics. (We don't have many Jews here.) Most of these groups met in people's houses until they got enough members to build a cinder-block church somewhere on cheap land. They were fringe people. They didn't attend city council meetings or the beerfest or the high school football games. They were both secretive and proselytizing. Their churches spread by word of mouth, and none of us knew exactly who these people were.

Warren Nixon started one of these groups, the Church of the Major Prophecy. He was divorced, forty-something, and had a large nose and a crewcut. He sold home, car, health, and life insurance out of a one-man office on First Street. For years he'd been a member of the Presbyterian church across from the Safeway, and one day out of the blue, on the golf course on a Sunday afternoon, he had a vision to start his own church. How he had this vision and what it entailed didn't concern or excite most of us. Who believed in such miracles? But over a couple of years he attracted enough people of like mind to build a church out on the highway. He sold his house in town to do it and rented an apartment above the Gambles' dry-goods store.

None of these developments had anything to do with us, and if we'd thought about it, we'd have assumed they had nothing much to do with the Olshanskys, either. None of us had ever heard Del mention God or Jesus Christ, except as swear words. Billie Jean might have been more of a churchgoer — we learned later from her sister she and her ex-husband had been in the Living Springs Church in Sioux Falls, South Dakota, but what difference did that make? She hadn't been in a church here, and she wasn't a member of the Church of the Major Prophecy.

But Del and Billie Jean sent Carlos to the church school. By then Danielle had graduated, and Marya, to pursue her basketball career, was boarding with a family in Colorado Springs. Carlos was in ninth grade, and when he was taken out of the public school, we heard about it. Carlos was the star the other children looked to, the one whose existence made theirs hopeful. He was the boy about whom they would talk the rest of their lives. "I knew this boy once," they'd say, "Carlos Olshansky, who was the most beautiful boy in the world."

And then he was gone.

We all admit that was one of the signs. When he was sent to that school we knew something was wrong, but we couldn't see it clearly. Perhaps we were afraid to look. The social service agencies, the sheriff for all his vigilance, the community volunteers — the people you'd expect to observe such things — didn't notice anything particularly wrong. Carlos went to the church school. It was the Olshanskys' choice. They had the right to send him there.

Of course, there were small details we thought about later — Danielle's missed appointment at the dentist, Billie Jean's not showing up a day here or there at work (though she called in sick each time), Marya's coming home for two weeks in the middle of basketball season. But what should we have read into these things? What did they mean, separately or taken together? A family in chaos, a dissolving of a psyche, a catastrophe about to unfold? Besides, we had our own lives to lead, our own grocery shopping, mortgages to pay, children to raise.

It was the fire through the snow that first caught Frieda Darius's attention out her kitchen window. She was making soup for Ivo, laid up in bed. It was February, a Thursday, early dark. The wind was hurling snowflakes sideways, and when she saw the flames, she thought the piñon trees were on fire. Ivo couldn't get out of bed, so she investigated in her Jeep, getting close enough to see the Olshanskys' trailer burning.

By the time the fire trucks got there — they carried their own water — most of the trailer had melted. There were two bodies burned beyond recognition in the kitchen, and one in the neighboring bedroom. The fire chief said chicken grease had ignited on the propane stove. But when the forensics experts identified the bodies — Billie Jean and Danielle in the kitchen, and Marya in the nearer bedroom — we learned they'd all been shot beforehand.

We couldn't find Del or Carlos. The truck wasn't there, so the first theory was that Del had done it and had taken off with his boy. The sheriff put out an all-points bulletin on Del and the Dodge, but almost before the APB had circulated, Claudia Reese, the rural mailperson, found Del's truck, with Del's body in it, parked in front of the Jeffersons' house on County Road 268. He was slumped against the passenger door with a single gunshot wound in his forehead.

The sheriff dusted the wheel for fingerprints, but it was cold, and whoever shot Del was probably wearing gloves. The window on the driver's side was open, and snow had blown into the cab. Whatever footprints there might have been were obliterated by snow, and underneath the snow, the ground was frozen rock-hard. Being on the passenger side, Del could have been shot anywhere and driven there, but of course then there would have had to have been at least two of them, two perpetrators, because they'd have needed another car to get away.

The Jeffersons' ranch house was the only house within a quarter of a mile of the truck, the original homestead on the mesa, where a five-acre subdivision had been recently approved. Emily Jefferson was home that night — Larry was in Pueblo at a seminar on computer programming — but she hadn't seen or heard anything. It had been windy and snowy, and she'd built a fire in the stove.

Random chance: That was the next predominant theory. A couple of psychos had turned off the highway — that explained the extra car — and the first place they'd come to was the Olshanskys'. They'd wanted money. In what was left of the trailer there were signs of a hurried search. In the back bedroom, drawers had been ripped open, and a purse was opened. But why kill everyone? Why was Del in his truck two miles away? Why had they kidnapped Carlos? Or had they killed him too? We searched for Carlos's body in a half-mile radius around the trailer, but found nothing but deer scat and rabbit tracks in the snow.

So there we were without clues. No insight. Nothing. All that weekend we talked about the Olshanskys — who they were, why they'd come to town, why anyone would want to kill them. So far as we could ascertain, they were ordinary people, like other families everywhere, nothing special.

Del had no relatives we could find, but Billie Jean had mentioned to Agnes Day at the hospital she had a sister in Rapid City, so the sheriff called her. We learned their mother was still alive in a nursing home, and from the way the sister reacted, we understood there were hard feelings between the sisters, apparently because Billie Jean had run off with Del. Billie Jean had married into evil.

Then late Saturday it came to light from Wilferd Barkley that Del's truck had been parked at that same turnout several times before. Wilferd was a stonemason who lived farther out the country road in an A-frame built thirty years ago in the hippie days. He kept a few sheep and goats, and he poached deer that wandered into his yard (he'd been fined for it twice). He wasn't the most trustworthy of witnesses — he drank up his disability check every month — but he knew Del's truck, and why would he lie?

After a few inquiries, Emily Jefferson admitted seeing Del, though she denied anything was going on, and Wilferd couldn't contradict her. Nobody believed it, though. Anyway, a possible motive was established for Larry Jefferson to have killed Del, and, in a rage, perhaps, the whole Olshansky family. So that evening the sheriff drove to Pueblo and hauled Larry out of his seminar. It was obvious right from the start Larry had no idea who Del Olshansky was. He'd heard of Marya, the basketball star, but that was the only family name he knew. He didn't know Emily was seeing Del, but it didn't surprise him. She was cold as ice to him. He called her a mousy woman with bad teeth.

That threw the situation into the same muddle as before, back to the idea of random chance.

Then on Sunday, another body turned up — Warren Nixon. He hadn't appeared at church, and when his phone was busy for half an hour, Jeff Bates, the assistant minister, went to look for him. Warren was in his apartment, face-down, bludgeoned with one of his own golf clubs.

In this day and age, with kids shooting other kids in the schools, oil spilling into the oceans, and people flying airplanes into buildings, nothing is bizarre anymore, but for our town this was bizarre. Warren Nixon had photos of boys lying around, a computer full of child pornography, movies. All young boys. Beautiful boys like Carlos Olshansky.

Just like that, Carlos became both a victim and a suspect.

*

That Warren Nixon lived in this community so long and kept his predilection hidden surprised us. We discovered he had gone to Denver, to Chicago, to Los Angeles to gratify his base desires, but here, he must have been tormented because right in front of him, practically handed over, was the most beautiful boy any of us had ever seen. He had to be careful; he had to work slowly, to curry favor. But something had gone wrong.

We imagined this scenario: there was another lover, a visitor, perhaps, with similar perverse tastes. This hypothetical person was in league with Warren Nixon, a disciple, a fringe character none of us noticed. This unknown person fell in love with Carlos, and, in a moment of rage and jealousy (who knew what Carlos felt?) beat Warren to death. The man took Carlos back to the trailer to get Carlos's things, and Billie Jean intervened. There was an argument, and the lover happened to have a pistol and shot everyone. It was at that moment Del drove up in his truck.

Was Carlos involved? Who else but Carlos could have driven the second car? Or was there a second car? Had Carlos acted alone? He might have killed Warren Nixon and then his family, driven his father's truck to Emily Jefferson's, and then walked to the highway. It was less than a mile. He could have hitchhiked from there.

Most of us think Carlos must have been drugged or otherwise coerced into participating. Perhaps there were two other men, or another couple. Carlos was the innocent casualty of someone else's perversions, the prey. He was frightened and threatened by someone bigger and stronger, a person in a position of power, a church person. Beautiful Carlos, still to be looked for.

Since these events, in their divorce, Emily Jefferson admitted to an affair. She confided to a friend Del insisted on making love every which way — in a chair, against a wall, from behind. Had he abused Carlos? Or had Billie Jean? Or one of the sisters? It came to light Marya had been expelled from her school in Colorado Springs for punching a teammate at practice. Marijuana was found in Danielle's room at the back of the trailer, and her raft company friends said she was a heavy user. Who knew about this family?

It is hard to inquire after the dead. Only Carlos might tell us the truth. And where is he?

*

There is one recollection we've wondered about, a story several people have come forward with — Arne Bullard, Donna Snow, Linda Sayles — all of whom have businesses downtown. They remember the day eight years ago, Carlos was five or six, when Danielle and Marya dressed him up as a girl. They had put makeup on him — eyeliner, rouge, and lipstick — that's what Donna Snow recalled. "He was a girly boy," she said, "with his hair curled and fixed up in blue ribbons. He was walking in a pink dress, and so pretty. They paraded him up and down Main Street, past all the shops and stores." Arne remembered it, too, seeing them through his barbershop window. "He was having a good time," Arne said. "He was holding the girls' hands and laughing, not resisting in the least. Of course, what did he know? He was a little kid."

Now there are other things people remember about Carlos, like his teachers at school and the boys on the football team and the girls who watched him in the halls. He was a smart kid, but so quiet, shy, and respectful. Though he was friendly with everyone, he had no girlfriend. He let people come to him.

Maybe Carlos is dead. That would explain why no one has found him in the year since this happened. The town has moved past the killings; people don't talk about it so much. The remains of the Olshanskys' trailer have been removed and the land sold to a developer, though Luther Warren and Ivo and Frieda Darius are protesting the rezoning to one-acre lots. Marya's class graduated from the high school, and in another two years, Carlos's will be gone, too, dispersed with their stories. The Church of the Major Prophecy has disbanded and the sign's been taken down. No other church has seen fit to establish itself there, so the cinder-block building is empty, the spire tilted a little to one side. Recently a cabinet company has been interested in the site.

In our town businesses go on, children are born, the old people get sick and die: there's nothing new about that. And in the wider world, the space shuttle has broken apart, the war in Iraq is past, the suicide bombings continue. No one can change what happens, but the events recede, especially now when we know so much. We are lucky, aren't we, that in the history of our town and our country, in the history of the world even with its wars and famines and plagues, no one has been able to stop time.

DANIEL OROZCO

Officers Weep

FROM *Harper's Magazine*

700 Block, First Street. Parking violation. Car blocking driveway. Citation issued. City Tow notified.

5700 Block, Central Boulevard. Public disturbance. Rowdy juveniles on interurban bus. Suspects flee before officers arrive.

400 Block, Sycamore Circle. Barking-dog complaint. Attempts to shush dog unsuccessful. Citation left in owner's mailbox. Animal Control notified.

1300 Block, Harvest Avenue. Suspicious odor. Homeowner returning from extended trip reports a bad odor — a gas leak or "the smell of death." Officers investigate. Odor ascertained to be emanating from a neighbor's mimosa tree in unseasonal bloom. "The smell of life," officer [Shield #647] ponders aloud. Officers nod. Homeowner rolls eyes, nods politely.

3900 Block, Fairview Avenue. Shady Glen Retirement Apartments. Loud-noise complaint. "What kind of noise?" officers ask. Complainant simply says it was "a loud report." "A gunshot?" officers query. "A scream? Explosion? What?" Complainant becomes adamant, shakes walnut cane in fisted hand: "It was a loud report!" Officers mutter, reach for batons, then relent. Officers report report.

700 Block, Sixth Street. Public disturbance. Kleen-Azza-Whistle Cleaners. Two women in fistfight over snakeskin vest. Each declares ownership of claim ticket found on floor by officers. In an inspired Solomonic moment, officer [Shield #647] waves pair of tai-

lor's shears and proposes cutting vest in half. Approaching the contested garment, he slips its coveted skins between the forged blades. And thus is the true mother revealed!

3600 Block, Sunnyside Drive. Vandalism. Handball courts in Phoenix Park defaced. Spray-paint graffiti depicts intimate congress between a male and a female, a panoramic mural of heterosexual coupling that spans the entire length of the courts' front wall, its every detail rendered with a high degree of clinical accuracy. Officers gape. Minutes pass in slack-jawed silence, until officer [Shield #647] ascertains incipient boner. Officer horrified, desperately reroutes train of thought, briskly repositions his baton. Second officer [Shield #325] takes down Scene Report, feigns unawareness of her partner's tumescent plight, ponders the small blessings of womanhood. Vandalism reported to Parks & Rec Maintenance.

900 Block, Maple Road. Canine-litter violation. Homeowner complains of dog feces on front lawn. Officers investigate, ascertain droppings are fresh, reconnoiter on foot. They walk abreast, eyes asquint and arms akimbo, their hands at rest among the ordnance of their utility belts: radio receiver, pepper spray, ammo pouch, handcuffs, keys and whistles, and change for the meter. Officers jingle like Santas. Their shoulders and hips move with the easy dip and roll of Classic Cop Swagger. "That business back there," she says, "with the snakeskin vest?" He grunts in acknowledgment, scanning the scene for untoward canine activity. "I — I liked that." Her voice is hoarse, throaty, tentative, as he's never heard before. He nods, purses lips, nods some more. She nervously fingers butt of her service revolver. He briskly repositions his baton. A high color passes from one steely countenance to the other. Officers blush. Midswagger, elbows graze. And within that scant touch, the zap of a thousand stun guns. Up ahead, another steaming pile, whereupon poop trail turns cold. Officers terminate search, notify Animal Control.

9200 Block, Bonny Road. Vehicular burglary. Items stolen from pickup truck: a pair of work boots, a hardhat, safety goggles, and — per victim's description — a cherry-red-enameled Thaesselhaeffer Sidewinder chain saw, with an 8.5-horsepower, two-stroke motor in a titanium-alloy housing, a four-speed trigger clutch with auto-reverse, and the words DADDY'S SWEET BITCH stenciled in flaming orange-yellow letters along the length of its thirty-four-inch saw bar. Victim weeps. Officers take Scene Report, refer victim to Crisis Center.

5600 Block, Fairvale Avenue. Traffic stop. Illegal U-turn. Officer [Shield #325] approaches vehicle. Her stride longer than her legs can accommodate, she leans too much into each step, coming down hard on her heels, as if trudging through sand. As she returns to Patrol Unit, a lock of her hair — thin and drab, a lusterless mousy brown — slips down and swings timidly across her left eye, across the left lens of her mirrored wraparounds. Officer tucks errant lock behind ear, secures it in place with a readjustment of duty cap. Her gestures are brisk and emphatic, as if she were quelling a desire to linger in the touch of her own hair. Officer [Shield #647] observes entire intimate sequence from his position behind wheel of Patrol Unit. Officer enthralled. Officer ascertains the potential encroachment of love, maybe, into his cautious and lonely life. Officer swallows hard.

700 Block, Willow Court. Dogs running loose. Pack of strays reported scavenging in neighborhood, turning over garbage cans and compost boxes. Worried homeowner reports cat missing, chats up officers, queries if they like cats. "Yes, ma'am," officer [Shield #325] replies. "They are especially flavorful batter-fried." Officers crack up. Levity unappreciated. Officers notify Animal Control, hightail it out of there.

2200 Block, Cherry Orchard Way. Burglary. Three half-gallon cans of chain-saw fuel stolen from open garage.

7800 Block, Frontage Boulevard at Highway 99. Vehicle accident and traffic obstruction. Semitrailer hydroplanes, overturns, spills cargo of Southwestern housewares down Frontage Road West off-ramp. Officers redirect traffic and clear debris: shattered steer skulls; fleshy cactus chunks; the dung-colored shards of indeterminate earthenware; the mangled scrap of copper-plate Kokopellis and dream shamans; and actual, honest-to-God tumbleweeds, rolling along the blacktop. "Tumbleweeds!" officer [Shield #325] exclaims. "Yee-haw!" Roundup commences, and her face gleams with exertion and sheer joy. Her stern little mouth elongates into goofy smile, teeth glinting like beach glass in the sun. As they divert traffic, officer ascertains being observed keenly. The watchful and intimate scrutiny makes her feel, for the first time in a long while, yearned for, desired. Officer [Shield #325] gets all goose-bumpy and flustered, and likes it. DPW Units arrive in their orange trucks, unload sundry orange accoutrements, erect signage: CAUTION, SLOW, OBSTRUCTION. Officers secure scene until State Patrol arrives, with their state jurisdiction and their shiny boots and their funny hats.

200 Block, Windjammer Court. Tall Ships Estates. Criminal trespass. One-armed solicitor selling magazine subscriptions in gated community. Forty-six-year-old suspect is embarrassed, despondent, angry, blames his bad luck on television, on fast food, on "the fucking Internet." Officers suggest cutting fast food some slack, then issue warning, escort suspect to main gate, buy subscriptions to *Firearms Fancier* and *Enforcement Weekly*.

2200 Block, Orange Grove Road. Criminal trespass and vandalism. Winicki's World of Burlwood. Merchant returns from lunch to find furnishings — burlwood dining tables and wardrobes and credenzas, burlwood salad bowls and CD racks, burlwood tie caddies and napkin rings and cheese boards — ravaged. Officers assess scene, do math: Burlwood + Chain Saw = Woodcraft Apocalypse.

800 Block, Clearvale Street. Possible illegal entry. Complainant "senses a presence" upon returning home from yoga class. Officers investigate, ascertain opportunity to practice Cop Swagger, to kick things up a bit. Officer [Shield #325] pulls shoulders back, adds inch to height. Officer [Shield #647] sucks gut in, pulls oblique muscle. Search of premises yields nothing. "That's OK," complainant says. "It's gone now." Officers mutter, blame yoga.

300 Block, Galleon Court. Tall Ships Estates. Criminal trespass and public disturbance. One-armed magazine salesman kicking doors and threatening residents. Scuffle ensues. Officers sit on suspect, call for backup, ponder a cop koan: How do you cuff a one-armed man?

2600 Block, Bloom Road. Public disturbance. Two men in shouting match at Eugene's Tamale Temple. Customer complains of insect in refried beans. Employee claims it's parsley. Officers investigate. Dead spider ascertained in frijoles. "Well, it's not an insect," officer [Shield #325] declares. "Spiders are arachnids, you know." "They're also high in protein," officer [Shield #647] adds. Customer not amused. Argument escalates. Scuffle ensues. Officers take thirty-two-year-old male customer into custody, and — compliments of a grateful and politic Eugene — two Cha Cha Chicken Chimichangas and a Mucho Macho Nacho Plate to go.

6700 Block, Coast Highway. Officers go to beach. They park Patrol Unit at overlook, dig into chimichangas, chew thoughtfully, ponder view. The sky above is heavy and gray, a slab of concrete. The ocean chops fretfully beneath it, muddy green, frothy as old soup. Officer [Shield #647] loves how the two of them can be quiet together. There is some small talk: the upcoming POA ballots; Tasers, yea or nay; the K-9 Unit's dog-fighting scandal. But mostly there is only the tick of the cooling engine, the distant whump of surf against shore, the radio crackling like a comfy fire. Officers sigh. Officer [Shield #647] gestures with chimichanga at vista before them. "There's a saying," he says. "How's it go — ?

> Blue skies all day, officers gay.
> If skies gray and clouds creep, officers weep."

Officer [Shield #325] chews, nods, furrows her brow. "It's an old saying," he adds. "You know. Happy gay. Not gay gay." She laughs. He laughs, too. Relief fills Patrol Unit. A weight is lifted. A door eases itself open and swings wide. His right hand slips from steering wheel and alights, trembling, upon her left knee. Her breath catches, then begins again — steady, resolute. Officers swallow, park chimichangas carefully on dash. Officers turn one to the other. Suspect in back seat asks if they're done with those chimis, complains he's hungry, too, you know, complains that *some*body in Patrol Unit didn't get to eat his combo plate and can they guess who? Officers terminate break, split Mucho Macho Nachos three ways, transport suspect to Division for booking.

400 Block, Glenhaven Road. Criminal trespass and vandalism at construction site. Four pallets of eight-foot framing two-by-fours chainsawed into a grand assortment of useless two- and four-foot one-by-fours. Officers walk scene, sniff air. Sawdust, gas fumes, chain oil. It is a pungent mix, complex and heady. Officers inhale deeply, go all woozy.

2600 Block, Frontage Boulevard at Highway 99. Injury accident. Soil subduction collapses shoulder of 44th Street on-ramp. Three vehicles roll down embankment. Officers notify EMT and DOT Units, assist injured, secure scene. State Patrol pulls up, kills engine, emerges from Patrol Unit like starlet at movie premiere. State Patrol is starch-crisp and preternaturally perspiration-free. State Patrol thanks officers for their assistance, flashes horsey smile, tips dopey hat. Officers sit slouched on Patrol Unit, watch State Patrol strut about. "Prince of Freeways," officer [Shield #647] mutters. "Lord of Turnpikes," he says. Partner suggests that a more collegial relationship with State Patrol is called for. "King of the Road," he continues. "Ayatollah of the Asphalt." Officers giggle, get all silly, love that they can be silly. DPW Units swing by, offer wide range of orange gear and signage: SLOW, CAUTION, choice of SOIL SUBDUCTION or SUBDUCTED SHOULDER.

2200 Block, Felicity Court. Domestic disturbance. Man with golf club pounds on washing machine in garage. Woman in lawn chair applauds his every blow, whistles, barks like dog. Dogs next door whipped into frenzy by noise, bark like woman in lawn chair. Soapy water jets in jugular arcs from innards of crippled washer, streams down driveway, gurgles into gutter. Officers linger in Patrol Unit, assess scene, swiftly reach unspoken agreement, gun engine, hightail it out of there.

1000 Block, Clearview Terrace. Traffic obstruction. Sinkhole reported in street, measuring twenty-five feet across by four feet deep. Officers peer down hole, whistle. DPW Units flush restraint down crapper, go whole hog in establishing perimeter — orange barricades and flashers, orange arrowboards and signage, orange-garbed personnel braiding Reflect-O-Tape throughout scene like carnival light-strings. Sinkhole perimeter is now a secure and festive perimeter. Officers clash with tableau, sent off to disperse rubberneckers: "Move along, folks, nothing to see here, move along."

2200 Block, Oak Street. Public intoxication and urination. Outside Ye Olde Liquor Shoppe. Sixty-four-year-old male taken into custody. During transport to Division, officer [Shield #325] confesses: "I've always wanted to say that. You know: 'Move along, nothing to see here.'"

5500 Block, Pleasant Avenue. Vandalism. Eighteen mailboxes destroyed along roadside, lopped neatly off their posts in a bout of mailbox baseball, but with chain saw instead of baseball bat. "Mailbox lumberjack," officer [Shield #325] muses aloud. Shot at whimsy misses mark. "Har-dee-har," complainant says. "Ha-fucking-ha." Officer [Shield #647] wonders aloud if somebody maybe put their crabby pants on today. Officer [Shield #325] adds that maybe they OD'd on their potty-mouth pills, too. Argument escalates. Scuffle ensues. Fifty-five-year-old male complainant taken into custody.

2200 Block, Felicity Court. Domestic disturbance. Woman wielding shovel hacks at wide-screen television set in driveway. Under canopy of tree in front yard, shirtless man sits on case of beer, pounding brewskies, watching woman, offering profane commentary. Above him, slung into limbs and branches, wet laundry drips heavily — hanged men left in the rain. Dogs next door yowl and bay. Officers cruise by, tap brakes, assess scene, nod assent, hightail it out of there.

2500 Block, Fairmount Street. Criminal trespass and vandalism. Spivak's House of Wicker. Wicker chewed and chopped chain-saw style. Officers move silently into gray wicker haze, powdered with wicker dust, in awe of the sheer totality of wicker havoc.

1900 Block, Cypress Avenue. Illegal assembly. Demonstrators blocking access to public health clinic, refuse order to disperse. All available units dispatched for crowd control. Officers gathered at staging area, briefed on use-of-force policy, on arrest and intake procedures, then sicced on crowd. Officers stoked, fired up, ready to rumba. Hand-to-hand maneuvers seemingly long forgotten — arm locks and chokeholds, the supple choreography of baton work — all return facilely to muscle memory. Crowd control progresses smoothly. Officer [Shield #325] musses hair clobbering balky demonstrator. A scrawny little hank slips loose, nestles against her right cheek, framing the side of her face like an open parenthesis. A semaphore of possibility, officer [Shield #647] muses, spotting her while clobbering his balky demonstrator. Amid the tussle and heat of arrest and intake, she looks up, seeks him out, finds him. She smiles, waves shyly. From across the tactical field, he smiles, waves back, sticks out tongue. She is suddenly overcome, startled at how the sight of him affects her. It is not just love, or desire, but something profoundly less complex, as unadorned and simple as the Vehicle Code. Officer laughs, cries. Tearful and giddy, she whales on her demonstrator with joy in her heart. Demonstrators cuffed, processed, loaded onto County Transport Units. Assembly dispersed. Scene secured. Officers spent, pink and damp in the afterglow of crowd control. Cop camaraderie ensues. Shirttails tucked, batons wiped down, cigarettes shared. Backs and butts slapped all around.

6700 Block, Coast Highway. Officers go to beach, park at overlook. Officers pooped, reposed. They do not speak. They sip double lattes, ponder view. A gash in the bruise-colored sky bleeds yellow. Sunshine leaks into the ocean, stains its surface with shimmering light. He looks over at her, notices a discoloration, a swelling on her left cheekbone. His hand reaches out, his fingers touch the wound, touch her. "You're hurt," he says. She smiles, whispers, "You should see the other guy." They park their double lattes on dash, slip off their sunglasses, avert their eyes. They screw their faces against the jagged harshness of an unpolarized world, slip sunglasses back on. His hands reach for hers; their fingers clasp and enmesh, roil and swarm at the fourth finger of her left hand. Officers tug and pull, remove and park ring on dash. He reaches for her. She leans toward him; it is like falling. Officers fall. Afterward, they linger over their coffee. Wedding ring on dash glints in the shifting light, harmless as a bottle cap or a shiny old button, something a bird might snatch up. Officers watch a ball of sunlight flare up at earth's edge like a direct hit. Officers assess scene, ascertain world to be beautiful.

2200 Block, Felicity Court. Domestic disturbance. Officers pull up, kill engine. They dawdle in Patrol Unit, fiddling with the mirrors and the radio, double-checking the parking brake. Officers sigh heavily, climb out, and assess scene. Garage door closed. Curtains in windows of home drawn. Officers walk up driveway, pick their way through the detritus of television set and washing machine. They knock on door, ring bell. No answer. Neighborhood quiet. Dogs next door quiet. Birds quiet. Everything, in fact, is quiet. The quiet of earplugs, of morgue duty, and of corridors at 3 A M. The quiet before an alarm clock goes off. Officers backtrack down driveway, approach west side of house, move toward a gate in the fence that leads to backyard. They move gingerly across a saturated lawn, squishy beneath their feet. Soapy water oozes into the tracks they leave. Up ahead, against an exterior wall of house, a pile of freshly cut wood comes into view — one-by-four posts and white-washed flatboards painted with black block letters. LIFE one of them reads. MURDER reads another. Chain-sawed picket signs. Officers' napes prickle, butts clench in autonomic response. They thumb the release tabs on their holsters, move toward gate. They lift latch, ease gate open. Above them, the sky clears and the sun breaks. The shadow of a distant airplane skims over them, glides across the lawn, disappears. Officers enter backyard. The back fence sags forward. Trellises and plant stakes list at crazy angles. A brick barbecue sits crumpled atop its sunken hearthslab. The deck along the west side of the house is a corrugation of collapsed planking. It is as if the earth here simply gave up, shrugged, and dropped six feet. Officers move along periphery of sinkhole, to-ward the sliding patio doors that open onto deck. Their panes are shattered. The ground glitters with pebbles of safety glass. From within, cool air drifts out. And then they are hit, bowled over by a surge of vapors foul and thick — the redolence of mimosa, clawing at their eyes and throats, like some monstrous blossoming from somewhere inside the house. And then the noises. First, a loud muffled report — the only way to describe it. Then, rising from the basement — or from someplace deeper still — the robust glissandi of a chain saw, its motor throttling up and down, laboring might-ily. And within this an indeterminate overtone — the cadence of voices, urgent and shrill. Shouting, or laughing. Or screaming. Officers unholster service revolvers, position themselves at either side of patio entry. They slip off their sunglasses, take this moment to let their eyes adjust to the dark inside. They look at each other. His eyes are dark brown, like coffee, or good soil. Hers are gray, flat as lead except for the glint of a pearly chip in one iris. They do not speak. They love that they don't have to say anything. Instead they reach down, check ammo pouches for extra clips, wipe palms on duty trousers. Eyes adjusted, they draw and shoulder their weap-ons. They brace their wrists, release their safeties, silently count three, and take a breath. Whereupon officers cross threshold, en-ter home.

DAVID RACHEL

The Last Man I Killed

FROM *Eureka Literary Magazine*

THE DREAM IS ALWAYS THE SAME. Of the last man I killed. I
had the dream again the night after Dr. Schofield told us he was
leaving the department. This was back in 1965. The dream always
wakes me. I keep a copy of von Clausewitz's *On War* beside my bed
to read until I fall asleep again.

Dr. Schofield was not only leaving the Department of German
Studies; he was leaving O'Connell State University and the Midwest
and returning to Georgia, where he would take up a position as
dean of arts at his alma mater. He made the announcement at the
end of the monthly department meeting. Warm applause followed
his statement. He was well liked, and the department had run
smoothly under his direction. He might have preferred the news of
his departure to be greeted by cries of anguish, but he accepted
our congratulations with a good grace.

I left the meeting with John Duncan. "Let's have a beer," he suggested. "Mulroney's in half an hour?"

"Going to try for it, Tomas? I'll nominate you," Duncan offered
as soon as we sat down. He was born in the U.S., like half the department. The other half, including myself, were German-born.
Duncan was overweight, and hadn't published for ten years. He
saw himself as a fixer.

"Hell, no," I said. "Thanks for asking, John. I don't want to com-
pete against Anna. She's earned it."

Anna Scheinberg and her late husband had befriended me
when I first arrived at O'Connell State, and I had gotten to know
her quite well. But it was not loyalty that prevented me from com-

peting with her for the headship. I'd already figured out the voting,
and I knew she would beat me easily.

"You're the only alternative. Everyone else is either too near retirement or too young or just plain incompetent." Duncan himself
was approaching retirement.

"She's the obvious choice," I said. "Assuming we go internal."

"The president will insist on internal. It will save one salary. Sure
you don't want to run? If you're going to move up, now's the time.
You're what, Tomas, forty?"

"Thirty-seven," I corrected him. We were sitting at a table in one
of the booths. The bar was quiet, furnished in dark wood with a lot
of black leather. "Right now, my work on Clausewitz demands all
my time. It'll be a good way for Anna to end her career. She's a people person first and foremost."

"She is," Duncan agreed, lighting his second cigarette. "But I
wonder whether she's sufficiently formidable? Can she ride herd
on the young lions?"

He always called them the young lions, because they gave him a
hard time. He was referring to Nick Jonas and the two Neomarxist
clones Nick supervised, nominally under my direction. Naturally,
in a Midwest university in the 1960s, they didn't call themselves
Neomarxists. They preferred the terms *critical theorist* or *postmodernist*.

"I had a word with Wisnesky right after the meeting," Duncan
was saying. "As you know, he's just started his sabbatical. He's going
to spend the year in Heidelberg. If he thought you were going
to run, he'd delay his departure in order to block you." Doug
Wisnesky had never forgiven me for discovering, a few years previ-
ously, that one of his favorite students had plagiarized several pages
of her master's thesis.

"I wouldn't want Wisnesky to stick around any longer than necessary. Why don't you nominate me for the Search Committee? Then
he'll know I'm not running."

I wouldn't have called Duncan a friend, but he had allied himself
to me ever since early in my time at the university, when a fortunate
event had allowed me to establish in everyone's mind the fact that,
unlike him, and unlike Anna Scheinberg, I was formidable. A small
body of women had gone public with the allegation that certain
professors were engaging in sexual relations with their students.
Without waiting for anyone else to react, I had issued a statement

requiring that they declare unequivocally that I was not one of this unnamed group of professors. If they did not do so within twenty-four hours, I would initiate proceedings for libel. Other faculty soon followed my lead, and the women had to withdraw their accusation unreservedly. This earned me the respect of my colleagues across the university, and the gratitude of those professors who actually were bedding their students.

The president believed in being proactive, and the university had subsequently established regulations that, for the time, were relatively strict regarding sexual activity between faculty and students. Not that the new rules deterred many people.

Although the war was the formative experience of my life, I came to an early understanding of academe, because my father was rector of the University of Erfurt. He had lost a leg and won the Iron Cross in the First War. I remember him as a remote and austere figure, who demanded the same standards of achievement from his family as he did from his staff. In my first year as an undergraduate, before the interruption of military service, I stood top of my class, despite the severity with which professors assessed my work on account of my father's position.

I had invited Nick Jonas to borrow my copy of a new book by Habermas, one of his favorite authors, and he came by my office the day before Anna Scheinberg's presentation to the Search Committee. Jonas was halfway through his second two-year term as lecturer, and he was desperate to get a tenure-track appointment. He hadn't yet accepted that no one at O'Connell State was going to let any kind of Marxist get a permanent foothold in the faculty. But he did know that his chances would further diminish if Anna became department head.

I was the nearest Jonas had to a confidant. Like myself, his background was in history; the Department of German Studies encompassed history, culture, and politics, as well as language and literature. I was no Marxist, but I knew the jargon. I'd made it my business to grasp the abstruse doctrines and the convoluted terminology of the Freiburg and Frankfort Schools. Jonas was in his early thirties, with prematurely thinning hair and a prominent Adam's apple. I never saw him smile, but his eyes would warm a little whenever I dropped the names of any of his heroes: "Marcuse used to say," or "I asked Adorno that question once."

I had been expecting him, and I waited for him to bring up the issue of the headship. "I'm concerned about the future of this department," he said.

"Got time for coffee, Nick?" I asked. "Why don't you close the door?" I kept a small fridge and a coffeemaker in my office.

"A lot of us are worried about the prospect of Anna Scheinberg heading the department," he said. "We'd much prefer you as head."

We didn't speak for a moment as I ground coffee beans, filling the room with their rich aroma. "That's kind of you, Nick, but I have no administrative ambitions. And Anna's much the best person for the job. Nobody else has thrown his hat in the ring. The only thing that would prevent her appointment would be if some impediment came up. And I can't see any way that could happen."

"So the department will just continue its reactionary drift for another five years?"

"Anna's no reactionary," I said. "Her liberal credentials are impeccable."

"Liberals! Democracy in retreat. At this of all times." The protests against the war in Vietnam were just beginning.

"She'll be good for the department's teaching side," I commented.

"Sure. Holds her graduate seminars at her house. False consciousness served up with wine and pizza. All the students on the Search Committee are in her pocket." Jonas very much resented not being appointed to the committee.

"Well, Nick," I said, "Anna's really a different generation. She left Germany soon after Hitler came to power, and she missed what some of the rest of us lived through — and people like yourself, who've made a conscientious effort to understand that experience."

"It was her generation that elected Hitler," Jonas said.

"But did they know what they were doing, Nick? Many who voted for Hitler in the early thirties were naive, even idealistic. Even Anna has commented how naive she was when she was young. She shared the ethos of most people in her part of Germany." The coffee was ready, and I handed Nick a mug.

A light had begun to come into his eyes. "How old is Anna?" he asked.

"Late fifties, I believe."

I watched him jot down a couple of figures on his yellow notepad. "So she'd be in her twenties at the time of the 1932 election."

"I'm not sure that's a fruitful line of inquiry, Nick," I remarked. "Some things are best left unsaid, best forgotten and forgiven." Forgetting and forgiving were not part of Jonas's personal equipment. "Tell me now, how are our two master's students coming along?"

I let Jonas work with the master's students. I supervised three doctoral candidates, and was about to add a fourth.

"We need people to look after my students," Dr. Schofield, the outgoing department head told me. "And Doug Wisnesky's, while he's on sabbatical. Any preferences?"

"Thought I might be able to help one of Dr. Wisnesky's," I offered. "Belinda Segal. She was in my class last semester." Doug Wisnesky, satisfied that I was not running for the headship, had left the previous day for Heidleberg.

"She's working on Schiller," Schofield said. "Bit out of your field, isn't it?"

"Won't hurt me to expand a little. She's a good student."

There was a very good reason why I wanted to adopt Belinda Segal as my student. We met in my office the following day. She was dark-haired and soulful. She wrote poetry in both English and German. I gave her coffee, told her I'd been assigned as her supervisor, and asked if she was comfortable with that arrangement. I flattered her on her thesis proposal, on "moral idealism in the early poetry of Friedrich von Schiller." Today she looked more than usually tragic.

There was no desk between us; I kept a couple of comfortable chairs in my office for conversation. While we talked, I began to synchronize my breathing with her own, and to copy her gestures and body posture. I kept eye contact while she was speaking. Her defenses began to soften. Eventually she indicated her feelings about Doug Wisnesky.

"You're fond of him?" I asked.

Belinda looked at me, and tears came into her eyes. "He promised he'd take me with him. To Heidelberg."

I passed her the box of Kleenex from my desk. "You were intimate friends?" She nodded. "Please excuse me asking this, Belinda," I said gently. "I don't want to be intrusive. But I do want us to have a trusting as well as a productive relationship, and I can assure you that I will respect your confidence. Do you mean you were sexually intimate with him?"

"Yes," she replied.

I expressed my sympathy for her distress, and assured her that we would work together successfully and professionally. After she left, I closed the door, opened my desk drawer, and switched off the tape recorder.

The open meeting of the Search Committee was well attended. Anna Scheinberg had taught modern German literature for more than twenty years, and was regarded affectionately in and beyond the Department of German Studies. The nine members of the committee were seated round the long table in the boardroom, and visitors sat in chairs against the paneled walls under the oil paintings of previous deans. Several of Anna's students were present, as were almost all members of the department, and half a dozen other faculty. Jonas and his two acolytes sat at the back, together with a graduate student who worked as a stringer for the local newspaper.

Anna's was the only application for the position. Everyone recognized that this meeting was a formality, an opportunity to honor Anna and launch her as the new department head.

She came into the room accompanied by the dean. She was wearing a blue dress with a darker blue scarf round her neck. Her short hair was still golden, skillfully blended with lighter streaks. She wore her years gracefully, her face rather full and not deeply lined, her manner combining dignity and friendliness.

Anna's presentation was well crafted. She reviewed the state of research in German studies, modestly mentioning her own contributions and interests. She paid tribute to the work of the faculty, including that of the outgoing head. She said nice things about my work, and even complimented Nick Jonas on his most recent research grant. It would be a privilege to lead such a distinguished body. Her role would be to encourage and support her colleagues in making this one of the most respected centers of German studies in the country. She sat down to prolonged applause.

The dean, chairing the meeting on behalf of the president, opened the questioning by asking her to talk about her plans for obtaining a greater share of money for research. She scored additional points by stating her intention to tap research funds in West Germany. Other members of the committee were then invited to participate, and two or three tame questions were asked. Then the dean asked if there were any questions from visitors. At the back of the room, Nick Jonas rose.

"I'd like to alter the line of discussion a little, if I may," he began. "Your own work, Dr. Scheinberg, has focused very perceptively on the interaction of the personal and the public in modern German literature. For many of us, one of the events of twentieth-century history when the personal and the public interacted most critically was the German election of July 1932 which gave Hitler a plurality in the Reichstag. May I ask how you voted in that election, Dr. Scheinberg?"

Izzie Neumann, sitting next to the dean, spoke up immediately: "I don't think —"

But Anna was already replying. "I was twenty-three years old in 1932. I voted for the Nationalsozialistische Deutsche Arbeiter Partei." I felt a rush of adrenaline.

"I deplore that type of interrogation," Izzie was declaring. "For one thing, in this country, we honor the principle of the secret ballot. For another, very few people realized in 1932 how National Socialism would develop. Germany was in economic and social chaos. Hitler promised order, economic development, and recovery of national honor. I don't think we should pillory people on the basis of ahistorical judgments made with benefit of hindsight." Izzie, who had lost two grandparents and innumerable other relatives in the Holocaust.

"I second Dr. Neumann's point," I said. "I myself was a soldier in Hitler's army. I fought for the Reich. I acknowledge my own interest in this question. All of us who grew up in Germany struggle with the issue of collective guilt. Certainly those who lack that experience are entitled to draw their own conclusions. But it's not as simple as a single question and answer might suggest." Jonas had done his job, and I didn't need him any more.

The dean tried to bring the meeting back to its earlier mood of bonhomie, and one or two people asked helpful questions, but the atmosphere had become deflated. There was applause for Anna when the meeting closed, but little conversation as people drifted out of the room.

Not everyone showed up that evening at the party Izzy was hosting for Anna. "They're waiting to read the editorials before they know what to think," Izzie observed disgustedly as he poured me a drink in the kitchen. "As for that little shit Jonas, I'd like to kick his sorry ass to kingdom come. Trying to create one more victim for Hitler." He handed me a glass and took my elbow as we went back into the living room and joined the group standing with Anna by the fireplace.

When there was a pause in the conversation, I remarked, "That was real style this afternoon, if I may say so, Anna. Just hang in there. Lot of people behind you." There was a chorus of agreement.

Anna was lighting a filter-tip cigarette. She had lost none of her customary dignity and composure, refusing the easy options either of defiance or of apology. "I can understand people's concerns," she said. "How can anyone recapture the way things were in 1932? Even we who were there. Our memories are so conditioned by later events."

The conversation remained supportive. There was a lot of talk about honesty, integrity, and retrospective justice. I looked around Izzie's living room at my intelligent, liberal colleagues, and reflected that in a community of reasonable people, power devolves on the one who is prepared to be most ruthless.

I understood this principle long before I read von Clausewitz's remark that "He who uses force unsparingly, without considering the bloodshed entailed, will achieve superiority over a less determined adversary." Like myself, Karl von Clausewitz saw his first military action as a teenager. He served in the Russo-German legion against Napoleon, and rose to the rank of major general and chief of staff of the Prussian army. He died of cholera at the age of fifty-one, and his magnum opus, the thirteen-hundred-page *Vom Krieg*, was published posthumously. My own work, which was on the ways in which his thinking was influenced by Immanuel Kant's notion of universal principles, had been supported by grants from foundations that were ultimately funded by the Pentagon.

Clausewitz is best remembered today for his statement that "war is a mere continuation of politics by other means." ("Der Krieg ist eine bloße Fortsetzung der Politik mit anderen Mitteln." *Politik* can also be translated "policy.") The reverse is also true: politics is a species of warfare.

President McKay asked me to drop by his home the following evening. He lived in one of the fine brick and white clapboard houses that lined the leafy streets around the university.

"Scotch, isn't it, Tomas?" he said. "Stopped off in London on my way back last week. There's a little shop in Soho, sells five hundred single malts. I think you'll like this one. Stag's Breath." He poured me a generous slug. McKay was tall and silver-haired; he was wearing a tweed jacket with a tie in the navy and maroon Harvard colors. A grand piano stood at one end of his living room. The walls were hung with pleasant landscapes in watercolor painted by his wife.

"How did things go in Bonn, Alistair, if I may ask?"

"Very well, Tomas, thank you. Many compliments on the paper. Your translation must have been faultless. And I don't think I made too many errors of pronunciation, thanks to your coaching."

We talked a while about McKay's increasing involvement in the UNESCO Forum on Higher Education. I was very happy to be his translator. I took an interest in him and his work, partly because I intended to be a university president myself one day.

McKay topped up my glass and said, "We have a problem with Anna Scheinberg's candidacy for the headship of German Studies. You and I both know that she would be a popular head. A solid scholar, even if her best work is behind her."

"And extremely good with students," I commented.

"Quite. There's really not much problem internally. A few of the more radical students might carry on a bit, but nothing she couldn't deal with. The problem is external."

"You mean her having voted National Socialist?"

"Exactly. It was a very small item in the local paper yesterday. But I've been fielding calls all day from the national media. If that was all, we could deal with it. Take a firm line on academic freedom. Now this is in the greatest confidence, Tomas."

"Of course."

President McKay filled his pipe and lit it. "I had a call this afternoon from Ivan Belinsky."

"The Belinsky Foundation?"

"The same. We've been in dialogue for almost a year. We were all set to go public at the beginning of next month. Twelve point five million for a new library, along with a seven-point-five million endowment."

I nodded slowly. "Lots of money. New library is long overdue."

"You know how library costs have escalated in the last decade. We had to cut back twenty percent on periodicals this year, and ten percent on open hours. The building itself has close to a mil-

lion dollars of outstanding repairs. My feeling is that this dona-
tion might be the beginning of a long-term relationship with the
Belinsky Foundation."

"What did Belinsky say?"

"Indicated that members of his board were asking questions
about the appointment. Wanted me to confirm yes or no, had the
new head of the German Department been a Hitler supporter? I
told him that I could only report what Dr. Scheinberg had stated.
But I also advised him that the appointment had not yet been
made."

"People change, Mr. President," I said. "If every human action
was held up to scrutiny, we'd all be in trouble."

"That's generous, Tomas, but it won't cut much ice with the media, or with the Belinsky Foundation. This is why I needed to talk to
you. The Search Committee has the prerogative to make whatever
recommendation it thinks prudent. If it nominates Dr. Scheinberg,
I shall have to turn its recommendation down. I will do so on the
basis of her lack of recent groundbreaking scholarship. I hope it
won't come to that. It's too late to go external now. The committee
could recommend an interim head pending an external search
next year, but we'd look like idiots. Or you could stand."

"Me?"

"You, Tomas. You have an excellent scholarly record, you're a
good committee man, and you're respected by your colleagues."

The Scotch was a light amber, with a warm aftertaste of smoke
and peat. While I appeared to consider the president's proposal, I
held up my glass against the light of the fire, lit more for effect than
for warmth. The cedar logs crackled in the fireplace, and I found
myself hearing the cacophony of artillery and small-arms fire on
that May evening twenty years before, and seeing the smoke-red-
dened sunset lighting the face of the last man I killed.

"I'd have to think about that," I said. "I have several reservations.
I'm only an associate professor. I have very little administrative experience. What's more to the point, I could be subject to the same
criticism as Anna. I fought for Hitler."

"That's the whole point, Tomas. You never freely supported Hitler. You never voted for him. You were conscripted into the Wehrmacht. You've always been completely open about your war service.
You were very young. Served only a few months, and never rose
above private. You were as much a victim as — as anyone. That is

the way I shall put it to the Search Committee. And to the Belinsky Foundation. And don't worry about your promotion, that will go through easily once you're head."

"Well, Alistair," I replied. "I'm very grateful for your confidence. But I want to put two things on the record. The first is that I regard Anna Scheinberg as a friend, and if she decides to maintain her application, I shall support her completely. The second is that if I were to accept the nomination, it would be with great reluctance, and only because it was essential to the best interests of the university."

"Duly noted, Tomas. I shall have a word with Anna in the morning. I suspect she'll withdraw her application on her own initiative when she reads tomorrow's papers. She's a very decent person, always has the well-being of the university at heart. I'll tell her I want to nominate her to a UNESCO committee. It will mean a free trip to Europe twice a year."

He needed an answer before I left his house, and in the end I gave it to him. I would let him have my resignation from the Search Committee first thing in the morning. The next afternoon, the president would meet with the committee in camera. I spent the rest of the evening updating the list of publications in my vita.

As it happened, the next day was May 4, which was an anniversary for me. It was on that day, in 1945, that my life changed forever.

The soldier was running fast, crouched low, holding his rifle level with and barely above the ground. The Russians were on the other side of the river at the edge of the town. In the river floated the bodies of scores, perhaps hundreds, of women. They had despaired of escaping the Russians, and had drowned themselves, many with their children. Shells were exploding in the ruins of the town, and Soviet snipers had taken up positions in buildings and trees on the far bank. Hitler was already dead, and the fighting had stopped almost everywhere except here in eastern Bohemia.

I stepped out from behind the broken wall.

"Halt!" I was right in front of him, pistol in hand. He recognized me as SS immediately from my camouflage jacket, which was issued only to SS troops. He stopped, eyes fixed on me, but did not straighten up. "Drop your weapon. Hands up. You are deserting." I raised my Luger.

"Nein, nein, herr Haupsturmfürher," he said desperately. His face was streaked with dirt, his eyes red, his body trembling with exhaustion. Quite young. "The Feldwebel sent me back to find ammunition. We're down to —" His next words were obliterated by a shell landing thirty meters away. I was protected by the wall on my right.

"Get under cover." I motioned him behind the wall. He picked up his rifle. I kept the pistol in my hand. "Where is your unit?"

"About eighty meters," he answered, pointing. "There are seven of us, holed up in a warehouse."

"What weapons?"

"Rifles and one Spandau. A few grenades. We've had no food for two days."

"There's no ammunition or food to be had," I told him. "You'd better wait a bit. Sit down."

"I've got to get back," he said.

"That's an order. You're no use to the Reich dead. You can head back when it gets dark." I returned the Luger to its holster. He sat down on the ground and leaned against the wall. I took out my brandy flask. "You might need a shot of this."

"Thanks." He took a big swallow, then a deep breath, and handed me back the flask. The evening was warm and he opened his jacket.

"You look all in, kid. What's your name?"

He told me. He was a private in a rearguard unit of Army Group Center. He relaxed when he realized I wasn't going to shoot him. He was eighteen. At twenty-one, with more than three years of service, I was middle-aged by comparison. He was from Grossenhain, in Saxony. Father killed at Stalingrad. Mother still alive, he hoped. He prayed God the Russians had spared his mother.

I gave him more brandy. I had him describe his unit and the names of his comrades and officers, his family, his town, his school, the subjects he'd studied, even the marks he'd earned. As the May evening darkened, the firing began to slacken. I cleaned my Luger as he talked. I took the flask from him now and again, but did no more than moisten my tongue. He hadn't slept for two days. I kept him awake with questions. The flask was almost empty. I handed it to him, and as he tilted it for the last swallow, I shot him through the heart.

I stripped his uniform fast, to avoid more blood on it than I could readily explain. He looked different in the smart boots, and with the SS lightning flashed on the helmet and the collar patch of the jacket. Within hours, the Russians would overrun his unit. He'd end in a mass grave, and no one was going to examine the body; nevertheless, I fired another bullet so that there would be an appropriate hole in the SS jacket.

I was now Tomas Landsberger. Complete with identification disk, pay book, photographs of my family, and a detailed life history. I had become three years younger. Along with the uniform, I had left behind Captain Helmut Schlosser of the SS Security Police. An officer who had worked with Heydrich, and had once shaken hands with Adolf Hitler. After the assassination of Heydrich in Prague, our assignment had been to eliminate the Czech intelligentsia — academics, clergy, journalists, artists, historians, musicians, psychiatrists. I specialized in academics. Before they died, many of them had much cause to regret their choice of career.

I had hidden a motorbike a short distance away. The American lines were almost three hundred kilometers to the west, halted by Eisenhower's order to allow the Russians to take Prague. To avoid SS patrols, I rode at night, mostly cross-country, and without lights. I detoured south of Prague, where a savage battle was in progress between the SS and a popular uprising. The next day I surrendered to a unit of Bradley's Third Army near Pilsen. Three days later, the war ended.

Like Clausewitz, who was captured at the Battle of Auerstädt in 1805, I was sent to a POW camp in France. All the prisoners were Wehrmacht. There were no SS; the Allies had declared the entire SS war criminals, and they were imprisoned in separate camps. I had managed to conceal a small amount of gold on my person, and I used some of this to bribe other men to take my place whenever there was a physical inspection that would have revealed my SS tattoo. Years later, I had the tattoo removed by a surgeon in Brazil.

I kept my distance from most of my fellow prisoners, especially any from Saxony. There were almost no veterans of Army Group Center; its remnants had been surrounded and captured by the Soviets outside Prague. I spent much of my time learning English. As soon as I was released, I registered at the University of Stuttgart. I studied incessantly, and was viewed as a recluse, traumatized by the war and separation from my home and family, which were now in

East Germany. My single aim was to get either to Australia or to the United States. One of the many foundations that came to Germany with the Marshall Plan offered me a graduate scholarship at the University of Wisconsin. I completed my doctorate in three years, obtained residence status, and got a tenure-track position at O'Connell State.

The day after the president announced my appointment as department head, the phone rang in my office.

"You son of a bitch!" Through the static on the line from Germany, Doug Wisnesky's voice rang in my ear. His former student and lover, Belinda Segal, had just left my office.

"I'm sorry you're taking it that way, Doug," I said.

"How could you do that to Anna Scheinberg?"

"You must be misinformed, Doug. It wasn't I —"

"Don't try to tell me you didn't put Jonas up to it! Listen, Landsberger, your troubles haven't even begun. I'm going to make your life hell on earth. You're going to wish you'd never seen O'Connell State."

"I don't think so, Doug. I don't think so at all. By the way, Belinda Segal sends her regards."

There was a momentary pause. Then, "You bastard!" and the line went dead.

The axioms of von Clausewitz continued to guide me as I rose through the administrative ranks of academe: It is the destiny of the weak to serve the will of the powerful, and war is the means by which we compel them to do so. Strike only when you have the probabilities on your side. Surprise is the most powerful element in victory. The best strategy is always to be very strong. I ended, as I had planned, as a university president. Von Clausewitz spent most of his later years as director of the Prussian Military Academy in Berlin, and I like to think that his reflections on war came out of his experiences in the academy as well as from his military service. For what is academic life, after all, but a continuation of war by other means?

JOSEPH RAICHE

One Mississippi

FROM *The Baltimore Review*

IF FIRED CORRECTLY, a bullet can instantly kill whatever it is intended to kill. When fired incorrectly, it can still kill quite handily,
it just takes a little longer. Sometimes it can take a lot longer. It can
take days and even weeks to achieve its full potential. Truthfully,
there are those bullets that are fired with no intention of coming
into contact with a living thing. A firing range might be a good example. Yet, when we examine it further, we see that the targets are
silhouettes with the highest points awarded, of course, for a shot to
the heart, or the head.

I try not to watch the news. There are only cosmetic differences
from one night to the next. "A shot B! Tonight at seven" or "A arrested in connection with whatever! Tonight at seven." The radio
or local paper isn't much better, but a person needs to stay current.
I usually skip the front page or tune out the late-breaking stories.
The fringe is where most of what I need to know is anyway. I never
thought that I would be part of the news. Not the "tonight at seven"
part anyway, but then there I was on a subway car that had come to
an unexpected stop.

It seems a twenty-four-year-old man named Mathew Hunstad
filed a grievance at his job stating that he wasn't adequately com-
pensated for his travel expenses to get to and from certain job
sites. This forced him to take all of his materials with him on the
crowded subway rather than allowing him to drive his own car. Of-
tentimes the subway would be too full for him and all of his things,
requiring him to wait for later runs. This caused him to be late for
jobs, costing him money, and as the grievance stated, credibility.

Well, his employer told him that if he wanted the luxury of driving his own car then he would have to pay for it, either that, or he would just have to *make* more space on the subway.

It couldn't have been eight o'clock yet when the subway appeared from the tunnel and breathed to a halt, pushing me back a step. It was already crowded from the stops that it made further out in the city on its way in. My wife, Jennifer, and I went to work together every day except Thursdays, when I have the day off. We stepped onto the near full car and luckily found seats next to each other. Usually one of us ends up standing so that we can talk. Usually that person is me. That day we were just lucky.

The doors closed and the engine started to pull us forward to the heart of the city. Then, halfway through a rather long tunnel the whole subway came to a stop. Since most people riding were regulars like Jenny and me, a few people stumbled, not expecting the stop. The lights in the car stayed on, helping people to stay calm. One other time I had been stuck on a subway car. The lights went out, though, and people started to panic. A few individuals had cigarette lighters that they would flick on from time to time just to make sure nothing was going on until we started moving again. This time the lights stayed on. Besides the slight irritation of possibly being late for work, no one complained very much.

From the front of the train we heard a single shot. I dismissed it as something else, but it was quite clearly a gun being fired. No more than ten seconds later, the sound of a second gunshot popped into my ears, followed by a third, and a fourth, and a fifth. Excluding the first shot, the subsequent ones were very rhythmic. I counted to myself: "one mississippi, two mississippi, three." Each time I got to three, the gun would go off. Each time the gun went off, it got louder. People started to panic. Looking through the window at the end of the car into the next, I could see a man walking down the center isle. Every few steps he turned and fired a shot at one of the passengers. He wasn't doing it randomly though. After watching for only a few seconds, I could see he was shooting every other passenger.

He made his way into the car next to ours and began his routine. "One mississippi, two mississippi, three." Of course, a few people tried to stop him. They would come at him from behind and try and wrestle one of his guns away. They tried, and failed. Every other person, "one mississippi, two mississippi, three." He was almost to the end. The doors slid open and he stepped onto our car. He would reload in the short time it took the doors to close behind him and open in front of him. Some people tried to escape, but the door to the next car was barricaded and the walls of the tunnel were too close to escape out the window. The people in the next car had taken an old man's cane and wedged it so that the door wouldn't automatically slide open.

The first good look I got of him was when he stepped through the door. He didn't hesitate, but my mind took a still picture of him. Nothing stood out. It was frightening to think that there was no discernible trait that separated him from anyone else, including me. Yes, he was a man. Yes, he was white. Beyond that I could just as well describe myself.

His first step was met with screaming, and then it began. "One mississippi, two mississippi, three." He was going back and forth across the rows. The first person on one side followed by the second on the other. "One mississippi, two mississippi, three." First, a secretary that worked for some law firm that specialized in mortgage foreclosures. I had talked to him a few times during the morning commute. "One mississippi, two mississippi, three." Next, a black woman who worked in a department store downtown who kept to herself most mornings. "One mississippi, two mississippi, three." Then, some woman who I never really talked to, but Jenny told me that she . . . Jenny. I was so terrified I had completely forgotten about Jenny. Counting out the seats, I realized that I was sitting in a "safe" chair. For a moment, I felt relieved.

Jenny had grabbed my arm and buried her face into my back. I pulled her toward me and tried to sneak to her other side. She hadn't been watching the shootings and so wouldn't know why I was doing it. My hope was that I hadn't been noticed. No sign made me think I hadn't been successful. The shootings went on. "One mississippi, two mississippi, three." Only a few people away now and the sound had grown to deafening claps against my ears. "One mississippi, two mississippi, three." Two people down from me, a body went limp and slid to the ground. Turning to the other side, another three seconds passed. He turned to me. "One mississippi, two mississippi," I just closed my eyes.

Nothing happened. No feeling of pain. No loud explosion.

Nothing. I opened my eyes and he was just staring at me. He could tell that I was scared, and now confused on top of that. A soft grin appeared on his face as he leaned into me. His lips were almost touching my ear. He whispered, "There's no switching places." He stood back up and turned the gun at Jenny. He fired a single shot. It wouldn't kill her instantly. It would take almost four and a half days to do that. She would never regain consciousness. A single shot that stole all the color from the world. He turned to the other side of the car. "One mississippi, two mississippi, three."

Someone from one of the front cars had made their way to the engine and started the subway back up. The sudden jerk sent everyone falling, including the lunatic on his rampage. Once on the ground, a man and a woman jumped at him, holding his arms. Another stepped on his hands until he let go of the guns. She broke two of his fingers in the process. All in all he had shot seventy-three people. Sixty-eight of them died. Most never made it off the subway.

His name was Mathew Hunstad. He would admit that after his employer refused his request for traveling expenses, he got mad. He said he was taking a suggestion to make more room on the subway literally. Thinking that if he killed half the people who rode at the same time he did, there would be plenty of room for him and all of his materials. He wasn't insane, he was just angry, and now faced five counts of attempted murder, on top of the sixty-eight counts of murder for those he had successfully executed.

The trial was nothing to speak of. More than a hundred people watched him methodically assassinate one after another of his fellow citizens. Hunstad never even hinted at an insanity plea, and when it came time for sentencing, he fully accepted, and expected, the death penalty. He made no mention of an appeal, making it very easy to feel relieved it wouldn't drag on and on. He was sentenced to death by lethal injection. The date was set by the court, and for the first time I could look beyond Mathew Hunstad.

I didn't mark the date on any calendar, or call my family to tell them. It was all absurd to me. I hoped that I could forget it altogether. His execution was front-page fodder, real headline news. The stuff three-part series are made of, but for me it was already over. Then the phone rang.

The voice on the other end of the line asked for me and gave me condolences when it was confirmed that I was, in fact, myself. She told me she represented the state prison at which Hunstad would be executed. She asked if I was aware of the lottery taking place to be a witness to the execution. I hung up the phone.

It rang again, and the same sweet voice assured me that she did represent the prison. The only way I would talk with her was if she gave me her number and extension and then I would call her back. When I did, the man at the switchboard routed me through to her. I asked why she was bothering me. She said that they had held the lottery and my name was chosen as one of the twenty-five individuals who would be able to see, in person, Hunstad's execution. I told her that I had entered no such lottery and just about hung up on her when she said that someone else must have. The lottery had only been open to those on the subway and the immediate families of those killed. Someone must have known me from the train and entered me. I told her I didn't want it. She told me that was none of her business and that she was only responsible for informing me I had been picked. The last thing she said before she hung up was that I was the very first pick, which meant I would be in the front row, the center seat.

Somehow my name got out to the public. Instantly, my phone began to ring. Some were calls relaying their envy because I got to be right there when the "sick bastard eats it," as one person put it. Most calls, though, were from those people asking if they could have my seat. Some offered money, others offered season tickets, home electronics, anything. It seemed everyone had become obsessed with watching a man die. One individual, who had no relation to anyone on the subway that day, called offering me three ounces of hash. I turned off the ringer and unplugged the answering machine. The daily newspaper was sitting by the sofa, so I picked it up. I crumpled up the front page without even looking at it. Nothing much seemed to be happening in the world. Maybe it only felt that way.

Jenny had always done the grocery shopping. There was nothing left in the apartment by this time and so I had to go out to get something. Down a few blocks from where we lived was a sandwich shop that we always used to go to. I hadn't been there in some time, but it was the closest place where I knew I could get something good. Inside the shop, I could smell wild-rice soup simmering in the back. The lighting was low with soft, unintelligible music playing. I always thought they kept it that way so that a person's sense of smell would take over. Jenny always said it was to save on electricity.

I got in line at the counter behind a tall man that looked to be in his early thirties. He didn't notice me come up right away. Once he recognized who I was, there was no way to get him to stop talking. He kept telling me how lucky I was. The condolences for my loss came after this, showing the importance of lost life to people fixated on the potential loss soon to come. He kept talking even after he had ordered. Telling me about how the execution works. The chemicals they use. The pain the body feels. Then he told me that from the time Hunstad is injected it will take about three seconds, and then his body will start to die. When I asked him to be quiet he looked at me like I had insulted him. In a way, that's what I had hoped to do.

A week before the execution, hundreds of family members of the deceased demanded their right to watch Hunstad die. What law gave that right I didn't know. It's like saying I want to be able to sit outside the cell of the man who robbed my home for his entire sentence. Regardless, the people demanded their right, and the state gave it to them. The prison would send a live feed of the execution to a closed-circuit television set up in the prison's common area so the people could watch. There wouldn't be just one television. There would be several, all around the room. All of them far bigger than any I've ever owned.

Hunstad was to be executed on a Saturday. This was to allow for most people who wanted to be there to not have to worry about work. On the Thursday before, I got a call from the prison asking if I could come down and take a look beforehand at how security would work, and where I would be sitting. Also, they said if I wanted to take a look at the room itself I could. Although I never worked on Thursdays I told him that I couldn't and asked him if he could just tell me over the phone. I felt bad for lying, especially because I hadn't been to work at all since it happened. They didn't know that though. So they went through it over the phone. What gate I needed to come to. Identification I needed to bring. To make sure not to bring any weapons with me. I thought this last rule was a little strange until I realized that there will be hundreds of people in a single building who are all there to watch someone die. I asked if you can go to prison for killing a man who is about to be executed. He said yes. Finally he described the room where the execution would take place. The room, as it was described to me, is no bigger than a bedroom of a cramped apartment. In it sits five rows of five chairs, each row a small step up from the one in front of it. On the wall that the chairs face is a large window that looks into another room of about the same size. In it there is only one chair. It sits on a round platform maybe a foot or so off the ground. About the arms and legs, various straps and locks are attached. To me it sounded like a theater. After flipping through some papers he said in an impressed tone that it looked like I was front and center. I thought the way he said it was in poor taste. We said goodbye and hung up the phone.

Saturday morning came and I got dressed. I didn't want to put on anything too fancy to make people think that this was an event, as if I were going to the opera. I gathered the two forms of identification that I needed. There were a few news cameras outside the building, but I figured most of the reporters had already found their way to the prison to watch the witnesses stroll in. The taxi that I had called for was parked on the street. The meter was probably running, so I tried to hurry. Once in the back, I told the driver I needed to go to the prison. He looked in the mirror and apparently recognized me from the papers. He said it was a shame about my wife, and that he felt just awful for what had happened. He said that he and his family had been praying for me ever since they saw it on the news. It was such a strange feeling to hear someone not talk about the execution, and rather about what had already happened. I thanked him, and for the first time in a long time I could force a smile on my face.

As we approached the prison, there were cars everywhere. The lot had overflowed onto a field where people just started making their own rows. The news vans lined the street with their towers reaching into the sky. Some protesters stood near the entrance to the prison. They were protesting for the execution, though. It seemed strange. Large groups of people stood around as if they were waiting for the last few tickets to a sold-out rock concert. The taxi driver started to slow down. He put on his blinker and waited for oncoming traffic to pass. When they had, I told him to stop.

I told him not to turn, and to just keep going. After a few seconds, I gave him a new destination. It was a small park near the center of town. He looked at me in the mirror. Not with a confused look. He knew who I was. He knew that I was supposed to be back there in the front row. He just looked at me for a second and kept driving.

The wind had picked up a little from earlier in the day. It felt good to feel it through my fingers. I sat on a bench where Jenny and I met for lunch as often as we could when we were working. I sat and just stared down one of the avenues. Time passed, I couldn't be sure how long, I made it a rule never to wear a watch. Mathew Hunstad was dead, though, that was for sure. It would be a lie to say it brought me any relief. I always knew that it wouldn't. Loss doesn't die. I thought of the man in the sandwich shop, how he said that it takes about three seconds for the body to start to die. I counted it in my head, "One mississippi, two mississippi, three."

JOHN SAYLES

Cruisers

FROM *Zoetrope: All-Story*

EMMETT TOSSES HIS BREAKFAST CRUMBS off the jetty and watches the shitfish rise to check them out. Blue-green, almost translucent, they wiggle listlessly in the shade of the hull all day and congregate at the surface near the vapor lights at night. "Shitfish got no 'urry," the locals say. "Just weat for somebody flush."

He hands the plate back to Muriel onboard. "I'm going to see if Roderick is there yet."

"He never comes in till eight." Muriel drops the plate into the plastic suds bucket to soak.

"I thought maybe because of this Whitey and Edna deal —"

"He'll probably sleep late. They called him down, it must have been what — ?"

"Four-thirty."

"See if the paper is in yet. And don't make a nuisance of yourself."

They get the Sunday edition of the St. Augustine paper once a week — news, want ads, employment, real estate, and funnies crammed into their little PO box at the marina office. Emmett needles Muriel for reading the obits first.

"There are people dying now," he says, "who never died before." Muriel pretends to ignore him.

They are moored in the section Emmett likes to call the Lesser Antilles, where most of the smaller liveaboards are concentrated and the walk to the security gates and harbormaster's office is farthest. The shadow of the Ocean Breeze Lifestyles complex barely reaches them in the morning. The buildings went up rapidly, replacing the funky collection of waterfront businesses that had stood since before Emmett and Muriel came to stay. LET THE FUN BEGIN! says the banner strung up on opening day, still hanging a year later. There are several units left unoccupied. The marina itself is only two-thirds full, peak season a few weeks off, and many of the boats lie sheathed in blue vinyl, owners off the island or sleeping in town.

Bill and Lil are up on the *Penobscot* though, Bill prepping the cedar decking while Lil pries open a gallon of goldspar satin.

"Ahoy."

Lil nods. "Morning, Emmett."

"Still working this varnish farm, eh?"

Bill, grimly sandpapering the foredeck, snorts something like a hello. Bill and Lil are in their late fifties, small, sun-baked to a tobacco-stain brown with nearly identical short-cropped gray hair.

"You're at it early."

"Got to stay on top of these babies," says Lil. "Lot of nasty stuff floating out there." Emmett had seen them take her out only once, and then just for a two-hour shakedown. Lil had been a registered nurse and was still handy with a remedy if you had something more than a headache, while Bill taught high school and had nothing good to say about it.

"You folks up for the ruckus?"

"Slept right through it. Bill heard voices but thought it was those party people in the motor cruisers."

"There were a dozen of them out there. Lights, stretchers —"

"We were dead to the world. Some wild stories were flying in the Crow's Nest this morning. But you know rumors on this island."

"It was the lights woke me up, not the sound," says Emmett. "Of course Muriel says I'm deaf as a post."

"I should be so lucky. This one" — Lil jerks her head toward the *Scavenger*, a daysailer owned by one of the locals — "has got his radio on all weekend. Rap music or whatever their version is called here. Makes Bill grind his teeth."

Bill wraps fine-grade sandpaper around a wooden dowel and goes to work on the mahogany trim. He and Lil wear the same brand of T-shirt and shorts, Topsiders, matching hooded windbreakers when they sit out at night. Emmett wonders if they swap clothes.

"I never figured — Whitey and Edna —"

Lil lays out her brushes. "I know. Edna was telling me just last week that they were looking into a condo here."

"My wife is convinced you can't live on a sportfisherman," says Emmett. He can see the tuna tower of the *Silver King*, Whitey and Edna's old Bertram, over the forest of masts. "Suppose they'll auction it right away. Unless Whitey paid their mooring through the year."

Lil frowns, staring at her varnish. "Condos. They must have been desperate."

"Well — storm season comes around, some folks like solid ground under their beds. What do you hear about this Cedric?"

Cedric is the tropical storm curling in from the Atlantic, possibly mutating into the first hurricane of the summer.

Lil glances out over the channel. Clear blue sky, flat water. "It'll blow itself out. Peaked too early."

"It does hit, it's gonna ruin your finish."

Lil shrugs. "Best way to protect the wood." She chooses a brush, riffling the bristles with her thumb. "No, you buy into that condo life, you're ready to throw in the towel."

"They've put up some real luxury boxes in the last few years."

"The ones we looked at, that Pelican Cove outfit? They'd blow down like a stack of cards."

Bill grimaces. "Pelican Cove."

Lil jerks her head toward her husband. "Says he'd just as soon ride it out in the marina."

"There's gonna be a big one hits this island sooner or later, Cedric or no Cedric. I can't say they've knocked themselves out preparing for it."

"Cyannot stop de wind, mon," mutters Bill, mimicking Roderick's island lilt. "She come, she come."

Lil dips the edge of her brush into the varnish, careful to avoid dripping as she starts to apply it. "We've been thinking about Curaçao."

"Dutch people."

"A lot of them speak English. And the prices are right."

"What's a rum collins?"

"Less than here, I can tell you that."

"I suppose. Muriel and I talk about Mexico now and again."

"Mañanaland."

Emmett shrugs. "The peso just keeps falling. Our checks could go a lot further —"

Bill wipes the section he's just sanded with a damp cloth. "Mexico," he says. "One good case of the trots and you're history."

A fishing skiff with a pair of locals aboard chugs around the reef of auto tires that serves as a breakwater and heads for the fuel dock. The marina was nothing much when Emmett first tied up here twenty years ago, rickety, unpainted wood crusted with gull droppings. As the cruisers and their money grew in importance, the mosquito fleet had been driven to shallower harbor farther west and a French corporation built the new jetty and facilities. Now ramshackle boats like this might wander in illegally to sightsee among the yachts or hustle up charters, but when Roderick is on duty they don't dare tie up. The man working the outboard waves lazily to Emmett and calls out.

"Golden Years," he smiles. "Bringin' the chat round."

A lot of the locals call him by the name of the boat, and Muriel endures being hailed as Mrs. Golden Years. "Could be worse," he likes to tell her. "If we had that catamaran on C Pier you'd be Betty Bazooka."

Rut Adams is up on the flydeck of the *Squire*, nursing a bloody mary and training binoculars on the new arrival at the far end of the marina.

"Anything to report?"

Rut brings his binoculars down, his eyes taking a moment to adjust.

"Emmett. Caught me spying."

"I don't suppose they spend their time looking at us."

It was just there one morning, looking more like a space-age hotel than a boat, dwarfing the Cheoy Lee and Broward hundred-footers in the Land of the Giants. A forty-plus sportfisherman was perched like a toy on the aft deck, and the heliport had been used once so quickly nobody saw who jumped in or out of the chopper.

"They got manned submersibles on that thing — those Jacques Cousteau things? Decompression chamber in the lazarette, satellite dish, large-format screen like a movie theater. Got two Jacuzzis, personal trainer, cook with a full staff —"

"You saw all this?"

Rut shakes his head. "Archibald, the local fella who comes around with the crabs? He's been onboard a bunch of times. Got a thing going with one of the maids. Filipino gal."

"I've still never seen the man," says Emmett. "Just people running around in uniforms setting things up."

"He's been here once or twice."

"Imagine being the center of all that. You get a whim to go out and dozens of people jump into action." Emmett had walked on the pontoon beside it once, pacing off at least eighty yards, staring up at his reflection in the tinted Plexiglas cabin panels. Nothing stirred aboard. Muriel calls it the Mother Ship and says it's crewed by bulb-headed aliens. "So what's he look like?"

Rut clears his throat, recalling. "Swarthy fella — remember the one Nixon used to hang out with? Relleno — Refugio —"

"Rebozo."

"Looks like him."

"Drug money?"

"Not enough security hanging around. I don't think he's Spanish of any kind. Not an Arab either — Arabs don't dive."

"They don't?"

"Hell no. My guess is he's some Greek, owns one of these international dot-com outfits. Making money out of thin air."

"What you think it runs him to keep it floating?"

Rut always knows what things cost or has an educated guess. He stands on top of his big Hatteras, calculating, face glowing red with his first drink of the day. "Damn if I can even imagine. Meggy was here the other day" — Rut's wife, Meggy, lives in their cliff house and only visits on weekends — "her Daddy owned half the state of Delaware and even *her* jaw dropped when she got a look at it. I'd say crew and staff alone is a good fifty, sixty grand a week."

Emmett whistles, looks back toward the massive yacht. "A thing that size, hardly know you're on the ocean."

"You sail people," Rut grins, "wrestling a hunk of canvas and puking your guts out."

"Dacron," says Emmett. "Things have progressed a little."

"If there's no wind you're still fucked. Hey, what's the deal with Whitey and what's-her-name?"

"Edna."

"Edna."

"No details yet. I'm hoping to track Roderick down."

They both look toward D Pier, to the yellow tape cordoning off the *Silver King* in its berth.

"I think of him sitting out there every evening in his fighting chair, knocking one back."

"G and T," says Emmett.

"That what it was? I'm a Scotch man myself. I could see him from up here — he'd raise his glass, we'd toast the sunset."

"A real gentleman, Whitey."

"Health problems?"

"Not that I know of."

"That age, it can go fast."

"They brought in a black marlin last month. Whitey was in the chair — fought him four, five hours before he made his last run. Boated him, cut him loose, but he just floated sidewise on the surface so they circled around and gaffed him in before the sharks could gather. Good seven, seven-and-a-half feet. You can't swing that with health problems."

"Fish like that will take up a lot of wall space."

"They'd caught it before."

"What?"

"Edna said that when they got it onboard they recognized the marlin. Scars, the shape of its dorsal. They were sure of it, couple years ago in the Dry Tortugas."

"That's one for Ripley."

"She said Whitey was pretty upset about it."

"Killing the fish?"

Emmett nods. "Either that or that it was the same one. He was always saying, 'I like to beat 'em, not beat 'em to death.'"

"Stick a hook in your lip, drag a quarter mile of line through the ocean for a couple hours, what's he think is gonna happen?" Rut shakes his head. "Moody bastards, fishermen. That Hemingway —"

"Whitey never cared for Hemingway. He liked the dog fella —"

"Dog fella."

"Call of the Wild, White Fang —"

"Jack London."

"Loved him."

"He wrote about boats?"

"I guess so."

"London. Think he drowned himself. Or drank himself to death." Rut kills the last of his bloody mary. "'Death, where is thy sting?'"

"He died of TB." Chase Pomeroy steps out on the *Rockin' Robin* in the next slip, rubbing his eyes. "Or some shit like that. Sailed to the South Seas and brought back all these really gnarly diseases."

Chase is a currency trader still in his thirties who has recently traded up from a little Sea Ray to a Sunchaser Predator.

"That thing get airborne?" asks Emmett, eyeing the boat.

"It'll move." Chase climbs on top of the cabin and lies on his back, covering his eyes against the sun. "Make the Caymans in under three hours."

"What's your hurry?" Rut complains about Chase speeding in the channel but always comes on deck when he brings a new girlfriend around.

Chase shrugs. "If I wanted to float with the current I'd find some Haitians and build a raft. What can you do in that thing — twelve knots, max?"

"It depends." Rut's face gets redder. "You hear the brouhaha last night?"

"Saw it. I was at Zooma till two — dead night, lot of dental hygienists off a cruise ship — then I hit the Daquiri Shak with Ricky G. till it closed. We got back from the Dak and there's the whole sorry excuse for a police department and the even sorrier excuse for a rescue squad —"

"They couldn't rescue a turd from a toilet bowl," says Rut. "I ever get in the shit out there I'm calling Key West and taking my chances on the wait."

"They asked us for ID. You imagine that? Ricky goes up to the captain, whatever he is, the one in charge, and says, 'You know me. I used to bang your sister when she worked in my restaurant.'"

"That must have cleared things up."

"Ricky's slipping payoffs to every one of these guys, what're they gonna do?"

"You see anything?"

"Lotta lights, lotta local constabulary. I think the old folks were already out of here by that point."

Emmett nods. "You heard anything more about the storm?"

"Just that it's supposed to be coming." Chase shifts his arm away from his eyes to squint up at Rut. "I'm taking this out today, pollute the environment. You see Stephanie —"

"That's the new one? Redheaded gal?"

Chase nods. "Yeah, with the wide butt. Tell her I'll be at Zooma by ten."

A trio of frigate birds sail over the marina, gradually losing altitude and seeming to pick up speed as they swoop down into the channel. It is already hot. A film of diesel oil swirls in rainbow colors around the pilings and a single turtle paddles between the moored boats, head just breaking the surface. Emmett likes to think of the marina as a community, maybe a few more transients than usual, but with reliably suburban rhythms. A bit of bustle at sunrise, morning errands, buckling down to serious work by midday, and then the relaxing slide to cocktail hour. He likes to hear the hardware rattling as the boats rock in their slips, the squeak of rope and cleat, the sharp luffing of plastic boat covers. He likes to hear the motors coughing into life, thrumming as they pass on the way out, likes the smell of polyurethane and deet. Emmett likes the long tines of the jetty with their evenly spaced slips, hundreds of boats with distinct outlines and personalities moored side by side, the blazing, primary blues and reds and yellows of gear, the stunning white of fiberglass and Dacron. He liked the gulls and pelicans in the old days, too, but the feeding and dumping regulations have had their effect and they only pass over now, heading for the smelly chaos of the locals' wharf.

Roderick is talking with Ricky G., who sits looking disoriented at the fore of a shiny new Beneteau. Ricky is wearing a shirt with a Day-Glo parrotfish design and has marks from fiberglass deck beading on one side of his face.

"Looks like somebody passed out on the deck," says Emmett.

"I needed to rest." Ricky never seems to shave yet never has a full beard, sporting a perpetual morning-after stubble. "These people are up in Vermont or something."

"What if I trespass you," says Roderick, "sleep on Ricky bar some night?"

Ricky tends bar at the Y-Ki-Ki, which he co-owns, the only bar locals of all colors go to. He squints at Roderick. "I've pulled you out from under the table more than once."

"Never 'appen beyond closing time. Surprise me them authority don't 'carcerate you while they here last night."

Emmett steps closer. "Listen, Roderick, what —"

Before he can say more Roderick puts his big hand up for silence.

"Mr. Alphonse already vex me wit instruction. I got nothing to tell till official version has been spoken."

"Were you here?"

"Drag me ass out of bed, got to open every gate in creation." Roderick shakes his head. "Why they don't weat till sunup, spear a mon his sleep?"

"It was an emergency."

"Nothing in that boat that wouldn't keep till sunup."

"Remember the dude two Christmases ago," says Ricky, "washed up by the old turtle works?"

"Accidental causes."

"That's what they always say when they don't know shit. Didn't know where he came from, what boat he was off of, nada. And nobody ever claimed him."

"Plenty of that on this island."

"But the watch he had on, the guy was obviously a tourist —"

"Black mon drown," says Roderick, "authority don't inquire. White mon drown they declear mystery."

There is a pause as they all watch the blond divorcée from Sarasota and her teenage daughter in matching bikinis pass on the parallel pier. Ricky moans quietly.

"I could go either way with that."

"Them womens kill you, Ricky. Rum has sap all your powers."

"I heard a rumor," says Emmett, "that it happened three days ago. Whitey and Edna."

"No way. He came in just yesterday." Ricky spends so many of his waking hours shooting the shit behind the bar that he never has a tan. "About four. Sat at the end, three G and Ts, paid his tab and left."

"You didn't talk with him?"

"There were these Belgian girls, I was feeding them yellow birds — you know, with the amaretto? They were starting to loosen up so I didn't pay much attention to Whitey."

"Whitey always drink his cocktail on his boat," says Roderick. "Why is he paying double to you?"

"Psychology's not my field, man. I just pour 'em what they ask for."

"How'd he look?"

"Like he always did. Like he just stepped off that battlewagon of theirs with some twenty-foot sea monster in tow. He had that squinty-lookin' smile —"

"Muriel called him the Ancient Mariner."

"He wasn't so ancient."

"Couple years older than me, and I'm getting on." Emmett turns back to Roderick. "I think as a resident of this marina, I deserve —"

"I give you a groundation and everybody want to ax me same story."

"You tell Emmett here," says Ricky, "and the news will *fly*."

Roderick just smiles and starts away. "Weat for official story. Then I tell you what part is a lie."

When Emmett last talked with Whitey he'd been fine, upbeat even. They ran into each other at the local grocery, the one a mile walk from the marina but half as expensive as the Captain's Larder at the Ocean Breeze condo complex.

"Only thing she'll eat anymore," said Whitey when he caught Emmett checking out the four loaves of white bread and dozen tins of ham spread in his basket.

"I thought you liked to cook?"

"Used to. Used to do a three-course layout in that little galley of ours. Baked bread, pies. Now, it's just — you know." Whitey shrugged. "It's another meal."

Emmett nodded. "Mine won't have anything to do with fixing dinner. Twenty-five years of feeding the kids —"

"Yeah."

"So I just fire the old hibachi up —"

"Grilled what — was it amberjack last night?"

"You can smell it."

"No problem. Just don't let day man catch you."

"Roderick and I have an understanding." Emmett pushed his items forward on the counter to make room for Whitey's case of bargain gin. "How the fish been treating you?"

"Oh, fair." Whitey and Edna didn't keep much of what they caught, but they went out almost every day. "Punk Loomis got into a bunch of wahoo the other day off the east tip, we might try that."

"What are the locals catching?"

"Infectious diseases."

They laughed. As more kids drifted down from the States there were fewer and fewer locals working in the bars and restaurants, and Ocean Breeze advertised that it had "fully professionalized" its staff, which meant most of the black faces were gone. The little market was one of the few places Emmett still rubbed elbows with people born on the island.

"It had to happen sooner or later," Whitey said. "That 'no problem, mon' thing only goes so far and then you need some service. It's something we thought about a lot before we made our commitment here."

"But the culture —"

"Nobody comes here for the culture."

There was a carnival once a year that Emmett tried to avoid, people passed out in unusual places and a couple local bands that played loud enough to be heard over the water several miles away. What amazed Emmett most about the island was that it was populated at all, with no fresh water and almost nothing edible grown in the interior. European sailors had tried leaving pigs and goats on it for provision, but they quickly died of thirst, and cane and sisal plantings hadn't done much better. The locals were descended from the workers on these destitute plantations and escapees from slave ships that ran aground in the early 1800s.

"All dem other crop feel," Roderick liked to say, "but tourist business been very good to we."

"You circle the globe between ten and twenty-five degrees above the equator," said Whitey, laying a sack of limes on top of the gin, "one port isn't much different than the next."

"So you're here for a while."

"Oh, we're here to stay. Like it says in the brochures," Whitey winked at Emmett, "'It's always smooth sailing in our island paradise.'"

The Schmecklers are behind the pilothouse of their big Frers headsail ketch, spreading engine parts on a tarp. Emmett knows the father and son are Fritz and Stefan but can never remember which is which.

"Part still hasn't come in?"

"Customs," says the father. "They steal it."

"One focking injector." The son stares down at the disassembled machinery. "They don't know what it is, but they steal it."

They are tall and wide-shouldered, relentlessly enthusiastic, with thick beards bleached by the sun. The first day they sailed in Muriel thought somebody was shooting a beer commercial.

"You were a friend of the diseased?" asks the father.

"Diseased —"

"The one who is dying."

"Deceased. Whitey — yes. They were neighbors, sort of. D Pier."

"Your boat is?"

"The *Golden Years*? Island Packet cutter?"

"I have seen this."

"Nothing compared to your rig, but we call it home." Mrs. Schmeckler, Greta, smiles as she steps up from the cabin to shake a mat out over the starboard side. "Whitey and Edna were eight or nine slips down from us."

"They were having some problem?"

Emmett considers. "I got the impression they were living their dream. Down here in the sun, chasing fish, nothing on the horizon but more of the same —"

"Our dream now is to circle the world in the *Liebenstraum*," says the father. "It keeps us moving forward."

"And when you finish?"

"Then we start on another dream," says the son. "You have been to Havana?"

"Havana, Cuba? No, I'm — we're Americans."

"We go there next."

"Could be some serious weather coming."

"If this cylinder is not fixed," says the father, "we will grow old here. Become native people."

Emmett thinks it's a joke, but he's never sure with the Schmecklers. "There are worse fates."

"Men have woyage for centuries without a motor," says the son. "Maybe we go on with only our sails."

"Don't think it's likely you'll find a Mercedes injector in Havana. Pretty lean times, what with the embargo and all. And berthing this baby without an engine in a strong wind —"

The father smiles. "Sailing is easy, ja? Only the landing is hard."

*

It had been another perfect day, maybe two weeks ago, heading northeast in a bracing dance with the wind, hull slicing through the swells, a half-dozen gulls coasting in their wake. Muriel's feel for trimming the sails was instinctive and they barely spoke, one anticipating the other's next move, making a leisurely ten knots into a slight breeze.

At first Emmett thought a cloud had drifted in front of the sun — a sudden chill, a dimming. Then he felt the hole inside of him, expanding. There was nothing on the horizon in any direction, nothing. But it wasn't fear or feeling small in the vast ocean. He had always preferred cruising to somewhere, somewhere they'd at least stay overnight. A destination. Going out and coming back to the same port, no one waiting for them, only the mute variables of tide and weather to define their passage — he felt suddenly disoriented, tempted to let the wheel go, to turn off all the systems, sit back and see what would happen. The feeling didn't last more than a few minutes. Blood sugar maybe, or just some random fantods. He told Muriel to come about and she gave him a look but didn't question. The trip home was just as spectacular.

Larry is nestled in a pile of life preservers at the base of the mast on the *Zephyr*, pecking at his laptop. The power cord loops over his bare feet and disappears down into the cockpit.

"When you wanted to crew a ship in the old days," he says without looking up, "you hung out at the sailors' bars till a couple likely ones drank themselves stiff, dragged them off, and threw them in the hold till you were a full day out of port. Now I'm on the fucking Web."

"What happened to your girls?"

Larry hit the marina three weeks ago with a pair of girls in their twenties he'd introduced to Emmett as his galley slaves.

"Bugged out on me."

"The both of them?"

"They came as a team. I saw the skinny one, Kim, in town yesterday. Hanging all over one of those boogie-board guys with the blond dreads. Bitch just waves, 'Hi, Captain Larry!' like she and her dumpy little pal haven't totally screwed me."

Larry is in his early fifties, salt-and-pepper beard, a regular at the Y-Ki-Ki since his Catalina sloop limped down from the Bahamas.

He was gradually heading for Tahiti, he said, once he got the right crew onboard.

"You know there's a couple young fellas on the island know their way around on a boat," says Emmett cheerfully. "Skip Andersen's boy there, Nicky, and that one that works at the bait shop — Jay? Jordan? —"

Larry shakes his head. "Only room for one hardtail on this bucket."

Emmett shrugs. "You're the skipper."

"They do that passive-aggressive thing. My wife was the queen of that. She could say 'Oh, don't worry, it's fine,' so it came out 'You blew it again, you insensitive piece of shit.'"

He seems more agitated than usual. At first, from the bile invoked when he spoke of his ex-wife and her evil lawyer, Emmett thought Larry's divorce must be recent, the wound still raw. But he'd been single a full eight years, cruising for five, a computer-dating Ahab chasing a wet dream.

"Even if they don't learn jack about sailing," he says, "these young ones get to practice their routine on me."

Emmett keeps smiling. "So is there some kind of computer shape-up where all the able-bodied sea ladies advertise?"

"Something like that. But you hire one, they bring their whole damn sorority along. If this wasn't too much boat to single-hand I'd be off this rock by now." He looks up to Emmett. "You hear the scuttle on the old couple?"

"Roderick won't talk."

"What does Roderick know? He didn't go inside the boat."

"You did?"

Larry logs off, closes the laptop, and sets it beside him. Emmett sees now that his eyes are red, his hands trembling slightly.

"I saw the old guy, Whitey, there at Ricky's place just yesterday afternoon. Then last night I couldn't sleep, so I get up, take a walk around the jetty —"

"This is late —"

"After three, at least. I get down at their end of D Pier and I hear the radio. Just weather reports and shit, somebody calling in the update on this Cedric."

"Edna was a real weather junkie," says Emmett. "We'd be sitting here, she'd tell you it was raining over in the Sea of Cortez."

"Fairly useless information."

"She explained the whole hurricane thing to me once. Most people think it's like straight wind pushing you over? But really you're being pulled, sucked in to fill a vacuum. Like going down a drain." Suddenly Emmett doesn't want to know the details, dreads the responsibility of passing the news to others. "All that noise and activity," he says, "but inside there's this big nothing."

Larry frowns at his hands. "The thing is, it was *loud.* The radio. I passed by, but on the way back I figure at that hour, not a light shining on the boat, they must have spent the night in town and left it running. So I'm gonna do the Good Samaritan thing."

Emmett suddenly feels a little dizzy. He looks across the channel. Something, not clouds exactly but a different kind of sky, is coming together in the north.

"You hesitate to step on somebody's boat without an invitation. Especially the liveaboards."

"You just don't do it," says Emmett, upset. "It's an invasion of privacy."

"I'm feeling pretty fucking invaded right now," says Larry, "if you want to know the truth."

"We haven't actually seen Edna for a while," says Emmett, stalling.

"No. I don't suppose you have." Larry wiggles the power cord with his toes, thinking. "You know that shark gun he kept by his chair when they went out for big stuff?"

"Short-barrel forty-four —"

"About as much wallop as you can get from a rifle. You can imagine, point-blank range, not shooting through water — he was just down on the saloon couch, the rifle was still between his knees. And the wife — the blood on the pillow and sheets was all dried. He must've caught her sleeping."

Emmett sees a trio of jellyfish working their way along the pontoon, no color, no edges, just a slight lack of focus in one part of the water. "Was she on her back? Looking up?"

"Yeah —"

"So she could have been awake. Knew it was coming, even."

"Like some kind of mercy-killing deal?"

"Why not?"

Larry considers this. He is shivering a bit, the shadow of the Lifestyles complex covering them both. He shrugs. "Who knows what the fuck goes on in people's heads? I figure she was already gone three, four days when I sat with him at Ricky's. I asked what was new and he said they were thinking about tarpon."

"That's all?"

"'We've been thinking about tarpon.'"

They are quiet for a long moment, a breeze picking up and tinkling the wind chimes on the back of the converted tug two slips down. A succession of hippie-looking people come down to use it on some sort of time-sharing deal. Muriel calls it the Love Boat.

"I hauled my ass back here and got my cell phone, tracked down the cops. I didn't go back in a second time, just gave them my statement. I'd forgot about the damn radio. Took the locals an hour before they turned it off." Larry looks out past the breakwater. "The fella calling in the weather said he thought this Cedric might turn into the real thing."

Emmett nods. The channel water has a little chop to it now. The frigate birds have disappeared.

"The way I feel, just let it blow," he says. "Be good to clear the air."

SAM SHAW

Reconstruction

FROM *StoryQuarterly*

ON A BRISK, beautiful autumn day, Guinevere accidentally killed my neighbor, Len Haynes. We were sniping chipmunks from a blind I'd constructed out of scrap tin when his head appeared over the crest of a hill. As if compelled by an innate marksman's instinct, she squeezed the trigger, and he vanished with a little spray of blood and what must have been brain matter. A cry escaped Guinevere's mouth.

"What," I said. "What did you do?"

"Oof," she said.

We were out of the blind and running across the field.

Haynes lay on the blond grass in the strangest position, arms and legs splayed like he had been interrupted in the performance of a dance. A cardboard box rested nearby, and objects that might have been hailstones had spilled from its mouth. Gwen licked one and said, wonderingly, "Mothballs."

I'd never seen a dead man before, not even Sid, whose ashes my brother and I had strewn in the fourth-hole water hazard at his beloved Pasquaney Club. Haynes looked almost serene, but blood of a startling red color streamed out of an opening an inch above his right eye. I dabbed his brow with the cuff of my shirt.

"Hey," I said to Haynes. "Hey, pal."

Haynes was not a good neighbor — often he left trash bags outside his door, and animals littered my yard with their contents — but I saw at that moment with perfect clarity that our fates were linked.

"It's OK," Guinevere said. "His eyes are moving."

But they weren't. Wide and glassy, they gaped at the cold expanse of the sky. I bent down, took his wrist in my hands and shook it.

At that moment, we heard what we took for a second shot, a screen door banging shut, and Guinevere and I both bucked upright. Haynes lived with his very large wife and a menagerie of desperate-looking cats and dogs in a green house some hundred feet from my own. Mrs. Haynes stood on the porch, holding a silver colander in her hands. It glinted terribly in the sun.

"You sonofabitch," she cried, in her grim baritone. To which, for reasons I still can't fathom, Guinevere lifted the rifle she had somehow neglected to drop, drew a bead on the woman, thought better of this, and fired a shot in the air. Mrs. Haynes loosed the colander and darted into her house.

We drove first to Guinevere's trailer, to collect some personal items and to think. As soon as we passed into its beery gloom, she thrust a stack of hardcover library books into my arms. The volume on top was called *Parrots of the World*. It must have weighed five pounds.

"I'm keeping these," she said. "It's wrong, I know, but I am."

I set the books by the door, then sat in the kitchen on the scuffed Formica counter while she filled a suitcase with clothes. Her faucet was busted, and a weak stream of water murmured in the sink. It was the bleakest sound I'd ever heard.

"What are we doing?" I asked her.

Through a half-opened door, I could see her standing over the suitcase. She held a sheer yellow blouse at arm's length as though contemplating a purchase. I took this opportunity to finish a roach I'd stowed in my wallet.

"Gwen? What are we doing, really?"

"I'm packing," she said, breathless, "and you're — I don't know what. Panicking."

"I'm not," I said. "Listen, you and I both know what happens next. We drive into town and straighten this thing out. Think for a second and you'll see I'm right."

"Getty, don't," she said.

"We've done nothing wrong, when you get down to it," I said, exhaling blue smoke.

She gave me a long, incredulous look. "See what you can find in the fridge," she said. "We're driving to Mexico."

Or rather I was driving — Gwen was unlicensed. What can be said about this plan? It sounded reasonable at the time. We piled into my Volvo, the two of us plus the bird.

Guinevere had acquired Cheyenne the prior Christmas from a war veteran in Sausalito. She was a cockatoo, an enormous creature with glistening feathers and imperious black eyes and an unsettling habit of turning her head 180 degrees to regard you over her shoulder — if a bird can be said to have shoulders. It was bad judgment, I thought. Exotic pets attract attention, and a getaway car ought properly to blend in. And there was the border crossing to consider: certainly the bird would not be welcome in Mexico.

"We'll burn that bridge when we come to it," Guinevere said. "I'll let her go if I have to. Who knows — could be she'll find us on the other side."

"She'll die," I said, and immediately I regretted this.

We didn't speak until we'd reached the highway. Everywhere, billboards. She put her hand on my leg, kneaded my thigh, and suddenly, exuberantly, I was erect.

"Look who's awake," she said.

Gwen had a special animal confidence, like she'd invented the concept of sex. We kissed there in the car, at eighty miles an hour, under a hemorrhaging sky.

I'd been stuck in a kind of emotional holding pattern for going on seven years. Not that things were desperate. I wasn't about to do myself in, for example, though I'd threatened it once in a letter to Sid. But I was looking down the barrel of turning thirty and there were days when I never put on pants, and nearly everything I ate emerged futile and gray from the maw of a George Foreman Grill. I'd moved to Port Wescott in '97, with the project of ruining my life. The place fairly reeked of disappointment. Everyone you met wore the same dazed look, as if the shovel of life had caught them square in the face. They were all former somethings: grounded pilots and injured farm-league phenoms, failed actors and businessmen, the disbarred, displaced, and dispossessed. As for me, I was a former son, doing everything I could think of to avoid becoming Sid. He'd built a pharmaceutical empire by the age of thirty-five; I took potshots at rodents from a half-collapsed porch. I was ready for a change.

One thing about flight: the sex is incredible. I've done breakup sex and makeup sex, sex with strangers, sex with old friends, sex in public, sex in closets, sex with several partners, sex with none; believe me when I tell you that there is nothing in the world like fugitive-from-justice sex.

We stopped for the night at a motel designed to resemble an African village: stucco office, empty kidney-shaped pool, and a corridor of suites with artificial thatching on the roof. I gave a false name and plate number to the desk attendant, a squirrelly Asian guy who might himself have been a wanted man. I was tense and depleted, and Guinevere fell on me as soon as we'd reached the room.

We screwed intermittently throughout the night. She pulled at my hair, bit my ear, cried and cursed, came like thunder. At dawn, swaddled in bedclothes, I told her that I loved her. She held me in a kind of wrestling lock with her legs and kissed my neck. I had said the words before. To Astrud Faison, dressed in her whites and smelling of tennis; to that French lifeguard, 1989; to Colleen, the night I left Antioch, not to return. Things have a way of ending.

"Have you been to Central America?" Gwen asked.

"No," I lied.

I lit a joint. The rotors of the ceiling fan did interesting things with the smoke.

"There are mangoes you eat right off the tree," she said. "And birds that you wouldn't believe. Serious birds. Everybody freaks over raptors, like the bald eagle is the greatest thing since bread. Try the resplendent quetzal. Emerald green with a three-foot tail."

As it happened, I had seen one in the wild. Guatemala, with Sid and Phyllis — or Syphilis, as I called my parents even then. As usual, they had spent the week indoors, shellacked on rum and cokes. I'd spotted the bird on an afternoon hike. The half-dozen tourists in our group, whose T-shirts attested to other vacations they'd enjoyed ("*Pura Vida* Costa Rica," "Oahu Nights") all clutched at their chests and swooned. Perched on a high branch, the resplendent quetzal looked to me like something you'd use to dust a chandelier.

"What I meant is, I love this," I said.

"I know," said Gwen.

She stood up and walked to the bathroom, perfectly naked and unashamed, urinated with the door open, then climbed back into bed.

"What's that?" I said.

"What?"

"On your back. ESP." I traced the letters with my finger.

"Extrasensory perception," she said. "I've got it like crazy. Think of a number between one and fifty."

"The E is darker," I said.

She put my hand on her breast.

"Because it's new."

I thought about this.

"Who's SP?"

"Just someone," she said.

She was undoubtedly the most beautiful person I ever knew.

"Guess where I'm heading once we get down south," she said. "Veracruz. Guess why."

"Have a swim?"

"I'm going to get my degree and become an ornithologist. They've got a very good program. Maybe the best."

"Hey. Hey." My finger was in her mouth. "We really killed that guy."

She laid my hand on the bed and sat upright.

We were back on the highway, then, traveling south. The car was a wreck, bird shit on the seats, snags and holes pecked in the dashboard upholstery. It was exhilarating in a way: we rode with the windows down, air howling in our ears so that we had to shout to make ourselves heard; Gwen held Cheyenne in her lap, smoothed her feathered head; I played the radio like an instrument, tuning gospel and swing and roiling Spanish talk.

It was a mistake, I knew, but I couldn't help worrying over Haynes. Probably laid out on a gurney somewhere on a paper sheet, and cruisers parked outside the house, hounds pursuing odors through the grass. I hadn't packed. So many objects I would never see again: my brother Antietam's trophy from the state geography bee, my journals, a Fender telecaster that had once belonged to Jeff Beck. And the eye, prized from the stony head of a bobcat at Pasquaney, when I was fourteen. Sid had shot the thing himself and presented it to the club as a monument. It was worthless, as far as I could tell. But of all his many treasures — all the asinine curios he'd found to throw his fortune at — the bobcat stood closest to his heart. Whenever he saw it he stopped and raised his glass as if toasting the honor of some great storied rival he had smote on the fields of war. I'd replaced the milky ball with a backgammon chip. Five minutes with a penknife while my parents drank cordials in the trophy room.

In spite of all that, it was good to be driving. From time to time, I would look over at Gwen and see the way she tended to her bird, and I'd want to pull over and stretch out in the back seat — not to make love, even, but to hold her and to feel the shock wave of passing trucks. It was as if I'd been granted a second chance. Now that Haynes was dead, I felt duty-bound to love and be loved, to build something real and true from the pieces of our three wrecked lives.

We lunched at a truck stop, in a fast-food place flanked by gray, skeletal hedges. I waited in a line of bedraggled kids and parents while Gwen made calls in the lot. Behind the counter, women in striped shirts dispensed hamburgers and vapid, lipsticked smiles. Unplugged pinball and arcade machines lined the wall like monuments in an antebellum graveyard. I was contemplating the plate glass windows when a hand touched my leg. It was attached to a boy in flannel pajamas.

"You're in the water," he said.

The floor was a vastness of blue tiles breached at intervals by islands of white. He leaped from one to the next, arms extended comically.

"I like a swim," I told him.

"There are sharks," he said soberly, and a woman seized his arm and dragged him off.

Gwen returned, dug her hand into my back pocket, and kissed my cheek.

"Everything all right?" I asked. She frowned in a way that suggested my question had endangered us both. All at once, I felt very anxious and not at all hungry. We ate without pleasure in a narrow booth.

Outside, she said, "We stop tonight in Arizona. Truck is going to meet us with money and a fresh car."

"Wait," I said. "What happened to Mexico?"

"Nothing happened," she said. "Except they'll be looking for your plates. And as far as money, Truck's got two thousand dollars, maybe more. We need every dollar we can get."

"I have money. I can get us — I don't know — five or six hun-

dred, plus another thousand on the first of the month." Those
were the provisions of my trust fund — a slow intravenous drip, interest from a principal I couldn't touch.

"Not enough," she said, and shook her head disgustedly.

"Enough for what, sunscreen? The whole point of Mexico is it's
cheap."

"It's called tuition," she said. "Ornithology, remember?"

"The thing about grad school, you don't just drive up at orienta-
tion with a suitcase full of cash. There are tests. You need transcripts and letters."

We got back in the car. Cheyenne cried out in salutation or complaint.

"And who or what is Truck?"

"Truck's my cousin," she said. "He's a genius at getaways. An escape artist practically."

Gwen was fishing in her bag, laying makeup compacts and emery
boards on the dash. There was something else in there, among her
women's things — a little revolver with a pearl handle.

"What's that for?" I said.

"In case something happens."

"In case what happens, exactly?"

She weighed it on her palm. "Something unforeseeable."

"If it's unforeseeable, you can't plan for it."

"Later," she said, "you may thank me."

It was dark when we left the highway. We drove a while on desolate
back roads before reaching our destination, a whitewashed motel
on the rubbled lunar plain. Our headlights caught the fender of a
station wagon, and Gwen shot upright in her seat.

"That's him," she said. "That's Truck's car."

It was an old model Chevy, taupe-colored with polyps of rust on
the side and cardboard in lieu of a window. The night air had a
vague chemical taste, and it was clear that I had made a serious mistake.

I parked behind a Dumpster, then followed Gwen across the lot
toward a half-opened door. All I could see of the room was the corner of a bed and a pair of large, vegetably feet. My stomach was doing a particular stock car maneuver I remembered from my glory
days on the junior tennis circuit. Once, on a grass court in Flag-

staff, I'd rallied with Ilie Nastase. It was a pristine day: high wind, and planes crossing overhead, contrails etched against a soft blue sky. The careering in my gut was such that I could barely execute a serve. Now with every step I took, the idea of return seemed more remote. As if sensing my doubt, Gwen hooked a finger in my belt loop and gave it a tug.

Truck wore a hunting cap and a suede jacket with tassled arms, and his eyes never strayed from the television screen, not even when you asked him a question. For the most part, he spoke to me through Gwen, as if I were immaterial, a phantom she alone could see. As for Gwen herself, she seemed positively enraptured by his company. She took off her shoes, sat on the dusty carpet, and laughed at all his comments, none of which were funny in the least. When she asked me to pick up whiskey, sandwiches, and corn nuts ("for baby Cheyenne"), I felt something close to gratitude.

It was twenty minutes to the store and back, and the bird flapped plaintively all the way.

Truck took so long with the door that I wondered momentarily if I'd knocked at the wrong room. I could hear the shower running in the bathroom, and Gwen's things were piled on a chair. Truck lay across the bed. On TV a couple of old-fashioned pugilists boxed primly in black and white.

"Getty," Truck said to the screen, testing the sound of it. "What kind of a name is Getty anyway?"

"You'd have to take it up with my father," I said.

"I don't like it much."

"It wasn't my idea," I told him. Why was I defending myself to a person called "Truck"?

After a while, I said, "That's an interesting car you've got."

"You expected a PT Cruiser?" he asked.

I said that I hadn't. Still, his Chevy wasn't worth the speakers in my Volvo, and I told him so. He frowned at me and looked away. His fists were balled, and he tensed now and then as if to deflect televised blows.

"Actually, you're a help," I said. "Otherwise we'd have to steal something. And I wouldn't know how to begin."

"Thought you were outlaws," Truck said, glancing vaguely in my direction.

"That's Gwen's thing," I said. "Honestly, I'm not built for it."

"You said it, not me," Truck said, and snorted.

The bathroom door opened, loosing generous clouds of steam. Gwen appeared, her hair wrapped in an elegant nautilus-curl of towel, and briefly the room was an alpine spa. She had changed into sweatpants and a T-shirt, which read: IF YOU LOVE SOME-THING, SET IT FREE. IF IT DOESN'T COME BACK, HUNT IT DOWN AND KILL IT.

We ate our sandwiches on the double bed, with a fresh towel for a picnic blanket. Truck took the whiskey bottle and poured tall drinks into plastic cups provided gratis by the motel staff. I held mine for a minute or two, then set it down on the floor. Truck regarded me warily.

"I don't drink," I said.

"That's right," said Gwen, as if I'd answered a question that had plagued her all week.

I rolled and lit a joint. Truck watched it hungrily as I smoked, but he never asked and I didn't offer. We all lay down on the bed, Gwen in the middle. The two of them drank and talked about old friends who had come into money or disappeared or suffered unexpected injury. As far as I could tell, half their friends were either locked in jail or on their way. It was all surprise and reversal. Presumably there were others, friends who persisted stubbornly in their same dull orbits, but Gwen and Truck neglected to mention them. Time passed and the two of them grew louder and happier.

I suggested that we get on the road.

"The room's paid," Gwen said.

"That may be true," I said. "Still, I'll be tired in the morning."

"Then Truck can drive."

She leaned over as if to embrace me. Instead she collected my cup from the floor and passed it to Truck.

"Tell Smokey to relax," he said. And then, buoyant, "Relax, Smokey."

I told Gwen I had to speak with her privately, and we left the room and walked to the rear of the motel. Overhead a harsh yellow bulb flashed to life, and suddenly we were exposed among beer cans and other flotsam.

"*Truck* can drive?"

She blinked. "It's his car."

"You're saying that Truck is coming with us. That's what you're saying, isn't it? Jesus."

"Hey," she said, touching my chest.

"And for another thing, it's clear he's not your cousin."

"Of course he's my cousin," she said. "He's my favorite cousin, and the only one I've got."

"If this gets strange, I'll kill him," I said, and let this sink in. "That's what I am, a murderer, same as you."

She moved in close and clasped her hands on my sides. Together, we managed a lurching backward dance step.

"Trust me," she said.

She wore that beatific white smile of hers under which, ordinarily, I was defenseless as a fawn in a poacher's beams. But some change in the timbre of the night — the dogfight of moths around our heads — cleared my mind of love and sex, and perhaps because I sensed that my anger could not possibly survive the ordeal of her holding me for even fifteen seconds more, I shook her off.

"This whole ornithology deal," I heard myself say. "You know what it is, don't you? It's a joke. It's fucked. First off, you don't have a bachelor's degree."

Gwen didn't flinch.

"I mean — let me ask you this. Did you finish high school even?"

"And you're supposed to be some kind of role model? So the point of life is wearing your robe all day like a schizo patient. Well excuse me for trying to improve myself. There's more to life than weed and Cinemax."

Back in the room, Truck had removed his shirt. He was muscular in a Byzantine, plated way that made me think of lobsters in a tank. He spread out on the floor, with his pants and shoes on. Gwen gave him the bedspread and a pillow, and shut off the light. I undressed and inched carefully into bed, listening to the faint oceanic sounds we made. Gwen lay very still. I would have liked to hear her voice.

Some time later there was a cry of sirens in the distance, and cold fingers probed the flap of my shorts. All I could think of was Truck, three feet away. I turned over and fought my way to sleep.

In the morning sun fell on the lot in golden sheets. Gwen and Truck were sleeping, and I sat on the hood of my car.

Inside, the bird was dead. You could tell by the way she lay there on the seat, sideways like a tiny person, her wings askew. I didn't care. I had a new plan, and I was silently mulling it.

If I was going to live in Mexico, which apparently I was, and with Guinevere, and also temporarily with Truck, I would need money. And something else, something more elusive, like authority. And both of these were readily available, not three hundred miles east.

We would drive to Prospect, to the Chateau Syphilis — where my mother lived alone, or with some callow tennis coach or gardener from the third world. In the master bedroom, there was a safe that contained, among antique coins and articles of jewelry, a stack of bonds as thick as a phone book. I would borrow against the trust that was rightfully mine. It wouldn't be theft, only a form of accounting.

Gwen emerged from the room wearing her gauzy yellow blouse, through which her bosom showed clear as a Christmas present wrapped in cellophane. I was so transfixed that I forgot to prepare her for the spectacle waiting in the car. She held her stomach and bent as if she might be sick.

"Take it slow," I said.

The doors were still locked, and when I offered her the keys she looked at me with such utter desolation you'd have thought it was her infant laid dead across a bier of accordion-fold state roadmaps. For a long minute, she didn't move. She clambered across the seat and lay down awkwardly next to her bird. When she touched it, I half expected the thing to shudder into flight. She was talking, but not to me. It was the sort of voice TV parents adopt when they're tucking their kids into bed. Then she climbed back out, and it was just as if the channel had been switched. She cradled Cheyenne in her arms and said some terrible things about God, the world, me and Truck, and also herself. "Human love is fucked," she said, poisoned with self-centeredness, jealousy, and doubt. "But an innocent bird loves with its whole heart." It struck me that the organ in question is roughly as large as a cashew, but I reserved this thought for myself. Truck stood shirtless in the doorway, looking lost. We were no comfort to Gwen in the least.

Truck drove with one hand and smoked with the other, and I watched through a gray window as houses reeled by and receded. It seemed incredible that each of these structures was someone's home.

After an hour or so, I said to the horizon, "We're going to make a detour not too far ahead. You'll both have to trust me."

Truck whistled. "He's your mess," he said to Gwen. "You clean it up."

When I turned and looked, her eyes were red from crying.

"Whatever he says," she told Truck. "Getty and me are in it together."

When the highway split, we proceeded east, toward Prospect and a house I hadn't seen in seven years.

When you're wanted for murder, and you're high on Humboldt Gold, even teenage girls in Saturns look like undercover cops. We were nearly home. Truck lay sprawled across the back seat, asleep with a hand thrust down his pants. He looked almost childlike, except for the lightning bolt tattooed across his neck.

Hours had passed since Guinevere had opened her mouth. She just sat there pulling loose hairs from her scalp and holding them up to the light. My brain ran hot and dry imagining the many trials ahead. As if conjured out of thin air by my dread, a convoy of sleek, malignant eighteen-wheelers bloomed in the rearview and overtook us. The trucks were full of cattle — lean, pathetic things. They crowded at a line of portholes, angling their noses like dogs on a Sunday pleasure drive. Did they know, in their dusky bovine skulls, about the holocaust to come? It seemed a glimpse into my own future. A road sign promised gas and food in half a mile; there were sure to be police. Nothing would be simpler than to turn myself in. But to do so would mean parting ways with Gwen. In spite of everything, she filled me with the kind of grievous longing I hadn't felt since seventh grade. She was all I had left.

"Look," I said. "Cows."

She unbuckled her seatbelt and hugged her knees to her chest.

"I wish I hadn't done it," she said. There was a perfect freckle at the corner of her mouth. The sight of it gave me a feeling of hope.

"It's plain shoddy luck is all," I said. "One of those wrong time wrong place deals. Think of it this way. The night you were conceived, if your parents had gone to see *Rocky* instead, or if they'd ordered in Chinese. If your father wore a different pair of slacks, whatever, you could be skiing down the Alps right now. You could be a world-famous tennis champ. You could be chauffeuring those cows around. Blame the stars." I took her hand in mine. It was utterly dead in my grip. "Accidents happen," I said. "Everyone's a victim in this thing."

"No," she said. "It wasn't though. Not really. I just — wondered if I could."

I looked straight ahead through the windshield. The sky was a rusty wash. Through an aperture the size of a volleyball, two gaunt Herefords peered back at me. One opened its mouth, disclosing a pink slab of tongue. Eventually I risked a glance at Gwen. She looked like somebody's daughter, perched there in the passenger seat. I gave her fingers an exploratory squeeze.

"OK, but my point is, you regret it, right?"

She squeezed back then, twice, as if signaling in code. A giddy warmth settled over me.

"We'll make up for it in Mexico," I said. "Plant a tree or something. It's going to be a whole different deal down there." I meant it. I could see the whole thing, with the vividness of recollection: sand in the sleeping bags and afternoon dips and the tang of grilling fish on the air.

"I wish I could take it back," she said.

"So do I," I told her. And as soon as I'd said it, I knew it was a lie.

We waited until nightfall, then made for the house. It stood atop a low ridge, a grand stone structure with wings that embraced the sculpted grounds, though coldly. We stopped at the gate. I directed my instructions to Truck. Kill the radio and headlights. Relax for a while. Then I got out and eased the door shut.

The night was electric with that wide-open amphitheater sound of insects chirring in grass. Right then, I knew that Gwen and Truck would be gone when I returned to the car. I stopped and held both hands open in the air. *Ten minutes.* The red point of Truck's cigarette bobbed a little, but if either of them waved I couldn't tell. The chalky driveway shone like a river in the dark. There was a wind, and I could hear the knell of cords lashing the flagpole in the yard.

In the 1980s, Sid had hosted lavish dinners at the house, big raucous affairs attended by some of Arizona's wealthiest and most influential drunks, people who filled our house with cigarette smoke and braying laughter. Those evenings followed a time-honored protocol: after an hour of cocktails in the foyer, the peal of an antique bell summoned all present to the dining room where, through the addition of leaves, a table would be set for as many as thirty guests. An hour later Sid would charge his glass and deliver an interminable toast, thanking Phyllis and God and the GOP. Then he'd call out to his children. We came in from the hall. Antietam led the way, beating a slow somber march on a drum, and under the rheumy watch of my parents' guests, I would sing all five verses of Julia Ward Howe's "Battle Hymn of the Republic." On a good night I was allowed to leave without fanfare. Usually, though, there were compulsory handshakes and kisses, and occasionally I had to sing it twice. Then in junior high, a girl I knew vaguely from school accompanied her parents to one of Sid's soirees, and the sight of her leering through the bit about "the beauty of the lilies" so riled me that afterward I kicked a six-inch hole in my bedroom wall. It was the first shot fired in a war I'd been fighting ever since.

There were no cars at the house, and no lighted windows, which came as a relief but no surprise. My mother lived her life on an outpatient basis, dividing time between bridge, church, and her philanthropies. Often she was gone for weeks at a time, to places like Antigua or Palm Springs, for symposiums, concerts, or luncheons. Anything to save her from the house and its photographic memory, its clutter and familiar smells.

I found the front door locked, so I stole back to the greenhouse where we'd kept a key in a rusted watering can. To my great satisfaction, I found it with ease. I walked back to the door and unlocked it and stood for a minute, breathing. Then I crossed the threshold and shut the door behind me.

The house was mausoleum still. You could almost hear dust motes falling. I moved across the floor in small, uncertain steps, hands extended as if I were blind — which, temporarily, I was.

On the second floor, tall windows surveyed the grounds. My mother's topiary, once a skyline of Platonic forms, had assumed a kind of gothic disarray. Moonlight skipped across the parquet floor. I crossed the threshold into my father's office. The room was crowded with furniture under painter's tarps, so that it appeared as if I were standing among the ghosts of tables, chairs, and lamps. I sat down on a long sofa. Time passed, and I spread out so that my face touched the plastic sheet.

Then the lights were on, and I lay there stiffly.

"Don't even breathe," came a voice from behind me. "I'm heavily armed." Unmistakably, this was Antietam, my brother.

There was the sound of a lamp overturned.

"Hey," I said from the sofa. "Ant, it's Getty. It's me."

"The hell it is," he said. And there he was, white and disheveled, his hair so long and unruly that I took it, at first, for a wig. He wore a jersey with a picture of Che Guevara on it, and his arms were full of what appeared to be a Confederate infantry rifle, complete with bayonet.

"Unbelievable," he said, with something like a smile on his face, but he didn't lower the gun. "You're the spitting image of Sid, do you know that?"

"That's very funny," I said. "Shouldn't you be at school?"

"Hung up the gloves. Same as you."

"Same nothing," I said. "I was twenty. You're what, seventeen?"

"I'm a regular prodigy," he said.

I thought if I moved to embrace him he might be inclined to put down the rifle; instead, I found myself holding its barrel, the bayonet's point grazing my chest. What ensued was a kind of reverse tug of war, with each of us gently thrusting the weapon toward the other. This exercise was cut short by a clamor from the doorway.

"Drop it," Truck said, presumably to my brother.

Antietam did as he was told, and so did I. The rifle met the floor with a regrettable crack. Truck picked it up and admired the stock while Gwen considered etchings on the walls. I made sheepish introductions.

"This is your place?" Truck wondered. "Who burgles his own damn house?"

"It's not burglary," I said. "I was going to leave a note."

"Where's your room?" Gwen asked me.

"He doesn't have a room," Antietam said. "Sid turned it into a den. Anyway, take what you like. I don't give a shit."

Feeling inexplicably tired, I sat back down on the shrouded sofa.

Gwen had discovered Sid's collection. One by one, she lifted the plastic tarps, and the bounty took shape: threadbare Union flags, bugles and blue velvet petticoats, sabers, firearms, pulpy documents, medals, and daguerreotypes, all in somber glass vitrines.

"God," she said. "What is all this?"

"Our father had a thing about the Civil War," said Antietam.

Truck picked up a silk top hat and set it on his head. "What's this shit worth, anyway?" he asked.

"More than me and Getty," my brother said, and coughed up a single dry laugh. "Probably more than the house, but a bitch and a half to sell. Anyway, I've got a lady guest upstairs. Try to keep it down." And he left us to manage on our own. I invited Gwen and Truck to make themselves at home while I conducted some business downstairs.

The master bedroom was on the ground floor — cloistered like a bomb shelter two stories below Antietam's and my own. I had some trouble opening the safe (was Sumter 1860? '62?), and when finally its tumblers fell with a satisfying clap, I found it empty. Or not quite: there was a lowball glass — with a desiccated lime in it, and lipstick on the rim — which I opted not to take. It was the sort of night that makes you want to crawl in bed and sleep for several years.

When I came upstairs, the front door hung open. Truck was loading objects through the smashed side window of the car, which he'd backed against the steps. Gwen's arms were full of antique guns.

"Look at him," Truck said after a while. "It's like he's foreman or something." And as they passed me on their way back upstairs, he nodded and called me "Sir."

I walked outside and peered into the car. It had become a traveling museum, full of glinting metal shapes, field maps and military drums, a faded Choctaw headdress, a portrait of Ulysses Grant. Truck installed a couple of globes in the trunk and emerged with a can of beer, which he cracked and sipped and then emptied on the grass. Gwen came out with an object clasped like a baby at her breast.

"Jesus H.," Truck said. "I could sell snow to a Puerto Rican. But no way in hell is anybody paying us for that thing." It was my father's prized bobcat. Gwen set it on the gravel drive and the two of them plunged back into the light of the house.

What a strange and sad reunion. I touched the hole I'd gouged thirteen years earlier. It was rough and dry. Had the club returned the trophy after Sid's death? As always, the animal was frozen in attack, tongue curled between painted teeth, fusty paw outstretched. A taxidermist's lie. Sid had shot it at a game park, in a pen; for all I knew the cat had been asleep. The miserable thing never stood a chance. I felt a wave of pity — for the bobcat, for Antietam, and even for Sid. He'd been a drunk and a tyrant, but also a man, and a father of sons who had failed him.

Truck urged me out of the way. Apparently, he'd tired of antiques: there was a widescreen television in his arms, and Gwen stood behind him, clutching the cord as if it were a wedding train. I watched him struggle to fit it in the car.

"Hang on a second," I said.

Truck set the TV on the ground and began hastily to unload the back seat, handing objects to Gwen more quickly than she could take them. She stacked Sid's life on the roof of the car.

"We need to put it all back," I said. "I'm sorry. I've made a mistake."

Truck had hefted the television onto his knees, and he labored under its weight.

"Move that puma," he said to Gwen. She slid the bobcat out of his way.

The week I'd left school, Sid rewarded me with dinner at his club. He maintained an eerie poise through three courses and dessert. Afterward, through a curtain of smoke, he told me, "Rest assured, I saw it coming long before you did." This wasn't quite true: since boyhood, I'd felt failure in my bones, a dull, constant ache. I had always been predictable, above all to myself. It came as a surprise, though, when I saw Gwen's bag on the passenger seat, reached in, and took her gun. I leveled it at Truck.

"Put it back," I said. "All of it."

"Oh, honey," said Gwen.

Truck watched me for a long moment. Slowly, he bent and put down the television. He squinted, as though performing long division in his head. Then he nodded and spread his arms, palms open, inviting me to shoot.

"I'll do it," I said. And I wanted to. My hand wavered. We stood there talking with our eyes.

Truck moved carefully toward me, and took the weapon from my hand. He lowered it and fired. There was a barking sound and a fierce blazing pressure in my thigh. Tears rushed to my eyes and I folded, almost gracefully, to an Indian position on the ground.

"Get in the car," Truck ordered Gwen.

She looked into my eyes with a lovely mournful calm. She had killed a man, and her bird was dead. She kissed my head and opened the passenger door.

The car tore away in a storm of Union relics, and I sat there in the inky silence, bleeding. The bobcat stared with its one good eye. Soon enough, I would limp inside and find a phone. For the moment, though, I held my leg and counted — breaths and heartbeats, birches, aircraft in the sky. They would get at least a small head start.

The Love of a Strong Man

FROM *The Ontario Review*

THIS IS A STORY that does not begin and end; it simply crept up on those involved, without warning, and will continue to haunt us, to hang over us after the trial is over, after he has died. We will remember. How can it be told? It started, perhaps, when we met: I, fourteen, new white sneakers, tight jeans, and long brown hair to the middle of my back, chewing gum; he, seventeen, shaggy blond hair brushing his chin, tight white T-shirt stretched over his muscular chest, torn jeans, and a posed cigarette drooping out of his mouth. He said, "Nice weather we're having," in a low, grim growl, and of course I had to respond to that, the bold contrast of the everyday phrase and the tough-guy voice straight out of the movies. Then, I loved his strength, loved the way his huge arm draped around my thin shoulders, the fact that everyone knew that he could have rubbed their boyfriends' faces in the dirt had he wanted to, yet he didn't, and had never been in a fight. He still hasn't so much as been punched. Later, when we married, his strength seemed to be a mirage, like the muscle builders who do nothing more with their muscles than rub oil on them and pose, and I wondered when the strength, the dominance, the love I always wanted had slipped away.

But that can't be where it started, because I knew nothing at fourteen, and he had done nothing. I don't believe that the snatched packs of gum slipped into his pocket at the grocery store, or the school suspension that resulted because his teacher said his constant habit of falling asleep in class was insubordination, were related to the things that happened later. I did not find out until a couple months ago, when it had been going on for years, and we lived on a cul-de-sac with wide open manicured lawns, and a strange, grainy suspect drawing appeared in the papers and all over town, and the wide chin and long nose looked uncannily like him, and of course the arrest several days later confirmed my suspicions. In some moments I wonder if it is all a horrible coincidence, or if a disgruntled patient framed him, and we will soon be on CNN talking about the incompetence of our local police force. But I have no proof of this. I refuse to go to the trial; I cannot be one of those pitiable wives who stands by her husband professing his innocence, crying and wringing her hands in court, wearing a nice blue skirt suit and borrowed pearls, whining, "He's such a good man; he's innocent, dentists don't do these things!"

Only if I start with the arrest, then you will never understand how I came to be his wife, the way that there can be a marriage in which so much is unknown, and unknowable. I will never know much of it, much of him. Aren't all marriages like that? After years of breaking up and making up, we eloped just as he entered school to become a dentist, a job he chose because I mentioned that it pays well, and it comes with none of the life-or-death decisions of being a doctor, just thoughts about cavities and crowns. A low-stress occupation, just as my job at the makeup counter is low-stress. We went to work, we took vacations to Hawaii, shopped for antique furniture in flea markets.

How can someone live with another and not see things, you will wonder, how could anyone marry, or love, such a person? Maybe I should back up and start earlier, perhaps even to his childhood, and show how he was the victim, the abuses that he suffered from *his* father, and let those make him less of a monster. But he did not speak to me of the nature of those abuses, other than the cold sweats of his nightmares, and I did not discover the details about them any sooner than any other regular, newspaper-reading citizen: "Accused Was Victim of Child Abuse," the papers claimed in bold 30-point font on the Local Interests page. I am married to a local interest.

Friends have asked me how I am doing, say "Are you OK, honey?" with their brows furrowed as they pat me on the arm. But I know that what they really want to know is how could he do those things, how could I be married to him, and when am I finally going to break down into a hysterical mess in public so that they can tell all their friends and the *National Enquirer* about it. I just keep telling them, "Oh, you know," when, of course, they don't, and probably thank God that they are not living my life. Recently, they've stopped calling.

I reach up over my head and grab the remote from my bedside table and flip on the television. A pregnant reporter in a beige suit stands in front of the county courthouse and says, "All seven victims are scheduled to testify during the trial of accused rapist Henry Calston, which will begin next week. Calston faces seven counts each of sexual assault, kidnapping, and breaking and entering. It is rumored that there may be other victims who have not yet come forward," and I quickly turn the television off. My heart pounds and I scan the expansive master bedroom with the fireplace he always said provided great ambience but never used because that would have made it ash-filled and dirty, and I look over the stacks of cardboard boxes just to make sure that no one is here. I walk over to my closet and open and shut the door, then return to my space on the carpet with my back against the wall, my body against one of the matching cherry tables that frame our king-size bed. From here I can see the two windows that overlook our street and the bedroom door. A worn romance novel, sent to me by his mother, sits on my bedside table, and I flip through it, watching the black and white merge into a gray blur as the pages move faster and faster.

I put down the book and remember the time that we went to see a romantic comedy about a lonely violinist and her truck-driving suitor and Henry said, right in the middle of the scene where the truck driver filled the violinist's bedroom with handpicked daisies, "People that different don't fall in love," loud enough that he was shushed from all sides. I answered, "But would she really have anything more in common with another violin player? Or any stringed-instrument player?" Henry laughed, grabbed my hand, and kissed the back of it. Moments like this seemed inconsequential at the time, but now, I search for meaning in every memory. I wonder if he kissed my hand because he felt too guilty over what he was doing to kiss my lips, or if he was trying to act normal and hand-kissing seemed like the regular husband thing to do. But, thinking about that day at the movie theater, and how Henry took off his sweater and gave it to me, so that I wore my own ribbed red crewneck sweater underneath his huge gray wool sweater, and the way my nose was filled with the spicy, dominant scent of his sweat, I cannot find anything other than a couple at the movies. It makes me shiver.

I cannot watch movies anymore because I always hear what Henry would say about them, I cannot read, I cannot watch television, and I don't really want to have to see or talk to anyone at all. I have nothing to do but pluck stray dark fibers out of the white of our carpet and think about what my husband did. So, I sit on our white bedroom floor in my worn black sweatpants, stare at the lines in the beige wallpaper, and think of the answers to your questions.

Now, all of my memories are contaminated, the picture on my table that shows him in his dark gray suit standing next to Elvis in the Chapel of Love where we eloped mixed with a scratchy pencil drawing of a victim sobbing on the witness stand, to-do lists written on Post-Its that I find still stuck inside of the closet and medicine cabinet juxtaposed against the pleading letters sent to me from jail, and it is the same handwriting, and that does not seem fair. It should be easy to separate, to split the lover from the rapist, to cut them apart, to distill my memories, to pasteurize them. That is what I am most angry about: he has left nothing untouched.

I glance at the clock: 1:00 AM. I crawl onto the bed and lay flat on my back on top of the comforter. I leave the overhead light on and stare at the ceiling until the morning sun creeps through the windows. I shower, get dressed, and then sit at our huge dining room table with a cup of coffee and wait until it is 9:00 and I can leave for work. I sit on his side of the table now, so that I don't have to stare at his empty chair and picture the way he sat up perfectly straight while he read the comics — never the front page or even the business news, Henry only read the Lifestyles and Sports sections of the paper. He always sat up rigidly, though his eyes were heavy with sleep. I try to remember ever seeing Henry relax, and I can't. He reminded me of a dog just given the command to freeze, poised and waiting for another command so he would know what to do next.

I drive through the thick suburban traffic and wonder if the other drivers, all alone in their cars as I am in mine, know who I am married to. I wonder if they know who they are married to. Perhaps their husbands are worse than mine, perhaps my husband is innocent and one of them will soon be in my place, hiding in the master bedroom and searching for the illusive moment when her life went wrong.

At the pastel-pink makeup counter, I give makeovers, to encourage women to buy skin creams and lotions that we both know will not remove their wrinkles and leave them with a younger, happier life, and I almost forget his supposed crimes. I pick up the phone to call him, careful to hold the white receiver away from my cheek so that my foundation does not leave a light brown stain, and then remember that he is in jail, not performing root canals, and he doesn't have a phone, and even if he did, charming anecdotes about the abuses of eye shadow are not what he would want to hear. It is not as easy as it should be to cut off your now-criminal husband, not like a hangnail or even a gangrene-infested limb. I could deal with the ghost pains left after amputation, but I cannot will myself to amputate.

"Making a call, Darlene?" says one of the other makeup girls, Ali, who wears black fishnet stockings every day. I wonder if it's the same pair.

"No," I answer, and put the phone back onto the receiver. She crosses the small space from the sunless tanning creme display to where I stand, by the phone, the cash register, and the sticky sweet newly released perfume called Luminescent Honey. Ali and I used to go out for margaritas after work, but after Henry's arrest, I caught her on the six o'clock news saying that she always thought Henry was a little too quiet, and that I once came to work with a black eye. That black eye had been from a skiing accident, in which I tumbled down the slope and kicked myself in the face with my ski, and she knew it. I haven't spoken to her, except for work-related conversations, since I saw that clip.

"How are you?" says Ali, stretching out the word "are" so that it covers the space three words normally fill in her rapid babble.

"Really, how are you?"

"I'm considering suicide," I say, just to see what she will do. Her face freezes into its pat expression of concern and her eyes double in size so that she looks exactly like the life-sized doll head I had as a kid that you could put makeup on and then wash clean before curling its hair into a huge synthetic bouffant. "But then, who would you have to talk about?"

She pulls down her white lab coat, the kind that we all wear over our black clothes, that I suspect are intended to make us look like experts. My husband wore a white lab coat, too. I wonder what he wore when he did those things, if he had a special outfit, or if he wore his clothes, the clothes that I always bought for him because he hated to shop. My stomach rumbles and I worry that I will throw up all over Ali and her fishnets and lab coat and green eye shadow. She is still staring at me. Two of the girls over at one of the other makeup counters are looking at us and talking in low voices, as they have been for the last few months. I want to tell them that I know what they're talking about, that they're talking about me and Henry, but I don't want to mention his name.

"How about that new perfume, that Luminescent Honey? It's something, isn't it?" I call over to them in my most threatening voice. They smile wide with their glossy lips and nod, the way that you smile and nod at the corsage-wearing women who try to get you to join their church.

Ali shakes her head at me. "Have you thought of a professional, Darlene? Because this problem of yours is getting to be too much for me. I can't help you. Maybe you should see a professional." She walks back over to the sunless tanning creme and stays on the opposite side of the makeup counter.

The day passes quickly; when there are no makeovers to give, I concentrate on stacking the tiny boxes of eye shadow in neat rows, making sure that the labels all point out and are right-side up, and that each of the 136 colors are in the correct slot. I ignore Ali, who has crossed over to the rival makeup counter and whispers with the other two girls, and I do not take a lunch break. One woman who comes to the department store to replace her powder says, "Looks like you're doing all the work around here," nodding toward Ali and the other girls who are now sipping on lattes, which Ali went to get for them all, without asking me if I wanted one. I smile at the woman, just like those girls smiled at me earlier, feeling my berry-glossed lips crackling under the effort, and take her money. I wish I had never met Henry. At seven, I return home, kick off my heels at the door, change into my sweatpants, grab my saltines and 7-Up, and return to my seat on the master bedroom floor.

The phone rings and I stand up and sink my toes into the thick white carpet as I walk over to his bedside table, which holds our smooth white replica of a 1940s phone with a gold-colored mouth and ear piece and rotary dial.

It is his mother, who asks me to go see him for the third time in as many days, says "Darlene, darling," which is how she's always addressed me when trying to get something, perhaps thinking that the alliteration will sway me, "He's all alone in that jail. It's been months."

"I am all alone here. You're all alone in Wichita, Eleanor. Loneliness is not a reason." In fact, Eleanor moved to Wichita after her husband's death, perhaps to escape her memories of him, and has since created a life centered on being alone. The only time that she has any kind of voluntary interaction with people, as far as I know, is when she goes to church, or calls us.

"What about all those lovely gifts he always got you, to show how much he loves you? That monthly subscription to the flower-delivery service? He took care of you when you had that lump scare."

"I left the order form for the flowers on the counter. And that was a false alarm. This is different." Even if he did go with me to the doctor to get it checked out, he probably wouldn't have continued to hold my hand and go on doctor visits if it had been cancer, if I had gone through chemo. But the moment I think that, I know it's not true. I remember how, at the doctor's, he brought me all seven types of soda from the vending machine because he wasn't sure what I wanted. He always went anywhere I asked him to go. I chew on a cracker. All I've been able to eat since it started is salty, flat things: anchovies, beef jerky, saltines. I don't know what that means.

"Different how? Husbands and wives stand together in a crisis." I wonder how to get her off the phone. She isn't here, visiting her son, standing by his side, she just sends checks to his lawyer, and she probably would try to send care packages full of gingerbread and clean underwear if they would let her. "Or they cause a crisis," I say. The cracker sucks my mouth dry and makes it painful to talk. I wish I hadn't said that.

"Oh," she sucks in through her teeth, as though I've punched her in the stomach. There is silence for a moment, then she continues. I can tell that she's decided to be sweet to me during this conversation no matter what, even if I tell her that her son is a creepy fucker like I did the last time we spoke. "Those things with my ex-husband are years past. Henry loves us. Handmade cards, that's love."

I swallow my cracker, wash it down with 7-Up. I drink 7-Up during any turmoil, it seems to calm my stomach. It hasn't been working. "How do you know he does?"

Her voice shifts and becomes harder, deeper, and I can hear the rough edge in her throat left over from her twenty-seven years of smoking. "I always told Henry you should have renewed your vows."

This was the type of comment that, if my husband were still sleeping underneath our deep blue down comforter and not the worn blanket I imagine in his jail cell, would have made me laugh. We were married by someone who asked, "Do you promise to hang on to your hunka hunka burning love till he croaks?" But I have found myself drawn to churches in the last months, pacing up and down streets in front of their imposing permanence, wishing that I could bloody my knees from too much prayer. I wonder what type of responsibility I have in what my husband did. He always prayed, when he thought that I wasn't looking, mumbling softly just after we got into bed, his hands clenched in a double fist. Why had he prayed, I wonder. Guilt? Solace? Forgiveness? Or was it just an automatic habit instilled by his Presbyterian mother that he simply could not stop performing, like a trained circus elephant's tricks?

I realize that Eleanor is talking again. "Did you hear what I said?"

"I've got to go. Bye," I say, then hang up the phone, hearing her screeches of "Darlene? Darlene!" as I move the handset toward the receiver. It's unfortunate she didn't have any other children. None of her other eggs were strong enough to withstand her.

What did she know, I wonder as I return to my seat on the carpet. Perhaps I can blame her, for staying with a man who beat her and her son, for not putting my husband in enough baseball leagues, for failing to notice signs of his criminal future. But what signs were there that I did not notice? He was a professed atheist who prayed, for one, and he always had insomnia and I, a heavy sleeper, never even knew which nights he wandered through our house and which nights he lay beside me. I should have known that, at the very least I should have recognized his physical presence. My stomach lurches, then drops, leaving me with a queer bottomless feeling.

I slip on my pink flip-flops and go outside. I wander up and down my street in the cool night, as though his insomnia has been passed to me, and search for signs. In crazed moments I think that I might redeem myself as his wife by catching another man trying to assault a teenage girl or, better yet, a grandmother, a sign of an even more depraved mind than my husband's. All of the houses on our street have the shades drawn, and there's no sign of people, other than the muted yellow of my neighbors' lights and the occasional blue flicker of a television. The night air makes me shiver, but my body is covered in a kind of sticky sweat, and I rush home to take a shower. I exfoliate and scrub hard so that my skin turns red. I use two kinds of perfumed soap and a body wash, and blast myself with water so hot that I cringe, but I cannot come out feeling clean.

The running water fills the silence of our three-bedroom two-bath, a new house in which the master suite takes up an entire floor, and I've filled it with heavy cardboard boxes. But why, though I have been able to box up his striped ties, the music boxes he gave me each year for our anniversary, and even the picture of the three-hundred-pound Elvis impersonator holding me, looking frightened and pale, that my husband took on our wedding day, can I not just throw them all out? I can't even put the boxes in the basement, so they wait at the foot of our bed, next to his dresser and in his walk-in closet, a testament to the purgatory I've been forced into.

I curl up into our huge bed and stretch my hands across it and try to grasp its edges, but fail. I hear his voice in my head, teasing me, saying, "Did you think your arms grew since the last time that you tried, Darlene?" Our last fight took place on this bed, the night before they arrived at his office and arrested him early in the morning, before his first checkup. It was an old fight, as all fights and discussions in our married life seemed to be, filled with a strange sense of déjà vu that I, always practical, brushed off as a side effect of allergy medication. But now, it seems that we had to replay our fights until we got it right, until the truth finally emerged, and I always failed to uncover anything, to move on to a new fight. I wish I could say that I've gained perspective and insight in the two months since his arrest, but really all I've gained is a constant mix of anger, sorrow, and loss that fills up my stomach.

"Ali's boyfriend came by work today. He surprised her with sesame chicken, and a bouquet of orchids," I told him that night, curled up on top of the bed in a lacy slip.

"Huh. Sesame — that's the spicy one, right?" He kept his eyes on his sports magazine.

"No. Kung Pao's spicy." I took a deep breath, and said, "We could do that — go to lunch. On a weekday. You can take me to lunch."

"I'm busy this week. Back-to-school surge of teeth cleaning."

"You know what I mean. You can surprise me sometime, take me on a champagne picnic."

"You can come meet me at the office. Or, on Saturday, we can go out, after we run to the store for the light bulbs and carpet shampoo." He flipped a page and rubbed his nose.

I tried to keep my tone light, flirtatious. "Carpet shampoo? I'm worth a little effort, aren't I? A little romance, a little bit of you taking the initiative. Y'know, grabbing me and kissing me. That stuff." Then, I was beginning to redden because he did not understand what I meant, but now, I think that he did. He always understood, that I wanted him to be the one to start things, to be the aggressor, to complete the role I thought he played when I first met him by clutching me to him, in the rain, and kissing me hard. He just didn't want to. He didn't want me.

The argument that night eventually escalated into our common argument. "Why do you always have to push?" He exhaled into the folds of his magazine. "Let's just talk about this in the morning."

"Every other week, Henry. That's what it's come to."

"It's like eloping. You just can't drop it, and so you shove until I agree."

"Shove? Stop changing the subject. Admit it. Just admit it!"

"What?"

"You're just not attracted to me any longer." I sat up straight, while he sunk further back into the pillows surrounding him and kept his eyes on the magazine, as if he were praying that one of the football players pictured would leap off the page and save him.

"I'm tired. Let's talk about this tomorrow."

"You always want to talk about it tomorrow," I whined, a line I knew I had heard and repeated countless times. He reached over and flipped off the light. I hissed, "Get yourself a dick, Henry," and then curled up as close to the edge of the bed as I could. I didn't expect to sleep; my whole body tingled as if someone kept pricking me with pins, and I wanted to stay awake until one of us apologized, and then fall asleep with my hand on his chest. But I did sleep, almost immediately, as though I were drugged, before either of us said anything more.

That night, I dreamed of the first time we ever slept together, on a heavy wool blanket spread out at night on a golf course, underneath the stars, when I thought that his soft, bumbling hands were because of inexperience, not the bland constant in our sex life that they were to become. Afterward, we lay naked on the blanket and Henry invented constellations and told me fairy tales to go along with them, just Sleeping Beauty, Snow White, and Beauty and the Beast, but with the characters' names changed. His arms had wrapped securely around me, solid against my body, and I was thrilled by the thought that, if he squeezed just a little too tightly, he could have crushed me.

When I woke up the next morning, I had wanted to tell him about my dream — I always talked about my dreams on lazy weekend mornings, while we sipped coffee in bed — but it was a weekday, and he'd already left for work, where the cops waited in his aquarium-filled lobby to arrest him. One of the victims had recognized him — his picture was in the paper on page B5 in an article about the top five dentists in the city, the same day that the grainy suspect sketch took up half of B1 — and a DNA test matched him up to the semen in a condom he'd left, carelessly, at another girl's house, at the base of the toilet, neatly wrapped in tissue. Henry kept his books in alphabetical order by author, in a separate bookshelf from mine. He would not miss the toilet.

The judge denied bail, saying Henry's past travel history and the nature of the crimes made him a flight risk. In the first days after the arrest, our house was a flurry of reporters and police officers, and a high-profile lawyer with a manicure who'd just defended a quarterback in a domestic violence case offered to represent Henry. He pushed the trial through quickly, so that the prosecution would have less time to add to its growing pile of evidence, and for that, I am thankful. The attention at our house has drifted away, and focuses now on the courthouse, and on images of young, thin, tearful victims, all college students of the type who visit the makeup counter in giggling groups of five and tell us they're getting married so that we will give them a free makeover.

*

The shrill ring of the phone wakes me. I know it is Eleanor before I roll across the bed to the phone and pick it up; no one else calls me.

"Look," she says, "I can't come out there." Her voice has lost its brittle, bullying edge and is softer, almost apologetic.

"I didn't ask you to."

"Well, I can't. I stayed with that man for him. And look what it did." She begins to sob into the phone. "They'll stone me right out of town. I should be stoned. But I can't travel five hundred miles just for that. I've got a bad back."

The strength of her guilt overwhelms me and I sit down on the floor. "You don't have to come out, Eleanor. That's all right."

Her jagged sobs travel across the phone lines to me. "He's still my son, though. Maybe he didn't do it, Darlene. Maybe not. But if he did, he's a monster, and I created him."

I stay sitting cross-legged on the bed with the phone pressed against my ear and listen to her cry for what seems like hours, before she slips the phone onto the receiver and the dial tone buzzes across the line.

I stay seated, with the phone cradled in my lap. I watch the light crawl across the floor toward me as the sun rises. Eleanor has not disowned him, and she will not disown him, despite her anger and sadness. But I might still be able to cut myself off from him, to save one of us from this mess. I know I have to see him first, though, with the same kind of irrational deep-in-my-bones knowledge that Eleanor knows that she cannot come out. I need to know what I pushed him to. I wash my face and get dressed in a pair of gray slacks and a cream sweater, then slap on some makeup so that I don't look like a ghost. The rouge only succeeds in making me look like an eerie combination of a corpse and a clown. I shrug and walk out the door.

I get into my car and begin to drive the silvery blue convertible, the one that my husband gave me for my last birthday, that I now think of as a guilt present, and hear the bass-voiced DJ mention him on the radio. It's nothing more than they've been saying for the past month: crimes committed, neighbors interviewed, victims' mothers crying, but somehow, it seems like it means something. Perhaps there are no coincidences, and, when our fat Elvis married us, after he asked, "Is there anyone to object to these two getting hitched?" and the Priscilla look-alike in a white minidress and tall black beehive who was taking pictures at the ceremony fainted, it meant something. I put my foot on the accelerator and drive faster toward the county jail, tell them who I am, submit to their weapons check, and find myself sitting across a scarred wooden table from my husband.

His hair looks darker than it has before, smoothed tightly against his skull, and his dry lips are riddled with cracks. "Darlene," he says, then falls silent.

We stare at the table. My nail polish has chipped, and I can't seem to move my eyes away from the jagged red. I blink, and, with my eyes closed, say, "Did you do it? To those girls? When I was at home, sleeping, did you?"

He says my name again, softer.

"I need to know." I open my eyes, but I still can't look at him.

"Are you leaving me?" His voice breaks.

"I'm trying." I look up now at his face, the lines that have deepened, that I did not even notice when staring at him across our dining room table. "What, I mean, did I . . ."

He cuts me off, his voice stronger now. "Do you remember that last fight that we had? When I told you that you pushed me to elope? I was glad you pushed me, I am glad. If you leave, I understand, but I'm glad. Since I've been here, I've had this dream . . ."

"You've been sleeping?"

"Listen, I've had this dream," he continues. He sounds so certain, more certain than I've ever heard him before. He looks so weak, but his voice, his conviction, seems so solid. I can't quite find my soft-spoken husband in this Henry. "In it, you were cutting out my patient's wisdom teeth, and then you handed things over to me to finish up."

"Oral surgery?" I mumble. "I was performing oral surgery?"

He continues. "That dream." He takes a deep breath. "The good stuff, Darlene, that was because of you."

He is only saying this, I think, to get me to stay. I can't only be responsible for the good parts, and imagine I had nothing to do with the rest. I wonder how many times I let him lie to me in the past several years. "Is this what you prayed about?" I ask.

"No, that was about us."

I shake my head at him. I don't believe him.

"Darlene, it'll be all right," he whispers, as though my name means something to him, as though it will mean something to me to hear it on his dry lips, and I recognize the man that I lived with, the way he chanted the same words again and again, until the words became a soothing white noise like the sounds of a heavy rain, when we waited together for the results of my lumpectomy.

"I'll plead, if that's what you want me to do. I'll plead any way you'd like. We can still settle."

"Stop. Please," I shake my head. I do not want to know these details.

Then, he looks down at his hands, and I follow his glance. His hands look stiff, and weak, no longer the strong, smooth hands that had wrapped around my shoulders, and I suddenly know for certain, in a way that I had not known until now, that he did it, and that I loved him, all of him, while he did it. My chest heaves. Hadn't I loved his strength, his ability to move all the furniture into our first apartment without help, and tried to make him stronger, to make him more forceful? Hadn't that been how he did it, force, muscles?

These are the same hands that touched me, caressed my belly and breasts with shaky, unsure strokes and left those bruises, heavy welts, swollen eyes, and split lips on those girls, wrapped ropes around their wrists, shook them and tore them and held them down in their own beds. My lungs tighten and seem to quiver within me, then I close my eyes, stand up, and walk out of the room. He calls after me, but I do not answer. I'm afraid of what I'll push him to, what lies I'll let myself believe, if I stay. I always wanted a more aggressive lover, someone to grab me and dispense with the foreplay, someone who I would not have to seduce. That was what our arguments were always about — he was not strong enough, not man enough. Not to me, at least. It is horrible, what happened to those girls, but my shame is that I feel worse that it was not enough for him to do those things to me. If he had truly wanted me, with an overpowering desire that obliterates all thoughts, wouldn't he have done those things to me? My hair would have been ripped from my skull, welts left on my neck from his grip, nose bloodied when he shoved me into the headboard, bite marks left on my breasts. Isn't this what I dreamed about, the love of a strong man, a man who, in the middle of the night, stormed into my room and threw me down on the bed, twisted my arms behind me swiftly, tore off my nightgown and, with it, bits of my flesh, and left me covered with his sweat and semen and my own blood, forever changed by him? Had he truly loved me, it would have been me, and not them, and I have to leave him. This is the truly unspeakable, I think, as I look down at my own thin hands, their bony frailness, desperately in need of a manicure.

SCOTT TUROW

Loyalty

FROM *Playboy*

THIS HAPPENED, the first part, four or five years before everything else. In those days I was still sweeping a lot of stuff under the
rug with Clarissa, and we didn't see the Elstners often, because my
wife, given the history, was never really at ease around Paul and
Ann. Instead, every few months, Paul Elstner and I would take in a
game on our own — basketball in the winter, baseball in the summer — meeting first for an early dinner usually at Gil's, near the
University Field House, formerly Gil's Men's Bar and still a bastion
of a lost world, with its walls wainscoted in sleek oak.

And so we were there, feeling timeless, telling tales about our
cases and our kids, when this character came to a halt near our table. I could feel Elstner start at the sight of him. The man had a
generation on us, putting him near seventy at this point. He was in
a longhair cashmere topcoat, with a heavy cuff link winking on his
sleeve and his sparse hair puffed up in a fifty-dollar do. But he was
the kind you couldn't really dress up. He was working a toothpick
in his mouth, and on his meaty face there was a harsh look of in-
grained self-importance. He was a tough mug, you could see it, the
kind whose father had come over on the boat and who had grown
up hard himself.

"Christ," Elstner whispered. He'd raised his menu to surround
his face. "Christ, don't look at him. Oh, Christ." Elstner has always
run a little over the margins. Never mind the dumb stuff twenty
years before when we were law school roommates. But even now, a
married grownup with two daughters, Paul would ride around in
the dead of winter with his car windows open so he wouldn't kill
himself with his own cigar smoke, a pair of yellow headphones

mounted over his earmuffs so he could rock with the Rolling Stones despite the onrushing wind. Looking at him with the two sides of the menu pushed against his ears, even though he was twice the size of the guy he was hiding from, I figured, It's Elstner.

"Maurie Moleva," Paul said when the old guy at last had moved on. "I just didn't want him remembering I'm still alive." Elstner swallowed hard on the hunk of schnitzel he'd stopped chewing when Moleva appeared.

I asked what it was Paul had done to Maurie.

"Me? Nothin'. Nada. This isn't about what anybody did to Maurie. It's about what Maurie did to somebody else." Elstner looked into his Diet Coke while the racket of the restaurant swelled around us. "This is obviously a story I shouldn't be telling anybody," he said.

"OK," I answered, meaning I was not asking for more. Elstner rattled the cubes in his drink, chasing a necklace of tiny brown bubbles to the sides of the glass, plainly reconsidering it all, the secret and its consequences.

"This was a long time ago," he finally said. "Before the earth had cooled. No more than a year after you and I finished law school. I was still working for Jack Barrish. You remember Jack. Wacky stuff was always going on around that office. He's defending hookers and taking it out in trade, or trying to give me something hot — a camera, a suit — instead of half my salary. You remember."

"I remember," I said.

"Anyway, Jack, you know, his business clients are all Kehwahnee hustlers just like him, and this guy Maurie Moleva is one of them. Dr. Moleva. PhD. Research chemist who went into business. A few years back now, he sold off his company to some New York Stock Exchange outfit, Tinker and Something, one of those conglomerates. I read about it in the *Journal,* forty million bucks, fifty million, you know, pocket money to them but a piece of change. Back then, the time I'm talking about, the company was still Maurie's.

"Moleva started out making household products, bleach and spot remover, off-brand stuff that they'd sell at the independent grocers, but by then he's really ringing the gong selling to the military. One of his biggest contracts is for windshield washer fluid. For jeeps. Airplanes. Tanks. Helicopters. And of course, the kind of guy he is, whatever he's got, he wants more, so the government is like, We need some chemical, HD-12 or whatever, in the washer fluid, in case we're in the desert, the sand won't stick. And Maurie, he's a smart guy, we've got several hundred thousand troops in the jungles of Nam, no sand there, and the HD-12, I don't know, it adds two bucks a gallon, so he tells them on the assembly line, 'Leave it out.'

"Now the guys on the line, they're all to a man Maurie's people from the old country. Including Maurie's cousin Dragon. When Cousin Dragon was about nine years old, he started in writing to Maurie, 'America's my dream, I need to come to America, I hate these commies over here, they're godless tyrants, they crush the spirit of every man,' and Maurie read these letters for about a decade. He'd never set eyes on Dragon, but like every tough SOB I ever met, he's sort of a softie on his own time, very sentimental. So Maurie pays Dragon's way, meets his plane, kisses Dragon's cheeks, gives him a diamond medallion with the American flag surrounded by some vines that are a big symbol in the homeland, and puts Dragon to work on the line. Then Maurie goes off to tell everybody at the church men's club what a hero he is for rescuing his young cousin.

"Anyway, Dragon's here for a while and he begins to get the lowdown. Maurie's sons are driving shiny cars, they got lovely wives and big houses, and Cousin Dragon is bustin' his hump on the line, starting at six AM every day because Maurie doesn't like his employees stuck in traffic. And long story short, Dragon begins to remember what's so great about communism. He starts in asking, Where's a little more for the workin' stiff? He even, God save the poor son of a bitch, talks on the assembly line about a union. Not smart. Maurie gets his two sons and they throw Dragon's butt out. Literally. They toss him through the door in the middle of winter without his hat and gloves. 'I bought your fuckin' hat, I bought your gloves, I brought your ungrateful pink heinie here from the old country. Go.'

"Bad news for Dragon. And worse news it turns out for Maurie. Because within a few months, an Army helicopter gets caught in a desert storm and goes kerplunk in the Mojave. One survivor. Who says they went down because they couldn't get the sand off their frigging windshield.

"So we have a big federal grand jury investigation started up. Which is where my boss Jack comes in. The G, of course, has figured out that their windshield wiper fluid doesn't have any HD-12 in it and Maurie's answer is, 'Darn it, can you believe what knuckleballs I got on my line? I need better help.' That's not so bad, right? As a defense? That could sell?"

It sounded OK to me, but I'd never practiced criminal law.

"It didn't," Elstner said. "Nope. The AUSA says, 'Nope, we're gonna put Maurie in the pokey, let the big boys call him Sweetie. We're gonna forfeit Maurie's great business 'cause he's a racketeer.' 'How you gonna do that?' Jack says. 'This is a terrible accident.' 'Nope,' says the AUSA. 'Nope, I got a witness.'"

"Dragon."

"You can move on to the Jeopardy round."

"So Maurie did some time?"

"Hardly. Negative on that one, flight commander. Maurie strolled. Here's where I come into the picture," Elstner said.

I made a sound to show I was getting interested.

"There was this night," Paul said. "I get a call. Past midnight. It's Maurie. Says he's been phoning Boss Jack everywhere and can't find him. When I tell Maurie that Jack went to take an emergency dep in Boston, you'd think from the sound that old Maurie was passing a stone. Finally he tells me to meet up with him instead. Now, I don't even own a car. I have to go wake up my sister across town. And I'm following Maurie's directions, which take me to East Bumblefuck. There are moons of Jupiter that are closer. I'm in cornfields. And here near one of these roadside telephone booths, here at two-thirty in the goddamn morning, here is Maurie Moleva. It's springtime. The earth is soft. Stuff is growing. The air smells of loam. There's a bright moon. He's in a rumpled seersucker suit. With mud up to his knees. He's got on a straw fedora and he's carrying a briefcase. He gets in the car and tells me to drive him home. That's all he says. Not hello. Not thanks. Just, 'Drive.' The Great Communicator. At his feet he's got the briefcase, which won't quite close because the wooden handle of something is sticking out of it. He's got a ring of grime under his polished fingernails, and every so often he's jiggling a chain in one palm. In time I see the medallion — diamond, flag, vines. I didn't have a clue right then whose it was, but still and all, this is bad voodoo. I'm definitely scared, especially a few days later when it turns out that good old Cousin Dragon is AWOL."

"Isn't that big trouble for Maurie?" I asked. "Prosecutors aren't going to have to summon the oracle to figure out who'd want to disappear Dragon."

"Yeah, well, Maurie's not stupid. Nobody will ever hang that on him. In about a week, Dragon's beater car turns up at the airport. So the FBI searches all the flight manifests and, can you imagine, one of them shows Dragon boarded a plane home the same night Maurie was taking mud baths in the boonies. Had a reservation and all, paid his ticket in cash. Bureau questions the guys on Maurie's line and some are saying Dragon was talking about making some bigtime money. Couple of them are even hearing from Aunt Tatiana who heard from Cousin Lugo how Dragon's back in the old country and acting real flush.

"Now the G, of course, they're up Maurie's hind end with a miner's light, because they just know he paid off dear old Dragon to boogie. Feebies tear up every bank account, they stick Maurie's bookkeeper in the grand jury, hoping to trace the money, but no luck. So they call Interpol to find Dragon, but he left no trail once he stepped off the plane.

"And of course, I'm young and dumb, and this is really killing me. Attorney-client, I can't talk about what I know, and I'm too petrified to do it anyway, but one Sunday I mosey back to where I picked Maurie up, just hoping to figure all this out for my own sake. Which I pretty much do. Maurie's in the chemical business, right? Ever hear of hazardous waste?"

"That's how Clarissa describes our marriage."

Elstner stopped to laugh. "Yeah, right. Well, this place, these days you'd call it a brownfield, a disposal site. My guess, it was owned by the outfit that hauled Maurie's stuff. Today, with the EPA, you probably have to have the Marines posted at the perimeter, but back then there's just a chainlink fence, and you can see somebody did a number on the padlock. Inside there are all these trenches, each longer than a football field, set about twenty yards apart and filled with rock and soil. The last one's open, maybe three, four feet deep with Styrofoam liner, and a couple dozen fifty-five-gallon drums of shit in there waiting to be buried."

"And 'RIP Dragon' written on one of the drums. Is that how it adds?"

"That's my arithmetic. I figure Dr. Maurie told Dragon he'd send him home rich, then took the guy down instead. Fella like Maurie, he'd kill you sooner than let you put the squeeze on him."

"And who got on the airplane with Dragon's passport?"

"My bet? One of the sons. Cousins, there's probably some resemblance. Besides, something like this stays at home."

"That's why you quit on Jack?"

"Hey, after this one, a nice real estate deal, that sounded just right. And even so, I've been scared all these years Maurie was gonna come for me with his meat ax or his latrine shovel or whatever it was he had in that briefcase. That's why this tale never got told. I mean," Elstner said, looking across the table, "how can you tell anyone a story like this?"

So that was what my pal Paul Elstner had told me several years before. By now I was seeing a good deal of Paul, because I had left Clarissa. I barely got out at first, but one of Paul's partners had deserted Elstner on their season tickets for the Hands basketball games over at the university, and I was happy to buy in.

Like most people who split up, I had told myself that I was starting a new life, a better life, a life in which I'd finally become my true self, but turmoil consumed most of my private moments, confining me within walls of pain. It is such a mystery, really, that you can stop loving someone. You grow up believing love is one of the epic forces of nature, like tidal patterns and the creeping of the earth's crust, an indomitable element. So how can it just go away? I would turn this question over in my head for hours at a time, sitting in my bare high-rise apartment and watching the city twinkle desolately at night.

I didn't know if I had married Clarissa for the wrong reasons or if she had changed, with the babies, the years at home, the death of her older sister and her mother. I could not explain why a somewhat wry, laconic woman, whom I'd found thrillingly bright when I first met her, became so obsessed with her children's health that barely a week passed without a visit to the pediatrician, or why at the age of forty a person who had been a defiant atheist returned to the Catholic Church and insisted, with the same ferocity with which she had once spurned religion, that the boys be baptized in a faith I did not share. I could not explain any of it, the passions or the quirks that had grown unbearably grating over time, but we had ended up like most couples who don't make it — embittered rivals who saw each other as emblems of life's shortcomings.

My sons had remained with their mother. At all moments, I seemed to feel them behind me, like passengers left on some pier. They were both in high school, a sophomore and a senior. I felt awful for them. But I felt worse for myself.

I moved into an apartment building in Center City, not far from work. The building's population was mostly young, late-twenties just-getting-starteds. I was weirdly aware of the number who moved out each week. Common sense suggested that they had fallen in love and were relocating to begin a life with someone else. The sight of furniture on dollies, of bags and boxes piled in the service elevator, seemed to seize all of my attention, like somebody calling my name.

I turned into one of those people who arrive home for a night alone, carrying as much as possible — the cleaning, something I'd had repaired, and a few groceries for dinner. Twice a week I saw my sons. The other nights I tried not to drink too much, certain that this cataclysm would finally make me the gentle alcoholic my father was in his later years, always waiting for sunset and the first Manhattan. I had been told that women would find a successful single man in his late forties magnetic, but I felt too sad even to start in that direction. Eventually, I began attending the kind of tony intellectual events around the city at which I'd envisioned myself when I first came here for law school and which Clarissa for years had derided as a complete bore — art openings, symphonies, lectures. There were few singles at these events, and I often felt out of place, but I was desperate to make some effort at self-improvement.

One of these evenings, involving a fundraising dinner and a reading by a poet celebrated in circles too narrow to mean much to me, was held in the West Bank condo of old acquaintances, Leo Levitz, a shrink, and his wife, Ruth, whose industrial-design firm has been an off-and-on client of mine for years. In their late sixties, the Levitzes had achieved an enviable settled grace. Vivid paintings and objects of primitive art they'd gathered from around the world crowded the track-lit corridors of their apartment. Alone, I studied each piece, deeply struck that a congenial married life could be reflected by such tangible beauty.

By ten, the gathering had thinned and I prepared to shirk the pretense I had made of being cheerful, humorous, of feeling I was of interest to other people. Shortly, I would again be on my own. I bade the Levitzes goodbye. Waiting in the small corridor outside their door for the elevator, I heard a vague thudding. I swore out loud when I realized it was the skylight overhead.

"I'm sorry?" A tall woman with straight black hair was working the key into the lock of her apartment across the hall. I'd noticed her once or twice during the evening, especially as she'd departed immediately before me. She smiled sociably, revealing a front tooth lapped over its neighbor. She had a long face and dark eyes, a woman close to my age who knew she still retained much of the appeal of youth.

"Is it raining out there?" I asked. It was fall, late November, and the prediction had been snow rather than rain. Without an umbrella, my topcoat would become sodden and emit a repellent scent that would taint the close air of my apartment.

"Take a look." Across the threshold, she gestured to her living room window. Staring down, I could make out both rain and snow, leaving a lethal glister on the streets. The smarter taxi drivers, who valued their lives and property, would already have called it a night.

She introduced herself as Karen Kolmar. Her apartment had soft yellow walls and deep Chinese rugs. A book about Coco Chanel was open on a cocktail table. We talked about the poet who'd read.

"His work seemed cold to me," she said. "But I suppose a lot of it was just over my head." She shrugged, not much concerned.

I would have said the same thing, I told her, but lacked the strength of character to admit it.

"I'm at peace as a middlebrow," she answered. I liked her. Self-awareness seemed a particularly appealing trait at the moment.

She asked whether it was the Levitzes or poetry that had brought me around, and in no time I had explained my situation in life, saying far too much about Clarissa. Karen Kolmar smiled philosophically. She was not wearing a wedding ring and no doubt had encountered her share of guys like me.

In fact, I soon picked out a photo of a fellow I figured for her beau, given the prominence with which the picture was displayed on the closed ebony lid of a baby grand in the corner. A healthy-looking older guy, he seemed mildly familiar, if only for his buoyant smile that appeared all too obviously manufactured for the sake of the camera. Looking at the photograph, I sized up my hostess's situation. A divorce. Some money. This guy who was at least ten years too old for her but who probably paid a lot of attention. That, I was slowly coming to realize, was one more sadness in divorce, not merely getting to the middle of your life and confessing that the most basic things had not worked out but finding that you're one of life's bench players waiting to get on the court again with the rest of the second string.

"That's my father," she told me when she caught my eye. "I just put up his picture a couple of days ago. We're having a rapprochement. My mother died and so we're being nice to one another. It might not last. We didn't speak for two years before this."

She asked if my parents were living. Neither was. Like her, I'd lost my mother recently. I wondered all the time if I would have left Clarissa but for that, if I'd hung on to my marriage for years for my mother's sake. I thought I might have. I told her that — I seemed willing to say anything, and she to listen to it appreciatively.

"I'm trying to figure out if my father is why I have trouble with men," she said.

She didn't seem to me to have much problem with men. She knew what she was doing.

"Three-time loser," she added and waggled the fourth finger of her left hand.

"God, three times," I said, before I could catch myself. "I'd throw myself under a train."

That could have gone badly, but her look was sadly sympathetic.

"It gets easier," she said. "Unfortunately." She didn't have kids, though. That was different. She asked if I was thinking of going back. I wasn't, although Clarissa, after weeks in which she'd been shrill and recklessly accusing — no one person could ever love me as much as I wanted to be loved; I was trying to change her because I could not change myself — had recently turned plaintive. After all this time, she asked me. After all this time? It was the only thing that ever had any resonance.

When I got ready to leave, Karen emerged from another room with an umbrella.

"I won't melt," I said.

"You can bring it back." She smiled, enjoying the fact that she was so far ahead of me. Walking me to the door, she took my arm.

I was quite happy until, halfway downstairs in the elevator, it came to me that she looked a good deal like Clarissa.

*

I brought the umbrella back, naturally. I called ahead, and then it started to rain as soon as I got there, which led to a pretty good laugh. We just dashed around the corner and sat on the stools in a little coffee bar, talking about ourselves.

She ran the sales division of a chemical company her father had founded and sold several years ago to a big conglomerate. I figured she was one of those sleek women I noticed in airports, always looking resourceful and self-possessed in their dark tailored suits, able to climb onto the plane at the last instant and still somehow get their luggage into the overhead.

"You don't really seem like a salesman," I told her. "Too sincere."

"That's why I'm good. I don't lie," she said. "I never lie." Her dark eyes rose over her paper cup in a measured warning. "I didn't believe I could handle sales. But I needed a job after my first divorce. And when I was a kid, I was always jealous that my brothers went to the office with my father." Her father, pushing seventy-five now, still ran the company under the terms of his buyout.

"How'd that work when you weren't talking to him?"

"E-mail." She laughed.

I was impressed with her rugged sense of humor about the way life had turned out. Her last name, for example, was her second husband's.

"You really wouldn't really call that a marriage. He was a country-club buddy of my father's, older and very polished, but it just never took. We were together six weeks, and kind of split up at a party one night and never were under the same roof again. I thought, Oh god, I'm not going to change all my credit cards again. I just did that. They were still coming in the mail, a different one each day. At some point, you have to start moving forward."

As we walked back to her place, a huge clap of thunder rattled the street, and the rain suddenly fell as if poured from a bucket. The small umbrella offered little protection, and I pushed her into a street-corner bus shelter, where I kissed her. I was afraid it might seem like a moment from a movie, but I guess everybody wants some of that in her life.

"That was very stylish," she said, and rubbed one finger under her lip to deal with the lipstick smudge. "You're a stylish guy."

The next time I saw her, we ended up walking down to the river. It was drizzling again, but there'd been plenty of winter weather, and the River Kindle was covered by a solid frozen sheet. Standing on the ice, you could still feel the lurking movement beneath, the vibration of the Cory Falls a hundred feet away, the telltale swirls of the water and its many enigmas.

Rain glossed the surface, refracting the lights of Center City and making it possible to skate along. Karen had trained as a girl and did wonderful, graceful movements, skidding ahead on a pair of Keds, encouraging me to follow her. She's an adventure, I thought. This woman's an adventure. My skin went electric, not just about her but for myself.

"You're not going to say anything to her. Tell me you're not." Elstner and I had stopped for a beer after the basketball game, mostly so Paul could have a final cigar before he got home, where Ann did not permit them. "Maurie will dissolve my bones in a vat of acid."

I had figured it out a while ago, probably by the second time I saw Karen. The details were a while coming back to me. But by then, as I told Elstner, I was involved.

"For crying out loud," I said. "I won't say anything. I thought you'd think it was funny."

"Sure. Funny. I'll laugh as soon as I change my diaper." Elstner blustered his lips. "Have you met Dr. Moleva yet?"

I had, in fact, only a few days before, when I'd picked Karen up at their Center City office. His smile was disturbing. He had bad teeth, like a farm animal whose poor bloodlines couldn't be concealed. To his daughter, he was a source of never-ending vexation. At work he was imperious, then blamed his subordinates when his orders turned out to be wrong. As a father, he attacked her often and made a habit of overlooking what was important to her. He hadn't been able to remember my name, although she gave it to him three times in the few minutes we were together.

"Kind of your run-of-the-mill jerk," I said.

"And murderer," added Paul.

"She hates him, I think. You know. Underneath."

Elstner shivered again. "Christ," he said. "Why don't you go out with twenty-five-year-old women like other guys your age?"

"Hey, cut me some slack. It won't make any difference."

Elstner groaned. "You think you can just know something like that about somebody and it won't matter?"

"Paul —"

"Listen. Did I ever give you advice about women?"

In our third year of law school, Elstner went out with a tall dark girl, an undergraduate who had the lean elegant moves of a whippet. Very moody. Very attractive. She smiled with notable reluctance. She seemed exotic because she knew a lot about motorcycles and introduced us to mescal — the saltshaker, the lime, the worm in the bottle. After their third date, I told Elstner I didn't think she was really right for him. To this day he seemed to agree, but two or three months later, on a whim, I called her myself. That was Clarissa. Elstner for one reason or another never said much, not even the kind of jokes you might expect, not when I married her or lived with her for twenty-two years, not even when I told him that our life together had become a barren misery and that I'd asked for a divorce. Maybe he thought I'd saved him. Or used him. He never said. I never asked.

"No," I told him, "you never gave me advice about women."

"Well," he said, "that's the only reason I'm not gonna start."

When you're having great sex, it seems to be the center of the world. Everything else — work, the news, people on the street — has a remote, second-tier quality, as if none of it will ever fully reach you. The rest of life seems a pretext, a recovery period before the shuddering starts again.

Over the holidays, Clarissa and I divided time with the boys. For Christmas she took them on the annual journey to Pennsylvania and her parents' home. Knowing their absence would be hard on me, I accepted when one of my partners offered his cabin up in Skageon. Clarissa hated the cold, and it had been years since I had passed any part of winter in the woods. On a chance, I invited Karen and she accepted, eager to avoid the annual holiday collisions with her father.

We left late on the twenty-fifth and made an elaborate Christmas dinner while it stormed outside. What followed were three of those crystalline days that occasionally bless the Midwest, when the snows magnify the available light and the lack of clouds leaves the air thin and exciting. We snowshoed for hours, then, exhausted by our treks, passed the long dark nights in bed, an intermittent languor of sleeping and reading, lovemaking and laughter. Driving back to the Tri-Cities, to the year-end deadlines of my law practice and the turmoil of my broken marriage, I felt the exhilaration of having finally, briefly, lived the life I'd longed for.

I spent the next couple of nights at Karen's apartment. I had second thoughts about the Levitzes, who also knew Clarissa, but they were away. Even in her own bed, Karen slept poorly. Initially I was afraid it was my presence, but she said she never got more than three or four hours in a row, which seemed somehow at odds with her resigned exterior. She would buck awake, thrashing with the demons of a savage nightmare.

"What was the dream?" I asked the second night.

She shook her head, unwilling or unable to answer. She was naked and had her arms wrapped about herself. When I laid my hand on her narrow back, I could feel her heart hammering.

"Go back to sleep," she said. "I'll get up until I calm down."

I asked what she would do.

"I have my things. I like cognac. I like Edith Piaf, in some moods. Or big symphonies. It's a good time to reflect."

Clarissa also did not sleep well. She read. In the middle of the night I'd find her propped on her pillow, a minute lamp clipped onto her book. The only pleasure I ever took in business travel was in not having to sleep with a pillow over my head.

Without warning Karen said, "I was dreaming about a fire." She was looking at the ceiling and a plaster rosette sculpted where a gas lamp had hung decades before. "I was in a fire with my father. I was watching the fire come toward him and there wasn't anything I could do."

"Frightening," I said.

"It's not what I dream that doesn't make sense to me. It's the way I react. All I had to do was shout, 'Watch out.' But the person I was in that dream — she didn't even know that shouting was possible. Why do you think you're yourself in a dream when you don't know the most basic things?"

Perhaps that was how life really was, I said, full of blind spots and the inability to do what seems obvious. She didn't take much to the suggestion.

"Do you dream about your father often?" I asked.

She wrinkled her mouth. "Why would you ask that?"

I didn't have an answer, not one I could speak. She went for her robe and told me again to go back to sleep.

"You know, my father likes you," she said in the morning, as I was driving her to work. "He says you're solid."

I wasn't sure what basis Maurie had to comment, although it was a remark that, a year before, I might have made about myself.

"He has a lot of good qualities," she added. "He's not all one way. Did you know he was a war hero?"

"Really? What kind of hero?"

"Are there kinds? A hero. He has medals. From Korea."

"Did he kill anyone?"

"God," she said. "What a question. Like I'm going to say, 'Daddy, who'd you shoot?' It was a war. He saved some people. He killed some people. Why else do they give you medals?" She kissed me before leaving the car, but bent to eye me from the curb. "What's your thing with my father?" she asked.

Karen and I spent New Year's Eve with the Elstners, enjoying dinner at their home, then, as midnight approached, a few minutes of revelry in the local hangout where Paul made an appearance most nights to smoke a cigar. I thought it had gone well — Elstner and I had engaged in our usual good-spirited mocking of one another, amusing the women — and when Paul and I went to a game later that week, he made it a point to say how much Ann and he had liked Karen.

"The only thing is," Elstner said, as he drove to the University Field House after dinner, "I nearly soaked my socks every time she mentioned her father. She always talk about him that much?"

"She works with him, Paul. He's her boss."

He gave an equivocal nod, clearly not inclined to question my hasty defense.

"Truth is," I added, "I always wonder how she'd be about her father if that story you told me had the right ending — you know, if Maurie got nabbed for offing his relative, and Karen knew it. Probably make a big difference, don't you think?"

"How's that?"

"She has no perspective on him. I mean, he's her dad. So whenever he clobbers her, she's inclined to think maybe it's her fault, that he's really a good guy underneath. But if she knew what a cruel character he is, an actual killer, that would have an impact." I was moving full throttle with the idea that had propelled me for months now, the belief that new perspectives and new information could make life a happier enterprise.

"Well, that didn't happen," he said. "Maurie's roaming free. And nobody's going to be diming him out now. Right?"

"Right," I said. "But it's strange knowing."

Paul had been keeping a close eye on the traffic. We were caught in the pregame rush, staggering a few feet and then stopping again as the cars funneled into the lot, but Elstner turned to me fully now. He might as well have said I told you so.

"Maybe strange is what you want, champ," he said.

"Meaning what?"

"Meaning you could have walked away as soon as you figured out who she was."

"Hey, I like this woman. More than 'like.'"

Paul had worked his mouth into a funny shape as he reflected. "Here," said Elstner, "mind if I tell you a weird story?"

"Another one?"

He paused to give me a sick smile, then asked, "Remember Rhonda Carling?"

"Rhonda Carling? The woman you went out with before Ann?"

"Her. Did I ever tell you about our sex life?"

"Christ, I don't think so."

"This was the bad old days, right? Virginity mattered." He grimaced. "Listen to me. 'Bad old days.' A man with two daughters."

"Don't act like a Cro-Magnon. Rhonda Carling and her virtue. I have the context."

"Well," he said, "she liked to play halvsies."

"Halvsies?"

"You know. To go just partway. So she remained, you know, intact."

"No," I said.

"Oh yeah," he said. "Now, I really dug Rhonda. And this halfway stuff, it had its moments. Kind of like surgery, very exact, and very exciting, with all the fuss and bother and holding back. And all the danger. I mean, I'm always trying to figure out what happens if we go one angstrom too far. Am I engaged or dead on the side of the road?"

Only Elstner, I thought to myself.

"But it was also pretty frigging strange. The whole thing really bugged me. What was wrong with her? Or me? It was bizarre, but it went on the whole time I was seeing her. Finally, I met Ann at her brother's at Thanksgiving, which is just about when Rhonda got interested in a guy she was working with, and we sort of faded away.

"One night, say six months later, I bumped into Rhonda at the A&P and we went out for coffee, just to sort of officially throw the dirt on the grave, and she tells me this other fellow has popped the question and something else. 'Are you hurt?' she says. 'My pride,' I say. She smiles, nicely, we liked each other, she says, 'Halfway's all you wanted, Paul.' And soon as she said it, I knew she had that just right."

Paul lowered the window to pay the parking attendant, then surged forward into the lot. As ever with Elstner, I was having a hard time following his logic.

"Meaning what? I should think about marrying Karen?" Even saying it seemed preposterous. I was still at the stage where I couldn't imagine being married to anyone but Clarissa.

Safely in a space, Paul threw the car into park and studied me.

"Forget it," he said finally. "It's just a story."

My law firm followed the quaint custom of holding a formal dinner at the conclusion of the firm's fiscal year in January. It was intended to celebrate our successes, but was frequently an occasion for teeth gritting among those who were upset about the annual division of spoils. I looked forward to having Karen with me, both to buffer me from the simmering quarrels and to show her off to my colleagues, before whom I'd suffered the shame of not holding together my home. Already in my tux, I swept by her office to collect her. She walked to the car mincingly, trying not to dirty her silk shoes on the icy street. She was in a long gown, its revealing crepe neckline visible in the parting of her coat. I whistled. She smiled as she peeked down through the car door, but made no move to get in.

"I can't go," she said. "There's a presentation tomorrow. My whole staff is upstairs. Somehow my father forgot to mention he had rescheduled with the customer, until he saw me dressed. I must have told him ten times how excited I was to be going with you tonight." She leaned inside. "Will you kill me?"

"Not you. Better not ask about Maurie. I thought you said he liked me."

"He does. You're not the issue. Believe me." She shook her head in sad wonder. "Why don't you come back when you're done?"

She gave a salacious little waggle to her brow. "I'll letcha take me home."

When I returned near midnight, I found her unsettled. She'd had words with her father, the usual stuff about his indifference to her. I was angry enough with him to relinquish my customary restraint.

"Have you ever kept track of how much time you spend being upset about Maurie?" I asked her.

"Who knows? Sometimes it seems as if I've lost years that way. What's the point?"

"I guess I wonder now and then why you put yourself in harm's way."

"You mean cut myself off?"

"Keep a distance. Nobody forces you to work with the guy."

"It's a family business. I'm in the family. And I refuse to just hand it all over to my brothers. You don't like my father, do you?"

I weighed my options. "I don't like the way he treats you."

"Neither do I, sometimes. But he's my father. And my problem." She did not speak for the rest of the ride.

I suspect we were each ready to call it a night. But we hadn't had many disagreements, and experience had taught us both the perils of parting angry. I came up. We had a drink and talked, then got around to doing what we did best.

As we groped, she slid from my arms, already naked below, and with a naughty grin pulled the belt from my trousers. I thought she was going for my fly, but instead she pushed me to a seated position on the bed, then threw herself across my lap. She bent one leg from the knee and touched her lip impishly. She put the folded belt in my hand.

"Spank me," she said.

I looked down at her behind as if it were a face. This was a new note between us. All I could think of to say was, "Why?"

"Why not? I feel like it."

"I don't think I can do that," I finally said.

"I'll enjoy it. I'm asking you to do it. This isn't whips and chains. Use your hand, if you'd rather. I'll enjoy it."

I tried one swat.

"Hard," she said. "Harder. Keep doing it. I'll say when I want you to stop. I'll enjoy it."

But I didn't.

"No," I said suddenly, and pushed her off my lap. I went for my clothing.

"What?"

"I don't want to be this to you," I said.

"Be what? The man who pleases me?"

"Not like that."

"It's what I want," she said.

"No," I said again and left.

"I think I have to tell her," I said to Elstner the next night. "About her father."

Paul took his time now. I'd been late and we'd skipped Gil's, settling instead for dogs we were gobbling down as we stood at a little linoleum table fixed to one of the elderly pillars in the Field House.

"You can't tell her," Paul said then. "That's all. You can't. You can't for my sake. And her sake. And your sake. You can't. This isn't comedy. This is real life. This guy is a murderer. And smart enough to realize there's no statute of limitations. He killed a man to keep from getting caught. You think he wouldn't do it again?"

"Paul, she wouldn't say anything to Maurie. I'd make her promise."

"Like you promised me?"

"I'll keep you out of it."

"He'll figure it out. She knows we're friends." Paul seldom took advantage of his size, but he'd drawn himself up to his full height. I wanted to explain what it was like to be alone, to feel you have a chance to regain the purpose love alone imparts.

"Paul, it might make a difference. It might open her eyes. To this whole thing with her old man. I really think it might."

"You think people open their eyes just because you tell them to look? There's no happily-ever-after on this. You're dreaming."

I kept shaking my head. "This is your fault, Elstner."

"My fault? Because I told you a story years ago about the father of some girl you didn't even know existed?"

"No," I said. "No. Because of what you said last time. About stopping at halfway? I'll say it to myself now, if I don't do this. I want to go for it all with this woman. To see if she can really be what I need. So don't tell me it's her or you."

Elstner stalked away to drop his little paper basket, now bearing only a few specks of relish, into the trash. When he came back, he said, "I'm not telling you it's her or me. I'm telling you that you don't have that choice. You gave me your word. And I have a God-given right to sleep at night. So you can't tell her." He stared at me, giving no ground. Instead he was calling in the cards guys like to think they have with one another, especially honor and loyalty.

Inside the arena, the horn blared, indicating the end of the shootaround. It was game time. Paul's eyes had never left mine.

"I can't tell her," I said at last.

I told her anyway.

I didn't see Karen or call her for several days after that encounter in her bedroom. Four or five nights along, I returned from work to find two items at my apartment door, a little bud vase with two sweetheart roses in fresh water, and a narrow box. Inside was a pair of suspenders with a note. "Forget about your belt. . . . Sorry to mess up. . . . Call me. Please."

I met her for lunch the next day.

"I offended you," she said, as soon as the waiter had left us in peace.

"No."

"I know I did. I didn't think. We've been so compatible that way, I just got caught up in my own stuff. I was stupid."

"It's not that." I felt she was taking me as puritanical or blinkered. "There are just some things I have in my head."

"What things?"

"I can't explain."

"Try," she said. "Please. This doesn't have to be an impasse."

I avoided several questions and she grew more imploring.

"What is it?" She leaned across the table to touch my hands. "What's the problem? What aren't you saying?" In her long face, I saw an urgency no different than my own, a will to connect and to escape the complexities of what had left us alone, to be a better person with a better life. In the end, it was exactly as I had told Elstner. I could not stop halfway, without taking the chance.

"There's something I've been told," I answered. I was surprised at the smoothness with which the tale emerged. I'd heard a story. From a reliable source. Someone I knew. A former prosecutor. I was so intent on the telling that I did not at first notice her draw away on the other side of the table, but when I finished, she was watching me with a bitter smile.

"That?" she asked. "That ridiculous, moldy rumor? Do you know how long people have been saying that? It's absurd."

It was one of those moments. In the crowded dining room, I thought I could somehow hear my watch tick. After a confused instant, I decided she had simply not understood. I repeated myself, more slowly, but her look soon hardened with suspicion. That glass wall I had smashed against so often with Clarissa had descended. Karen stared through it with appalling remoteness.

"And why are you telling me this?" she asked then. "Is that how you see me? Is this something genetic?"

"Of course not."

"So what is the point? I'm neurotic? Because my father is supposedly some hoodlum?" With vehemence, she shifted in her chair. "You know, every divorced man I meet either has had no therapy or way too much. Go shrink somebody else's head." I reached for her as she marched from the table. "No!" she said and swung her arm away violently. "It's me anyway. You don't want me. My father is just an excuse."

She disappeared around a pillar. In her wake, I was miserable, but I knew two things for certain. It was over. And I was never going to tell Paul.

In late March, the Hands ended a dismal season with one more agonizing loss. They took the game to overtime, then, while they were trailing by a single point with only a few seconds left, Pokey Corr, the Hands' only star, broke free on the baseline and ascended toward the basket. He wound up and slammed his intended dunk shot against the back iron of the rim. Along with everyone else in the stadium, Pokey watched as the ball floated along an arc that brought it down almost at center court as time expired.

Like a losing bettor at the track, Elstner threw the season's last ticket into the air. Then we started up toward the exit, inching ahead as the crowd merged into the walkways. From one stair above, I felt the weight of someone staring. It was Maurie Moleva.

"Oh, Christ!" he said. "Look at this. The heartbreaker." His tone wasn't completely malicious. His crooked brown teeth even appeared briefly as he smiled.

"It was mutual," I said.

"Not how I hear it. How you keeping?"

I said I was OK.

"Gone back to your wife yet?"

I absorbed Dr. Moleva's estimate of my situation, which he must have shared with his daughter long ago. With Maurie, anything that came at Karen's expense was never waylaid by circumspection.

"Not so far as I know," I told him. Clarissa had lately taken to mentioning counseling, an option she'd adamantly refused during the years I'd suggested it. Now I had no idea how to regard her surrender. I was fairly sure I no longer had the strength or interest. Oddly, though, there were moments when I felt sorry for her, sorry to see that loneliness had broken her will. Clarissa liked to portray herself as a person beyond regrets.

Maurie introduced me to his companion, a woman not quite his age. Reliably himself, Elstner had stood, face averted, as if studying something on the empty basketball court behind us.

"Doctor, did you ever meet Paul Elstner?" Elstner went rigid as I placed my hand on his shoulder, but he turned and greeted Moleva.

"Not so as I recall," Moleva answered. "But I don't remember my own name these days. Bad eyes, bad back, bad memory. I'm beginning to think I'm not getting younger."

We all laughed as if this were original, then, when the crowd began moving, parted with a genial wave.

Elstner was still agitated when we settled in my car. "Thanks," he said. "Thanks a lot. I really needed to renew acquaintances."

"I didn't have any choice. And besides — he doesn't remember you. I really don't think he does. Not tonight anyway."

"Probably not most nights," said Elstner. "That's how he sleeps."

I edged my car out of the lot.

"So you never told her?" Elstner asked me. "I'd have bet a whole lot you told her."

"I told her."

He swore at me. "I knew you'd tell her."

"I thought it would make a difference, Paul."

"Screw you. You're too old to believe people change because you want them to. They change because they get tired of themselves."

"She didn't believe it anyway," I said. "And I knew you'd be fine, because she'd never tell her old man about it."

"And how's that?"

"Because she'd never take the chance on seeing it might be true."

The remark cast him down into silence as we swept into the lights and rush of the highway. After a few minutes his indignation rose up again.

"I can't believe you told her," he said. "Jesus Christ. Why do I put up with you?"

"Why do you?" I asked with sudden earnestness. The question seemed to exasperate him more than anything I'd said yet.

"Because you're part of my life," said Elstner. "How many people do we get in a lifetime? And I'm loyal. I'm a loyal person. Loyalty is an undervalued virtue these days. Besides, I have too much respect for myself to think I wasted twenty-five years on you. Or that I just figured you out. You've always been trying to find the Holy Grail with women. You haven't changed either."

"Well, apparently then, I expected better from her."

"Don't laugh, pal." My sarcasm had provoked Elstner to point a finger. "The older I get, the more I'm just watching the same movie. He's and she's, the attraction is that they're different, right? Everybody's looking for the other piece. And then nothing makes them crazier. She's upset because he's not like she is, or vice versa, and then there are nimrods like you who actually think different oughta mean better, all the time hoping that will make you better, too. Grow up."

With that blow delivered, he did not speak until we reached his house. I was furious, but also aware that I was due a lashing of some kind. A client, a trader from the exchange, had given me a couple of Cubans. I'd left them on the dashboard for Paul and remembered them now, fortuitous timing. Elstner studied the label with appreciation.

"Smoke one with me," he said.

Hanging around with Paul, I'd puffed on a short cigar now and then and saw the wisdom of a peace pipe. I rolled down all the windows. It was a fairly mild night for mid-March, and we lit up the Cubans and reclined the front seats and talked in a dreamy reconciled way, reviewing the season. The Hands, who'd been a Final Four team within the last decade, were not even going to the Big Dance this season. We tried at great length to discern the ephemeral difference between winning and losing, how coaching and spirit contribute to talent. We talked about great teams we'd seen and, by contrast, recollected our own failed careers as high school athletes.

Finally, Elstner decided it was time for him to get inside. I watched as Paul, with his sloppy loping stride, made his way to the house he'd lived in for decades. From the door, he gave an elaborate wave, like a campaigning politician. I thought he was marking the end of the season or the peace reestablished between us, but over time the image of him there on his stoop, grandly flagging his hand, has returned to me often, and with it the suspicion that he meant to acknowledge more. An intuitive creature like Elstner probably knew before I did that I was headed back to Clarissa, that she and I would find a new mercy with each other and make better of it, and that, as a result, I would see him less. Paul never required any explanation. In fact, I had no doubt that reviving my marriage was what he would have counseled, if I'd ever allowed him to lift his embargo on advice.

I remember all this because we lost Paul Elstner last week. He developed cancer of the liver and slipped off in a matter of months. I saw him often during his illness. One day he cataloged all the other ways he'd worried he might die — an extensive list with Maurie Moleva still on it — but he spoke the name without rancor. It turns out that there are far too many ironies as one's life draws to a close to linger much with a small one like that.

It was Paul's wish, another of his harmless eccentricities, to be buried in cigar ash. On a bitterly cold day, with the graveyard mounded with snow, the casket was lowered and the entire burial procession was presented with lighted Coronas. Paul had many friends, of course, and we formed a long, moving circle around the open grave, each person approaching to tamp whatever ash had developed since the last time she or he had gone past. The proceedings had all the comic elements Elstner would have savored, with designated puffers to keep the cigars going for the nonsmokers and many mourners making smart comments about the smell, which they figured would linger in their clothing forever, Paul's unwelcome ghost. This rite continued for more than half an hour, with the group dwindling in the cold. I was among the last. The ember by now was near the fingertips of my gloves. Before surrendering the last bit to the earth, I stood above the casket, desperate to speak, but able to summon only a few fragments to mind. All our longings, I thought. All our futility. The comfort we can be to each other. Then Clarissa and I went home.

SCOTT WOLVEN

Barracuda

FROM plotswithguns.com

THE BAG OF CLEAR LIQUID hung suspended above me, hooked to a metal pole, and ran into my right arm through a clear plastic tube. A nurse came in and looked at me, adjusted the flow of my drugs, and left. There were two other beds in the room, one empty and tightly made. The other bed had an old guy in it, rigged up to more bags and machines than me.

"What's your name?" he asked.

"Paul," I lied.

"Paul, you're in a bad way, but you're going to make it."

"I'm hurt," I agreed.

"Pain is just weakness leaving the body," the old guy said. "Learned that in the service."

I was silent.

The old guy indicated the empty bed. Next to it was a table full of surgical tools, bright and shiny stainless steel. I saw the raw rows of teeth of what I took to be a bone saw.

"There was a cop in that bed five hours ago," the old guy said. "Had some emergency operation, right there on the spot."

"Really," I listened. The bed was freshly made with clean white sheets pulled back and a white pillow. It looked as if nobody had ever been in that bed, ever.

The old guy kept going. "He had gray hair and didn't want to tell me he'd been a cop, when he first came in. I introduced myself and he didn't say anything, really, so then I heard the nurse taking insurance information from him and when she left I said 'Insurance? That must be nice,' and he said 'Well I earned it.' I said 'What did you used to do?,' tryin' to be friendly, get a little conversation going while I'm waitin' to kick off and he didn't answer, so I said it louder, 'Hey, what do you do?' and he says 'Private security,' and that put me onto it, right there."

"Really," I said.

"I said to him 'That's a job they give off-duty cops. You a cop?' and he mumbled some shit about being an MP in the service and coming out and getting a job as a radio patrol car officer years ago, in Jersey, and then coming up here and being a uniformed cop up here for thirty years."

"Sounds personal," I said. "On your end."

The old guy didn't let up. "Don't give me that crap, that you like cops. Come in here beat the hell up like you are and tell me you haven't been around." He moved to one side of the bed. "When I came out of the service, I got a job making parts on an assembly line. I got in a couple scrapes, more than I should have, but I worked there till I retired and I'm lucky I got a pension. The collection agency still calls all the time from when I was in the hospital four years ago. And don't tell me somebody didn't take a tire iron to you. I know what I'm talking about."

"I don't know what you're talking about," I said. "This was a work accident."

The old guy raised himself up on one elbow and looked over at me. "I've been around," the old man said. "You look like you've been around."

"Sure," I said. To shut him up.

"Don't kid yourself," the old guy said. "You're always all the men you've ever been." He quieted down as a nurse came in to check on him. She fed him some pills and water and left. The old guy pointed at the surgical tools on the metal table by the empty bed.

"Think those tools are sterile?" he asked.

"That's what they tell me," I said.

"You can't sterilize the inside. Those tools remember where they've been. Saving a life one day, killing someone the next," he said. "Those tools are playing a little game with the doctors. The doctors think they control the tools, but it's the other way around."

"OK," I said.

"The cop started to have some type of fit and they all came in and rushed around him and put up a movable curtain, but there was a space between the curtain panels. Right through that space I watched that saw and it bit too deep and I knew it as soon as it happened and I knew he was getting it back, getting done to him what he did to somebody."

The drugs the nurse had given him must have relaxed him too much to make him a good roommate anymore.

"Hey," he said. "If I asked you a question, would you tell the truth?"

"Sure," I lied again.

He stretched his neck up toward the dark, blank TV mounted from the ceiling in the corner of the room. He lowered his voice. "Whenever I'm in the hospital, I see a man in a black suit with a hat on, inside the TV, when it ain't on. He's looking out at me." The old guy paused. "Do you ever see that?"

"Yes," I said, to help him. "Sometimes."

"Bull," the old guy spit. "If you saw something like that, you'd shit the bed."

Two nurses and a doctor came into the room and began wheeling him out the next morning. I thought he was asleep, but as he passed my bed, his eyes were open.

"Watch yourself," he said to me. "They don't save everybody here."

After sixty-five days, I was allowed to leave the hospital. The doctor saw me during morning rounds and signed off on my discharge paperwork. One of the blond nurses I'd flirted with stood next to me and whispered in my ear. Goodbye Mister Whoever-you-are. They'd seen enough loggers float in, the facility being so close to the Adirondacks. Sixty-five days without a visitor and no phone in my room, no calls, Paul Wagner wasn't going to be paying any hospital bill or following up with occupational therapy. The insurance cards I vaguely referred to would never arrive and I'd sell the pain pills to my buddies, if I could make it through the day on a shot or two of straight hard booze. Paul Wagner died the minute I hit the exit door.

My truck sat in the parking lot with tiny deltas of mud near the tires, left there as the rain flowed into the lot's sunken storm drain. A layer of dirt and fine grit covered the windows. Dirty rain, over the largest forest in the Northeast. People talked about whole lakes being ruined, far to the north, but you hear a lot of things in the

woods. The toughest trick in the mountains and valleys was telling
where the shot came from, what was the echo and what was the
original report, what was reaching your ears and eyes. The shape of
the land gave birth to lies of sound and the same was true with people. The shape of their lives led them to lie. Sometimes they had no
choice. That's what I told myself about being Paul Wagner for sixty-
five days.

The truck started on the third try. It stuttered. The brakes were
stiff, they groaned and creaked a little. I jammed it in gear and left.
The foot-long ceramic spike that had caused some of the damage
to my right arm and head after my saw hit it rolled around on the
passenger's-side floor. I was on a job and spotted a chance to make
some extra money with a stand of straight maple, fifty yards off a
landing site. Seven thousand dollars covered in bark and leaves. It
was coming down. I ran the metal detector over the trees and nothing showed on the meter, so after the crew left, I took a saw to the
lead tree in the group. Two things happened at once. The chain
snapped and the saw kicked out of the cut with so much force, it
broke my arm and slammed into my head, digging deep into my
helmet as the chain shot one last revolution through the orange
plastic housing, like a deadly silver ribbon, flashing and slicing its
way to my bones. My Kevlar pants finally stopped it, but I was on the
ground, bleeding.

Someone had been protecting those trees. There are only two
reasons to spike trees. If you're an environmental whacko, who
doesn't realize that loggers need to eat, too. Or to protect something you own that's valuable. I doubt they were protecting the
trees against me specifically, just people like me. Because in the
world of the woods, there are a lot of people like me, who steal
good timber and once it's on the ground, it's long past late.

The landowner and his son pulled up in a king cab rig and the
old man must have puzzled out what happened right away. He
grabbed a ten-pound rubber mallet out of the lock-box on the
truck and hit me in the head and spine like I've never been hit before. I went unconscious from the pain and woke up in the hospital. The doctors thought a tree had fallen on me, that's what the
two guys who brought me in said. They left my truck in the parking
lot. A broken eardrum and severely bruised spine with a possible
cracked disk was thanks to that mallet. At least they left me my

truck. As I drove out of the parking lot, I reached under my seat. The old forty-five I kept there was gone.

I drove around the reservoirs, south, into my own territory. The western edge of Catskill Park, the Pepacton Reservoir. Mostly Department of Environmental Protection cops, state police. If something serious happened, the Bureau of Criminal Investigation, the BCI, handled it. They were the detectives of the state police. No local law. Once in a while, a Sheriff's patrol. When I got behind a long yellow school bus, with kids giving me the finger through the back emergency exit window, I realized it must be the first week of September.

My rented cabin smelled. Bad. It was chilly, because the temperature had been dropping at night and I hadn't been there to light the fire. Ladybugs clustered on the ceiling, trying to stay warm. Two months of bills sat in the mailbox, some of them soaking wet. The phone was cut off. Before I went on the job that day, I'd meant to pay the bill. I always meant to pay all my bills, but I never did.

It looked like a good time to start skimming timber. In my honest life, I was a timber appraiser and a good one. I gave people prices based on all the usual formulas. Felling and bucking, skidding cost, making sure all the wood was merchantable, all the current stumpage rates on standing timber. Landowners needed that information for tax purposes, to make a buy or sell decision, for due-diligence valuation. Any number of reasons. I loved the job, being out in the woods, working. Weather never bothered me.

But when I was short money, truth and honesty rested outside of me. My relationship with money was more important, like most people. I would skim. Skimming timber is a nonteachable skill. In the course of evaluating standing timber, I would mark a few trees — prime trees, like tiger maple, or northern white ash — and cut them, the day before the big crew moved in. It meant working alone with a fast saw, no hangers, nothing stuck or tipped or fucked. Straight trees on the ground, limbed up and ready to go, and my buddy Dave would come in with his cherry picker and load up, maybe twenty trunks depending on the size. Off he'd go. Usually to Maine, where we knew a specialty furniture maker who always bought from us. Always no questions asked, always cash. You didn't want to skim too much, because people noticed and you couldn't truck it out. Most timber companies know that appraisers make a little extra money on the side and nobody kicks too much. Most timber companies hand out cash themselves, to appraisers. The difference between a hundred thousand dollar appraisal on a hundred and twenty-five thousand dollars worth of wood is usually worth a thousand dollars to the timber companies. A low appraisal gives them leeway. In case some trees aren't straight enough for high-grade lumber, or if gas prices go up, or if weather begins to eat paydays for the crew. There was more than one way to skim and all of it was dangerous, lying work.

I drove to a gas station, picked up a calling card, and went to the payphone. I started calling all the big outfits I'd ever worked for. There was no work right now and I think a couple of them were skeptical that I was even calling. I put in a call to Molly Johnson at Hayes. I made it a point to know these people and had even taken her out to dinner once when I was in Canada and treated her to a Tim Horton's after. She seemed glad to hear from me.

"John, I'll tell you. You're welcome to this guy. I'll note it on the file that you're the one doing the work. But it has to be done right. He's got a couple friends up here and he's a big deal, know what I mean?"

"Sure," I said. I strained to hear her as trucks pulled into the gas station. "Molly, I appreciate it."

She paused, then went on. "They haven't assigned a supervisor to this project yet, we haven't even officially taken it, but I'm sure it'll go through. We're just waiting on the appraisal. We're actually holding his check," she said. "So do a good job, because there will be people up here who will listen if he yells."

"Thanks for the heads up," I said, and wrote the name and number she gave me on a slip of paper. Theodore Morrison. He had called Hayes to have his land in upstate New York logged off, but Hayes didn't operate that way. They liked to have an independent appraisal, in case the landowner changed his mind midway through the cut. I'd seen it happen. Change of heart, mixed feelings, a broken business deal. Half the trees were gone, and it was impossible to get an accounting from the sawmills. The appraisal was a smart thing. It was supposed to keep everybody honest, but the added layer just allowed for more skim. I called the Manhattan number Molly had given me and a secretary answered.

"This is John Thorn calling, is Mister Morrison available?"

"One moment, please. What's this regarding?"

"His upstate acreage," I said. "Logging it. I'm calling from Hayes-Canada."

"One moment," she repeated.

Morrison got on the line. He sounded like an older man with some kick left in him. "Mister Thorn, you're with Hayes?"

"John's fine," I said, "and no. I'm the independent. Molly Johnson at Hayes told me you were hiring an independent appraisal of standing timber in order to complete a clear-cut job and that I should call you. I work independent, call around every week or so, to see what jobs are available."

"Where are you located?" he asked. In his background, in the concrete woods of Manhattan, a faint siren moved closer, then further, then gone.

"Northwest of Roscoe, outside of the Catskill Park area. Do you know where that is?"

"I can find it on a map, I'm sure. Listen, what kind of credentials do you have and how fast can you get on this thing?"

It started to look good for me. "You can call Hayes, if you like, and get hold of Tom West, he's a supervisor up there and has seen my work and my clients."

"OK," Morrison said. "I'll do that." He paused. "How fast?"

The necessity of speed always works on the side of the skim, never against it. "What's the parcel and what are you doing?"

"Almost five hundred acres, and I've got two offers on the table right now, one from a condo developer and one from a lawyer in Albany with Indian connections, who wants to build a casino when that new legislation passes."

"And you want to sell the timber rights off first?"

"That's it. I haven't been up to the property in twenty years, my wife and I used to go camping up there years ago, but she enjoys warmer weather now, so it's Florida and the beach. Twenty-five years, I bet. We even put in a foundation. Never did anything with it. Taxes are all paid and I used to have a local guy look it over, a guy named Nolan, who I originally bought it from. But he's passed on."

I considered. "I can go get the survey map today, if you had it done local."

"The map is at Menden's, do you know them? Are you going to bill me or do I need to have a check sent to you?"

I was in the driver's seat now. "Wire transfer me two thousand dollars, I'll give the routing numbers to your secretary. I don't take checks anymore, they take too long to clear." I waited and controlled the pace. "I know where Menden's is, fine. I'll get the map."

He knew he was a passenger. "Fine. Just get in there and get it done. I'll put you back on with Karen."

"Nice to do business with you, Mister Morrison."

"It is nice to do business with me," he made himself laugh. The secretary was on the line and I gave her the bank instructions and numbers. I drove to Menden's office, twenty miles to get the maps, and then pulled into my bank. I told the head teller I was waiting for a transfer and I sat there. She came out from behind her desk an hour and a half later to tell me I was two thousand dollars richer. In the skim, checks are no good. You can't put a stop payment on a wire transfer. And you can't get it back, either. I withdrew all but two hundred of it and when I got home, sat and figured my bills. Three hundred was left when I got done paying. I was trying to live low. I was lucky. I went to sleep and dreamed of the site. Tried hard to dream myself up some tiger maple, a whole straight stand of them. My arms and legs hurt from the accident and beating and that night my back seized once. The pain pills helped, with a chaser. It wasn't going to be easy cutting trees.

The next day on my way to the site, I stopped and phoned Dave, my cherry picker man. He was home.

"Hey," I said.

"Shit," he said. "Saint Peter hand you the phone or what?"

"I got hurt and ended up in the hospital." He didn't say anything. "Look," I went on. "I've got a job."

"It will have to be within the next three days," he said. "Where is it?"

I told him.

"I've driven past that for years, used to be posted under the name Nolan. I've been up there hunting."

"That's the spot," I said.

"Park your truck where I can see it from the road," he said. "If I can't see your truck, I'll figure it's off."

"That's good," I said.

"See you then," he said as he hung up.

"See you then," I said to nobody.

Part of working in the woods means being able to see things and knowing how those things will impact the operation later. What soil will give way after a rain and heavy tonnage load of logs, bogging down equipment. I pulled my truck up an old dirt path, so I could pull it back down within sight of the road when I was ready for Dave. I took a can of red marking paint and drew myself a landing site on a slight hill and started to look the place over. Within ten minutes of walking, I'd found what I was looking for. Some of the best maple I'd seen in years. At least twenty of them, all straight up to the sky like God meant them to be. I tied some yellow area tape around them, then some orange, and when I got done walking the site, at least a couple of them were coming down today. I kept walking and making notes in my weatherproof book. It was always strange to me, to be doing an honest appraisal and keeping an eye out for trees to steal. I crossed a small stream and started up a rocky hill that had more timber behind it. This was a great spot and why Morrison wanted to sell was beyond me. It was funny that I hadn't seen any deer yet, but I figured they must be deeper in the woods. I got to the top of the rocks and it looked like there was a trail ahead of me.

The man leaning against one of the trees held a rifle. It was a stainless steel, wood-grip lever action, with a short barrel. He wore a black work jacket.

"I'm up here on a timber appraisal," I said. "For Morrison. He said anybody who knew Nolan was OK with him." I tossed in the only local name I knew.

The man nodded. "Come here," he said.

I didn't move.

"Come here or I'll shoot you and leave you there," he said. I walked toward him and we started down the trail together, with me in front. As we went forward, I heard noise. I'd heard the same noise once before, in a logging camp in Quebec. Dog fights.

There was an old barn, half falling down, and a bunch of guys standing on an old concrete foundation, looking down in. I could hear the dogs ripping into each other, low growls, yelps, then a sound like strips of Velcro being pulled apart. Bodies hitting the concrete walls. And the scraping of claws on the concrete slab floor. They had a long handler's stick set up and it looked like they yoked the dogs into a crate and then used pulleys to haul it up to the rim of the foundation. Nobody went into the pit except the dogs. That was the fight area.

A couple of the guys standing around were state cops, I sort of recognized them. A DEP cop stood right there in his uniform, giving his bet money to a man behind a makeshift desk in the barn. My escort with the rifle took me over to a fat guy sitting on a stool near the barn entrance. There was an old car there, a Plymouth Barracuda, light blue, and as I walked past, a pit bull slammed with everything he had against the window trying to get at me. I jumped back a few steps and the fat guy laughed at me. I looked at the chrome fish emblem on the car and thought about how barracuda are supposed to have rows of sharp teeth and the chrome brought me back to the surgical tools from the hospital. Fear made my mouth taste like hot metal.

"Christ," I said.

"He's in the car," Fatman said. "He ain't gonna hurt you."

"What's his name?" I asked.

"What's his name?" Fatman said. "What are you, five years old? Want to name your doggy? His name is bite the living shit out of anything that moves. He's a fighting dog, what the fuck does he need a name for? He'll be dead in a month." He coughed. "Call him Barracuda."

"I found him walking through the woods," my escort said, pointing the rifle at me.

Fatman shook his head. "What the fuck do you need a name for?" he asked, pissed, looking around. "Do you know anybody here, can you help yourself out of this? This is a serious fucking hole you're in."

I looked around. A guy with a ball cap on, near the foundation, I swore I had gone fishing with his brother years and years ago. I think the guy had just got out of prison. I pointed at the guy. "I used to go fishing with Russell Work and I think that's his brother Jimmy over there, the big quiet guy with the baseball hat on straight." Men were handing him money, so his dog must have just won the fight. They were starting to load the dog from the Barracuda into a crate, two big guys with the full-length leather gloves and another guy with a neck harness made from a belt wrench. The dog looked to be around a hundred pounds of pure black and white muscle. Once they had him in the crate, they lowered him into the pit.

Fatman yelled, "Hey Jimmy come here."

The guy I thought was Jimmy Work walked over to us.

"Know him?" asked Fatman.

His brother Russell and I had driven through a snowstorm once to visit Jimmy up in Dannemora. I think after he got out, he'd done more time somewhere. He was at least ten years older than me and I hadn't seen Russell in over five years. He looked at me hard. The scars on my face and the way I held myself after the accident and the beating. I must have looked totally different. His mind tried to place me.

"John," he said. "You're John, but I can't get your last name." He turned to Fatman. "He's OK. Friend of my brother's."

I started to breathe again. "How is Russell?" I asked.

Jimmy Work was already walking back to the dog pit. "Passed on," he said over his shoulder. My guard walked into the woods as sweat rolled down my ribs under my T-shirt. I sat on a plastic milk crate for a minute to cool down. It happened then.

The DEP cop shoved Jimmy Work over the edge of the concrete pit. I heard Jimmy hit the floor and the dog was on him. I got to the edge of the pit and the dog already had hold of his leg, clamped on, and had bit Jimmy in two spots on the arm. He was bleeding and the floor of the pit was covered in shit and blood and it smelled. Somebody shot the dog, and we all hit the deck, the ricochet buzzed out of the pit through the woods, sizzling through the leaves. Two guys jumped into the pit and cut the dog off Jimmy, they had to practically skin the thing to get at the jaw and get that loose. Blood was everywhere. The fucking DEP cop was next to me.

"Saw man," he said. "He just got hurt in logging accident and you and I are taking him to the hospital."

"Fuck you," I said.

"Yeah," he said. "And the next time we see a cherry picker with a single load going around the reservoir, we'll stop it. And the next time. And the next time. Until your eighteen-wheeled friend loses his license. You must think we're stupid, running single loads up here before the big crew shows up."

At the hospital, a different one from the one I'd gone to, closer to Syracuse, the doctor pulled me to one side, behind a curtain. He was obviously from India, very serious-looking. Concerned. His English was a little tight but good.

"These wounds, sir," he said to me. "They are from an animal, probably a dog. Not a chain saw, as you told me. As the officer told me."

In his world, you called people sir and expected them to act accordingly. With truth and honesty and human concern. I wanted to act like someone who deserved to be called sir, but I couldn't.

"It was a saw," I said. "He was climbing, way up, with the small limb saw and he fell, with the chain going, and really did a number on himself." I nodded to myself and him.

"Yes," the doctor said. "That is what happened in the lie the officer told you to speak. This man could die from his punctured arteries. Be honest with me now."

I wondered if in India they had trees and chain saws and men who fought dogs in the afternoon. "Chain saw," I said.

"Yes," the doctor said again. "Never." He shook his head and walked past the curtain back to the emergency room. The DEP cop hung around, to make sure Jimmy Work lived, then took off. It took Jimmy almost two months to recover. The cop had bet a hundred to one against Jimmy's dog and lost. I missed my rendezvous with Dave, I never turned in the appraisal. I knew Molly at Hayes wouldn't work with me again. If any Hayes crew ever came down to the site, they saw the marking tape. They're not stupid. I visited Jimmy Work twice and he stayed at my new apartment for a month. I had to move out of my old cabin because I couldn't make rent.

The first time I saw the DEP cop after that was in a bar, Cody's, a one-pool-table joint a mile off the reservoir. It was night and snowing. The DEP cop was parked behind my truck when I came out.

"Hey," he called out his window. "Where's your friend Jimmy?"

Jimmy had moved in with this woman he knew, not far down the road. "I have no idea," I said.

"Tell him I'm trying to get some money together," he said. "In fact, why don't you give me what you've got in your wallet?"

Nobody else was in the parking lot. "Piss on you," I said.

He took his foot off the brake of his patrol car and tapped the back of my truck. "I could total it," he said. "You're drunk, and this car isn't going to hurt me."

I couldn't afford a new truck. I took fifty dollars out of my pocket and handed it to him.

"You're a good boy," he said. The cruiser spit gravel at me as he pulled into the night.

*

I was off, headed to this girl's house, when through the park, behind me, came a DEP cop. He followed me for over a mile and then the flashers went on. I pulled over.

When he got next to the truck I recognized him and he had his gun in his hand. "Hey," he said. "You were speeding and weaving and out of control and then we had a high-speed chase." He was grinning from ear to ear as he said it. Behind him it was pitch black.

"Here's my license," I said.

"I don't want your license," he said. I could smell booze on him. "I want two hundred bucks." I reached into my wallet and pulled out some twenties and handed them to him.

"I bet you didn't know this was a toll road," he said.

I didn't say anything.

He took out a knife and stuck it in the sidewall of the front driver's-side tire. I listened to the hiss as he yanked it out of the split rubber.

"Front tire's flat," he said. "Flat flat flat. That's too bad." He had his gun in one hand and a knife in the other.

"Come on, man," I said. "Give me a break."

"Sure," he said. He started to walk back to the patrol car, stopped at the end of my truck and kicked out a rear light. The whole truck rocked. "Got a back light out too," he said. "That's a violation. Better get that fixed." He slammed his door and swung around me. I watched his taillights get smaller in the dark as he drove off.

A couple months later they found his patrol car empty on a logging road near the reservoir. The door was open, the cop radio was turned on. There was money and blood all over the place, like green and red leaves blowing in the wind, and as the investigation went on, the BCI determined it was his money. He came to that spot to pay someone for something. But they didn't take his money. They took him.

Contributors' Notes
Other Distinguished Mystery Stories
of 2004

Contributors' Notes

Richard Burgin is the author of eleven books, including the novel *Ghost Quartet* and the recent story collections *Fear of Blue Skies* and *The Spirit Returns*. Four of his stories have won Pushcart Prizes and thirteen others have been listed by the prestigious Pushcart Prize anthology as being among the year's best. His forthcoming *New and Selected Stories* will also include a CD of his musical compositions. He is a professor of communication and English at Saint Louis University, where he edits the nationally distributed and award-winning literary journal *Boulevard*.

■ "The Identity Club" grew out of my thinking about how enamored so many people are with celebrities. I imaged a secret club of people so obsessed with various famous dead writers or artists, etc., that they literally attempted to live their lives and die their deaths. To justify what they do, they devise a theory of reincarnation suited to their needs. New York City seemed a logical place for the Identity Club to exist. I also thought it important to make the protagonist an outsider from New England who innocently and enthusiastically, at first, becomes involved with this bizarre organization.

Louise Erdrich grew up in North Dakota and is enrolled in the Turtle Mountain Band of Ojibwe. She is the author of ten novels, including *Love Medicine*, which won the National Book Critics Circle Award, and *The Last Report on the Miracles at Little No Horse*, which was a finalist for the National Book Award. She has also published children's books, poetry, and a memoir of early motherhood, *The Blue Jay's Dance*. Her short fiction has won the National Magazine Award and appeared in the O. Henry and *Best American* short story collections. She lives in Minnesota with her children and runs a small independent bookstore, the Birchbark.

Daniel Handler is the author of the novels *The Basic Eight* and *Watch Your Mouth,* and serves as the legal, literary, and social representative of Lemony Snicket, whose sequence of books for children, known collectively as *A Series of Unfortunate Events,* have been alleged international bestsellers. He has worked intermittently and inexplicably in film and journalism, and has been commissioned by the San Francisco Symphony to create a piece in collaboration with the composer Nathaniel Stookey. An adjunct accordionist for the pop group The Magnetic Fields, Mr. Handler lives in San Francisco with his wife, the illustrator Lisa Brown, and a baby.

• On March 14, 2003, the novelist and short story writer Amanda Davis died in a plane crash. She was a friend of mine. We used to meet up at my local bar from time to time to chew over problems both literary and personal. When I was asked to contribute to an anthology of genre writing, I thought it would be a kick to try a locked-room mystery, and as my religious beliefs do not contain much in the way of an afterlife, I had the idea to place Davis somewhere she might enjoy. Discerning readers may also note some references to Davis's fiction within the story. I have an enthusiasm for complicated cocktails and perhaps there'll be some more rounds at the Slow Night, but among the lessons of Davis's death is that I ought not to make reckless promises about the future.

George V. Higgins (1939–1999) was the author of more than twenty novels, most notably his first, *The Friends of Eddie Coyle,* published in 1972 and filmed the following year. The short story collection from which "Jack Duggan's Law" was taken, *The Easiest Thing in the World,* was published posthumously.

Edward P. Jones is the author of the novel *The Known World,* which received the National Book Critics Circle Award and the Pulitzer Prize, and of *Lost in the City: Stories.*

• "Old Boys, Old Girls" began with the main character in "Young Lions," a story in *Lost in the City.* In the latter story, Caesar is a thief, not quite twenty-five, and growing into a not very nice man. Now, with "Old Boys," we have that fully formed man — a prisoner who has murdered two human beings.

Stuart M. Kaminsky is the author of more than sixty published novels and forty short stories; he has also plus produced screenplays, television episodes, two plays, and even a book of poetry and a graphic novel. He writes four different series, featuring the 1940s private eye to the stars Toby Peters; the depressed Sarasota process server Lew Fonesca; the put-upon Chicago police detective Abe Leiberman and his partner, Bill Hanrahan; and the one-legged Russian police inspector Porfiry Petrovich Rostnikov.

▪ "The Shooting of John Roy Worth" was written in two sittings. I had no idea what I was writing or what was going to happen. That's not the way it usually works for me, but I tried it successfully once before, enjoyed the ride, and decided to take another one. My hope was that this tale would surprise the reader just as it surprised me when I wrote it. I just let my central character come alive and followed him down the street.

Dennis Lehane is the author of *Mystic River* and *Shutter Island*, as well as five novels featuring Patrick Kenzie and Angie Gennaro. He lives in Boston, where he is currently writing a novel about, among other things, World War I, the great influenza outbreak of 1918, the Boston police strike of 1919, and the Tulsa race riot of 1921. The only thing he's sure of is that it won't be short.

▪ I'd had the first line of "Until Gwen" bouncing around in my head for a few years when John Harvey asked me to write a story for a British anthology called *Men from Boys*. The only requirement was that it have something to do with fathers and sons. The deadline was maybe a week off, at best, when I finally tried writing it. I was going through a lot of personal turmoil at the time and I've never been the kind of writer who can write directly about my own life, but I think I do OK when I approach it obliquely. So I took a notepad out onto my front porch, which is surrounded by a hundred-year-old wisteria, and this rainstorm hit, a huge one, bending trees, clattering all over the street and the roof. But the wisteria kept anything from hitting me. I wrote the first draft that night on my porch in this crazy storm. It was supposed to be a comic story — that first line, hell, the whole first scene, is pretty absurd — but page by page it kept getting darker and darker until it ended up being arguably the darkest thing I've ever written. The writing of it, though — that whole storm-within/storm-without, mad-scientist vibe — was one of my favorite creative experiences.

Since publishing her first Tess Monaghan mystery in 1997, **Laura Lippman** has won virtually every major American crime-writing prize including the Edgar, Nero Wolfe, Anthony, Agatha, and Shamus. She lives in Baltimore.

▪ "The Shoeshine Man's Regrets" came about through the usual combination of solicitation and serendipity that guides most of my short stories into print. Bob Randisi asked me to contribute to his jazz-themed anthology, and I gave my usual conditional reply: "Sure, if I can think of something." A few nights later, a strange white gob appeared on my boyfriend's shoe as we left a restaurant — and a shoeshine man appeared providentially from the shadows to clean it up. But the most important aspect of the story, in my opinion, is that it describes the local sartorial flourish known in these parts as the "full Towson" — white shoes, white belt, and white tie.

My laptop died, taking this story with it, and I became so frustrated in my attempts to find and salvage it that I almost reneged on my promise to Bob. I'm glad I persevered and finally recovered it.

Tim McLoughlin was born in Brooklyn, New York, where he still resides. His first novel, *Heart of the Old Country*, was a selection of the Barnes & Noble Discover Great New Writers program and won Italy's Premio Penne award. He is the editor of the crime-fiction anthology series *Brooklyn Noir.*

 ▪ I began writing a novel about a white graffiti artist growing up in a predominantly Hispanic neighborhood, and the story got away from me. It became a complicated tale about fathers and sons, one I was not yet prepared to write. "When All This Was Bay Ridge" is taken from the core of that novel, and I think it scratches the surface of the emotional landscape I found myself navigating. I hope to return to it on the broader canvas one day, older, wiser, and better girded.

Lou Manfredo was born in Brooklyn and holds a bachelor of arts degree in English literature from St. John's University in New York. A former New York City schoolteacher and legal investigator, he has recently completed a novel in which "Case Closed" appears as the first chapter. He is the father of one daughter, Nicole, and currently lives in Manalapan, New Jersey, with his wife, Joanne, and their long-haired dachshund.

 ▪ I always strive for a realistic character-driven flavor in my fiction, with strong attention to dialogue. That is what I attempted in "Case Closed." When I read fiction, or, for that matter, view a film or television show, I need to believe that the "who" and "what" being portrayed reflect reality. I feel that if a writer can successfully develop believable characters and dialogue, the plot will often develop on its own.

David Means's stories have appeared in *The New Yorker, Harper's Magazine, Esquire,* and numerous anthologies, including *The Best American Mystery Stories 2001.* His second collection of stories, *Assorted Fire Events,* won the 2000 Los Angeles Times Book Prize and was a finalist for the National Book Critics Circle Award. His third book, *The Secret Goldfish,* has just been published by HarperCollins.

 ▪ As I wrote this story, my characters moved according to their own wishes, and I watched as they became locked into the mystery of their relationship with each other, but also with the hard realities of postindustrial Michigan where they were venturing and the fact that erotic energies are most often best served between two people, not three. When I was doing the final edits on this story, I was staying in West Cork, Ireland, living for a few weeks in a small town called Durrus, working at a little table on the back patio. One day I looked up from the pages to watch a cow graze in the field just behind our cottage. As I watched, a farmer came out and began to pat the side of his cow, talking softly into her ear, and I thought: Man, I'm a long way from the world of Michigan and the place where these characters reside. I was happy to be away from all of that violence and chaos, but then I got back to work and was perfectly content to be amid the darker forces I'd set in motion.

Kent Nelson has published four novels and four collections of short fiction. His most recent novel, *Land That Moves, Land That Stands Still*, published in 2003, won the Colorado Book Award and the Mountains and Plains Booksellers Award. In addition, with his daughter, Dylan, he has edited *Birds in the Hand*, a collection of stories and poems about birds. Nelson has run the Imogene Pass Run three times and the Pikes Peak Marathon twice, most recently in 2001. He is also an avid birder, with 739 North American species on his life list.

- When my son was four or five, my older daughters got him into a dress and put lipstick and eyeliner on him, and he looked as beautiful as any girl possibly could. This was a fleeting image that stayed with me, and I meant to merge it somehow with some of my brutal experiences playing ice hockey in college. It was originally to be called "Girly Boy," but what emerged in the writing of it was a much darker story than I'd ever intended.

The point of view became important, too. I experimented with a perspective I'd never tried before — the general viewpoint of a town, as Faulkner uses in "A Rose for Emily." "Public Trouble" is not Faulkner, but at least the point of view worked well enough to get the story published.

Daniel Orozco was a Scowcroft and L'Heureux Fiction Fellow at Stanford University, then a Jones Lecturer in Fiction in the creative writing program there. His stories have appeared in the Best American and Pushcart Prize anthologies, and in *Harper's Magazine*, *Zoetrope All-Story*, and others. He currently teaches in the creative writing program at the University of Idaho.

- When I taught classes at Stanford, I commuted there by train. It was a short walk to the station, a short wait for the train, and a ten-minute ride after that, so I never had the space I needed to really read anything. I killed time thumbing through the free local dailies. The police blotters caught my eye, and I started clipping them:

> Woman yelling for help. Officers found man and woman arguing over trash.
> Citizen reported a suspicious man crouched down in a driveway. Man was gone when officers arrived.
> Citizen shooting BB gun.

Resident reported a bad odor and said it might be a dead animal. Officers
    determined it was pollen in the air.
Dogs running loose.
Phone fell off a truck.
Sterling silver ring found near bleachers.
Man found his watch in a pawn shop. His daughter had sold it.
Fourteen-year-old boy cited for allegedly possessing a cigar.
One student burned another with a penny.
Karate instructor suspected of injuring domestic partner.
Two men fighting. One ran away carrying scissors.
Four large women suspected of stealing from a beauty supply store.
Drunken nineteen-year-old crashed Jefferson High School prom and wouldn't
    leave.
Skateboarders causing disturbance.
Student out of control, yelling and screaming.
Suspicious person seen.
Suspicious person *spotted.*
Solicitor selling magazines was being abusive to residents.
A resident woke up and saw a strange man crawling on his knees in the living
    room of his house. Suspicious crawler escaped through sliding glass door.
Caller reported bald man in his late forties sitting in a white BMW for thirty
    minutes.
Caller reported a loose German shepherd. Officers couldn't find the dog.
Caller reported squashed watermelons on a car.
Caller reported lost tortoise.
Terrier found whose name is Owen.

I thought about the officers who would respond to such incidents on this
metaphorical day, and I thought about what *their* story might be as they attended to all these other stories. And I thought, How could I not at least *try*
to write this?

David Rachel has worked as a factory laborer, forest fire fighter, hospital
chaplain, massage therapist, letter carrier, teacher, professor, and professional storyteller. Author of several technical works, he now concentrates
on fiction and poetry and divides his time between Europe and North
America. His work has been broadcast on public radio stations and published in more than eighty literary journals in the United States, Canada,
Britain, and Australia, including *Antigonish Review, Dalhousie Review, Indi-
ana Review, Midwest Poetry Review, Pangolin Papers, Prism International,* and
South Carolina Review.

▪ "The Last Man I Killed" had its origins in two widely separated experiences. One was many years of observation of corporate decision-making in
universities. In this process evidence and logic, the stock-in-trade of academics, are seldom employed. In public, arguments tend to the personal

and anecdotal, while the important decisions are usually made behind closed doors.

The second experience was as a child growing up in wartime Britain in a village all of whose men of military age were away in the armed forces. For a prolonged period, the village was hit almost every night by high explosive and incendiary bombs jettisoned by German planes returning from bombing raids on London. This experience, exhilarating at that age, led to a lifelong interest in the Second World War, and with the innumerable moral fables it engendered.

Joseph Raiche was born in 1979 in Faribault, Minnesota. He currently is an obituary writer for a local newspaper in Saint Cloud, Minnesota, where he lives with his wife, Amanda. He graduated with a B.A. in creative writing from Saint Cloud State University and is soon to begin work on his M.A. at any school that will take him. Works of his have been published in *Upper Mississippi Harvest*, and the story "One Mississippi" originally appeared in *The Baltimore Review.*

• The idea for "One Mississippi" came from a report I had heard of people trying to buy tickets to witness a real-life execution. Space was limited, so they held a lottery for what space there was. It struck me as odd that watching someone die was an enviable situation and not something you would want to distance yourself from. I bounced the idea for the story off Ryan Hanson, a friend and fellow writer in Saint Cloud. He thought it was a good one and the story was born. With the character Drew Larkun I hoped to create someone who was both realistic with the pain that he feels, yet believable with the understanding he arrives at. I believe the character is unlike most people, but I hope not so unlike the person we wish we could be.

My mom thinks the story is a complete downer. I thought there was hope in it, if you looked for it. Maybe she was right. I hope that I am.

John Sayles wrote the screenplays for and directed *Return of the Secaucus 7, The Brother from Another Planet, Matewan, Passion Fish,* and other groundbreaking films. Twice nominated for an Academy Award for best original screenplay, Sayles has also written two short story collections, *Dillinger in Hollywood* and *The Anarchists' Convention,* and several novels, including *Los Gusanos.*

• I started thinking about "Cruisers" while working on a film in Alaska, meeting fishermen, charter captains, and other people who spent a lot of their lives on the water. It struck me that people's boats reflected their personalities, and that the "marina hoppers," especially the retirees, were always looking toward the next berth with a kind of eternal hopefulness, as if never staying put could ward off age and time. Humans have an innate yearning for community, even if it's a floating one with a high turnover in members. And I got to do research in sunnier places than Juneau.

Sam Shaw was born and raised in New York City, where, as a minor, he spent a good deal of his allowance money on detective pulps at the Mysterious Bookshop. A graduate of Harvard University and the Iowa Writers' Workshop, he is currently finishing his first novel.

• Typically I work my way into a new short story like an old man entering a pool — slowly, and with gritted teeth. "Reconstruction" presented an exception. In the end, the story would require many revisions, additions, and subtractions, but I dispatched a first draft in three short insomniac weeks, around Thanksgiving of 2002. The difference, I think, was the narrative voice, which I heard clearly almost from the start.

If you credit George Herbert, living well is the best revenge. But I've known a few sad, conflicted types (usually sons of successful, overbearing fathers) who avenge themselves by living badly — by willfully failing in the world. Such is the case with Getty, who, when we meet him, subsists in a limbo of dope smoke and bad TV, despite the fact that the father who set him on his course has been dead for years. The key to the story, for me, consisted in allowing the totems of his failure — his father's Civil War treasure — to play a role in his awakening.

Many thanks to Marylee Macdonald for improving this story, M. M. M. Hayes for publishing it, and Otto Penzler and Joyce Carol Oates for anthologizing it.

Oz Spies was born in 1978 in Kirkland, Washington, and raised in many places before settling in Colorado. Her work has been published in several literary journals, including the *Ontario Review,* as well as in a collection of short-short stories entitled *Women Behaving Badly.* She received an M.F.A. from Colorado State University and is currently at work on a novel. She lives in Denver with her husband.

• I wrote "The Love of a Strong Man" during the summer before my last year in graduate school. Earlier that year, in the spring, a man had broken into several students' apartments late at night, then assaulted the young women who lived there. Thanks to DNA evidence and a baseball cap, the man was finally caught. The only detail about this man that I can recall hearing on the news was that he was married. Though (or because) I knew nothing about her, I began to dream about this man's wife and imagine the life of someone married to a rapist. Out of those dreams came this story.

A native Chicagoan, **Scott Turow** is the author of six novels, all bestsellers, and two books of nonfiction. His works include *Presumed Innocent, The Burden of Proof,* and *One L.* He won the Heartland Prize in 2003 for his novel *Reversible Errors,* and the 2004 Robert F. Kennedy Prize for his book about the death penalty, *Ultimate Punishment.* Turow is a law partner at Sonnenschein Nath & Rosenthal, devoting much of his time in practice to public interest and pro bono projects. He lives near Chicago with his wife, Annette, a painter; they have three children.

▪ I began "Loyalty" in 1993, when I finished my third novel, *Pleading Guilty,* and I continued to work on the story in the intervals after completing my subsequent novels. I made a little headway each time but never could get to the end, even though the theme, about the interaction between male friendships and love relationships, felt like an enduring one to me. I always think I want to write more stories, but my ideas don't seem to fit the current mold. "Loyalty" solidified my conclusion that in my hands the short story is more de Maupassant than Joyce. I hope that recognition will allow me to write stories in the future at a faster pace than one every eleven years.

Scott Wolven is the author of *Controlled Burn,* a collection of short stories. For four years in a row, Wolven's stories have been selected for the *Best American Mystery Stories* series. One of his stories will appear in a plotswith guns.com hardboiled anthology, available from Dennis McMillan Publications. Scott Wolven lives in upstate New York.

▪ "Barracuda" is a violent story, filled with violent men. I once owned a Barracuda automobile; I once saw an abandoned concrete swimming pool in the woods. Part of the mystery here is small — for example, who is the man appearing inside the hospital TV? Some of the mystery is larger, because violence sometimes knows no path and has a before and after that is hard to trace.

▪ This story is dedicated to my brother Will, a great brother and fantastic artist who draws pictures that inspire my fiction. Anthony Neil Smith of plotswithguns.com, in which "Barracuda" appeared, deserves big credit for all the fine stories he piloted to success. It's a real honor to have my story published here. Thanks to D.W., M., A.J.C., S.H., and the team at WSBW.

Other Distinguished Mystery Stories of 2004

ANAPOL, BAY
  The Real Life Test. *Manoa,* winter

BICK, ILSA J.
  The Key. sciFi.com, August
BLESSINGER, JUSTIN
  Posse Comitatus. *South Dakota Review,* summer
BRACKEN, MICHAEL
  Dreams Unborn. *Small Crimes,* ed. Michael Bracken (Betancourt)
BRALY, DAVID
  A Trail on the Desert. *Alfred Hitchcock's Mystery Magazine,* June

CHAMBERS, CHRISTOPHER
  Doggy Style. *Shades of Black,* ed. Eleanor Taylor Bland (Berkley)

GREENBAUM, ADAM
  Killing Alex. smallspiralnotebook.com
GUERRIERO, LUCIANO
  Eating Italian. *Brooklyn Noir,* ed. Tim McLaughlin (Akashic)

HAMILL, PETE
  The Book Signing. *Brooklyn Noir,* ed. Tim McLaughlin (Akashic)
HIEBERT, MICHAEL
  My Lame Summer Journal by Brandon Harris, Grade 7. *A World of Words,* ed.
    Jack Whyte and Diana Gabaldon
HOCH, EDWARD D.
  The Theft of the Double Elephant. *Ellery Queen's Mystery Magazine,* February
HOWARD, CLARK
  Tequila Memories. *Ellery Queen's Mystery Magazine,* June
HUNTER, SANDRA
  Under Cover. *South Dakota Review,* fall

IRVINE, ALEX
  Peter Skilling. *Fantasy & Science Fiction,* September

LAMBE, PATRICK J.
  Union Card. plotswithguns.com, May/June

McCLURE, ROBERT
  Harlan's Salvation. *MudRock,* spring/summer
McKEE, ROBERT
  A Covert Operation. *Eureka Literary Magazine,* fall
McMEEL, CORTRIGHT
  Istanbul. plotswithguns.com, May/June
MALLORY, MICHAEL
  The Beast of Guangming Pass. *Sherlock Holmes: The Hidden Years,* ed. Michael
    Kurland (St. Martin's)
MEYERS, MARTIN
  Mr. Quincy's Different Drummer. *Argosy,* May/June

NEWMAN, SHARON
  Emily's New World. *Sherlock Holmes: The Hidden Years,* ed. Michael Kurland (St.
    Martin's)

O'DELL, CAROL D.
  Fascination. *Atlanta,* September

PARKISON, AIMEE
  Blue Train Summer. *River City,* winter
PAROTTI, PHILLIP
  Spot of Trouble. *Sewanee Review,* winter

SWIERCZYNSKI, DUANE
  Hilly Palmer's Last Case. plotswithguns.com, September/October

WATERMAN, FREDERICK
  Last Day's Work. *Hemisphere,* November
WATTS, LESLIE
  Crocodile Tears. *Revenge,* ed. Kerry J. Schooley and Peter Sellers (Insomniac
    Press)
WHEAT, CAROLYN
  A Long and Constant Courtship. *Death by Dickens,* ed. Anne Perry (Berkley)
WOHLFORTH, TIM
  Jesus Christ Is Dead. plotswithguns.com, May/June

YODER, JEREMY
  Bubble, Bubble, Toil and Trouble. *Who Died in Here?* ed. Pat Dennis (Penury
    Press)

THE B·E·S·T AMERICAN SERIES®

THE BEST AMERICAN SHORT STORIES® 2005

Michael Chabon, guest editor, Katrina Kenison, series editor. "Story for story, readers can't beat the *Best American Short Stories* series" (*Chicago Tribune*). This year's most beloved short fiction anthology is edited by the Pulitzer Prize–winning novelist Michael Chabon and features stories by Tom Perrotta, Alice Munro, Edward P. Jones, Joyce Carol Oates, and Thomas McGuane, among others.

0-618-42705-8 PA $14.00 / 0-618-42349-4 CL $27.50

THE BEST AMERICAN ESSAYS® 2005

Susan Orlean, guest editor, Robert Atwan, series editor. Since 1986, *The Best American Essays* has gathered the best nonfiction writing of the year and established itself as the premier anthology of its kind. Edited by the best-selling writer Susan Orlean, this year's volume features writing by Roger Angell, Jonathan Franzen, David Sedaris, Andrea Barrett, and others.

0-618-35713-0 PA $14.00 / 0-618-35712-2 CL $27.50

THE BEST AMERICAN MYSTERY STORIES™ 2005

Joyce Carol Oates, guest editor, Otto Penzler, series editor. This perennially popular anthology is sure to appeal to crime fiction fans of every variety. This year's volume is edited by the National Book Award winner Joyce Carol Oates and offers stories by Scott Turow, Dennis Lehane, Louise Erdrich, George V. Higgins, and others.

0-618-51745-6 PA $14.00 / 0-618-51744-8 CL $27.50

THE BEST AMERICAN SPORTS WRITING™ 2005

Mike Lupica, guest editor, Glenn Stout, series editor. "An ongoing centerpiece for all sports collections" (*Booklist*), this series has garnered wide acclaim for its extraordinary sports writing and topnotch editors. Mike Lupica, the *New York Daily News* columnist and best-selling author, continues that tradition with pieces by Michael Lewis, Gary Smith, Bill Plaschke, Pat Jordan, L. Jon Wertheim, and others.

0-618-47020-4 PA $14.00 / 0-618-47019-0 CL $27.50

THE BEST AMERICAN TRAVEL WRITING 2005

Jamaica Kincaid, guest editor, Jason Wilson, series editor. Edited by the renowned novelist and travel writer Jamaica Kincaid, *The Best American Travel Writing 2005* captures the traveler's wandering spirit and ever-present quest for adventure. Giving new life to armchair journeys this year are Tom Bissell, Ian Frazier, Simon Winchester, John McPhee, and many others.

0-618-36952-X PA $14.00 / 0-618-36951-1 CL $27.50

THE B·E·S·T AMERICAN SERIES ®

THE BEST AMERICAN SCIENCE AND NATURE WRITING 2005

Jonathan Weiner, guest editor, Tim Folger, series editor. This year's edition presents another "eclectic, provocative collection" (*Entertainment Weekly*). Edited by Jonathan Weiner, the author of *The Beak of the Finch* and *Time, Love, Memory,* it features work by Oliver Sacks, Natalie Angier, Malcolm Gladwell, Sherwin B. Nuland, and others.

0-618-27343-3 PA $14.00 / 0-618-27341-7 CL $27.50

THE BEST AME

Edited by Fran McC

is looking for the

Tribune). Offering t

trends, time-saving

celebrated chef Mar

0-618-57478-6 CL $26.0

> WGRL-HQ FIC
> 31057100818767
> SC BEST
> Oates, Joyce Carol
> The best American mystery
> stories, 2005

ok who

Chicago

e latest

word by

THE BEST AMERICAN NONREQUIRED READING 2005

Edited by Dave Eggers, Introduction by Beck. In this genre-busting volume, best-selling author Dave Eggers draws the finest, most interesting, and least expected fiction, nonfiction, humor, alternative comics, and more from publications large, small, and on-line. With an introduction by the Grammy Award–winning musician Beck, this year's volume features writing by Jhumpa Lahiri, George Saunders, Aimee Bender, Stephen Elliott, and others.

0-618-57048-9 PA $14.00 / 0-618-57047-0 CL $27.50

THE BEST AMERICAN SPIRITUAL WRITING 2005

Edited by Philip Zaleski, Introduction by Barry Lopez. Featuring an introduction by the National Book Award winner Barry Lopez, *The Best American Spiritual Writing 2005* brings the year's finest writing about faith and spirituality to all readers. This year's volume gathers pieces from diverse faiths and denominations and includes writing by Natalie Goldberg, Harvey Cox, W. S. Merwin, Patricia Hampl, and others.

0-618-58643-1 PA $14.00 / 0-618-58642-3 CL $27.50

HOUGHTON MIFFLIN COMPANY www.houghtonmifflinbooks.com